Crimson Hearts

Copyright © 2016 Georgiana Fields

All rights reserved.

This book or parts thereof may not be reproduced in any form without permission in writing from the publisher, Georgiana Fields. The scanning, uploading, and distribution of this book via the Internet or via any other means without the permission of the publisher is illegal and punishable by law. Please purchase only authorized electronic editions, and do not participate in or encourage electronic piracy of copyrighted materials. Your support of the author's rights is appreciated. The publisher does not have any control over and does not assume any responsibility for author or third-party websites or their content.

All characters and events in this book are fictitious. Any resemblance to persons living or dead is strictly coincidental.

ISBN: 978-1-7260-3809-6

Cover Design: Gina Dyer
Photography: Gina Dyer
Depositphoto
Interior Design: Melba Moon
Editor: Mary Marvella

Crimson Hearts

Crimson Series
Book Two

Georgiana Fields

Crimson Series Reviews

Caitlin MacPhee is a badass, blood-sucking, murder-solving reporter/heroine you can root for. Crimson Hearts is a fast-paced and exciting read.
~ Raven Hart, author of The Vampire's Seduction

Crimson Dreams is a keeper, and I'll be looking for more books by Georgiana Fields. This book is quite something for a debut novel, and I'm exceedingly glad that it is a series!
~Linda Nightingale~author

Wow! What a fantastic read! Romance, time travel, mystery, and vampires - seems like a lot for one book, but Georgiana Fields weaves it all together beautifully with vivid details and clear story lines. She is truly a gifted writer. I can hardly wait for the next book in the series.
~S. Light

An excellent first novel. If you like paranormal romance, this is a must read. Unique, creative, and a wonderful read.
~Saphira

Dedication:

To John for putting up with my ghoulish inquiries. To Gina for understanding my Georgie-isms. And a special thanks to all my readers You're the best.

Prologue

She shuffled the Tarot cards then placed them on the table using the Celtic cross spread. She wasn't a devout believer, but lately, the cards had been right. "According to the cards, I'm moving back in with my husband."

"If that's what you want. But don't come crawling back to me when your husband starts running around on you again." Lenard slammed the cabinet door then walked to the windows, and closed his blinds.

She looked up at him. He stood with his back toward her. He'd been a close friend, even a lover at times over the past four years. He could be a little odd and opinionated at times, but he was still a friend. "Lenard, I'm sorry if I've hurt you. I don't mean to."

"Martha, don't *ever* call me by that name." He turned and glared at the cards in front of her. "I told you not to bring those things here again. They're evil." He made the sign of the cross, glaring at her as he did. "Get rid of them."

Martha rolled her eyes at him. "Oh, grow up! It's just a game."

He stormed over to the table and swept the cards to the floor. "They are the instruments of the devil," he growled, gritting his teeth as he spoke. Splotches of color crept into his cheeks, and his right eye twitched with anger.

She jumped up, hands to her hips. "Sometimes I think you're crazy."

"I'm not crazy." His voice sounded strangely high pitched, almost frantic. He leveled his eyes at her, staring as if seeing her for the first time. He was angrier than she'd ever seen him. Before she could say anything to calm him, he drew back and slapped her.

Stunned, she merely reacted. "Go to hell you, you *insane* son of a bitch!"

"Witch!" He grabbed her. "Zigana sent you to seduce me. Didn't she?" For the first time since they'd been friends, she was afraid of him.

Panicking, Martha clawed at his fingers, trying to pry free of his grip. "You're mad." Her words were more of a gurgle than real speech.

"God, protect me from this witch. Give me power over her darkness."

She staggered, her nails dug deep into his forearm until tiny blood crescents appeared. If anything, he tightened his grip. "Please," she gasped.

"Black magic killed Mother. I must destroy you." His eyes blazing with rage and fury bore into her.

"Not . . . witch." She kicked at him.

"Destroy all of you." He shook her like a ragdoll. "Mother believed in Madame Zigana's evil potions, and she's dead because of that witch." He squeezed his fingers tighter around her throat and shook her again. "You're just like the other witches Zigana sent after me. Black magic won't save you. Forsake your evil ways before I send you to hell. Save your unholy soul. Repent!"

Martha's eyes rolled back, her hands fell to her sides, and her legs buckled.

He dropped her to the floor. "I had to punish you, just like I had to punish Madame Zigana and her other followers. Her magic flows from hell and taints the women of this town." He opened a drawer and selected a knife. He was the town's only hope of salvation. He stared down at Martha's limp body. She'd be an example to the others. They would know she had been discovered and turn from their evil practices.

He knelt beside the body, stroking her hair. "Your long brown hair is the exact color of Zigana's. All of her followers have some part of her, her long hair, the color of her eyes, or some other part of her. You, my dear, have her eyes and her hair, that's how I know who you are. He laughed. She doesn't know I've figured out how she's transferred her powers to her living followers." He cut a clump of the woman's hair then carefully combed it through his fingers, relishing the feel against his flesh. He leaned down and whispered to the cold body. "I killed you too quickly. You didn't suffer enough for your sins. You didn't repent." He'd have to be more controlled if he wanted to save their souls before sending them to hell.

After several hours, he rocked back on his heels. Mother had spoken to him. To save her soul, he must hunt down all the witches. It was his duty to make them repent before he destroyed their evil black hearts and sent their souls to hell. Killing them was the only way Mother could rest.

Chapter One

"Love, personally, I'd throw him to the floor, have him a time or two then bite him."

Caitlin nearly dropped the phone. "Mother! I can't do that to Raven."

"Sure you can. Trust me men love it. How do you think I got your father?"

"Father rescued you from being burnt at a stake."

"Details, details, details, besides, we are not talking about your father and me. We are discussing you and Raven. You do realize that just because we are long-lived, your Raven is not. He's human. Besides, you're not getting any younger, so when are you going to act?"

Caitlin tapped a pencil on her desk and stared at her reflection in the office window. She was a successful, award-winning journalist, who was still intimidated by her mother. Caitlin loved talking to her mum, but every time the same question came up. When would she claim Raven O'Brien as her soul mate? "I don't know. These things take time, Mum. I can't go up to him and say hey, you're the other half of my soul, my one true mate. Let's get married."

"Why not?"

"So how's Victoria?" She tried to change the subject. "I haven't heard a word from my wayward sister in over a month. And by the way, she isn't mated either."

"Don't you worry about your sister? I'm working on her as well. She's fine. At least she was when she came home two weeks ago. For some strange reason, she had to cut her holiday short. Now, don't you believe it's time you claimed this man?"

Caitlin groaned. Thank God her mother was on the other side of the Atlantic Ocean. Otherwise, she'd be here harassing poor Raven.

"You've known him for two years," her mother continued. "What's the holdup? Caitlin, are you listening to me?"

"Yes, I'm listening. I haven't told Raven about myself yet. Raven is a no-nonsense detective. If he can't see it, smell it, or taste it, it isn't real. I have to find the right time to tell him."

"Love, there isn't a right time to tell someone that you are, for no other word, a vampire. No matter if we call ourselves Dhampir, Vampyr, Vurvulak, or Day-walker. The meanings are all the same. We are Vampires."

A movement caught her attention. Caitlin looked up as Raven strolled down the dark and empty aisle between the office desks.

He smiled and sat on the edge of her desk then flopped a copy of the afternoon edition of *The Herald* newspaper in front of her. The paper opened to her story.

"I'll be with you in a sec," she told him. "Mum, I've got to get back to work."

"Hi, Mom," Raven said and loosened his tie then undid the first two buttons of his shirt. Even wearing a rumpled suit, and sporting a five o'clock shadow, he made her heart beat faster.

"Tell him," her mother urged.

Caitlin leaned closer to the phone. "Mother." She smiled up at him. "Mum says hi."

"I did not."

"Got to go, love you, Mum." She hung up and leaned back in her chair. No wonder Vicky always cut short her holidays.

Caitlin gazed up into Raven's black, unfathomable eyes, and licked her dried lips. She could spend eternity staring into those dark pools. "What brings you here, Detective?"

He motioned to the paper. "The guys and I just wanted to thank you. It means a lot to us, having someone in the press on our side." He chuckled as he scanned the article again. "I even sent a copy to my folks in Chicago."

"No problem. I know you're doing all you can to catch this creep."

"I stopped by your house, but your roommate said you were still here. I frightened her."

"How?"

"I knocked on your door. Inky was grooming himself on your porch, and I know Stacey doesn't permit him outside, so I opened the door to put him inside. Stacey screamed so loud I think she broke my eardrum."

Caitlin covered her mouth, stifling her laugh. "It's not funny. Stacey has been uneasy lately. Everyone in town has been."

"She also told me to tell you to hurry home." He pointed to the wall clock. "It's after six, and you were supposed to be off today."

"I was. I treated myself to a spa treatment then came in to work on this story. I had to. Anne Thomason makes the third victim killed by this maniac in eighteen months. And his sixth total. He's increasing his timeline between victims." Her throat tightened. She had to keep reminding herself this was only a story. Damn. Anne Thomason was only seventeen years old. She'd had her whole life ahead of her.

Raven's gaze roamed over Caitlin, sending a tingling sensation through her "Your hair looks the same." He glanced at her hands. "Nails look the same." He gave her a suspicious look. "Spa treatment huh, what did you have done?"

She stared into Raven's black eyes, licked her lower lip then rose and leaned toward him. "From my lower eyelashes to the tips of my well-manicured toes, I'm a hairless cat," she whispered in his ear. Caitlin sat back down enjoying the delightful expression on his face.

He closed his mouth and coughed, clearing his throat. "Sounds painful."

Caitlin laughed. "Okay, Raven, what's your real reason for being here?" Caitlin tapped her pencil on his knuckles. She hoped he'd stopped by to take her to dinner. After all, it was her birthday. She tried to read his thoughts. But, Raven kept them and his emotions so buried she had difficulty sensing his feelings. Raven, a man of mystery. One more reason he drew her to him.

Raven brushed a lock of his dark hair from his eye and gave her that grin that always had a way of turning her to putty. "I need a favor."

Four little words that had the same effect on her like ice water. Raven hadn't come to take her out after all. Hell, she could be sitting here in front of him bare ass naked, and he'd still see her only as a friend. "Sure. What are friends for?"

He reached into his coat pocket and pulled out a piece of paper. "Didn't you tell me someone in your family was a historian or something like that?"

"My grandfather, he's an archaeology teacher at Cambridge. Why?"

"Could I have his number? There's something I'd like to see if he could help me with."

"Sure. What is it?" She needed to look at it first.

Raven eyed her then reluctantly handed her a piece of paper.

She studied the drawing, turning it one way then the next. "What's this? It looks like a strange cross."

"It may be nothing then, on the other hand, it could be important. Could your grandfather check this out and see if it has any meaning? He can call me. I wrote my number and email on the back." He placed his hand over hers, and his expression grew serious. "Cat, this has to remain confidential."

She eyed him speculatively. He had a brother in the FBI who had helped with information before. Why wouldn't his brother help him now? "What about Edgar? Can't the Feds help this time?"

"I asked. Edgar couldn't find anything on file. I thought that maybe you . . . never mind." He reached for the paper. "Sorry. I'm wasting your time and grasping at straws."

"You're not wasting my time." Caitlin snatched the scrap of paper back, holding it to her chest. "I'll ask Grandpapa, and don't worry this will stay between us. I don't want you to get your hopes up, that's all." She sighed, studying the slip of paper. The drawing looked ancient Celtic. For Raven to be so uptight, it had to have something to do with the case. "Does it have something to do with the case? Is this the killer's calling card?"

"Possibly."

"Does that mean yes?"

"It means maybe."

She frowned. "It means you're not telling."

"You're right." Raven picked up Anne's graduation picture from the pile of papers. He stared at the photo. His jaw twitched, a sign this case was getting to him. "Her parents reported her missing two days ago. They didn't hear from her over the weekend, and Anne hadn't slept in her bed according to her roommate. She figured Anne slept over with her date Friday night. Since Anne spoke with her parents regularly, we were looking for her. Otherwise, she may have been like the first two. Found, before we knew she was missing."

Raven paused. His eyes took on a faraway look. "Dr. Whenn said she'd been dead for about six or seven hours when we found her Monday morning." His voice sounded hollow and emotionless.

Caitlin stared into Raven's empty eyes. "Give me some comfort. Tell me Anne was dead before he did all those things to her. Tell me he'd overdosed her like his previous victims." The bleakness in Raven's eyes told her otherwise.

He took the pencil from her hand. "Not this time. Whenn told me Anne knew and felt everything that bastard did to her. He'd drugged Anne just enough to overpower her. Cause of death, strangulation. The bastard is getting off on their pain before he kills. The only good news is we now know what toxic cocktail he's using. He's using GHB along with a mix of toxic plants. Oleander for starters and something called pasque flower. According to Whenn, the flowers' toxins slow the heartbeat."

Caitlin shuddered. Such a horrible way for that child to have died. "Do you think Anne's boyfriend, what's his name?" She flipped through her notes. "Here it is. Do you think Dennis Wilson is the murderer?"

"Nope, not the type."

"How do you know? Do you have hard facts?"

Raven twirled the pencil between his fingers. "Off the record?"

"Yes."

"First of all, according to Mr. Wilson, they stopped off at the coffee shop before he took her back to her dorm. He walked her to the door, kissed her goodnight then left. Two other students saw him. I've already spoken to them. They both swear Anne went into her room alone."

"What are their names?" She picked up a pen, ready to write. "They could be covering for him. You told me a second ago that her roommate said Anne hadn't made it back."

"Nope. Anne's roommate assumed she hadn't come home because of her bed. As for Mr. Wilson, he wasn't in the state when the other two murders occurred. He moved here eight weeks ago. And before you ask Sherlock, we've checked his background. One more thing, he's right-handed." Raven's jaw twitched.

She made him angry. Too bad, at least he was talking. Keeping his emotions locked inside would drive him mad someday. One more question should do it. "So that means, the killer followed them and abducted Anne after the boyfriend left. How did the killer get to her after she'd entered her room?"

"Hell if I know. Perhaps he knocked on her door. If she knew him, it's common sense that she'd open the door."

"And if she didn't?"

Raven slammed his hand down, breaking the pencil. "I wish I had all the answers. All I know is this SOB is choosing his victims then dumping their bodies in a churchyard before they're reported missing."

"Raven?"

He tossed the broken pencil into the trash. "Look, I'm sorry, Cat. When Mike and I went to the Thomason's house, there were pictures of this child covering the walls." He pointed to the photo of Anne. "Despite what that bastard did to her, I recognized her eyes. Her mother," Raven's voice cracked, and he turned away. "God, I hate this part of the job. She asked if we'd found her baby."

His shoulders dropped, and he lowered his head. His dark hair shielded his eyes. "In thirteen years, I haven't seen anything like this. I'll get this animal. Even if it costs me my badge, I'll get him."

She knew Raven would keep the vow he'd just made, even if he got booted from the force or dropped dead from exhaustion. He devoted himself to his cases. That had been the problem in his marriage. She couldn't blame Beth for leaving him. The man was a workaholic. Just like Caitlin was.

Caitlin squeezed his hand. "I know you will. This creature will make a mistake if he hasn't already, and you'll catch him."

"I hope you're right."

"What does the lab say about the paint splatters found on the victims? Do you think he's keeping them in a warehouse? Can't you search all the warehouses in the nearby area?"

"Sure. All we'd need is a thousand search warrants and about a hundred extra men."

"Sorry I asked."

Raven cast a cynical look at her. "Sure you are. The lab test confirmed the paint is a common brand. A million people in this state have the same hunter-green spray paint in their garages and basements. You used the same brand when you painted your porch furniture."

She saw his point. "Okay so going door to door won't solve this case. I'm about to head home. Why don't you call it quits for the night and come with me? I can cook."

"How about we order out, I know how you cook."

She tilted her chin up and chuckled. "Smartass."

"I've been called worst." One side of his mouth turned up. "I'll warn you, I haven't eaten since morning, and I'm starving."

"From the look of you, you haven't slept in a week either."

"You offering to share your bed?"

"I might be. Any takers?" She pushed away from her desk and stood as Raven's partner, Mike, entered her office.

"Hi, Cat." Mike glared at Raven. "Birdie, you said you'd only be a second."

"What can I say? She put me in a headlock."

"Hey. How's Jeanette?" Caitlin asked.

Mike shrugged. His light brown hair and weathered tanned skin made him look older than his forty-five years. His suit looked as wrinkled as Raven's. "Fine. She's agreed to move back."

"That's wonderful." She admired Mike for his devotion to saving his marriage.

"Yeah, that's great," Raven, muttered under his breath. "Jeanette is one in a million. You're a lucky son-of-a-bitch to have her."

Mike rolled his eyes. "Don't mind him, Cat. He's been in a pissy mood all day. Jeanette and I talked last night, and we agree twenty years is a hell of a long time to throw away."

He turned to Raven. "Hate to pull you away from Mountain Spring's number one reporter, but the Captain wants us."

"Damn." Raven's dark eyebrows slanted in a frown.

Mike motioned to the door. "Let's go."

"All right. Cat, it looks like I'll have to take you up on dinner later. How about tomorrow?"

"Can't, I've got a date."

"With who?" Raven grabbed the edge of her desk and loomed over her.

"I don't think you know him."

"Try me." His eyes narrowed to small dark slits.

"Come on, Birdie, leave the Cat alone, Captain is waiting," Mike said.

"*Whom*, are you going out with?" Raven asked again.

"All right, big brother, if you must know, Jeff Morgan. He's Caren's brother. You know, she's in distribution."

"You're right. I don't know the guy." Raven straightened and turned. "Enjoy yourself," he said as he walked through the open door.

Caitlin stared after him as he and Mike made their way through the empty office area. Raven hadn't even remembered today was her birthday. He drove her nuts. One minute he sounded jealous and the next unconcerned. "Maybe I will take your advice, Mum," she huffed, turning back to her computer.

She read over the previous six murders, comparing them, and making notes. All six women had been found wearing a crude handmade shift. Residue on their hands and feet indicated she was bound. All of the victims had their hair chopped extremely short. The only thing that differed was the method in which he'd killed them.

Caitlin rubbed her blurry eyes. *What a way to spend my birthday. But at least I get another birthday. These women won't ever celebrate another one.*

The first victim, Martha Hawkins, worked at the bank, African-American, and newly divorced. Her body discovered posed with her hands crossed over her chest, in a church graveyard. Martha's hair had been cut off. She'd died from strangulation. Evidence showed he'd beaten and mutilated her body after death.

The killer had burned the next three victims to death and also left their bodies in Church graveyards. The fifth victim, Susan Holloway, Caucasian, a single mother. She worked days. He'd overdosed her, but still mutilated her body and also left her in a church graveyard posed liked the first victim.

Race didn't seem to be the deciding factor. Other than having shoulder-length hair, none of the women looked alike. However, both the first and second victim had green eyes. Martha Hawkins wore green colored contacts. Susan Holloway's eyes were naturally green.

Caitlin scrolled down. The sixth victim, Anne Thomson, a college student. Blue eyed. All three single women had busy daytime schedules. He had to be grabbing them at night. How did the killer know them? Did he see them during the day or did he pick them randomly? Why choose them? Were they merely in the wrong place at the wrong time?

Tapping a pen against her desk, Caitlin stared at the computer screen. What connected these women? The stores they shopped? The clothes and jewelry they wore? Something had to be the common thread?

Her eyes blurred. She closed them and leaned back in the chair. Images of when she covered the Vietnam War flashed in her mind. For some reason, she could understand the carnage of battle better than these senseless murders.

She opened her eyes. The knowledge that this murderer, this monster, this animal had tortured those poor women enraged her. She ran her tongue over the tips of her fangs. If she ever ran into the creep, she'd make him pay. *Dearly.*

"This sucks," she said and closed her notebook.

A million questions surged through her mind with no answers. And she knew some if not most of her questions may never be answered.

She flipped open her notebook again, and reread the notes she'd taken from the police interviews. She knew the police wouldn't release some of the evidence to the public. No similar murders turned up when ran through ViCAP, the Violent Criminal Apprehension Program, and NCAVC, the FBI's resource center for the collection of violent crime data. She didn't like the FBI's profile on the murderer either. It described him as someone who blended in with his surroundings. Someone his victims would feel comfortable being with alone, a doctor, lawyer, or even a schoolteacher. Someone the victims knew and trusted.

The police knew the suspect was left-handed from the directionality of his cuts from the way he tied the knot around Anne's neck. Or, the A-hole was ambidextrous, that would near down the suspects. They suspect he uses a predator drug commonly known as a date rape drug, on his victims. Possibly GHB, Rohypnol, or ketamine and now according to Raven the killer is mixing it with poisonous plants.

The phone rang, shattering Caitlin's thoughts. She snatched up the receiver. "*The Herald,* Caitlin MacPhee, speaking."

"How's my wonderful Granddaughter?"

Mishenka's voice washed over her. "Grandpapa! You just made my evening."

"Happy Birthday, Kitten."

"Thanks. You always know when I need to talk to you."

"I know when all of my grandchildren need me. What's dampening your birthday?"

She told him about the murders then waited. There was a long pause before he spoke again.

"It sounds as if he punished them for witchcraft."

"Grandpapa, in this day and age?"

"Kitten, as long as I've been around, I've learned some people, no matter how well educated, fear witchcraft. Do you know if he stripped them?"

"They were found wearing handmade shifts. The police haven't released much information."

"Probably a wise decision."

"Raven gave me a sketch tonight. He thinks it may have a hidden meaning. It could help solve this case. He asked me if you would mind looking at it."

"Fax me the drawing, and I'll have a go. If I can't help, then I'll have your cousin, Royce, or your brother run it through the Yard. I'll let you know something as soon as possible. How's Spacey-Stacey doing?"

"Grandpapa, that isn't nice. You and Raven have to stop calling her that."

He chuckled. "Stacey is one of a kind."

"She hasn't been handling this too well. She came home the other night pretty upset. I think Doctor Whenn will take her off the case."

"Tell me what she's told you about the autopsies," Mishenka gently urged.

"He mangled the fifth victim's birthmark on her lower back. What kind of person is this man?"

"He isn't a person, Kitten. He's an animal needing to be destroyed."

"Raven called him an animal tonight, too."

"Oh, how is Raven? You do realize he won't live forever in his current state of being."

She groaned. "Good grief, it's bad enough I get it from Mum, now you?"

"Are you sure he is your heart's mate? Choosing a human can have complications. Will he be able to leave his job and everything that is familiar, for you, when the time comes?"

She closed her eyes and squinted against the tears. After Raven's wife left him, he'd thrown himself into his job even more. Then there was his family. "I don't know."

"I feel your sorrow, Kitten. I didn't mean to upset you. I'm only concerned for your happiness. If you like, I will influence him."

"No."

"That's what I wanted to hear, Kitten. Had you said yes, I would have. You know that."

"I know, but I want Raven to love me for myself. If you influence him, I'll always have doubts."

They talked about everything from the latest family gossip to the local soccer team. Somehow, over the course of their conversation, they came back to the subject of Raven. She told her Grandpapa about her mother's suggestion. Mishenka laughed so hard she held the phone away from her ear.

Talking to her grandfather lifted her spirits. She glanced up at the clock. "Oh, pooh. Grandpapa, I have to let you go. I'll fax you that photo. Love you."

He wished her happy birthday again then disconnected.

After faxing him the photos, Caitlin picked up her sweater and purse then strode out of Mountain Springs' only newspaper, *The Herald*.

Caitlin breathed in the night air. The spring air smelled of pending rain. The serenity of this Pennsylvania town reminded her of the village where her parents lived. Sadly the tranquility of this town has been shattered by this killer.

The grinding gears of a truck coming from the college broke the silence. Caitlin smiled, watching the truckload of kids roll past. She envied them the joy of being young and worry-free.

She pulled the scrunchy from her ginger hair, letting it tumble to her waist. Today had been long and tiring, and she still had one stop to make before heading home. Caitlin ran her fingers through her hair then glanced at her watch, 08:45. Good thing the bookstore stayed open until nine.

The bell over the door chimed as she entered Books and Java, her favorite bookstore. It was also the only bookstore in town. The delicious smell of rich, brewed coffee teased her nose.

"Hey, Lambert," she greeted the lanky owner who looked just as comfortable behind a computer as he did behind his counter.

"Evening, Miss MacPhee. Are you now getting off work?"

She nodded. "Yeah. Is the book Stacey ordered in?"

"Got it right here." His smile reached his brown eyes. "It's thirty-two fifty."

"That's fine, and can I get a large mocha to go?"

He poured her coffee. "Here you are. Have a good night."

The drive home seemed longer, and she swore she'd hit every red light on her way. She pulled down a street with houses built in the mid-forties. A few seconds later, she turned into her driveway. The two-bedroom, yellow clapboard house with its white trim had never looked so good to her as it did now. With the fortune she'd accumulated over her lifetime, she could have purchased a larger home, but she liked simple things, and this house fitted who she was now.

Inky, Stacey's black Persian jumped from his perch on the railing and strolled down the steps. Caitlin reached down and petted him. "What are you doing out here? Stacey will have a fit if she knows you've escaped again. Come on, little man, let's go in."

A familiar tingle told her one of her family was here, and they were blocking their mind from her. Crap. She paused before opening the door, trying to figure out who it could be. It couldn't be her parents or her grandfather. Her brother, Glen, was still in London, and her sister, Victoria, was somewhere on the continent. Maybe it was *Babushka*?

Inky pushed between Caitlin's leg and the door. He darted over to the fireplace and stretched out as if he'd been there all night.

Caitlin gaped at the countless colorful balloons that filled her living room. Hundreds of peach colored roses sat arranged in vases on her bar, separating the living room from the kitchen.

"Many happy returns," Victoria shouted and jumped from behind the door. She hugged Caitlin. "How does it feel to be two hundred?"

"The same as yesterday. No different." Having her sister here made this a happy birthday after all.

Stacey, Caitlin's roommate, came out of the kitchen carrying one of her gourmet chocolate cakes, glowing with three candles. "Happy Birthday," she sang, slightly off-key.

"Thanks."

"I made your favorite, chocolate raspberry. For dinner, I made my special lasagna with cheesy garlic bread. I figured you're only this age once, why not have dessert first." She grinned. "Like the candles? I thought putting the number candles on would be safer than lighting two hundred individual candles."

Stacey placed the cake on the large, travel-sticker covered, steamer trunk they used as a coffee table. The light from the candles reflected on the gold chain, and rose crystal Stacey always wore. It had been a gift from Grandpapa.

Caitlin met Stacey's gaze and grinned. "And the smoke detectors won't go off either."

"Make a wish and blow them out," Vicky urged.

Caitlin blew out the candles and watched as white smoke curled up from the three candles.

"What did you wish," Vicky asked, pulling the number two candle from the cake. She licked the icing from the candle then removed the two zeros and did the same. A habit of hers, Caitlin had learned to ignore.

Flopping into an overstuffed chair, she realized how tired she was. Ice cream and cake was the furthest thing from her mind. Her feet ached, and her head still throbbed. She just wanted to go to bed and sleep for the next month. Maybe by then the demon terrorizing this town would be caught and this nightmare over. "I didn't make a wish. I couldn't make up my mind."

"Well, what were your possibilities?" Stacey cut the cake then handed a slice to Caitlin.

"I don't know. Maybe for Raven to capture this maniac."

"I meant for you. What do you want?" Stacey sliced another piece of cake and handed it to Victoria.

"Let's see. I want a guy to know the color of my eyes before he knows my bra size. I want Raven to see me as a woman instead of his best bud. And I want Mum to stop interfering in my love life."

Vicky laughed. "Well, you might get two of your wishes, but Mum won't stop prying until you're mated with a bairn on the way, and then I'm not sure that would stop her. Interfering that is."

Caitlin sank deeper into the chair and kicked off her shoes. "Vicky, your being here has made this a wonderful birthday. How long can you stay?"

"Only through the weekend. I have a client coming in on Tuesday to purchase several oils. I wouldn't have missed sharing your birthday with you. You know that. By-the-way, I thought you had today off."

"I did. I went to the spa. I had a complete body waxing. I told Raven what I did. God, I loved the expression on his face, even if it only lasted a second, it was worth it. Then I went in to work on this story. Part one should be in tomorrow afternoon's edition."

"Stacey told me about the murders. Is Raven stopping by tonight? Or has he already given you your birthday spankings?"

"He didn't even remember what today was, not that I can blame him with everything going on."

Stacey placed the phone on the coffee table near Caitlin. "You may need this. Glen, Royce, and Vaughn have all tried to call tonight. They informed me you weren't answering your cell and your office phone was busy. I told them to try back after nine. Oh, and this card came with the flowers."

"I've already spoken with the guys. They each called me at work. So did Grandpapa." Caitlin opened the card and smiled. "They're from Glen. One for each year of my life, he writes."

"The last time Glen sent flowers was when you told father you wanted to be a Pinkerton agent," Vicky said.

"Dad was more upset over the cutting my hair than about my wanting to be a detective."

"Well, you should have known better. Women didn't bob their hair back then," Victoria said, licking the icing off her fork.

"Do you realize that was the only time I've had short hair?" Caitlin scooped up a large amount of icing herself. "I love chocolate."

Victoria stood, placed her plate on the bar then pulled a large brown paper wrapped package from behind the counter. "Here." She handed Caitlin the package. "I know you're going to love what I got you. I saw it in an art gallery. Open it."

Caitlin eyed the brown paper. Her stomach knotted with dread. She suspected what was under that paper. *Please don't let it be so.*

Slowly she tore away the wrapping. The gray eyes of the portrait stared at her. The same eyes she saw every morning and night in the bathroom mirror. "Vicky, I wish you hadn't."

Chapter Two

Caitlin stared at the oil painting of Kate Marlow, reclining on a burgundy velvet chaise. She wore a timeless off-the-shoulder gown of midnight blue silk that clung to her figure. Her platinum blond hair swirled around her shoulders.

The portrait's eyes haunted Caitlin. She saw the sadness in them and remembered the pain that caused it. The one chapter in her life she hated. "Why did you purchase this?"

Victoria inhaled deeply. "I thought you would like it. But I see I made a bloody hash of it. What gives?" She sat back, waiting in silence.

"Do you honestly want to know?"

"I asked, didn't I?" Vic eyed her and nothing, but honest flowed from her. She wasn't her usual catty self. No, Vic wanted answers.

Caitlin sighed. Time for the truth. "Let's go into the kitchen."

Stacey rummaged through the freezer. "Will this be cookie dough or a banana split moment?" She held two quarts of ice cream in her hands.

"Banana split. I'll get the spoons," Caitlin said.

Victoria pulled out a chair and sat. "Why don't you like the portrait?"

Caitlin removed the lid from the ice cream then scooped out a large amount. "Because it reminds me of a time in my life I hated. Everyone thought more of the illusion they'd created than the person inside." She tasted the cold, creamy treat. It smoothed the lump in her throat.

"Then why did you decide to become an actress? You knew what it would be like, we all warned you." And nothing said Victoria like, 'I told you so.'

"Because I wanted to be like you, Vicky. You had everything I wanted, friends, wit, and every man in England fighting for your attention. I wanted the spotlight on me for once. Do you know what it was like living in your shadow?

Every one of my suitors wanted to get close to *you*." She thrust her finger at Vicky. "Do you know how many frigging times I was called *little sister*?"

"You wanted to be like me? Caitlin, I never had any real friends other than you and Aileen. And as far as the men were concerned, we both know what they were after." She rested her chin on her hand, and a sad smile curved her lips. "I envied you for your voice. Me, I sound like a sick cow in a hailstorm. I wish I could sing like you."

"You don't sound like a sick cow."

"Moo."

Stacey laughed and spooned a heap of ice cream into her bowl. "From what you've told me about Hollywood back then, it sounded like one big party."

"That's right," Vicky said. "You were on everyone's A-list."

"No, *I* wasn't!" The spoon dropped from Caitlin's hand, splattering ice cream. "Kate Marlow was."

Vicky rolled her eyes. "But you were Kate Marlow. You had it all and threw it away."

"I had nothing. I wasn't free. The studio owned me. They changed my name, told me what to wear, and who to see. They bleached my hair and my eyebrows. They made me get rid of my Scottish accent. They changed everything about me. Kate Marlow was just another character I portrayed. The problem, I had to be her twenty-four seven, until I hated her so much I hated myself."

Vicky covered Caitlin's hand with hers. "Why didn't you tell us?"

"How could I after the fuss I'd made? The whole family was against my going into acting. I couldn't admit I'd made a mistake. One morning I woke up and decided to take a drive on Highway 1 right over the cliff and into the Pacific."

Stacey shook her head, and her golden tresses swayed. "Talk about dramatic. You should have gotten an Oscar for that performance," she laughed.

"I got this." Caitlin lifted her bangs, revealing a thin scar over her right eye. "And the studio gave me a nice memorial service. I have to admit I did get a kick out of the rumors about my alleged murder. The scandal sheets gave me more publicity after I'd died than they did when I was alive. Three of my movies became box office hits, and all of my recordings went gold."

"What happened to all of your royalties?" Stacey asked then quickly covered her mouth. "I'm sorry. I shouldn't have asked that."

"Nothing is personal in this family," Caitlin reassured her. "In my will, I left everything to my dear niece and namesake. Me." She stood and took her bowl over to the sink. "I'm just glad that part of my life is over. It did teach me a valuable lesson."

"Which was?" Stacey asked. She threw away the empty carton then opened the oven door. The marvelous smell of baked lasagna made Caitlin's mouth water.

"It's not driving off the cliff that hurts like hell. It's the sudden stop."

Vicky held up the last spoonful of ice cream. "All wasn't a total waste. With the time you needed to create a new life you realized your love for journalism."

"True. I guess it's better for our kind to be writing the news than being the news."

"Here, here. Now tell me, what do you want me to do with that picture?"

"I don't care what you do with it. Use it for a dart board for all I care."

Vicky frowned. "That wouldn't seem right."

"Why?"

Vicky's lips parted in a wide-open smile. "I love you too much."

~ ~ ~

Raven turned into Caitlin's driveway. The lights from the house gave off a warm glow. How could he have blown it? Hell, it wasn't every day your best friend turned thirty. Best friend, damn, who was he kidding? Cat was more than his friend. She was his life preserver, his shrink, his—Hell, she knew he needed to vent tonight, and she let him. Not once did she throw it back in his face he'd forgotten her birthday.

Caitlin was something else. She'd always been there for him. She'd been there when Beth left. The first time he saw Caitlin, he knew she was something special. She deserves someone just as incredible as she was. Someone who would be there for her, someone she could lean on.

He wanted to be there for her.

Raven hit the steering wheel. She deserved better than a cop who was on the job, twenty-four hours a day, but the thought of her with anyone else sickened him.

He stared up at the house. Well, at least she was still up. He picked up his present from the seat, opened the car door then climbed the steps to the house.

The smell of Italian food made his mouth water. Stacey must have made her incredible lasagna. His stomach grumbled even after the burgers he'd grabbed earlier.

Raven pushed the newly painted rockers back and forth, imagining sitting there with Cat, and watching their kids play.

Damn, there I go again, dreaming of things I shouldn't.

He pressed the doorbell and stepped back.

Caitlin peered out the curtain. She smiled at him. At least she wasn't mad at him for forgetting her birthday.

She flung open the door. "What brings you here?"

"My car. I saw lights on, and well." He held out the square box he'd wrapped in pastel purple paper and tied with white ribbon. "Forgot to wish you happy birthday earlier."

"You shouldn't have. Come in." She took the present and almost dropped it. "It's heavy. What is it?"

Brightly colored balloons filled her small living room, and hundreds of peach roses covered the bar. *Someone had spent a bundle on her. Wonder if it was that Jeff guy, she has the date with tomorrow night.*

He removed his jacket and draped it across the back of the couch. He eyed the gift he'd brought. His wrap-job sucked with the crumpled paper and smashed bow. In his defense, the package looked better this morning. And the contents of the box wouldn't compare to the flowers. He'd tried. "I hope you like it."

"I'm sure I will. Have you eaten? Stacey made lasagna and a chocolate raspberry cake. We ate all the ice cream."

"That's okay. I grabbed a burger on my way over." He turned as an unfamiliar woman entered the room.

She smiled at him and her gaze roamed from his head to his toes. "I thought I heard a man's voice," she said in a sultry tone. Her gaze fell to his shoulder holster. "Mmm, armed and dangerous. I like that."

Heat rose in his face. Who the hell was she?

Caitlin motioned to the other woman. "Raven, my sister, Victoria."

Sister?

Looking from one to the other, he could see the resemblance. Caitlin and Victoria were the same height and size. The shapes of their faces were the same. They even had the same smile. He also saw the sharp differences in their looks. Victoria's short black hair and ice blue eyes gave her a harsh, but exotic look. Caitlin's thick, waist-length, rich red hair, and gray eyes made her appear touchable. He smiled politely and offered his hand to Victoria. "A pleasure. Caitlin's told me a lot about you."

Victoria took his hand and smiled seductively at him. "Really? That's odd. She hasn't ever mentioned you."

"Oh." His guts twisted.

"Victoria," Caitlin snapped.

"I'm only teasing. Of course, Caitlin's mentioned you, Raven, quite frequently. So, how long have you known my little sister?"

"Two years." He eased onto the couch next to Caitlin. He didn't know why, but the knot in his stomach eased as soon as he heard Caitlin had mentioned him to her family.

He watched her opening his gift and chuckled as she fought with the tape. "Do you need help?"

She slid her fingernail under the tape and popped it open. "No."

Stacey leaned over the counter. "I thought I heard your voice."

"Hey, Stace." He waved at her. "I'm glad to see Whenn let you come home."

She fingered the gold chain around her neck. "I guess we all will be putting in some late hours until this creep is caught or killed. Guys, I'm exhausted. I'm calling it a night." She wiggled her fingers at them and disappeared down the hall.

He scooted closer to Cat as Victoria slid onto the couch arm next to him.

She placed her hand on his shoulder, and he noticed more differences between the sisters. Victoria wore strong perfume that announced her presence, while Caitlin always had a clean spicy scent. Cat's nails were short and natural not long, red talons like Victoria's nails. How could anyone work with fingernails like that? He tried not to stare at her hands. Those things were lethal weapons.

"Raven, do you know the color of Caitlin's eyes?" Sugar dripped from Victoria's words.

"Huh. What? The color of Cat's eyes? Sure." Why did Victoria want to know that? She's Cat's sister. She should know that answer. "They're dark gray, like storm clouds, but her eyes tend to turn almost lavender whenever she gets mad. I like that. It gives me a three-second warning." He watched Cat slowly unwrap his gift, trying not to tear the paper. Why didn't she just rip it and open it already? "Why do you ask?"

"Just wanted to know how well you know my sister. Caitlin, dear, that should give you one of your wishes."

A touch of pink teased Caitlin's cheeks, and she cleared her throat. "Yes, well let's not go for two, or I'd think you were Mum."

Raven sat back and glanced from one sister to the other. He was missing something here, something important.

Caitlin lifted the lid of the box and gasped. "A bowling ball. Raven, you shouldn't have spent so much." She flung her arms around his neck.

The ball rolled onto his lap. He caught it just in time. "It's the one you wanted, right?"

"Yes. You didn't have to do this." She set the ten-pound crimson ball on the floor then hugged him again. "Now I have two balls."

He bit his tongue, fighting the urge to respond. Instead, he slid his arms around Caitlin's waist. "You embarrass me with that old black thing you use." He leaned toward her and brushed a kiss to her cheek. "I'm glad you like it."

"A bowling ball?" Victoria said with mock surprise. "I would never have guessed." She slid from her perch and strolled over to the bar then bent over and picked up a partially unwrapped picture, tore the remaining paper from it then turned the painting toward him. "Raven, what do you think of this?"

That face, I know that face. "That's Kate Marlow. Where did you get that? I love to hear her sing. I've downloaded every song of hers I can find on the net. I don't know why the record company won't re-release her music."

He looked at Caitlin and quickly looked at the painting then back to Cat. "My God, it could be you!" He stood and went over for a better look at the portrait.

"You can say that again," Victoria mumbled.

"Cat, I never realized how much you resemble Marlow." He took the painting from Victoria and studied it. "If you ever decided to go blond you'd be a dead ringer for her."

Caitlin snickered, "Boy do you have a way with words."

Victoria pointed to the fireplace. "Raven, darling. Don't you think it would look great over there?"

"Yeah. Cat, where do you want to hang it? I can do it tonight if you'd like."

Caitlin rose fluidly then came over to him. She took the painting, turned it, and leaned it against the chair. "Anywhere, but in this house. It's just not my style. You like her so much, why don't you take it home? You could put it with the rest of your movie memorabilia."

"As much as I'd like to, I couldn't. This painting must have cost your sister a bundle."

"Two bundles." Victoria picked up the painting and pushed it at him. "Take it. That's settled then. I think I'll call it a night. It was nice to meet you." She brushed a kiss to his cheek. "Do you have any brothers?"

"Two, but they're married."

"That's not a problem." She winked and left the room.

Caitlin sighed and collapsed on the couch as if her legs had given out. "Please forgive Vicky. She's always a little forward."

"It's because she isn't as sure of herself as you are."

"Not sure of herself?" Caitlin coughed. "Trust me. She's the outgoing one. I've always been," she paused and lowered her gaze. "Never mind."

"You shouldn't envy your sister."

Caitlin watched Inky as he pounced on the discarded wrapping paper, kicking the ribbons with his hind feet, acting as if he were a kitten again. "Raven, do you honestly think Vicky is insecure?"

"Yes. Cat, you're the one who knows what she wants and where she's going in life. And speaking of going." Raven glanced down at the painting he held. "I should be heading home." He met her gaze. "Cat, I really can't accept this. I know what your sister must have paid for it."

"Please take it. I don't want it."

"Why? What's the story behind this portrait?" He looked at the portrait's eyes. The artist had captured the sadness shimmering in Kate Marlow's eyes. The woman had everything, fame, fortune, and a country in love with her and she still killed herself.

"I don't like it. That's all."

He nodded and walked to the door. He'd find out what dark secret Cat was hiding.

"Let me get that for you," Cat said, opening the door. "Thanks for the ball. I can't wait to try it out." She went up on her toes and kissed his cheek. "Goodnight."

He tilted his head, pressing a kiss to her mouth. Caitlin's lips parted, tempting him to taste her sweetness. He lifted his mouth from hers. "Hope you enjoy your date tomorrow night." He left, praying she had a miserable time.

Chapter Three

"I don't feel right going out and leaving you here, especially when I don't get to spend a lot of time with you." Caitlin picked up her cell phone and called Jeff's number. She didn't know the guy and wasn't that keen on going out with him. She hated blind dates. You never knew if you would get a prince or a toad. She'd only agreed to the date to make Raven jealous, but that plan failed. Raven only saw her as a good friend, or worse, a little sister.

Vicky snatched the phone from Caitlin and tossed it on the bed. "You're going out, and I won't be alone. Stacey and I are going to the cinema."

"Today is Friday, and you're leaving Sunday night." Caitlin shut her closet door and leaned against it. Her tiny bedroom looked even smaller with Vicky's suitcases stacked in the corner. "I want to spend time with you, not some guy I don't know."

"Hell and damnation! The last time you went out on a date, the Hustle was hot! Go out with this gent and give Raven something to worry about."

"He has enough to worry about with this case." Caitlin fell across her bed, wrinkling the four rejected dresses she'd flung there. "And it hasn't been that long since I've been on a date," she sputtered.

Vicky rolled her eyes. "I'm talking about his status with you. He needs to think you won't wait around for him. He needs to feel threatened."

"No, he doesn't. I don't want him to think I'm like his ex." Caitlin sat up, clutching a pillow to her chest. "His wife got tired of him putting in long hours, so she started having an affair. Raven put all the blame on himself and gave her a divorce. She remarried a few weeks after their divorce was final. I know it hurt Raven more than he lets on and I know it affected him in other ways. I don't want him not to trust me. I don't want to ruin our relationship."

"Relationship? What relationship, Caitlin? He sees you as nothing but a bowling chum," Vicky huffed, flopping on the bed.

"That's not so. We have a very deep friendship."

"Take off your rose-colored glasses. You're Raven's chum, not his lover. As long as he knows you will always be here when *he* needs *you*, you will never be anything more than chums."

Victoria's honest words ripped open old heartaches. As much as Caitlin wanted Raven's love, she knew the truth. They were only friends. Maybe someday, he would fall in love with her. She could enter his thoughts and force him to love her, but then she'd live with the knowledge he hadn't given his love freely. "He'll come around."

"Aye, and someday I'll be a natural blond. When was the last time Raven took you dancing?"

"Never."

"Films?"

Caitlin shook her head. "We don't like the same movies."

"Dinner then?"

"Well, kinda."

"Kinda?" Vicky eyed her with a calculating expression. "What kind of dates do you two go on?"

"We bowl on Thursday nights, and sometimes on Saturday, we'll play a game or two of racquetball. Sometimes we'll grab a burger and watch a game at Malone's Sports Bar."

"Oh good grief, burgers, bowling, and brew, you call that a relationship? Give me a break."

"What's wrong with that? I enjoy myself. I don't have to get dressed up, and I can be me."

"No roses, no romance. Face it. You are his spare tire. You are someone *he* can depend on when *he* needs you. What about when *you* need him?"

"If I needed Raven, he'd be there for me. You don't understand. He isn't ready for a relationship. He isn't ready to get married again."

"And when he is ready to get married again, then what? You'll be his best man?"

Caitlin slid off the bed. "Fine, I'll go on the stupid date. But I won't enjoy myself."

~ ~ ~

Caitlin pulled into Capone's parking lot. From what she'd heard about the place, it resembled a speakeasy on the inside. And from how packed the parking lot was, it had to be good. The first available space she spotted was quite a distance from the door. Heck, she'd been closer if she'd just walked from her home. Caitlin pulled her Mustang into the parking space and cut her engine. At least she was under a light. Caitlin checked her watch. Maybe Jeff had grown tired of waiting for her and left. She could wish.

The Maître d' tipped his white fedora as she entered. "What brings a dame like you to a place like this?"

"I'm meeting a friend," she said. "Jeff Morgan."

While the Maître d' checked a list, she peeked inside the bar. The waiters and waitress wore pinstriped suits and black fedoras. On the walls hung photos of Al Capone, Bugs Moran, and John Dillinger. Over the bar were two Thompson machine guns. From where she stood, they looked like the real things.

She had to give a point in Jeff's favor. Capone's was an excellent choice for a first date. It beat the devil out of the bowling alley.

"I'll show you to his table, Doll." The Maître d' led her down a few steps and wove between tables to the back of the room.

Jeff sat in a booth near the dance floor.

Four empty glasses littered the table. Her *date* smiled and held up an empty glass in his left hand to a waiter. "Another whiskey," he said and glanced at her. "What can I get you?"

"A glass of your house red wine, please."

"You head the gorgeous lady."

Caitlin eyed him and slid into the seat across from him. His short-cropped curly blond hair, cleft chin, and brown eyes made him attractive. "Sorry, I'm late. I couldn't decide what to wear."

"It was worth the wait." His gaze roamed over her and his smile widened. "Damn, you look fine."

Thankful the semidarkness hid her embarrassment, Caitlin smiled. She never could take compliments, especially from people she didn't know well. "Thanks. Have you been here long?"

His left eyebrow rose a fraction. "No, I was early. But if it bothers you. . ." His eyebrows arched mischievously. "You can make it up to me later."

Some minds were just easy for her to read. The alcohol Jeff ingested made his mind nearly transparent. She didn't like the faint images filtering from him. She should leave. "That depends on what you have in mind." *Why in the hell did I come?*

Jeff motioned to the dance floor. "Care to dance?"

"Sure." Caitlin slid out from the booth. Maybe he'd burn off some of his buzz.

Jeff wrapped his arm around her waist. His hand slid to her buttocks. She firmly moved it back to her waist. *Or maybe I'll end up killing him. Hmm, tomorrow's headline, drunk dies on dance floor.*

Once on the dance floor, he held her close to him, too close. His pelvis brushed against her more than once. Keeping with the music, she twisted from his grip. Why was she even doing this?

Caitlin knew she shouldn't have come. Damn, she hated dating.

The number ended and they made their way back to their table.

"Maybe we should get something to eat," she suggested.

Jeff flagged down the waitress, placed their orders, and got himself another drink. "My sister tells me you're covering the *Rag Dress Murders*. You enjoy that?" His gaze intently lowered to her cleavage.

"I find it interesting."

"It would give me nightmares. How can you write about dead people?"

"They don't stare at my chest."

"Hey, I like what I see." He gave her an innocent look. "You are a beautiful woman."

"And I have brains, too. Talk to me, not my boobs."

He grinned, sat back against his seat, and looking at her face. "So tell me, are the cops any closer to finding this killer?"

"Not from the information I have."

The waiter brought Jeff his drink.

"My sister tells me you are friends with a couple of detectives. Jeff leaned closer to her. "Fill me in on all the good stuff. You know the juicy details."

She rolled her eyes. Writing the articles had made her sick, and this guy wanted her to tell him all the details. *People thrive on gore.*

"Over dinner? Really?" Caitlin folded her arms tightly over her chest. "All I can tell you is what I've already written."

Jeff frowned. "You reported that he cut off all their hair. Is that true?"

"Yes," she whispered. The image of Anne Thompson flashed in her mind, and Caitlin ran her hand down the length of her hair.

Jeff's gaze followed her fingers. "I like long hair. And yours is beautiful. Red is my favorite color."

She wrinkled her nose. "I've considered cutting it, but I've worn it this way so long, I'd feel naked without it."

His eyes flickered with desire. "Naked, huh? So were the victims, you know? Raped?"

Is this guy for real? "I don't feel like talking about it. Can we discuss something else? Why don't you tell me about yourself?"

Jeff reached across the table and took her hand in his. "I like dancing. I like to read fiction, and I'm in business for myself. It's your turn. I begged my sister to tell me everything she knew about you. Are you really from Scotland? I don't detect an accent."

She pulled her hand from under his and took a sip of her sherry. "I'm from Scotland, and I've lived in this country for oh, about twenty years."

A wolfish smile curved Jeff's lips. "I've got an idea. How about we blow this place and go back to my apartment. We can talk and get to know each other better."

Caitlin slid from the booth. "I think I know you as well as I care. Good night."

He stood and grabbed her by the arm. "Hey! We haven't eaten yet."

She slowly turned and glared at him. "Move it or lose it," she spoke in a firm voice. How easy it would be to snap his arm like a dried twig.

He quickly released her and held both hands up in surrender. "Look, Caitlin, I've had too much to drink. What do you say we start over?" He smiled at her and offered his hand.

"I don't think so." She turned, leaving him standing there. As she made her way to the door, she heard him order another drink.

She'd been in the nightclub just long enough for it to start raining. To add to her fun-filled evening, the light she'd parked under had burnt out. Her car sat in darkness. Good thing she could see in the dark.

Standing under the club's neon lights out of the rain, she searched for her keys. Somewhere in the black void of her purse, she found them.

It began to pour.

They found the last two victims after rainstorms. Crap, she knew she shouldn't have come here. She'd hoped to put the murders out of her mind for a little while. Last night she hadn't slept, and now, because of Jeff's questions, she probably wouldn't sleep tonight either. Every time she closed her eyes she'd seen Anne's face, heard the screams she knew Anne cried.

Jeff asked if the victims had been raped. They hadn't been, what that animal did to them was far worse.

Someone walked by her and stopped. She glanced over at the short man.

His grin sent shivers down her back. "Pretty babe like you shouldn't be out alone."

She ignored him and stepped into the pouring rain.

The man caught up to her. "Why not come back inside where it's dry, and I'll buy you a drink? You look like you could use one."

"No, thanks." She increased her pace.

She knew the man followed her. He kept his distance, but by the crunching of gravel and the sound of his breathing, she calculated him to be about ten feet behind her.

"At least lemme walk you to your car. It's dark out here and not safe," he shouted.

The hairs on the back of her neck stood up as every alarm in her sounded. Caitlin drew in a deep breath. She hoped he wasn't stupid enough to try something. Why had she parked so darn far away? Because it was the closest parking space available.

She ran the rest of the way to her car.

Three college-age men ran toward her, cursing the rain, and, trying to keep from getting wet. Their voices faded as she neared her car.

Caitlin pressed the button on her key fob, unlocking her car as she reached for the handle. Someone slammed her hard against the door. The sharp edge of a blade pressed against her throat.

"Scream, and I'll kill you," a voice hissed.

He's stupid. "Please don't hurt me." She coughed. The combination of his bad breath, cheap cologne, and her rage choked her.

"Hurt you?" he sneered and yanked her hair. "With pleasure."

Her temper exploded, and she twisted around.

He threw his head back, laughing. "I like a bitch with a lot of fight."

"Cat!" a familiar voice cried from the dark parking lot.

Her gaze focused on the man's hands. He held a clump of her red hair in his left hand and a long thin knife in his right. He'd cut her hair. "You bastard!"

He'd cut his victims' hair.

Uncontrollable rage boiled inside her as she reacted. She balled her fist and not pulling her punch, bashed him in the face.

The man flew against the truck parked near to her car. The force of his impact dented the passenger door. He slid down and fell face first onto the mud and gravel.

Oh, God. I've killed him.

Caitlin took a shaky step toward the man. She reached her hand out to feel for a pulse, but someone pulled her back. His accomplice?

She spun around, claws extended, ready to battle. "Raven?"

His dark eyes grew wide, his face paled, and he took a step back. "What happened?" The pounding of his heart echoed in her ears.

She brought her hands up to her face. Her nails were still talons. The sharp points of her fangs pricked her lower lip. She jerked away, turning her back. Raven had seen her like this. The icy fingers of fear gripped her. What could he be thinking?

"Cat," his voice sounded calm. "Are you all right? What happened?" He placed his hand on her shoulders. "Tell me." The concern in Raven's voice comforted her.

"He followed me to my car and pulled a knife on me. He cut a chunk of my hair." She ran her fingers through her locks, feeling their uneven length.

A car pulled up, and Mike jumped out. "What happened?"

Raven roughly turned her and pulled her into his embrace, holding her face against his chest. "This son-of-a-bitch pulled a knife on her."

The calm rhythm of Raven's heartbeat soothed her. In the dark, he couldn't have noticed her changed form and still be this calm. She sighed and breathed in, smelling the woodsy scent of Raven's aftershave.

"She all right?" Mike asked. He placed his hand on her shoulder. "Caitlin, do you need an ambulance?"

Raven held his hand firmly against the back of her head, preventing her from facing Mike.

"No," she mumbled into Raven's chest.

He removed his hand, but cupped her chin, tilting her face up toward him. "Cat."

"He'd cut Anne's hair," she whispered.

Raven's eyes turned black, and she felt his anger build.

"She's badly shaken," he said and opened her door. Keeping between her and Mike, Raven shoved her inside the car. He leaned toward her. "Stay in here and lemme handle this. *Do not* get out. I'll drive you home in a minute." He slammed her door.

Caitlin stared out the windshield and watched as other officers arrived on the scene. She flicked her attention to Mike as he processed the crime scene. He knelt beside her attacker, carefully placing the knife in an evidence bag. Once he labeled the bag, Mike picked up the cut strands of her hair and placed them in a separate evidence bag.

She was now part of an active investigation. Caitlin closed her eyes. The image of that man holding her hair flashed in her mind. "He's right-handed. He couldn't be the killer."

She grabbed the door handle.

Raven glared at her and shook his head. Stay put, he mouthed.

Slowly she removed her hand and crossed her arms over her chest. She'd tell Raven the guy was right-handed once Raven came back to the car.

Even with the windows rolled up, she could still hear the conversation, thanks to her sensitive hearing. She'd only knocked the man out, not killed him.

Relief poured through her, and she concentrated on the rest of the conversation. Raven wanted the unconscious man arrested for assault with a deadly weapon and attempted murder. He also wanted the man held as a possible suspect in the murder of Anne Thomason.

Raven came back to her car, got in, and started the engine without looking at her.

"You don't have to drive me home. I can drive."

Silently, he pulled from the parking space and turned left, keeping his eyes on the road.

The only sounds were the beating of the windshield wipers and the roar of the tires.

A red light stopped them.

"I was only protecting myself."

"Was he your date?" Raven's words were cold and hollow.

She noticed his white knuckles. If he gripped the wheel any tighter, he'd break it. "No. I left that jerk inside. Why were you here?"

The light changed, and they rolled forward.

"We found a matchbook from Capone's. We were staking out the place."

"Do you think this is his pick-up site?"

"It's a lead."

She turned in her seat. "I don't think the guy who attacked me is the murderer."

Raven continued to stare straight ahead. "Maybe."

"Maybe," she huffed. "This creep was too obnoxious. He wanted me to go back inside with him and have a drink."

"That's how we think he's drugging his victims."

"That's what I'm trying to tell you. No self-respecting woman would go back into a bar with a creep like that."

"If you say so."

She glared out the windshield. "I know so."

He stopped for a signal. "I don't need you to tell me how to do my job, damn it! I have enough on my mind with six dead women. I don't need to worry about some fucking copycat attacking. I know this guy isn't the killer. For one thing, he's right-handed. Just in case you didn't notice."

She glared at him. "I noticed."

He glanced at her and chuckled. "That evil eye of yours won't work."

She sat back and stared out the windshield, watching the wipers sweep back and forth.

Ten minutes later, they pulled into her driveway.

"How will you get your car? What if it's stolen?" She thought her tone was reasonable, considering her uncontrollable urge to hit something.

A chuckle burst from Raven. "Cat, that bucket of tin is fifteen years old. Trust me. If it gets stolen, the thief will be doing me a favor."

He looped his arm around her waist, and she pulled away. "Don't touch me."

"Look Cat, I'm sorry I snapped at you, and I'm sorry I shoved you inside of your car. I was only trying to," his words faded. "It doesn't matter. You're safe." He took her keys and unlocked her door.

Once inside, he flipped on the light and turned her in his arms. "Tell me again. Are you all right?"

She forced a smile for him. "I'm fine."

Raven nodded. "Then explain to me what I saw?"

"For the last time. My date was a dud, so I left, and as I made my way to my car, in the freakin' pouring down rain, this jerk came up to me."

"No. That's not what I'm talking about." He tilted her chin and looked her in the eyes. "I'm talking about you. Glistening white fangs, glowing red eyes, and nine-inch fingernails. You looked like Dracula's Daughter."

She swallowed. "You saw?"

He nodded. "I saw."

"And you're not afraid?"

"Should I be?"

Chapter Four

Where do I start? Caitlin glanced up at Raven's stony expression and sank into a chair. Her living room never looked as small as it did now. She rested her head against the back of the tan leather chair and looked up at the ceiling. Her answer wasn't there, but she noted the cobwebs she'd meant to clean and sighed.

After a few seconds, Caitlin kicked off her high heels, propped her feet on the steamer trunk, and picked up the remote for her sound system.

Yeah, she was stalling. Caitlin had thought about this moment a million times and never liked the outcome. Clearing her mind, she pressed the start button then tossed the remote back onto the trunk.

The sounds of Les Brown and his orchestra floated from the speakers. She'd fallen in love with the music of the 30's and 40's when she lived during that time. The tune brought back pleasant memories of when she'd stood on stage, singing. That was another life and another time.

Inky strolled into the room and leaped onto her lap. He kneaded her legs then settled down, purring. Strange, but his purr soothed her.

Raven sat on the couch. He folded his hands behind his head, propped his feet on the trunk and stared at her. "Whenever you're ready to tell me, I've got all night."

"How bad did I hurt that guy?" She stroked Inky's long coat.

Raven's left eyebrow lifted a bit. "Mike said you might have broken the man's jaw. You caused a hell-of-a-lot more damage to the truck you sent him flying into than you did him. Of course, they don't make side panels as they use too." His black eyes became unreadable pits. "Level with me. Who are you? What are you, Caitlin?"

She bit her lower lip. *Detective O'Brien is reporting for duty, and he means to interrogate me.* Very well, she might as well get it over.

Then what happens? What if he couldn't accept her for what she was? She couldn't think about that.

Caitlin chewed on her bottom lip and stole a glimpse at him. His dark eyes weren't angry like they'd been in the parking lot, nor were they condemning. Instead, they were warm. "I don't know how to begin."

"Take your time and start at the beginning." His calm, low, voice held no emotion.

In the quiet room, she listened to Raven's steady and soothing heartbeat. His relaxed manner put her at ease. This was the Raven she knew, the Raven she'd fallen in love with so long ago. What did she have to lose?

Him.

She was stalling, and Raven knew it. Caitlin shifted in her chair and tucked her feet under her, irritating Inky. The cat flicked his tail and jumped from her lap.

She stared at the cat hair on her dress. "I didn't turn thirty yesterday. I turned two hundred."

A rush of air escaped Raven, and she looked up, his eyes were a little wider than normal.

"Get serious," he said with calm authority.

"I am serious." The card Glen had sent with the roses rested on the trunk. She picked up the card and handed it to Raven. "Read this."

"Many happy returns, Sis. One rose for each year of your life. And the thorns for how much a pain in my ass, you were growing up. Love Glen." Raven looked up his lips moved as his eyes darted from vase to vase. The card slipped from Raven's fingers. "Two hundred."

Vampire. Nosferatu. His thoughts slammed into her mind. He pictured her sleeping in a coffin surrounded by candles.

At least he didn't bolt for the door or try to figure out how to kill her. That had to be a good thing. Right?

He glanced at the trunk she used as a coffee table. "Is your dirt in there?"

"My dirt? Oh good grief, you watch too many horror movies. I don't sleep in dirt. Jeez. I'm not a Vampire. Well, at least not in a sense you're thinking," she said. "I'm Dhampir."

"You're a damn what?"

She spelled out the word then slowly pronounced it again. "In the dark ages, we were called Day-Walkers. We've been called many things including Carpathian, vampire, Vampyr, and Vurvulak, to name a few."

"I see. Carpathian?"

"During the dark ages, Gypsies believed we were the children of vampires and could detect and destroy them. In-a-way, they were right."

He nodded slowly and reached inside his coat pocket, pulling out his notepad. "Vampire children."

"Put it back," she ordered. "You're not taking notes."

The strange look crept over his face made her laugh, and she threw her hands up in the air. "Once a cop always a cop. Is this how you interrogate someone?"

"Sorry." He stared at the notebook and shook his head. "Habit, I guess." He laughed, a deep rich sound that made his eyes water. He pocketed his notebook. "I don't believe I did that and I don't believe you're two hundred years old. Next thing you'll be telling me is that you drink blood."

"I have to."

He stopped laughing. "You're serious."

"Afraid so."

Raven sprang from the couch as if it were on fire and hovered over her, glaring at her. "You're two hundred years old, and you drink blood. You're telling me you're dead, that some bloodsucker made you this way? That everything I've seen in the movies is correct?"

She couldn't ever remember seeing Raven lose control like this. "First off, I was born, like you, not made. Secondly, my father is human, but my mother is Dhampir."

She stood slowly, bringing her toe-to-toe with Raven. If nothing else, he would see, she was alive. Keeping her gaze locked with his, she took his hand and placed it over her heart. "Do I feel cold to your touch? Do you feel my heart beating? Do I feel dead to you?"

"You're warm, and you feel very much alive." He pulled her passionately into his arms and buried his face in her hair. "Cat," he whispered near her ear. "You're my dearest friend and I trust you, but I have to know, what the hell are you?"

She eased from his hold, took his hand, and led him to the couch. She sat and patted the cushion next to her.

He dropped down beside her, taking her hand in his. "I can handle whatever you tell me."

Awkwardly, she cleared her throat and forced herself to meet his questioning gaze. "Before the Egyptians built their pyramids. Hell, before your ancestors moved out of caves, my ancestors landed on this planet. We believe our ancient technology helped create the pyramids in both Egypt and South America."

Raven stiffened. "You're an alien."

"If you call a race of beings that have lived on a planet for over ten thousand years aliens, then I guess I am. And by-the-way, we don't have green cards."

He didn't laugh. "How do you know this? Do you have a written history?"

"No." She shook her head. "The stories of our arrival that were passed down through the generations have become more like fairy tales. My grandfather has researched as much about our race as he could. Grandpapa's convinced our ancestors were responsible for blood sacrifices in several cultures. I'm not proud of that, but the facts are there. The names of the gods worshiped in these cultures came from our ancient language. I won't turn this into one of my grandfather's history lessons. I am Dhampir. A race of beings that heals quickly has a long-ass-life-span and superhuman strength. But needs human blood to survive."

Raven's eyes narrowed, and his lips thinned. "Before you say anything else, do *you* kill for this blood?"

"No. God, no."

"Thank God. I wouldn't be able to handle it if you'd said yes." He turned and took her hand in his and tilted his head to one side. Oh, she could see the gears spinning in his analytical mind. "You say, God. Do you mean God?" He pointed his finger upward.

"Yes, I'm a Christian and was brought up in the Church of Scotland. My mother used to follow *Yeva* but converted after she mated uh, married my father." Might as well lay it all out there for him. "Raven, Dhampirs have as many religious beliefs as humans, and many follow the same religions. Some Dhampirs follow *Yeva*, the Creator. The Mother of Life. Some are New Age, Wicca, Buddhist, Muslim, Jewish, we each have our own spiritual beliefs, and the rest of us try to respect that. We're like you Raven."

"No, not exactly." Raven's lips thinned. "Has any of your family killed for blood?"

And we're back to that again. "Not in a long time."

"So they have." His expression hardened. "Why?"

"Sometimes it's an accident because we have gone so long without blood. Other times it's in the heat of battle. Centuries ago we learned how to take without killing and began living among humans. However, there were a few of my kind who viewed humans as prey."

"Do they still exist?"

"Yes, but our lord passed an ordered prohibiting the killing of humans strictly for the sake of blood. To go against this law means certain death."

"Your lord? Is he your god? Who is he?" Raven stared at her and motioned with his hand for her to continue.

"I've already told you I'm Christian." She shook her head. "Looks like this will be a history lesson." Caitlin flicked a speck of dust from her black dress. She wanted to tap into his emotions, but she couldn't bring herself to invade his privacy. "Millennia ago my people were ruled by two brothers, Ibon and Raoul. Raoul was a monster. . ." She tried to think of a word to describe him, but couldn't. "He killed thousands of our people, and God only knows how many humans. With the help of the elders, Ibon overthrew Raoul. Unfortunately, soon after gaining control, Ibon was assassinated. Raoul stabbed his brother in the back and took his heart. Thus began and the clan wars. When all the dust settled, and the wars were over, a new lord was chosen to lead our people."

"Uh-huh. And this new lord?"

Oh God, Raven already thinks she's making all this up. Wait until she answers this question. Caitlin looked up, but couldn't bring herself to meet Raven's gaze. Instead, she chose to stare at a spot on the wall just behind his right shoulder. "The new lord was my grandfather. He ordered the execution of anyone who killed for the sake of blood. He stepped down and handed the reins of power over to my Uncle Alan. My family has ruled over our people ever since."

Raven grinned, and a chuckle erupted from him. "This is getting good. You're telling me that you are a two-hundred-year-old, alien, vampire-princess." He looked around her small living room. "And you couldn't afford better accommodations?"

Jerk. Bastard. Buttwipe. All of her life she struggled with who and what she was. Raven's flippant attitude just fanned her anger. She'd struggled with her emotions. How could she explain to him what she was, when there were times in her life she didn't understand the answer. Damnit! She didn't make any of this up. But she was too frigging exhausted to give a crap anymore. She wasn't going to defend herself.

"Leave." Caitlin stood and pointed toward the door as she headed toward her room. Her feet felt like cement. She just wanted to crawl into bed and pull the covers over her head. She should never have gotten out of bed in the first place.

Today sucked!

Raven grabbed her shoulder, stopping her retreat. Caitlin squashed the urge to remove his hand. Instead, she allowed him to turn her to face him. "Alien vampire princess? You've got to admit this is getting a little hard to swallow." His cocky expression just added more fuel to her fire.

"Okay, then try this. What you saw tonight was nothing more than your imagination brought on by an overdose of coffee and doughnuts. I didn't have red eyes, fangs, or talons. Goodnight."

A momentary look of fear crossed his face, and the smell of it tainted the air. Yeah, she knew her eyes were red again and not because she'd been crying. The tips of her fangs pricked her lower lip. Maybe giving him a good look at her in the living room light hadn't been such a good idea. Too fuckin' bad.

"You're . . . You're telling the truth. Everything you've told me was true."

In the past few hours she'd lost everything, she'd lost Raven. Never again would he see her for who she was, but the monster he thought she was. "No shit, Dick Tracy. I've told you the truth." With those words, her life drained from her, leaving her hollow and dreading what she had to do. She had to remove all memories of tonight from Raven's mind. Perhaps it would be best if she let him think that they were less than friends, only acquaintances.

"Please tell me you drink animal blood now." Raven cupped her face.

"It has to be human blood." Her voice sounded as hollow as she felt. It was time to do what she must. She stared into his dark eyes, brimming with tenderness and compassion. Damnit! Why did he have to look at her like that? Why couldn't she see fear, anger, or rage in his eyes? She turned away. Coward, party of one. Shit!

His thumb tenderly caressed her cheek. "Why? Why do you need blood—human blood?"

"You can't live on coffee alone, and I can't live on animal blood. It doesn't have the nutrients we need. Animal blood will act as a temporary fix in an emergency. Much like a candy bar helps when you're hungry, but we need human blood to live."

"Why?"

"I don't know." She turned and flopped down on the couch, drawing her knees to her. She wrapped her arms around her shins and rested her chin on her knees. Her cousin, Quaid, told her once he thought it was because of the antibodies in their bodies. Caitlin wasn't about to go down that road with Raven.

"So where do you get your blood?"

"Don't you know? We rob blood banks."

"Cat, stop with the jokes." He crossed his arms over his chest. "And just answer the questions." He sat beside her. "Help me understand. Please."

She couldn't deny him. Caitlin drew in a deep breath then let it out slowly. "We have friends, humans, who know what we are, who bleed for us. We also bleed for each other. However, giving us blood binds us to that individual. Taking a human's blood gives me the power to enter their mind. The humans who bleed for us understand this and accept us. To them, it's an honor. For us, it is the gift of trust and acceptance."

Raven leaned forward, resting his elbows on his knees and ran his hands over his face. "I haven't given you my blood. But can you read my mind now?"

"With you, I can already sense your emotions and see glimpses of your thoughts. If I wanted, I could force your thoughts, and change your mind about things."

"But I've never given you my blood."

"You're different." *Please don't let him ask how.* She didn't think she could have the whole, 'You're my mate,' conversation with him tonight.

Raven gave a faint nod as he drew his hand across his chin, eyeing her. God, she hated it when he did that. "I guess it's easy for you to read my thought because we're close friends."

She smiled, thankful he came up with the answer to his question. This conversation was awkward enough without having to add the whole mating-sex thing to the mix.

"If I give you my blood, could you make me do whatever you wish?"

Where was Raven leading her this time? She looked at him and smiled. Oh well, might as well tell him the truth. "I can erase parts of your memory. And I can give you suggestions, but I cannot make you do anything that goes against your nature. If it's any consolation to you, I'd rather you be my friend than my slave."

"Have you ever used your power on me?"

"No." Caitlin shook her head. "I've wanted too. God, I've wanted to so many times." She glanced at him. No matter how mad he'd made her, or how stubborn he could be in an argument. She'd never violated the trust between them.

Raven relaxed more and leaned back against the couch. He propped his feet on her steam trunk then cocked his head, looking at her. "I've seen you eat and I've seen you sunbathing. I've got photos of you, so I know you have a reflection."

"You've never seen me in the sun without dark glasses. Our eyes are very sensitive to light."

He edged closer to her. An enthusiastic gleam shimmered in his eyes. "So, all the stuff about not eating and the sun turning you into a pile of ash is a bunch of bull. So, what about changing into animals, like bats or wolves, can you do that? Can you walk through walls? Does silver affect you?"

The excitement in Raven's voice reminded Caitlin of a little boy finding out that Santa Claus existed. She didn't know if she should be pleased or offended. Oh, well at least he wasn't running for the door or trying to drive a stake through her heart. Not yet at least.

"We have heightened senses. In other words, I have great eyesight, hearing, and smell. We can't change into bats, but some of us can fly. I don't. Some of us can change into wolves and larger animals. My cousins can. I can't. Silver crosses don't affect us. I wear one. A few of us do have the ability to walk through walls. I can. We call the process fading."

"Whoa—wait—what? Can you? Why do you call it fading?" Raven's eyes looked as if they'd pop out of his head.

She'd laugh if this weren't such a serious discussion. "Well, I'll show you." Drawing in a calming breath, Caitlin relaxed and began to fade. She purposely slowed the process to give Raven the full effect. Her hands became transparent, followed by her entire body, and she merged with the couch.

"Oh, jeez!"

Raven's sudden outburst broke her concentration, and she became solid again.

"I didn't mean to frighten you," she offered, trying not to laugh.

He eased back onto the couch, even closer to her this time. "You didn't," he said quickly.

Liar. She could hear the fast beating of his heart.

"I wasn't ready to see the couch swallow you up, that's all. So, ah, how much blood do you need?" Raven's heart rate slowed.

"A pint every few days, I'm part human. Therefore, I don't require as much as a pure Dhampir. I have gone as long as a week before, but it was difficult. If we don't feed, the pain is excruciating. The worst part is the risk of losing control when we do take blood. We could harm our donor."

"Why did you go for so long without blood?"

"I had no choice."

"Are you going to tell me about it?"

"Do you want another history lesson?" Her time covering the war was a part of her life she had mixed feelings about discussing.

"I asked, didn't I?"

"I was a reporter during the Vietnam war. The platoon I was with was hit hard one night. So much blood, so many wounded, I couldn't feed, not when men were dying around me." She lost so many good friends that night. That part she hated. Caitlin tried to push the images of their faces and their screams for help from her mind. "There are times in my life I wish to forget. That's one of them."

"Sorry." Raven tucked a strand of her hair behind her ear. "And when you were Kate Marlow, was that another time in your life you don't want to remember?"

She lifted her head and met his warm dark gaze. "Took you long enough. So, when did you realize we were the same?"

"Just now, when you told me."

Raven pulled her into his embrace and calmly stroked her butchered hair. "I wish you had told me all this sooner, but I can understand why you didn't." He kissed the side of her head.

She exhaled almost as if she had been holding her breath the entire time. Her mum had been right, he had understood.

"Cat?" Raven stared at her intently.

"I can't believe how calmly you've taken all this. Earlier tonight in the parking lot, I saw and felt your anger."

Raven fingered her hair. His warm hand slipped to her face. Tenderly he stroked her cheek. "Mike and I were checking a lead. I saw you walk toward your car and a man following you. I didn't know if he was your date or someone parked nearby. I saw him push you into your car door and pull his knife. I shouted and went for my sidearm. Then all hell broke loose. You turned and slugged him." Raven paused and broke eye contact. "I've never been so damned frightened in my life, Cat, I thought I would lose you. I thought you would be killed right before my eyes. I wanted to break that bastard's neck." His shoulders shook with his laugh. "But you beat me to the punch."

"Very funny," she said and playfully punched his arm.

"When you saw me, I mean what I look like when I'm mad, what went through your mind?"

"You scared the crap out of me so bad I wanted to run. When I saw Mike heading toward us, and I knew I had to protect—prevent him from seeing you like that."

Caitlin sat there absorbing what Raven had said. He'd protected her, like a big brother. "Any more questions, Detective?"

"Just one. You told me your father is human. Is he the same man you call father now?" Raven held up his hand and shook his head. "I mean—oh hell, never mind."

She smiled. God how she loved the fact he couldn't put any of what she told him into a neat little 'logical' file. She laughed. Another square peg for all his little round holes. "My biological father is still very much alive."

Raven raised a dark eyebrow. "But you said he's human."

"Another difference in our race. When we take a mate, we exchange blood with them. Our mates live as long as we do, and we mate for life. With a true mate, there are no divorces and no cheating. We tend to be a little possessive."

A strangled chortle escaped him. "Not like us. We marry for the time being." He leaned forward, resting his arms on his legs.

She placed her hand on his thigh. "Raven."

He slid his arm around her shoulder and pulled her toward him. With his other hand, Raven smoothed the pad of his thumb over her cheek. "Vampire, alien princess." A faint smile curved his lip as he locked his gaze with hers.

"Yep." Somewhere in the back of her mind, she knew he would kiss her. Her heart pounded in anticipation, and she licked her dry lips as he lowered his mouth.

The front door flew open, and Raven jumped back as Stacey ran in. "Vicky told me what happened. God, are you all right?"

Stacey stood wild-eyed, staring down at them, waiting for some assurance.

Damn! Your timing couldn't be worst! Caitlin groaned inward and smiled at her friend. "I'm fine. I'm a little shaken that's all. You never think it could happen to you, you know?"

Stacey wedged herself between Caitlin and the couch arm, pushing her much closer to Raven, not that she minded.

Caitlin glanced over her shoulder. Vicky slowly and calmly closed the door then strolled toward them, putting a little too much wiggle in her hips.

"Are you all right?" Vicky asked fingering Caitlin's mangled hair.

Raven crossed his arms. His eyes darted from Vicky to Stacey. "You know what happened to Caitlin tonight?"

He'd asked it as a question, but Caitlin knew he'd meant it as a statement of fact. Especially after all she'd told him. She could practically see the wheels turning in his head.

Vicky nodded. "Of course, I wish we'd gotten here sooner. Thank you for staying with her, Raven."

"No problem. Just one thing."

"Sure?"

"How did you learn of Caitlin's attack?"

Vicky cocked her eyebrow, giving Raven one of her signature expressions that said she thought someone was the village idiot. She held up her cellphone, wiggling it back and forth. "Modern technology. Duh!"

Chapter Five

Raven locked gazes with Victoria and shook his head. He could picture her as a vampire more easily than he could picture Caitlin as one. "Cat didn't call you. Try the fact blood's thicker than water."

Victoria's mouth fell slightly. It amazed him how quickly she recovered her composure. "She finally told you. Good." The woman rolled her eyes.

"I take it being sisters each of you knows when the other is in trouble."

Victoria gave a faint nod. "We can feel when one of us is in trouble. The closer we are both emotionally and in proximity the stronger the connection. One thing you should know about us, Raven. We are a close family."

"I can see that. My family is also close."

He leaned forward and twisted in his seat so he could see Stacey better. He couldn't see her as a vampire. However, up until a few hours ago, he wouldn't have thought that of Caitlin. "What about you? Are you like them?"

"Me? No, I hate the sight of blood." Stacey shivered. "It grosses me out. Like, ew."

"You work in the damn morgue. How can you be grossed out by blood?" He stared at her.

Stacey flushed and blinked, her mouth slightly open. "That's different. The people I cut on are dead. It's not like seeing blood flow from a living body."

Caitlin toyed with her hair. "I can vouch for that. The other day I cut myself, and she went all white on me."

"It was a deep cut," Stacey said.

"It was a *paper cut*."

Victoria rolled her eyes. "Stacey, we all know you're unique. What I want to know is, if the bastard is dead or not?"

Caitlin looked up at Victoria. "He isn't dead. I lost my temper and belted him. I knocked him out. Mike, Raven's partner, thinks I may have broken the man's jaw." Caitlin's shoulders slumped. "I wasn't thinking. I just reacted."

"You should have broken his bloody neck. I would have." Victoria snapped. She drew in a deep breath and looked at Caitlin. "Did he see you?"

Caitlin's eyes grew wide. "I . . . I don't think so, but what if he did see? Oh, crap. I have truly made a mess out of this." Caitlin lifted her hands to her temples, rubbing tiny circles over the areas. "Oh, damn, damn and triple damn."

Victoria wedged herself between Raven and Caitlin, forcing him to stand. "If he did, no one will believe him. And if they do, then it's nothing we can't handle."

The chill in Victoria's voice set off every alarm in Raven. "What do you mean by that?" he asked.

Victoria turned and glared at Raven. Her eyes glowed, and her fangs became visible. "We will protect ourselves. If this man did see Caitlin, and he creates problems, he will be taken care of by any means necessary. That goes for *anyone* who poses a threat." Victoria flipped her hand in the air. "But rest assured Detective, phase one is always bloodless. However. . ."

He didn't miss the message that flashed in her eyes. "You don't have to worry about me."

Victoria smoothed her hand over Cat's hair. "We'll go to a salon first thing in the morning. You won't look bad in a bob. I think you'll look cute, even better than when you cut your hair. Don't you agree, Raven?"

"I think if Cat is feeling up to it, she needs to go down tonight and file charges against the son-of-a-bitch."

Caitlin pointed to her hair. "Like this? I can't be seen looking like this."

He drew in a deep breath and pinched the bridge of his nose. "Yes. Like that. They have to see what that bastard did to you." He offered his hand.

"Oh dammit." Caitlin frowned, but took his hand, and stood.

Victoria handed Cat her purse. "Do you want me to come with you?"

"No." Cat glanced up at him. "I'm in good hands."

Warmth spread through Raven hearing Caitlin's words.

He opened the door for her. "C'mon. I'll have you back before sunrise."

Caitlin stopped and stared up at him. "Aren't we the comic," she snapped.

He'd never understand women. One moment they're happy, the next they want to bite your head off. "No. Why? What did I say?" He asked as he closed the door.

She tugged on his arm and stepped off the porch. "Come on, Renfield. Let's get this over with."

Renfield? Raven opened her car door for her then shut it. He walked around and slid in behind the wheel. "Who the hell is Renfield?"

Cat turned to him. Her eyes were wide, and her lips parted in surprise. "Seriously? You've never heard of Renfield? You've never read *the book*?"

"Don't have the foggiest idea what you're talking about." He started the engine, put the car in reverse, and backed out of the drive.

"You're serious!" She turned in her seat, facing him. "You've never read *Dracula*?"

"That book? Nope seen several of the old movies with Christopher Lee, but never read the book."

She laughed. The sound washed over him like a warm breeze and the last of his fear for her vanished. His Cat would be all right.

Nevertheless, he didn't think he'd get the image of a knife held to her throat out of his mind for a long time. He hoped he could remain professional when he saw the son-of-a-bitch again. Raven clenched his jaw. If he'd been confident he wouldn't have accidentally shot Caitlin, he'd have killed the bastard. He loved her, and the thought of watching her murdered made his knees weak. He risked a glance at her. She had a sour look about her.

"What?" he asked.

"I can sense your anger. I wasn't laughing at you. It's just that I thought everyone had read that misbegotten book."

"That's not it. It's just—hell! You scared the shit out of me tonight. Not what you are," he quickly added. "But seeing you in danger and knowing I couldn't do a damn thing at the time. I felt helpless."

"Because of what I am, I wasn't in much danger. So you shouldn't feel the way you do."

He drew in a deep breath. "First off, I didn't know it at the time, and secondly, even if I had known, you were still attacked. I can't help how I feel. Period."

Caitlin's hand rested on his leg. "Well, stop worrying about me. If it happens again, remember there are only three ways I can die. Destroy my heart, cut off my head, and the last is what I prefer, old age." She patted his knee. "That doesn't mean I can't feel pain and a slashed throat, from what I've been told hurts like hell."

He covered her hand. He liked it when she touched him. God how he wished she saw him as a man, not just a friend. "So, the stuff about a stake through your heart is true?"

"Only if it's big enough, and stays in place until we die. My cousin, Royce, has been staked more than once and he's still alive and kicking."

Raven pulled into the police station parking lot. He circled the lot and finally pulled into his space. "I'm still going to worry about you."

He got out of the car, came around to her side, and opened the door. "Ready?"

Caitlin took his hand, stood, and glanced up at the police station. Raven could see it written on her face. Cat wasn't looking forward to going in there. "As I will ever be," she said, squaring her shoulders.

"There's no reason to feel intimidated. You've been inside there many times. The officers all like you. Trust me on this."

Tonight was different, and he knew it. Tonight Cat wasn't a reporter covering a story. She was the story. Hell, Cat was the victim.

"To be honest, I'm a little frightened," she confessed.

"You've got nothing to be scared about." He gave her what he hoped was his best encouraging smile. The one that said he'd be there with her.

"You're right. I'm just worried that . . . jeez, Raven, what if that creep did see my face?"

Raven put his large hands on her shoulders, giving them a firm squeeze. "What if he did see you, who'll believe him? Cat, I know how the guys feel about you," he gestured at the station. "They all like you. If he did see you and did run his mouth, it will only make him look as if he was under the influence of something. No one will take him seriously. He'll hang himself. Trust me."

She drew in a deep breath. "Let's go."

"By the way," he asked. "Which do you prefer, Dhampir or Carpathian?"

"Dhampir."

"I'll keep that in mind." He squeezed her hand then opened the door.

~ ~ ~

They entered the station. As many times as Caitlin had been here, tonight seemed like the first. The overhead lighting seemed brighter to her and the noises louder. Maybe it's because this was a different shift. She'd only been here during the day.

Caitlin followed Raven through a door and down the hall. An officer came toward them, escorting a man in handcuffs. As they strolled past, the officer glanced at her and smiled. She recognized his face, but his name slipped her mind.

"That officer looked familiar. Who is he?" she asked.

"Martin. You interviewed him. Remember? He discovered the first victim. By the way, he's transferring to arson next week." Raven pushed open a gray metal door then ushered her inside.

She looked beyond the swing gate. The rows of metal desks looked the same as the last time she'd been here. On the far left-hand side of the room, she spotted Raven's desk where a uniformed officer sat, using the computer. She glanced up at Raven. He didn't seem to mind that someone else sat at his desk. Guess he wasn't as territorial about his stuff like she was about her things.

The desk sergeant, Steve Higgins, glanced from his paperwork. "Caitlin, are you all right?" His kind blue eyes searched her face.

She nodded and fingered her hair.

Steve's weathered lips pulled into a thin line. "O'Brien, your partner's in room six. Jackson, from sex crimes, is with him."

"Sex crimes?" She stared at him in astonishment.

Higgins gave her a faint nod then looked at Raven. "One more thing, Barbara Barracuda Townsley is here."

"What! What's she doing here?" Raven turned and looked around. "Where is she?"

"Still out front, last I saw. The captain wouldn't let her go any farther. When she left town three years ago, I thought we'd seen the last of her. Guess, I was wrong. She's with the *Informer*, covering the murders. I thought you'd like to know."

"Raven, who are you talking about?" Caitlin touched his arm to get his attention.

He didn't look at her. "Barbara Townsley, the reporter you replaced."

"Oh." Now, she understood. Raven had told her about Barbara's unethical reporting. She also liked to smear the police department, never giving them any credit. Needless to say, she wasn't well liked. That could be a reporter's downfall. If the officers didn't like you, the only information you'd get would be what they'd released or what you heard on a scanner.

She'd like to see if this woman looked like the raving witch everyone had described. Heck, Raven had described Barbara Townsley as more of a monster than Jack the Ripper.

"C'mon, Cat. Let's get you on back." Raven guided her through the swing gate and back to his desk. The uniformed officer sitting there stood.

"Ma'am." He pulled a chair over for her and motioned her to sit.

She recognized him now. He was one of the officers at the nightclub.

Raven stood behind her. "Caitlin, Officer Wagner will take your statement. When you have finished giving your statement, and with your permission, we would like to take some photos of you. It would provide a record of your injuries."

"But I'm not hurt." She turned and glanced up at him. "You didn't say a word about having to have my picture taken."

"Is there a *problem*?" Raven bent down. "Caitlin, what's wrong?" he whispered.

"Nothing is wrong, silly."

"Miss MacPhee," Wagner said, drawing her attention back to him. "Your attacker cut your hair. The photo will provide evidence even after your hair grows back or if you decide to have it trimmed."

"Very well," she agreed.

"That's my girl." Raven squeezed her shoulder. "I'll be back in a few."

Forty-five minutes later, Caitlin wondered what had happened to Raven. She shifted in her seat as she read over her statement. "This looks right." She handed the paper back to the officer.

He took it and stood. "If you'll come this way, we'll take the pictures."

She followed him down the hall and into an empty office. An officer photographed her from four different angles. Once finished there, the officer escorted Caitlin back to Raven's desk.

Officer Wagner pulled out a chair for her. "Detective O'Brien asked that you wait here for him, Miss MacPhee. He shouldn't be much longer. If you would like something to drink there is a vending machine out by the Sergeant's desk."

"Thanks." She dug through her purse, found some change then went to get a drink.

A man and a woman stood by the machine. Caitlin studied the couple, wondering who they were and what was their story?

The man looked to be in his early twenties, tall and looked rather handsome with his long dark brown hair pulled back into a man-bun. His smooth-shaven face made him appear approachable. A good angle for a paparazzo. He wore jeans and a shirt. On the floor by his feet sat what looked like a camera bag. She narrowed her eyes. They could be reporters from a neighboring township.

Caitlin tried not to stare as she glanced at the overly made-up woman. Her extremely too tight and short tan skirt with a too low cut cream blouse made her look like a desperate woman trying to hold onto her youth. Her brassy hair hung loosely around her shoulder. The woman bent down and retrieved her drink can from the machine. She straightened, smoothed her hand over her skirt, and gave Caitlin a quick glance then moved aside.

Caitlin put her money into the machine and made her choice. She smiled at the couple before making her way back to Raven's desk.

From the clock on the wall, it was eleven-thirty. *How much longer would Raven be?*

She heard Raven's voice and turned.

He walked toward her and the smile on his face faded. Raven's gaze shifted from her to something or someone behind her. His eyes narrowed and darkened to black pits as his lips thinned.

"Ready, Miss MacPhee?" He took her arm, lifting her from the chair. "We'll go out through the holding area."

Miss MacPhee? "What's wrong?" She stumbled, trying to get her footing.

"Tell you later." He opened a door marked *Restricted*.

"Oh, goodie. The scenic route," Caitlin joked, trying to lighten Raven's mood.

Raven grunted and pulled her along.

"Slow down. I've never been back here before."

"You can sightsee later." Raven practically dragged her down the long wide hall.

She had to practically run to match his long stride, all the while trying to see as much as she could. On both sides were rooms with glass windows. Interrogation rooms, she surmised. They passed another room, and she glanced inside to see a man fingerprinted. "So this is where everything happens."

A door to her right opened. "I'm telling you what I saw! And I'm not drunk," a man argued.

Raven paused.

"Yeah, Buddy. Someone get him a garland of garlic for his cell," a uniformed officer said.

Caitlin turned to see the commotion going on. The man who attacked her stood in leg irons and cuffs with a swollen jaw from where she'd punched him. Guess she hit him harder than she'd thought. Good. Maybe he'd think twice before attacking another woman.

"That's her! That's the bitch!" He jerked away from the officer.

Raven grabbed her arm and rushed her through a back exit and into the night air. "Sorry about that. I shouldn't have brought you out this way, but I didn't want to take you out by the Barracuda either."

The tone of his voice sent chills down her spine. "Raven, what's going on?"

A flash went off, startling her. She dropped her drink can.

"This will have to go to the cleaners," a woman snapped.

Caitlin blinked, trying to focus her eyes again. She hated bright lights. When her vision cleared, she saw the man and woman from the drink machine standing in front of her.

The woman pointed at Caitlin. "You'll get my cleaning bill for this."

Raven pushed Caitlin behind him.

The woman looked at Raven with contempt. "Well, O'Brien, I thought you'd try to get away without telling me hello."

"Out of our way, Townsley." Raven took hold of Caitlin's hand and pushed past them.

"O'Brien," the woman called, "I came here to cover the *Rag Dress Murders*, but I think I've found another story. *Vampire Reporter.*"

Chapter Six

Curses flew from Raven's mouth as he shut Caitlin's door. Ever since he'd had that sick feeling about Caitlin going on her blind date, he knew tonight would be hell.

He closed his eyes briefly and drew in a deep breath. He couldn't explain it, but at times this strange feeling washed over him just before something terrible happened. He got that same sensation tonight when he saw Cat going into Capone's and again when he found out about Townsley's return. He could only guess her motive for returning, seeing that rag she wrote for didn't cover real news. They only covered gossip. Hell, Cat didn't need that bitch on her butt and he sure as hell wouldn't protect Townsley from Victoria. Of course, giving it a little more thought, he may have to protect Victoria from Townsley. Hmm, he didn't like that idea either, even if Victoria was Caitlin's sister. Cat was the one he'd defend, with his life. "Are you all right?" Silly question, but he'd ask it anyway.

"Take me home," Cat whispered.

He started the car and pulled out of the police station. "Well, I figured I'd take you to my apartment, and you can drive yourself home from there. Mike's picking me up in the morning."

"That's fine."

Raven glanced at her. How would Caitlin's family react to Barracuda's story? Ever since he figured out she had been Kate Marlow, he'd wondered if her family was behind her leaving Hollywood. To protect their secret would they insist on her vanishing again? He gripped the steering wheel tightly.

His life would be empty without his Cat. If her family sent her to the top of the world, he'd find her. "What will happen when your family sees Townsley's article?"

She shrugged, staring ahead. "I don't know. I'm hoping that Royce, Vaughn, and Glen, laugh about it. As for my father and Uncle Alan, they won't pay any attention to it. They realize no sane person believes that stuff."

Caitlin massaged her temples. "However, if this woman sticks her nose where it doesn't belong, or digs too deep into my life, I can't say what will happen."

"Will I have to get between Townsley and your sister?"

"No, if it comes to that I will."

"Like hell!"

"It's my problem. I won't let my sister fight my battles for me, and that goes for you as well."

He'd see about that. "Cat, be honest with me. Did your family force you to leave Hollywood?"

"No. I handled that problem. Quite nicely if I do say so."

"What manner of trouble were you in?"

"I wasn't in any trouble. I left because I got tired of being a puppet. Faking my death was the only solution I could come up with to get the press to stop hounding me. It worked. But, I don't think killing myself will rid me of this witch."

Despite her calm tone, he heard the anger seething from her. She usually let things roll off her back. Cat wasn't one to hold anything in, not like she was now. She had to release her pent-up anger before it consumed her. And he should know. Damn, how many times had he'd gone to the range during his divorce? Too many time to count. "Cat, you need to get it out of your system. Go ahead and vent."

"I don't need to vent. I'm fine."

"Don't know what you're so pissed about."

Cat glared at him. "Seriously?" She shook her head and clenched her jaw then pounded her fist against the car door. "I went on a crappy blind date with a total dick. Correction. A total drunk dick who only wanted to talk about the murders as if I don't think about them twenty-four-seven. I didn't want to go on the damn blind date in the first place, but I did just to appease my sister. I had to park fifty miles away from the fuckin' door, and when I finally left the loser, it was pouring and getting soaked wasn't the worst of it. Nope, to add the whipped cream and nuts to my fun-filled night, I had to get myself mugged in the damn parking lot. And for the cherry on top, I have a vindictive bitch on my ass." Caitlin hit the side of the car so hard he wasn't sure she hadn't dented the panel. "And *you* don't understand why I'm pissed!"

Raven pulled over into an empty parking lot and stopped. "Cat."

She growled low in her throat. Her eyes blazed with violet flames, and the tips of her fangs peeked from under her lips. "I've got a story to cover, and I know that skank will be watching every move I make. She'll be in my way, hampering everything I do. What the hell did I do to cause karma to bite my ass?"

Caitlin threw open the car door, got out, and slammed the door. She paced back and forth, her arms wrapped tight across herself.

Cat needed this. She needed to vent, to get it out of her system. Raven sat in the car, watching her. In all the time he'd known Caitlin, he'd never seen her so furious and hoped he never saw her anger again. Part of him wanted to go to her and comfort her, the other part of him knew better. Cat didn't need to be comforted she needed to rant and rave, to get it out of her system.

Raven watched her pace up and down the parking lot, cursing. The sway of her hips caught his gaze. For the first time tonight, he realized how gorgeous she looked in her simple black dress. It clung to her, accentuating her curves. Maybe he'd take her out to dinner one night, somewhere special.

Cat's shape mesmerized him. She was the type of woman a man could live with forever. Cat did tell him her people married for life.

Dammit, what was he thinking? Beth was right. Their marriage had failed because of him. Because his job always came first and he didn't have enough time in his life for anything else, let alone a relationship. Caitlin deserved someone special in her life, someone not like him.

A light drizzle began to fall.

Raven opened his door, got out and slammed the door. "Cat, it's raining."

She glared at him, turned, and marched away.

It began to pour.

He followed her. Her dress clung to her like a second skin. "You're getting soaked. Cat, get back in the car."

She turned and marched toward him. "I didn't take her damn job from her. Hell, she got fired weeks before I even applied for the position."

He slipped his jacket off, draped it around Cat's shoulders then pulled her into his embrace. "People like Townsley thrive on revenge. It doesn't matter to her you weren't working at the paper when they canned her. You replaced her. In her eyes, that makes you the enemy."

Caitlin's silver eyes pleaded for answers. "What else could go wrong?"

"Baby, don't ask that." Raven brushed a kiss to her lips and held her. He longed to kiss her deeper, to show her how he felt about her, but not now, not ever. He would never lead her to think they could be anything more than friends. He slipped his arm around her shoulders. "Let's get out of the rain."

Raven led her back to the car then pulled on the door handle. *Shit!*

The door was locked. Raven ran around to the driver's side. It was also locked. He peered in and stared at the keys dangling from the ignition. "You were saying, Cat?"

A faint laugh slipped from her. "This is nothing." She grinned at him, locking her gaze with his. Her body began to shimmer then faded, transforming into a faint whisper of smoke. Damn, he couldn't remember seeing anything more beautiful.

Caitlin's body reformed inside the car. She leaned over to the driver's side and opened the door for him. "See."

"Handy trick. You'll have to teach it to me someday." He started the car, pulled from the parking lot, and headed toward his place. "By the way, that dress looks great on you."

Caitlin smoothed her hands across her lap. "Thanks."

Raven turned into his apartment complex and followed the road to his unit. "Want to come up for some coffee?" He parked the car.

"No. I'd best be getting home. Victoria and Stacey will want to know what happened. I guess I should call my brother and let him know about Townsley's threat."

"I'll take care of her."

"Raven, I'll deal with her myself. I don't need you playing big brother."

Hell, that was the last thing he wanted to be. "I'm not *your* big brother." He got out. "Go home and get some sleep." He shut the car door then walked up the flight of steps to his apartment.

~ ~ ~

The Saturday mid-afternoon sun peeked through the last of the storm clouds as Caitlin left the salon. She ran her fingers through her newly cut hair, trying to get used to its shortness. "Well?" she asked Vicky.

She grinned. "I think it's cute. What do you think?"

Caitlin caught a glimpse of herself in the window. This look was entirely different from anything she'd ever had.

The stylist had layered Caitlin's hair so it would flip under in the back and parted on the left. Caitlin had always worn it parted in the center. "I've never had my hair this short. It feels funny. But I like it."

"You look great." Victoria beamed. "You know what you need, earrings. They always look great with short hair."

Caitlin bit her lower lip. "There are some diamond studs I've had my eye on." She grinned. "What do you say we go shopping?"

Victoria looped her arm through Caitlin's. "We'll have lunch first, right, because I'm starving."

"Yes, silly. I'm hungry too." Caitlin glanced at her watch. "I told Stacey to meet us at Books and Java around two if she could get away."

"A bookstore for lunch?" Victoria frowned. "You're kidding, right?"

"No, I'm not. Last fall Lambert put in a deli to compete with the mall. He serves great soups and sandwiches. Besides, it's only three stores down from here, and last night you said you wanted a Reuben."

"Let's go. I'm still craving one."

Caitlin pushed open the door to the bookstore. The smell of freshly brewed coffee and baked bread made her stomach more impatient for food.

They inched their way inside the packed place. "I guess everyone had the same idea for lunch today." Caitlin handed a tray to Victoria.

"A Reuben and a meatball sub please." Victoria took the tray. "Hmm, this place reminds me of that coffee shop you liked in L.A."

"It does, doesn't it?" Caitlin glanced around. Lambert had told her he wanted the place to look rustic. It did. The dark paneling came from an old barn. Lambert had a local blacksmith custom make the wrought iron light fixtures. The tables were old picnic tables Lambert refinished. The place had a very relaxed atmosphere.

"The pictures are for sale. Lambert allows the students at the college to display their work here," Caitlin informed Victoria. Perhaps her sister would find a local artist to showcase in her studio. She led Victoria to a table by the window.

"I like that oil of the sunset." Victoria pointed behind Caitlin.

She turned her head. "That one's new. I don't remember seeing it the other day." Caitlin turned back to her sister. "I wish you didn't have to go back tomorrow. It seems we never have enough time together."

"I know. If this sale weren't so big, I'd let my assistant handle it, but as it is I want to make sure everything goes smooth."

"Don't let Miranda hear you call her your assistant." Caitlin could imagine their cousin going all wolf on Victoria.

"Hey! I've just had a brainstorm. Let's make plans to take a holiday together. Just us single girls. We'll drag Stacey along with us. Heaven knows she needs to get out more.

"The four of us? Imagine the fun we can get into." Caitlin rested her elbows on the table. "So, where to?"

Victoria shrugged. "How about Monaco?"

"Sounds great to me, when do we leave?"

"June."

"That soon? I don't know if I can get off. I doubt Stacey can." Caitlin leaned back, trying to move out of the sun's rays.

"Whenever then." Vic sighed. "Heck we can go the second this murder of yours is solved."

The afternoon sun burned into Caitlin's eyes. She tilted the blinds by their table. "That's better. I guess Stacey couldn't get away."

"Do you want to get her something and take it to her?" Victoria asked.

Caitlin looked up toward the menu. The door opened. She cringed as Jeff Morgan entered.

He smiled and strolled over to their table. "Caitlin, you cut your hair. It's different."

She fingered her short locks. "Jeff, my sister, Victoria. Victoria, Jeff Morgan."

Victoria's eyes flashed and narrowed to blazing slits as she stared at Jeff. "Caitlin's lucky that the only thing her attacker cut was her hair and not her throat."

"Victoria," Caitlin warned.

Vic waved her off and continued, "My sister was attacked last night because you acted like an ass. You're no gentleman. Thank God, Raven happened by when he did."

Jeff turned to Caitlin and motioned at Victoria. "What is she talking about, Caitlin? Were you mugged last night?"

"Do you not understand English? I can repeat myself in French if that would help. *Ma soeur a été agressée hier soir.* My sister was attacked last night." *Where did you find this dweeb?* Victoria bit a hunk out of her sandwich.

You, insisted I go on the stupid date. Caitlin drew in a deep breath then exhaled. "You could say that, Jeff." She didn't want to discuss it anymore and particularly not with him.

Caitlin glared across the table at Victoria. *I wished your mouth had been full five minutes ago.*

It was either my sandwich or his throat.

"Are you all right?" Jeff slid into the booth next to Caitlin, forcing her to move. "What happened? Tell me."

She pushed aside her half-eaten meatball sub. "You can read about it in today's afternoon edition. It will be part two of my story, how not to become a victim. Something, I never thought I would be."

Jeff's gaze searched her face. "Can I have a preview? Tell me what happened. How did you feel?"

"What!" Victoria exploded. "I've known some jerks in my day, but you top them all."

He broke eye contact. "I'm sorry if I sound insensitive. I'm a writer and, well . . . call it research."

"A writer," Caitlin said.

"Yes, I write horror. I get my ideas from headlines."

"Leave." Caitlin glared at him.

He slid from the booth. "Look, I didn't mean to come off like an ass."

Victoria rolled her eyes. "You could have fooled me."

Jeff held up his hands in surrender. An act Caitlin remembered from the previous evening. "I'm just curious. What happened?"

Stacey entered the deli and waved at them.

"Aren't we all curious?" a new voice asked.

Caitlin looked up into Barbara Townsley's heavily mascara eyes. She looked older in the daylight.

Barbara's dark red lips parted in a smile. "Do tell us everything." She raised her voice. "And while you are at it, explain why that poor man keeps insisting you're a vampire." Barbara glanced around the deli, making sure she had everyone's attention. "He even said your eyes glowed blood red."

Caitlin drew in a calming breath and forced her fangs to retract. She kept her tone calm and indifferent. "I don't know why he said those things, perhaps for the same reason he held a knife to my throat. I was lucky he only cut my hair."

The witch tossed her head and gave a faint laugh. "When you've been a reporter as long as I have, you learn that there's some truth in every story. Maybe he did see something. I plan to dig until I find the truth. You see, I get my information from hard work, not by sleeping with the police force."

Clenching her teeth, Caitlin swallowed hard, trying not to reveal her anger. She'd love to fang-out, to scare the crap out of that beyotch.

Caitlin shot a glance to Victoria and winked. "Barbara, you've got me. I confess. I'm Dracula's daughter."

Victoria laughed. "And we know how much vampires love sunlight." She pulled on the blinds, bathing Caitlin in the bright afternoon sun.

Caitlin threw her arms over her face. "The sun. The sun," she laughed and looked up at Barbara, giving her a sarcastic smile. "Good thing I wear sunscreen. It prevents wrinkles too. You might want to try it."

"And soon," Victoria added then high-fived Caitlin.

Townsley's lips pulled into a thin line. "Laugh all you want."

Caitlin held up her sandwich. "Oops, I'm a vampire I shouldn't be eating this." She examined the sandwich. "And it's on garlic bread to boot. Talk about a double whammy." She dropped the sandwich to the plate and pressed her hand against her chest. "What's this?" She pulled her crucifix from under her blouse. "I guess I shouldn't be wearing this either. Oh jeez, I'm not doing anything right. Am I?"

Loud laughter filled the deli.

Stacey slid into the booth beside Victoria. "Ms. Townsley, why don't you do us all a favor and take a flying leap."

Townsley's nostrils flared, and she glared with reproachful eyes, before turning on her heels. She stumbled and fell, sprawling face down on the hard concrete floor. The contents of her purse flew across the floor.

Lambert strode over to Townsley and offered his hand. "Let me help you. Are you all right?"

Barbara slapped his hand away. "I'm fine." She stood, brushed off her skirt then gathered the contents of her purse. As she stormed from the deli, she glared at Caitlin.

When the door shut behind Townsley, Lambert shook his head. "This town didn't need that woman to return." He looked at Caitlin and picked up their bills. "Let me get these for you, ladies."

"That's not necessary," Caitlin protested.

"Yes, it is." He grinned. "While I enjoyed seeing you put Ms. Townsley in her place, I don't want customers harassed in my business. I should have asked her to leave when she started in on you. I'm sorry." Lambert pocketed the bills and strolled back into the bookstore part of the establishment.

"I loved it when you tossed your hands up against the sun," Stacey laughed. "I truly don't like that woman."

Caitlin glanced out the window and down the street. She had to admit she'd enjoyed herself, but at what price? A person like Barbara Townsley could be dangerous. Caitlin smiled at Victoria and Stacey then noticed Jeff still stood beside their table. He grinned at Caitlin then turned his attention to Stacey.

Jeff extended his hand to Stacey. "I'm Jeff Morgan. Tell me that I'll soon be rich and famous."

Stacey gave him a puzzled look. "Excuse me."

He chuckled. "You told Barracuda Barbara to take a flying leap, and she did."

Stacey laughed. "What can I say? The power of positive thinking."

Chapter Seven

The clanging alarm clock jolted Caitlin awake. She fumbled in the dark to shut the blasted thing off.

The clock crashed to the floor. Caitlin moaned. It couldn't be Monday morning already. She hated Monday mornings. Hell, she hated mornings. Period.

She rolled onto her back, only to be pounced on by Inky. The black Persian felt as if he weighed a ton. "I'm getting up."

Groggily, she pushed from the warmth of her bed and made her way to the bathroom. The pleasant smell of coffee and bacon teased her nose. Caitlin smiled. She was so glad Stacey loved to cook. She should have been a chef, working in a five-star restaurant, instead of a pathology assistant in the morgue. "I hope she's making crêpes." Caitlin quickly shed her nightshirt.

The warm water splashed on her face, waking her. Her thoughts were on the day ahead. She needed to call Grandpapa as soon as she got to work. Surely, he'd have something by now on the drawing she'd faxed him. She also needed his advice on handling Barbara Townsley.

Pushing that woman's face from her mind, Caitlin, poured a generous amount of almond-cherry shampoo into her hand and groaned. She'd squeezed too much shampoo into her hand for her short hair. Oh, well, old habits. She lathered her hair then rinsed it several times, making sure she'd washed out all the shampoo.

Caitlin finished her shower, dressed then made her way into the kitchen.

Stacey slid the last egg from the pan. "What time did you get in last night?"

"After midnight. Victoria's flight didn't take off until after ten. Then on the way home, there was a wreck. I wondered if I would make it back before noon. Can I help you do anything?"

"No. I've got it all under control." She pushed aside a pile of magazines and papers then set a plate of fried eggs and bacon on the table. "I made you some crêpes. I know how much you love them." Stacey turned back to the stove, took a plate from the oven then set it on the table.

She took her seat across from Caitlin. "So do you want to eat first or do you want the bad news first?"

Fear gripped Caitlin, and she stared at Stacey. "Was there another murder?"

"No. It's worse." She pulled a gossip sheet from under the pile. "You made the cover of the *Informer*." She handed the paper to Caitlin. "I must say it doesn't look anything like you."

Caitlin frowned. "My teeth aren't yellow and—" She tossed the paper on the table. "My forehead doesn't go Neanderthal either. That witch! I don't look anything like that when I'm fanged out."

Stacey giggled. "And here I thought you'd be pissed."

"Oh, God," Caitlin groaned. "I hate Monday's." She glanced at the headlines. *Transylvania in Pennsylvania*? Then read the article. "*Bizarre murders haunt college town of Mountain Springs, Pennsylvania. In the wake of these killings, reporter Kaitlin MacPhee. . ."* Caitlin looked at Stacey. "Did you read this? That witch even spelled my name wrong. No wonder she got canned."

Stacey lifted her cup of coffee. "God, no. The picture stunned me enough. I didn't want to be traumatized by the article. When did she take it and how did she get a picture of your fangs?"

"Friday night as Raven and I were leaving the police station. I wasn't fanged out. This piece of artwork has been computer enhanced."

"I thought so."

Stacey twisted the necklace she wore. She'd never taken it off since Mishenka gave it to her. It had been a Christmas present. Caitlin had convinced Stacy to go home with her several years ago right after she'd discovered the family secret. Caitlin smiled at the memory. It was also when Stacy was dubbed Spacy-Stacy by Glen and Royce. "What does Townsley say about you?"

Caitlin read, "Reporter Kaitlin MacPhee claimed she was assaulted in the parking lot of a local nightclub. She claims to have fought off her attacker, breaking his jaw with a forceful punch. Ms. MacPhee is of average height and weight. Her alleged attacker, Joe Fisher, is a man of incredible strength." Caitlin glanced up. "Bull-crap! He's a short, stocky, slimy creep." She continued reading. "According to Mr. Fisher, MacPhee asked him to walk her to her car parked in a dark corner of the lot. In the darkness, she transformed into a red-eyed, fanged monster, and tried to bite him. He defended himself with a knife he always carries."

Caitlin seethed with mounting rage. "That bloody bitch!" She threw the paper across the room. "Never mind the fact that poor excuse of a human tried to cut my throat." Her fangs cut into her lower lip. The taste of her blood only fanned her anger. She breathed deeply and snatched a piece of bacon from the plate. "She must have faxed her story Saturday night after we left the station. I can't believe this."

Stacey got up and brought the coffee pot to the table. Her hand shook as she poured Caitlin another cup. "I can. This type of journalism was what cost Townsley her job. I'm sorry I showed you the paper."

Caitlin forced a smile, sensing Stacey's apprehension. "Don't be. I'm glad I found out from you instead of seeing it at the checkout line myself."

"You won't have to move? Will you?"

"If she becomes a problem, I may have to. But it wouldn't be the first time, and I doubt that it will be the last time I'll deal with someone like her." Caitlin forced a smile for Stacey. "I'm like a cat. I always land on my feet."

She pushed from her chair. "I'll clean up when I come in for lunch. I'd best get to work. Mr. D.P. Hamilton isn't too pleased about this." She folded the paper in half and tucked it under her arm. "D.P. wants all of his reporters to keep a low profile. I'll get chewed out over this."

Caitlin glanced at Stacey, still at the table, eyes cast down as she pushed a piece of egg from one side of her plate to the other. "Stacey?"

She got up and turned her back. "Why did Barbara have to come back here?" Her voice shook.

Despite the fact she'd never taken Stacey's blood, Caitlin sensed her sadness and smelled her fear taint the air. Caitlin went to Stacey, placed her hands on her shoulders, and turned her.

Tears stained Stacey's cheeks. "You're the only friend I've ever had in my life. I don't want you to leave. I can't be alone again." She turned away and covered her face.

The thought barely crossed Caitlin's mind how Stacey's life would change. Her life hadn't been easy. She never got over being abandoned.

Caitlin closed her eyes against the stinging in them. Stacey's mother had been an alcoholic and placed Stacey in foster care when she was nine. As far as Caitlin knew, Stacey never heard from her mother again. She spent her teen years bouncing from one foster family to another. When she turned eighteen, Stacey aged out of the system. She found herself alone again.

Caitlin admired Stacey. She'd worked her way through college and found a job working with Doctor Whenn. And that was when they met.

Tipping Stacey's chin up, Caitlin wiped away the tears. "You'll never be alone, Stacey. I promise. I'll always be here for you. Wherever I go, you'll go. Didn't Daddy tell you that you were family? And whatever the MacPhee says is law."

Stacey's eyes widened. A soft gasp escaped her, and she flung her arms around Caitlin's neck.

"Honest. I'll call Grandpapa when I get to work. I'm sure he'll know how to deal with Ms. Townsley."

"While you've got him on the phone, do you think you can get him to quit calling me Spacey-Stacey?"

Caitlin bit her lower lip to keep from laughing and shook her head.

"Didn't think so," Stacey mumbled. She stepped back, wiped her hands over her face, and sniffed. "We'd better get going, or we'll both be late for work."

"You're right. Do you have class tonight?" Caitlin tossed the copy of the *Informer* into her briefcase, closed it then headed toward the front door.

"No, but I won't be home until after dark, so leave the light on for me. I ran into Jeff Morgan yesterday at Lambert's. I'm meeting him for dinner. He wants to ask me questions for his book." She grabbed her purse and keys.

"Stacey? Are you sure about this? I mean the guy drinks like a fish."

"It isn't a date and, I know how to deal with a drunk. I've had experience, remember?"

Caitlin stepped out of the house. She worried. Men like Jeff Morgan could easily manipulate someone as naive as Stacey. "Where are you meeting him?"

Stacey opened her car door and got in. "Pizza Max. I figure it's safe enough, the parking lot is well lit, and it's crowded with students. If I'm not home by ten, you can call out the Cavalry."

"I'll do it too," Caitlin shouted. She backed out of the drive. "If Jeff tries anything, he'll need a medic once I get done with him," she growled.

Caitlin drove to work. The driver beside her blew his horn. She glanced over at him. She hadn't cut him off so what was his problem? He held up a copy of the *Informer* and waved. Great, the locals have seen the story. Oh well, at least he waved and didn't hold up a garland of garlic or a cross. Maybe today wouldn't be too bad.

She pulled into the company parking lot and drove around to her space. She slammed on her brakes then rested her forehead against the steering wheel. "I knew I should have stayed in bed."

Some of her coworkers replaced her nameplate with a cardboard cutout of a coffin. They'd even painted the blasted thing black with her name in dark red paint resembling blood.

Today is going to suck. Really, really suck.

Forcing a smile, she got out and started toward the building. She hesitated before pushing the door open

As she passed editing, she noticed everyone wore black. Stifling the groan in her throat, she continued down the hall. Great, Halloween had come six months early this year.

"Morning, Miss MacPhee," Betty, Mr. Hamilton's secretary, slurred.

Caitlin turned. "Morning." She grinned, seeing Betty repositioning the large plastic vampire teeth in her mouth. Betty Meyers had been with the paper for thirty years and was the only one who could say what she thought to the paper's manager, D. P. Hamilton. "I bet those things are murder on doughnuts."

Betty pulled the fake teeth from her mouth. "Not only that, but you can't drink coffee with them in either." She placed the teeth on her desk then came over to Caitlin. "In case you're wondering, D. P. brought all this in with him today. I think its stuff he had left over from last year's Halloween party."

"Why? I thought he'd be madder than a wet setting-hen."

Betty laughed. "You and your sayings. He was. The old goat called me last night yelling up a storm." Betty reached over and placed her weathered hand on Caitlin's. "He wasn't mad at you, but at Barbara Townsley. He couldn't believe she would do anything like this, especially after what happened to you at the club. Are you all right?"

"I'm fine, Betty." Caitlin fingered her hair. "Thanks."

"I have to tell you I like your short hair. It looks great."

The door behind her opened. "MacPhee, in my office, now," called the raspy voice of her boss.

"Right away," she said.

Donald P. Hamilton filled his office door. He wasn't a tall man, but he commanded respect, even if D.P. Hamilton reminded her of an English bulldog. Short, stocky, and what little hair he had was graying. He also barked a lot.

His small black eyes gleamed at her. "My girl," he said, stepping aside for her to enter. "That poor excuse for a reporter has given me a wonderful idea for a promotion. I've had advertising working on this since yesterday." He turned the poster around.

Bloody hell, the man would use anything to promote his paper. Caitlin stared at the photo taken of her a few weeks ago, only the boys in advertising had computer-enhanced it. Unlike the one on the cover of the *Informer*, this rendition of her, she liked. First, they'd given her sparkling white fangs, a pleasant smile, and they'd left her gray eyes alone. The caption read; *The Herald,* news you can sink your teeth into.

D. P. Hamilton grinned. "What do you think? Great huh? I turned Barbara's little slam to our favor. Wonderful isn't it. I knew you'd love it. I went ahead and ordered three billboards. They should be up by the time you go home today. Fantastic, isn't it?"

"Yeah. Great." She was too surprised to say anything else. "Except it ends in a preposition." She laughed.

"Screw Editing. I love it. Have a seat." He motioned to the chair.

She sat in the black overstuffed chair positioned in front of his massive desk.

He stepped behind his desk, sat, and drummed his fingers as he stared at her.

She sat knowing she'd catch hell for something she did or didn't do.

"I liked your editorial in Saturday's and Sunday's paper. With this killer on the loose, we have a responsibility to our readers to remind them about safety. Besides, it makes us look good. However, do you think it was wise to suggest that people stay home after dark? Your commentary could hurt businesses that stay open at night. Businesses that advertise in our paper." He stared at her with a bland half smile and folded his hands together on his desk.

So, this was his ploy. Caitlin sat up straight and imposed an iron control on her temper. She wouldn't let him intimidate her. "Mr. Hamilton, in my article I simply suggested that if women had to go out at night to be sure they were in groups. I, for one, learned the dangers of walking alone. Had I not taken self-defense classes, I might have ended up as another victim."

He bolted up, leaning across his desk. "Is he the Rag Dress Killer?"

"No. However, the police are treating the guy as a potential copy-cat."

Hamilton fell back into his chair. "Great. If there isn't a full moon to bring the nuts out of the woodwork, then a killer would." He pointed his finger at her. "Do everything you can to get all the information on this Joe Fisher character." He waved his hand, dismissing her. "Get on it."

"Yes, sir." Standing, she gave him a quick nod and left his office.

Caitlin made her way down the hall to her desk. Mr. Hamilton wanted all the information she could find, all right. She'd get right on it-ish, just as soon as she made a call. Caitlin picked up her phone and dialed her grandfather's number.

He answered after the second ring. "Hello."

"Grandpapa."

"Kitten, what a wonderful surprise. Why are you calling? Is something wrong?"

She floundered. She didn't want to tell him about Barbara Townsley or the cover of the *Informer*, but she'd never kept anything from him before. "I've made the front cover of a magazine." Her voice squeaked.

"You don't sound happy about it."

"I'm not! Grandpapa, it's awful." She proceeded to tell him everything, including D. P.'s billboards.

He chuckled.

"This isn't funny, Grandpapa."

"It is if you step back and look at it from a different point of view. I, for one, like your boss's idea. However, I don't care much for the slogan."

"You don't think this will cause problems? What do you think Royce, Vaughn, and Glen will say?"

"Oh, I'm sure they'll be miffed."

"You are?"

"Oh yes, very much so, especially if you don't send them an autographed copy."

She laughed. "You had me there for a second."

"Kitten, of all people, you shouldn't worry about what your brothers and cousin think. You know first-hand what those three bounders have done in the past. This is nothing."

"But what about Townsley? What if she digs too deep?"

"Then she will be dealt with, bloodlessly of course."

"But—"

"Kitten, you cannot live in fear of this woman. She is nothing but a fabricator of lies. No intelligent person will believe her stories. Besides, common knowledge is vampires do not go out in the sunlight, or if they do, they sparkle. Do you wish for me to send your editor that photograph of you in Rio?"

His rich laughter washed over her, removing all her doubts.

"You're right. Have you found out anything about that drawing Raven asked about?"

"As a matter-of-fact, I'd just finished discussing it with him before you called."

Her stomach twisted. "You've talked to Raven?"

"I just said so, did I not?"

"Yes, so what did you tell him?"

"I gave him my *word* that the information would remain confidential. You'll have to ask him yourself."

"Grandpapa!"

Chapter Eight

Caitlin stared at the phone. She couldn't believe this. He was refusing to help her. "You're my grandfather. At least tell me something. I have a duty to report the news and keep the public informed. Maybe something you tell me will trigger a memory in one of my readers that will lead to the capture and conviction of this madman."

Mishenka chuckled. "My little kitten, you should be a lawyer like your cousin, Royce. Or, perhaps a speechwriter."

"You're *my* grandfather," she censored her tone.

"And if I go back on my word to Mr. O'Brien then how would you be able to trust me to keep my word to you? Caitlin, we are an invisible people. We do not exist. Over the centuries, we have lost our history and our heritage. We must always hide what we are. The only thing we have is our honor."

Humiliation twisted her stomach. She shouldn't have pushed the issue. Her grandfather was right. If he went back on his word to a stranger then what would keep him from going back on his word to her? "I'm sorry."

"No need to apologize. You are a reporter. You've always been curious." Mishenka laughed. "But don't forget what curiosity did to the cat."

Caitlan stifled a groan. "Will you at least shed some light on why he's cutting the victims noses?"

"How long has it been since you visited a library?"

"It's been a while. I surf the net."

"And not the part on the middle ages," he said. "I had wished one grandchild would take a liking to history, but 'tis not to be."

"Grandpapa?"

"Very well, young lady. During the height of the witch-hunts, Inquisitors followed the guidelines outlined in the *Malleus Maleficarum*."

"You're kidding? They had an instructor's manual? I can't believe this."

"Before the victims were tortured, they were told what would happen to them. They were stripped, humiliated, examined for marks of the beast, and their noses were cut. Sometimes completely off."

Caitlin gasped, "Why?"

"The Inquisitors believed it would prevent the witches from casting spells on them. They didn't wish to be turned into toads."

Bile rose in her throat. "Oh, dear God. How could they have been so stupid?"

"Fear makes people ignorant and dangerous. You should know that."

"I'm looking for a self-proclaimed witch-hunter."

"That is my thinking."

"Do you think he's," she lowered her voice, "like us."

"No, he or she is mortal."

Anxiety gripped her. Mishenka's not hers. "Grandpapa, are you all right?" He didn't reply. "Grandpapa!"

His choked whisper broke the silence. "Kitten, I want you and Stacey to pack your belongings and come home."

"I can't, Grandpapa. I have a job to do."

"Listen to me. This person could be a danger to you. Thousands of our kind perished during the Burning Time."

"I'm not a witch."

"No, but thanks to that woman, you're something much worse. You're a vampire, a lieutenant in Satan's army, a demon more fearful than any witch."

Never in her life had she defied her grandfather. "I'm staying."

"Kitten."

"Don't worry 'bout me. I can look out for myself." She held her breath and waited for his next argument.

"Very well."

That was too easy. "And don't tell daddy or send the guys here to babysit me either."

"If that's how you want it. You have my word. At least permit me to help you. After all, it's terribly lonely here by myself."

"Where is everyone?"

"Your parents are with your aunt and uncle. Sara is in the States with Vaughn, leaving me here with my books."

He was up to something. *I knew it.* Caitlin leaned back in her chair and stared up at the ceiling. "You like being alone."

"Only when everyone is here."

She ran her fingers through her hair. She knew her grandfather well. He wanted her to take pity on him and ask him to come over and help. She smiled. She had another plan. "If you were me, how would you catch this killer?"

"First, I would stay out of the way of the police and the task force, let them do their job. While I learned all that I could about the victims." She heard the interest in his voice.

"Why? I don't understand."

"You are an excellent reporter. Speak for the victims don't let them be forgotten. Tell their story. Get to know the victims, and in doing so, you may learn about the criminal. Talk to the victims' families, not as a reporter, but as someone who wants to know who these women were. What were their hopes and dreams? What were their habits? Talk to their friends, coworkers, and the people at the grocery store they visited. Find out everything you can. See if you can go back thirty days or so before their deaths and trace their every move. And yes, I realize your detective and the police have done this. But they are looking at this case as police officers. Kitten, you need to remind the public who these women were. And when the killer is apprehended, the jury will know who the victims were because of you."

"That will take time."

"I know. The police should always profile the victims as well as the criminals but, as you said, it takes time. Let Raven do his job. You do as I've told you."

"Grandpapa, what are you up to?"

"Oh, about six foot. I'm shrinking you know."

Caitlin huffed. "I know you too well."

"You have a suspicious mind, my dear."

No, she just knew him. "Well, no matter what you're planning, I'm sure Raven will apprehend this creep before long."

"I'm sure he will. I must say I rather like your Raven. I normally do not pass judgment on a person I have not met face to face, but I liked what I've felt from him. I think he will eventually make a valuable member to our team. I'm sure he will get along quite well with Royce and Glen. He may even get on with Vaughn. Tristan, on the other hand, I hope your Raven is a dog person. How do you think Raven will take to our Percy? Never mind. If he can get on so well with Spacey-Stacey, I'm sure Raven will get on with our family's other fruitcake."

"Grandfather." This conversation was going in the wrong direction. "You're worse than mother. Raven and I are only friends. That's all, nothing more. So he won't be on your so-called team."

"Really?"

She heard the laughter in Mishenka's voice.

She groaned. "Love you, Grandpapa." She hung up.

Great, now her grandfather was playing matchmaker. Caitlin snatched open her file drawer and yanked out the orange folder on Martha Hawkins, the first victim. Caitlin read over the papers then pulled out the folders on the other victims. Her Grandfather had a point. By studying the victims, she might learn why the killer picked them and possibly prevent another horrible murder.

She grabbed her purse, tape recorder, and the files. Today would be long and emotional.

Six hours later Caitlin got out of her car then went into Hawkins' Jewelry Store.

A handsome gentleman greeted her. His warm ebony eyes peeked out from thick lashes any woman would envy.

"May I help you?" he asked in a baritone voice that made her weak.

"I'd like to speak with Mr. David Hawkins, please."

The man offered her his hand. "I'm he. What can I help you with?"

Caitlin shook his hand firmly. "I'm Caitlin MacPhee."

"I thought you looked familiar. You were in here this weekend and purchased a pair of diamond studs. Are you pleased with them?"

"Very much so." She flicked her hair behind her ear, showing off the earrings.

"Can I show you something else, perhaps a matching necklace?"

"Not this time. I would like to ask you some questions about your ex-wife if you have time."

His kind smile faded, and his eyes turned icy. "I think you'd best leave. I've told the police all I know. And for the record, I didn't kill Martha." He turned his back and trudged away.

"Mr. Hawkins," Caitlin called after him. "I want people to know who your ex-wife was. I don't want her to end up as a faceless, forgotten statistic."

He stopped, keeping his back to her. His emotion washed over her. The heartache he felt from losing Martha pained Caitlin. David Hawkins had truly loved his ex-wife. They were even dating again. He hadn't killed her.

Caitlin eased from his mind and tried to speak in a calm voice. "Earlier today I spoke with her co-workers. From what I learned about Martha, she had a wonderful gift for making people laugh. All of her co-workers held her in the highest regard."

His shoulders relaxed slightly. "What do you want to know?"

~ ~ ~

Raven entered the station's briefing room and walked to the front. He placed the file on the desk and looked out into the room. Mike was always better at this than him. Raven clenched his jaw. He could interrogate a criminal, or interview a witness but, for some reason he hated speaking in front of a crowd, even when he knew everyone. He kept his eyes on Mike standing in the back of the room.

Raven cleared his throat. "According to the profile, our suspect will probably be a white male between the ages of twenty-five and thirty-five. He is an organized killer who plans every move. We believe our suspect may know his victims or, at the very least, be a casual acquaintance. We know he is drugging them."

"The Thomason girl didn't drink. And the toxicology results proved this," someone pointed out.

Raven hadn't seen who'd spoken. "True, but there are other ways of slipping a drug to someone.

"Our suspect will seem average in appearance. He may even be considered handsome." He glanced at the back of the room. "Lights."

Raven started the power point program. "This is the first victim. Our suspect brands his victims with a cross." He pointed to the photo on the screen. "As you can see, it is unique in design."

"Any idea as to why he's branding these women and is it done before or after death?" another officer asked.

Raven read from his notes. "From the autopsy reports, the brands are made while the victims are still alive. As to why?" He clicked to the next photo. "This is the second victim. Notice the lacerations on her back and lower legs and the lash marks across the victim's back and legs. Glass particles were found in the victim's wounds indicating whatever the perp used was tipped with glass shards." Raven pointed to the photo. "Here, you can see where her fingernails were pulled out."

A chair scraped across the floor, followed by the back door opening then closing as someone fled the room.

Raven glared at the interruption. "If anyone else can't stomach these pictures, leave now. I'll warn you now the pictures only get worse."

No one else left the room.

Raven described the final picture as the officers took notes.

"Lights," he said. "Now, you've seen just what this bastard is capable of doing. Let's catch him, and put an end to his terror. I want to re-interview every business owner and all of the victims' neighbors, and co-workers. What we are trying to find out is if anyone can remember seeing a man with any of the victims in the last few days before her disappearance. Any questions?"

Officer Johnson raised his hand. "Any idea as to what triggered this behavior?"

"The precipitating factor could have been the loss of a loved one, through death or a breakup. On the other hand, it could have been the loss of a job, maybe to a woman." Raven checked his notes then looked at the officers. "Through an expert in arcane symbolism, we believe our suspect could be punishing these women for witchcraft."

Another officer raised his hand. "Were these women practicing witchcraft?"

"No. However, something about the victims triggered our suspect into believing they were. It could have been a piece of jewelry, a book they read, or even something they said. Hell, it could have been a simple act he witnessed, like their knocking on wood, or throwing salt over their shoulder. Whatever the reason, we won't know until we catch him."

Mike stepped from the back of the room. "We have approximately thirty suspects we'll be re-interviewing over the course of the next few days. We will be going back to the beginning. We will revisit each victim's movements for thirty days before their deaths. Yes, we have already done this, but apparently, we've missed something. We will need to recheck everything, credit card receipts, canceled checks, and sales slips. You will be canvassing their neighborhoods, speaking with the victim's neighbors, and questioning friends and family members. Something tied these women together, and we have to find out what it was. And please, keep in mind these women were victims."

Raven glanced out into the room. "If there are no more questions then you're dismissed."

He waited until the room emptied. "Who ran out?"

Mike exited the program. He shut off the laptop then closed the lid. "Stewart. He'll be all right. Give him time."

"First time I saw photos like those, I slept with a night light for a week." Raven shoved his papers into their file. "Who do you want to speak to first? Hawkins or Thomason?"

Mike picked up the laptop. "I don't think Hawkins is our man. He didn't know the other two women, and we can't find anything linking the other victims to him. Oh, we got the credit card reports on Holloway and Anne Thomason."

Raven glanced up. "Anything of interest?"

Mike's lips thinned. "Nothing. They both shopped at the local stores and the mall, just like everyone else."

"There has to be something." Raven gathered up the folders. "C'mon, let's grab a cup of coffee before we talk with Coach Thomason. I also want to speak with Barbara Townsley." He opened the door and walked out.

Mike stopped. "What the hell do you want to talk to her for?"

Raven glanced over his shoulder. "That story she wrote." He continued down the hall to his desk. He had that feeling in his stomach again, the one he always got just before hell broke loose. "Barbara may have marked Caitlin as the killer's next victim. Dammit to hell, we have a maniac out there killing women he thinks are witches, and that bitch writes a frigging story naming Cat as a vampire. For all we know, our manic has already sharpened an arsenal of stakes."

Mike placed the laptop on Raven's desk. "Talking to Townsley will only egg her on, Birdie. You know that woman has it in for you and as soon as she knows you're in love with Caitlin—"

"What! You're crazy. I'm not in love with her, or any woman, for that fact. I learned my lesson with Beth and will never be that involved with a woman again." Raven tossed the file on his desk.

Mike smiled and picked up his mug. "Yeah, well, I've known you for fifteen years, and the other night when we witnessed Caitlin's attack, I saw pure unadulterated fear on your face."

"So, I was concerned for her. That's all."

"Uh-huh. Keep telling yourself that, Birdie, and she'll slip through your fingers. No woman will wait forever."

Raven slid on his coat. "You're full of it. Cat and I aren't involved. We're only friends. Period."

Mike set his mug down and grabbed his coat. "Look Birdie, you and Cat have been involved from the first time you two met. The only problem is neither one of you have balls big enough to admit it."

Raven glared at Mike.

The phone rang, and Raven snatched up the receiver. "O'Brien."

"Detective," Mishenka's voice came over the line.

Raven motioned for Mike to wait. "Mr. Lucard, what can I help you with?"

"It's Caitlin. I want you to convince her to come home."

Raven's stomach twisted. Hell just broke loose, or the egg sandwich he had for breakfast didn't agree with him. "Why?"

"She told me about that story. I found it humorous, but under the circumstances, I would feel better if she were in Scotland until this madman is apprehended."

Raven eased into his chair. "I'm concerned about that as well. However, Caitlin is an intelligent and careful woman, Mr. Lucard. I'm sure she'll be all right."

"So you won't talk to her," Mishenka asked sharply.

Raven cleared his throat. "I'll speak to her, but she's a stubborn woman. I doubt it will do any good."

"You've eased an old man's fears. Thank you, son." The connection ended.

Raven returned the phone to its cradle. "That was Caitlin's grandfather. He wants me to convince her to return to Scotland until this case is solved."

"Are you?"

Raven stood. He couldn't answer Mike's question. The answer was too painful. "Let's go. We'll interview the Thomasons first, and then I want to speak with Mr. Hawkins. Some men view divorce as a good reason to kill, particularly if there is something to lose."

Mike followed Raven out. "Speaking from experience, are you?"

Raven ignored Mike's comments, opened his car door, and got in.

Mike shut his door. "Birdie, are you going to talk to Caitlin?"

"Sure." Raven pulled out of the station.

"I mean about her going back to Scotland," Mike said.

Raven turned left. Caitlin's grandfather had reason to worry. Hell, the man had lived during the dark ages. He'd seen his people hunted down and tortured. They might be long-lived, but they weren't immortal. Shit. The old man was right. Caitlin had to go back home, just until things were over. The only problem, he didn't want her to leave. She was the only person with whom he could be himself. If he blew up, Cat understood. If he didn't feel like talking, she understood that too. Cat had always been there for him. He didn't want her to go back to Scotland, but he wanted her safe as well. Damn! Damn! Damn! He slammed his hand against the steering wheel.

Chapter Nine

Caitlin rested her forehead in the palms of her hands. This week had been one from hell. She glanced up at her office clock, four forty-five, and groaned. She didn't feel like bowling tonight. She just wanted to go to bed and pull the covers over her head. She was exhausted and mentally burned out.

The more she'd learned about the victims, the more they became people and not just names. Though she'd never known any of these women, Caitlin felt she knew them personally, now. They were women she would have liked. They had been well-respected, strong-willed, and independent women. Now, they were dead.

Caitlin rubbed her hands over her eyes. She hadn't felt this numb since Nam.

She pushed her hand over her desk, shoving the countless notes about the victims and the numerous photographs she'd received from their friends and families. Catlin's gaze fell on a snapshot of Susan Holloway and her small daughter. A child would never know the joy of having her mother's touch again. What bastard stole a mother from her child?

Caitlin drew in a deep breath. She needed to harden her heart and erect barriers around her rage. Otherwise, this case would drive her insane. She'd do just that, tomorrow. Tonight, she'd go home and try to put this carnage out of her mind.

Caitlin picked up the phone and dialed Raven's number, praying that he'd left for the bowling alley. She didn't feel like hearing him berate her for blowing off their bowling night.

It rang. No answer. Good. All week Raven and she had played phone tag. Heck, Raven hadn't even seen her haircut.

The phone rang again. Maybe Raven wasn't home.

Three more rings then his voicemail clicked. Good. Raven wouldn't blast her tonight. Caitlin exhaled, and the knots in her stomach loosened.

She left her message, hung up, grabbed her purse, and stood. Her legs felt like lead. Perhaps she'd soak in the tub before pulling the covers over her head.

~ ~ ~

Caitlin trudged up the steps to her home. She was so exhausted it felt as if she climbed a mountain. Never had her front door looked so good as it did now. The second she pushed open her door the sweet smell of rosemary greeted her. "Stacey, are you making soap again?"

"No. I made candles. Just cleaning up the kitchen." Stacey leaned on the bar and frowned. "Good grief you look like hell."

"Thanks. I'm glad I look as good as I feel. After a long hot bath, I think I'll go to bed. Wake me next century."

Stacey turned and picked up the teapot. "You've been pushing yourself extremely hard, more so than usual. I've placed some fresh cut rosemary in the bathroom. Put it in your bath water. It will help relieve some tension." She filled the teapot. "I'll bring you some herbal tea."

"You and your herbs."

Caitlin shut the bathroom door then began running hot water while she peeled out of her clothes. "Even though I like the scent of rosemary, I'm not putting *grass* in my bathwater." She opened the bottle of almond cream bubble bath and poured a liberal amount into the water.

As the tub filled, she washed her face removing the last traces of her make-up then brushed out her hair. It didn't take as long as it usually did. One positive about having her hair short.

She eased into the warm water then leaned against her bath pillow. Closing her eyes, Caitlin savored the water's relaxing effect.

A knock on the door shattered her silence.

"Caitlin, I've brewed you some tea. Can I come in?"

"Sure." Caitlin slid down into the bubbles.

Stacey frowned at her. "You never listen to me."

"Sorry, but I wanted my bubbles."

She placed the cup of tea on the side of the tub. "I went ahead and turned down your bed. Need anything else before I go?"

"No, thanks. Do you have a class tonight?"

"I'm meeting Jeff at six for dinner. He's a charming guy once you get to know him."

Caitlin rolled her eyes and lifted the cup of tea to her lips. "If you say so."

"Hey," Raven's voice boomed through the house. "Anyone home?"

Caitlin groaned and slid farther into the water until the bubbles were up to her chin. Why was he here? "Raven, I'm in the tub," she shouted. "Stacey, if it's something important, I'll talk with him, but if he's here to blast me for blowing off our game, I don't want to hear it."

"Don't worry," Stacey said. "I'll get rid of him. You enjoy your bath then get some sleep." She closed the door on her way out.

~ ~ ~

Raven shut the door. Cat should know better than to leave her front door unlocked. He glanced around the living room. Fallen helium balloons littered the floor. The two hundred roses Caitlin's brother sent her covered the bar separating the living room and kitchen. Damn, the man must love his sister, to spend that kind of money. Hope he had a better personality than Victoria.

Something brushed against his leg, and he looked down. "Hey, cat." He picked Inky up and placed him on the back of the couch. "Inky, stupid name for a black cat. Couldn't Stacey have come up with a more imaginative name for you?"

"What would you suggest I call him? Snowball?" Stacey stood in the hall glaring at him. "For a cop, you, of all people should know that you knock before entering someone's home."

"I was about to until I noticed the door was open. Forgive me for being concerned."

Stacey twisted her lips and marched over to the couch. She slung her purse onto her shoulder. "Caitlin isn't feeling well, so why don't you come back tomorrow?"

Inky flicked his tail and leaped to the top of the bookshelf.

"She sick?" He'd never known her to be ill.

"No, she's just exhausted. She's been pushing herself hard on this story." Stacey grabbed her keys and opened the door.

"Are you leaving?"

"No." He shook his head. "I need to talk to her. It's important."

"Raven," Stacey huffed.

"If it weren't important, I'd leave, but I need to speak to Cat."

Stacey flung open the front door. "Don't fuss at her. She's been staying up every night working. If she doesn't slow down, she'll make herself ill." Stacey strolled out the door then poked her head back in. "Don't fuss."

"I won't fuss."

She shut the door.

Inky jumped from his perch, knocking a large book to the floor.

"Nothing broke, Cat," Raven shouted, more to let Caitlin know he was still there. He bent down and picked up the album. Its corners were worn, and the gold lettering had long ago lost its luster.

Somehow, he knew it belonged to Caitlin. He opened the album and stared at the tin plate photograph. He remembered his grandmother having pictures similar to this one. That reminded him he needed to call his grandmother. He hadn't spoken to her in a week. Come to think of it he hadn't spoken to any of his family in days. His mother would have his hide.

Raven studied the photo and smiled as he recognized Caitlin and her sister Victoria, but didn't know the other three people in the picture.

Caitlin and Victoria stood on either side of a dark haired woman sitting on a wingback chair. The woman looked similar to Victoria. Standing next to Caitlin was a man dressed in a kilt. Behind the seated woman, stood a young dark haired man.

Raven slid his finger over Caitlin's image. She looked like she just stepped out of Victorian England. The photo had to be one of those novelty pictures taken at amusement parks. Yeah, that was it. He and his brothers had one made at Hershey when they were kids.

Raven turned the page. The next picture had yellowed with age. The three men in the photograph wore World War I British uniforms. He flipped a few more pages. This one was of four men, the same three men dressed in British World War II uniforms, and a dark-complexioned man, possibly Native American, dressed in an American Marine uniform. He was in the center, with the other three hanging on him. All four were smoking cigars.

He turned several more pages. The faces were of the same people, but the clothing changed. How could this be? He flipped the pages back and forth then turned to the last page.

The undeniable truth stared him in the face. These were not novelty pictures. They were originals. The proof of Caitlin's long-lived life. *Dear God.*

Raven sank to the couch and slowly turned the pages again, studying each photograph.

He'd always heard that you could learn a million things from looking at photos. He'd learned two tonight. One, Caitlin had a very loving family who appeared to care very much for her. The second and terrifying realization was the two of them had no future together. Their worlds were too far apart.

Caitlin was two hundred years old. He was human. He stared at the photo, losing himself in her eyes. What would she want with him in twenty or thirty years when she was still young and beautiful and him old and gray?

Raven's throat tightened. He knew what he had to do. He had to send her home, back to Scotland, where she'd be safe.

He turned the pages back to the one photo he liked the best. It was the one of Cat in a silky looking dress with her hair pulled back. She could have been a singer in a nightclub.

"Raven?"

Caitlin's voice startled him, and he looked up at her. She'd brushed her wet hair back behind her ears. She wore a white terrycloth bathrobe tied at her waist. He wondered if she had anything on underneath. Damn, she was beautiful. His gaze traveled down to her feet, and he laughed. "Bunny slippers?"

She planted her hand on her hips. "Yeah, got a problem with them?"

"No, not at all. Inky knocked this off the shelf." He stood and glanced at the open page. A photo of five people standing in front of a Nash with a black wolf sitting on the ground. The three men wore gray fedoras and held Thompson machineguns, while the two women, dressed as flappers, leaned against the car. "Lemme guess." He pointed to the picture. "This is you, and this is Victoria. Right?"

"Very good."

He pointed to one of the men. "And this is your brother, Glen?"

She smiled. "Nope, my Cousin Royce." Caitlin pointed to the dark-haired man. "That's Glen." She ran her finger over the image of the wolf. "And that's Tristan."

Raven stared at the picture then at Caitlin. "You look like your cousin."

She shrugged. "I take after my father. Glen and Vicky have my mother's black hair and ice blue eyes."

"I see. Who's the mountain standing behind you? An old boyfriend?"

"Oh, heaven's no. That's my brother, Vaughn."

"Brother?" He'd never doubted Caitlin before, but the man she called her brother most certainly didn't hold any resemblance to her, her siblings, or her cousin.

"Vaughn's parents were killed during one of the clan wars. My father and Uncle Alan took in Vaughn and his sister, Aileen. Vaughn lived mostly with my uncle while Aileen lived with my family."

"So, he's an adopted brother." That explained the difference in his looks.

"He isn't my biological brother. *However,* he is my brother. We have shared blood. Therefore we are connected." She spoke matter-of-factly. "In our culture, we don't have steps or halves. When you come into a family, you become a member, just as if you were born to it. When I claim my mate, he will become my father's son and my siblings' brother."

"Sounds like how my family looks at things. My parents fuss over my sisters-in-law as if they were their blood daughters." He shrugged. Guess there weren't as many differences between their families. Just the age factor and the blood-drinking thing, and the fangs. Shit. They were as different as night and day.

Caitlin took the album from him and sat on the couch. Her bathrobe parted at her knees, exposing her soft, smooth legs.

She patted the cushion beside her. "Have a seat." Cat opened the album to the first photo. "This was taken at Vaughn's wedding in 1900." She tapped the photo on the opposite page. "And this photo is of Rose, Vaughn's mate, and my sister Aileen." Caitlin turned the page. "That's Aileen and her husband, David Campbell. Father wasn't too thrilled about David, but he won my father over."

Raven joined her on the couch and looked at the photo. He turned the page back to the first photo. "I recognize you, your brother, and sister, but who are the other two people.

"The man in the kilt is my father and the woman sitting in the chair is my mother."

He felt his jaw drop. "You're kidding? They don't look old enough to be your parents."

Cat placed her hand on his knee. "My father's over three hundred years old. I think my mother was born around 1465, but I'm not sure."

Completely at a loss for words, Raven leaned back against the couch and stared at the photo again. Slowly he lifted his gaze to hers.

"What?" Caitlin asked.

"I can't comprehend all this. How old is your grandfather?" He ran his hands over his face.

"I have no idea, and I wouldn't even want to guess. Grandfather brags about knowing Charlemagne, and being his adviser during his reign."

Raven studied the photo then Cat. She didn't look any older in the picture than she did now. "You got your hair cut. It looks good."

"Thanks." She fingered her hair.

All he could say was he liked her short hair. What an imbecile. The woman had just announced her mother was nearly six hundred years old, and she had no idea how old her grandfather was, but he was alive in the late 700's. Hell, even if he were looking for a relationship with her, what chance did he have? In ten or fifteen years, if he lived that long, she wouldn't want anything to do with him. What did he have to offer her other than a cop's pension and sleepless nights?

Cat placed the album on the trunk then turned and drew her knees up on the couch. She pulled her robe over, covering her legs. "What's wrong? You didn't come here to look at my family photos. And you're not dressed for bowling tonight either. You're still in your suit."

He drew in a deep breath. He knew the decision he had to make. "I've been talking with your grandfather. He's been burning up my e-mail all day."

"Grandpapa? He's finally learned to use e-mail. Wow. Well, it's about time."

"Cat."

"I'm sorry, Raven, what's my grandfather up to?"

"First of all, I want you to know that I agree with him one hundred percent."

She shifted in her seat, sitting upright, and alert. "Okay, so let's have it."

Looking deeply into her pale gray eyes, he couldn't deny the evidence. He loved her and would always love her, but he had to do this. It was for her good. "We want you to pack up and leave town, as soon as possible. Tomorrow if you can."

She jumped to her feet. "What?"

"Cat, damn it to hell! Townsley has fingered you as a frigging vampire, and we have a maniac out there looking for witches. It's my guess, you've just moved to the top of his list."

Her lips thinned. Caitlin flung her arms wide, pulling her robe slightly apart. "I have to hand it to Mishenka. My grandfather kept his word all right." She turned her back to him and balled her fists. "Grandpapa, I'll get you for this," she snarled and glanced over her shoulder. "He promised me he wouldn't call in Royce, Glen, or Vaughn to drag me home. And hell, he kept his word. He used you as his pawn. Oh, he's good."

"Cat, it's for your safety. Don't you understand? He doesn't want you hurt, and neither do I."

She whirled around, her eyes blazing red, and her fangs peeked from her lips. "Bullcrap! All my life, whenever there was the slightest bit of danger, Daddy or Grandpapa would send one of the guys to drag me safely home. When I was with the French résistance, Daddy sent Vaughn after me. When Eliot Ness asked me to go undercover in Chicago, Daddy sent Royce and Glen both after me. Hell, I was about to blow the lid off Capone and his gang when those two had me tied up like a Thanksgiving turkey and on a boat sailing for Scotland. What I was in Nam was the only time Daddy or Grandpapa didn't drag my ass home, not that they didn't try. They didn't know exactly where I was, even after having the Wolfes try to sniff me out. And now this." She threw her hands in the air. "I thought Grandpapa would help me. Boy, was I wrong."

Raven stepped toward her. He knew convincing her wouldn't be easy, but Mishenka hadn't told him everything. Cat's grandfather was a crafty old geezer. "Cat."

She glared at him. "Don't Cat me. You, of all people, should know I'm not in any danger." She stormed over to the entry, snatched up her briefcase, tossed it in the chair then opened it. "He's after women he believes dabbles in black magic. All of his victims had shoulder length or longer hair and pale eyes. All of the victims wore some form of Celtic or new age jewelry." She shoved a file at him. "Our killer isn't looking for a vampire, and even if he was, I can defend myself. So I'm not going anywhere."

"Martha Hawkins didn't have pale eyes. She was African-American."

"Who also wore green contacts and a pendant of the goddess." Caitlin crossed her arms. "Her husband told me so."

Her robe opened farther.

His gaze fell to her round full breasts peeking from the V of her bathrobe.

All right, O'Brien, this isn't the time to think about her tits. He willed himself to look at her face. How would it feel to kiss her lush lips? Dammit! "What else have you found out?" He forced himself to speak calmly as his cock swelled and pressed against the zipper of his pants.

"Did you know that Susan Holloway took night classes at the University? She was taking courses on organic gardening and holistic healing. Her daughter had food allergies."

"Anne Thomason was a freshman at the University."

Caitlin's lips pulled into a smirk. "Exactly. I guess that our man may have met both women on or near campus."

He had to hand it to her. She had her grandfather's shrewdness. "Okay, Smarty, what's the tie-in with Martha? She didn't take classes at the campus. Where did our man pick her up?"

Her smirk faded. "I haven't figured that out yet, but I'm working on it. I did find out from her husband she liked to play with tarot cards. Maybe our killer saw her with them."

"Maybe. If that's the case, then you could still be a target. You *had* long hair. You have pale colored eyes, and sometimes you wear Celtic jewelry. So by your own logic, Cat, you're a likely candidate."

Her cool gray eyes flashed red. "I'm not going anywhere." She crossed her arms. "I can take care of myself, thank you."

"Fine. What about Stacey? Huh? She takes a night class, loves to play with herbs, and cuts up dead people for a living.

From what you just told me, she'd make a perfect candidate for our killer as well. Oh, I forgot one more thing that should seal it for her. Stacey resides with a vampire and owns a black cat."

Caitlin stared at him. Her eyes turned darker red with each passing second. She lifted her arm and pointed to the door. "Get the hell out. I can take care of myself and Stacey."

"No, you can't. The fact is Caitlin, you don't know who the killer is, and you can't be in two places at the same time. Pack your bags. You and Stacey get the hell out of this town and don't come back until its safe. For all you know, you could be living next to the killer."

She swiveled, turning her back. "Lock the door on your way out."

His blood boiled. Cat was the most stubborn woman he'd ever known, and he wasn't about to let her get herself killed. He had to convince her she was in over her head.

He lunged at her, grabbed her arm, pulled it up behind her back, pinning her against the wall. "And what if I told you, I'm the killer?" he hissed.

Chapter Ten

Raven's weight pressed her against the living room wall. How dare he use his macho male scare tactics on her! She knew he wasn't the killer. He'd only accomplished, making her lose her temper.

Caitlin drew in a deep breath. If Raven thought he could hold her, he'd better think again. "You want to play? Fine." She faded then reappeared behind him.

Raven glanced at the space between his hands. He whirled around to face her. "What the—"

Caitlin grabbed him, flipped him over her shoulder, and pinned him to the floor face down. "For someone, I like a lot you sure know how to tick me off."

She leaned over him and scraped the tips of her fangs across the back of his neck, just to let him know how angry she was. "To answer your question, I know you aren't the killer, because, I know you."

Raven turned his head to the side and looked up at her. "All the victims knew their killer." He tried to buck her off. He managed to roll onto his back.

She shifted her weight and held him firm.

Caitlin stared into Raven's dark brown eyes, knowing hers were glowing an unholy red. She smiled, displaying her extended fangs. Caitlin flexed her hands. Her fingernails were long, lethal talons. "Look at me." She drew a sharp nail down the side of Raven's face. "Do you still think I can't defend myself?"

"You've made your point, Cat. Pull in your claws and lemme up. All right?"

As fearsome as she knew she looked, she sensed no fear in him. He wasn't even slightly angry with her. Didn't he know she could easily drain him of his life's blood? "So why aren't you afraid of me? I could kill you. After all, I am a vampire."

He grinned. "Dhampir."

His gaze left hers and moved to her chest. "And. . . Uh, you may want to adjust your robe, not that I'm not enjoying the view."

She looked down at her bathrobe. During their tussle, it had pulled apart. She wasn't flashing Raven, but she wasn't far from spilling out of it either.

"Pervert!" She yanked the terrycloth robe tight and retied her sash.

His eyes glittered with amusement. "Pervert? Madame, you wound me. I'm merely a man. And if I may point out, one who is sprawled on your living room floor with you on top." He raised a dark eyebrow. "Come to think of it, the last time we worked on your judo, I ended up on top of you." He grinned. "Should I say, uncle?"

No matter how angry she'd been, seeing him pinned beneath her and joking about it made her laugh. "The only reason you won the last time we were at the gym was that I let you."

His expression suddenly changed to shock. "Pardon? You *let* me?" He sat up, circling her waist with his arms. "Are you telling me that all those times we sparred, you just *allowed* me to win?"

She stared into his deep dark eyes. Her heart fluttered. All she wanted to do was kiss those incredible lips. "Hate to say it, Bub, but I'm about six times stronger than you."

His smile faded, and he looked at her critically. "I like strong women."

"You do?" She asked, staring at his lips.

He nodded his approval and bent toward her. "Very much." His lips brushed against hers as he spoke. Raising his mouth from hers, he gazed into her eyes. Waiting.

Her heart pounded in her chest. "I've been hoping you'd do that for a long time," she whispered.

"Have you?" He covered her mouth again.

This time, she kissed him with all the hunger that raged inside her. Her tongue traced the softness of his lips then dipped into the recess of his mouth. He tasted of coffee and something wonderful. He tasted of Raven.

She didn't mind his beard stubble scraping her cheek. He was in her arms and kissing her.

Caitlin moaned as her hands explored Raven's muscular back. The bulge in his pants pressed against her, arousing her. He was big, thick, and hard as steel. She did that to him. Damn, she should have taken her mother's advice sooner. Oh well, better late than never. Caitlin pressed against his erection, sending faint trimers coursing through her. If she'd taken the time to put on some panties, they'd be soaked.

When this game started, she tossed him to the floor, planning on having him, but taking his blood? Caitlin wouldn't claim Raven as her mate until he told her he loved her. Until he finally opened up his heart to her and expelled the last bit of poison left from his ex-wife.

Shifting her weight, she rubbed over his very impressive shaft, pressing it against her mound. Never in her life had she come just from humping, but damn. There's always a first time. So, very tempting to tear his pants from him and impale herself on his cock. Just the thought made her even wetter.

The rich taste of blood tinged her tongue, and she broke off their kiss. "I didn't hurt you? Did I?" Dark, rich, crimson blood pooled on his bottom lip.

Raven stared at her. "Why are you mad?"

She licked his lower lip, tasting his blood and healing the wound she'd caused. "I'm not mad. I want you."

A seductive smile curved his lips. Hmm. I would have never guessed." Raven gently guided her hand to his dick. "Feel what you do to me?" He nipped her earlobe. "Every time I'm around you, I get a boner."

She palmed him, running her hand up the outside of his pants and feeling his hardness, feeling his desire for her. She squeezed him, drawing a moan from him. "Hmm, then we're even because it's no fun walking around with soaked panties."

~ ~ ~

Raven covered her mouth, to stop Cat from talking. One more word about how he made her wet, and he'd blow his wad like a pimply face teen.

A small drop of her blood tinged his tongue. It warmed him like a fine brandy and tasted as intoxicating. He wanted more. He wanted to taste more. He wanted to taste her.

"Cat," he moaned. What was he thinking? He had no business taking advantage of Cat, of her vulnerability. Yeah, he knew she told him she wanted him. But he also realized Cat felt like this because she'd spent so much time researching this damn case. She was looking for a way to reaffirm life and sex was one sure-fire way to do that. He wanted their first time to be special, not a 'feel-fuck.' Sure as hell, come tomorrow morning, she'd only feel worse. Another thing, making love to Caitlin, could demolish their friendship.

"Make love to me," she whispered. Her fingers tugged on his zipper. "I want you in me."

He stilled her hand as he stared into her eyes, trying to see the truth. Caitlin projected an intoxicating power. Despite her dark red eyes and dangerous looking fangs, he wanted her. Hell, he's wanted her for the past two years.

His hands slid under her thick terry robe, finding the softness of her skin. He cupped her breasts. His thumbs teased her nipples, making them hard little nubs. "Only if you respect me in the morning." He leaned forward, his tongue teasing her nipple.

Moaning, Caitlin pushed from him. Her red eyes glimmered. "I need you now."

Carefully, he traced her swollen lips with the tip of his finger, feeling the sharp points of her fangs. "Cat," he forced the words from his mouth. "I care about you. No matter what happens—"

"I'll always be your friend," she finished for him. Her lips covered his as she rocked against him. Her heat scorched him through his pants. Damn, she was hot. "I want you naked. I want to feel your skin."

His heart pounded as she freed him of his shirt. The tender touches of her hands drove him mad. Raven pushed her robe from her. "You're beautiful."

She spayed her fingers over his chest. "You're not bad yourself," she said and moved her attention to his pants. She ran her hand up the length of him before she tugged on his belt.

It would be heaven to have her touch him, to take him in her hands. He stifled a moan. If he didn't take her to bed, he'd be making love to her on the floor. He kept his gazed locked with hers, firmly gripped her waist. "Not here. Not on the floor." Cat deserved to be made love to in a bed. He maneuvered himself into a squat position. Still holding Caitlin, he stood. "You may be stronger than me, but are you flexible?"

"I'll show you flexible." She nipped his earlobe.

Laughing, he carried her to her bedroom. The bed covers were turned down. Raven dropped her on the large iron bed. Its size engulfed her.

He smiled and looked into her blazing eyes. "Are you sure about this?" He had to ask, had to make certain she wanted this as much as he did, even if the demon on his shoulder screamed at him to shut his pie-hole.

Caitlin slid from the bed and stood. With a quick jerk, she unzipped him and pushed his trousers down over his hips. "I've never been surer. So, stop stalling."

He snatched his wallet from the pocket, before letting his pants fall to the floor.

She glanced at him curiously. "Afraid I'll roll you?"

He laughed. "For six bucks and a lottery ticket, doubt it." He held up the foil pack. "We don't want any unexpected consequences, do we?"

A faint blush crossed her pale and beautiful face as she took the package from him. "Allow me." She pressed against him. "But first, we have to get rid of these." She pushed his shorts over his hips.

The second her soft hand gripped his cock firmly, he nearly came. Her tender touch was pure torture and pleasure. Her fingers lightly traced his tip. He locked his knees to keep them from buckling. He wondered if Cat knew the power she had over him.

~ ~ ~

Caitlin pressed herself against him and lifted herself on tiptoes. She knew in her heart Raven would merely be fulfilling a physical desire, but for her, it would be more. She loved him and would fight everything in her to keep from claiming him. She wouldn't take the choice from him. Caitlin pressed her lips against Raven as she took him in her hands, and slid the condom over him.

Her fangs throbbed and the scent of his blood teased her, excited her. She nuzzled the tender area between his shoulder and neck, wanting to drink from him, wanting to claim him as her mate as he was meant to be.

She gasped as Raven lifted her in his arms and passionately nibbled on her throat. Her body hummed with need. Her hand pressed his head tighter, wanting him to bite her harder. She moaned, "That feels wonderful."

"Does it? What else feels good to you?" he asked, his voice rough.

"You in me now." She smiled and licked her lips.

They fell to the bed, on their sides facing each other and clutching each other. The grin splitting Raven's face slowly faded as his hand moved down the length of her back. He rolled her under him.

Caitlin parted her legs and wrapped them around his hips as he reclaimed her mouth. Instinctively she arched her body toward him, as she caressed the strong tendons in his back.

The tip of him pressed into her. Then he stopped, and she thought she would die. "You're tight," he murmured, as he eased into her. "Cat?"

"It's been awhile." He wasn't going to deny her now, damn it. So what if it's been a couple of years. She tightened her legs around him and thrust her hips up, taking him into her.

He growled out something sounding too much like bossy before he eased back then slowly slid into her again.

The desire to mate with Raven pounded the blood through Caitlin's body. Raven tried to set an easy pace, but her passion and her primal need demanded she'd set the tempo of their lovemaking. She arched her neck, angling her mouth, so her fangs hovered briefly over the large vein in his throat. It was so tempting to claim him, make him hers in every way. The muscles in her jaw twitched before she closed her lips and turned her face from him.

Caitlin opened her mind and shared Raven's emotions. He wanted her. Her heart swelled with the knowledge, but she would not claim him tonight. She wouldn't know the full pleasure of his lovemaking.

Raven held her tightly and thrust deeply into her. He cried out her name with his release.

The sharing of his emotions gave her a false climax. Another difference between their kind. Males could get off no matter what, females only experienced an orgasm with their true mate. A tear ran down her cheek. Someday, he'd be hers. Someday she'd know true pleasure.

Raven rolled them, so he lay on his back, keeping himself inside of her. "Lady, you're something special." He lowered his lips, claiming her mouth.

His kiss excited her again. Waves of desire washed over her. Her hands slid up his chest and down his arms. She followed her hands with her gaze taking in his beautiful muscular form. "You don't look anything like a scrawny blackbird."

He chuckled. "Gee, thanks."

His hands glided over her thighs, stopping at her womanhood. He smiled as his fingers stroked her. "Hairless."

She squeezed her muscles, feeling him harden. "How did you get the name Raven, did your mom think she was having a girl?"

"Cat, I can't believe you want to talk now." He closed his eyes and moaned.

If she didn't keep some part of herself under control, she'd claim him this very moment and take away his right to choose.

Caitlin leaned over him, letting her nipples brush against his chest. "Is it a family name?"

His hands circled her waist, controlling her movement. "My mother adored Poe. She named my two brothers Edgar and Usher." He moved slowly in her. "My sister is Lenore, and I was dubbed Raven. Lucky me."

Caitlin tightened and loosened her muscles, enjoying the look of pleasure that crossed Raven's handsome face. "Your mother could have named you Al Aaraaf."

"You talk too much." Raven sat up and covered her mouth with his. She surrendered completely to his masterful skills. Her thoughts became fragmented with his, as hot raging passion took over.

He surged in her. "Cat!" He held her as his body shook.

The tips of her fangs lengthened. Blood.

The smell of it, the sound of it pulsating through Raven's body as he came, pushed her over the edge of sanity. Her body hummed with his release. All she had to do was take his blood, give him hers, and they would be bound together for eternity. She hovered over the large vein in his neck. No! She would not take the choice away from him. She loved him too much. She sank her fangs into her lower lip, tasting the bitterness of her blood.

Raven sank back on the bed, taking her with him. His hands encircled her, one hand on the small of her back, the other on her shoulders. His uneven breath teased her cheek.

Caitlin snuggled against him. She had no desire to move from his embrace.

"Cat," Raven said. "I still want you to go home."

She lifted her head. "I am home."

"You know what I mean." He drew in a deep breath and met her gaze. "I care a hell of a lot about you. It would kill me if anything happened to you. Take some time off and go back to Scotland. Please."

She stared at him. He cared about her. That's all? They'd just shared incredible sex, and all he could say was he cared about her. "The only place I'm going is to the bathroom." She slid from him and rolled to her side of the bed.

"Oh, jeez!" He groaned. "The frigging thing broke."

Caitlin turned and looked at him. "What broke?"

"What do you think? Please tell me you're on the pill. My God, Cat! If you end up with my kid..." Raven scrubbed his hands over his face and let out a heavy sigh. "Shit! Are you on the pill or not?"

His panic that she'd end up pregnant slammed into her. Raven's fear quickly turned to rage, and it cut through her heart.

"I'm not on the pill, but you don't have to worry. I'm not pregnant,"

He glared at her. "How can you be certain?"

"Because we didn't go all the way."

Raven's mouth fell open, and he rose up. "What? How can you say that after the kind of sex we just had? What do you mean we didn't go all the way?"

"I didn't take your blood."

"What does that have to do with what we just did?" He matched her snappish tone.

"Just did? You make it sound like we just finished a card game or something."

He rolled his eyes. "I didn't mean for it to sound like that. Cat, if you end up pregnant with my child, it will be my responsibility as well. Are you sure you can't be pregnant?"

The bliss she'd been feeling vanished, replaced by a sudden coldness. "I didn't claim you as my mate. The only guaranteed time I can conceive is when I first take the blood of my chosen while making love to him. So, you don't have a thing to worry about." Suddenly feeling exposed, she pulled the blanket from the bed and wrapped it around her. She blinked back tears and marched to the bathroom pausing briefly. "So you don't have to worry about being trapped by me." She slammed the door closed behind her.

Her heart broke. Raven didn't love her. She'd been right. She'd felt his fear that she'd trap him with a child and that cut into her. She'd just lost her best friend. Why hadn't she severed her mental link with him after they made love? No, they hadn't made love, they banged uglies.

Caitlin looked at her reflection in the bathroom mirror. Bloodstained tears ran down her cheek.

~ ~ ~

Raven stared up at the ceiling. Caitlin's words still echoed in his mind. She'd not claimed him as hers. She didn't want him. Beth hadn't wanted him either.

He'd leave before Caitlin returned. He never allowed Beth to see him upset and he wouldn't let Caitlin either.

Raven, bent over and retrieved his pants from the floor.

The sound of running water came from the bathroom.

He pulled them on, shoved his hands deep into his pockets, and left her room. He slid his shirt on over his bare chest then retrieved his shoes and coat.

He opened the front door. Something brushed by his leg.

He clenched his teeth. "Damn it's cold."

Raven drove home, not thinking, not feeling, only being.

Numb, he put his key in the lock and turned the knob. Darkness greeted him. He flipped the light switch and tossed his jacket, shoes, and shirt to the couch. He flopped into his favorite chair in front of the fireplace.

Raven stared up at the portrait hanging above the mantle. No longer did he see Kate Marlow. He saw Caitlin.

He closed his eyes and leaned his head back. What went wrong tonight? Why hadn't she wanted him? Shit! He'd knew making love to Caitlin would be a mistake, but he couldn't resist.

Raven scrubbed his hands over his face. Superstition said a vampire couldn't enter one's home unless invited. Maybe the same law applied to Caitlin. Perhaps she couldn't take his blood unless he offered it to her. She did tell him some people willingly bled for her kind.

Raven folded his fingers together forming a triangle. Had she taken his blood tonight while they were making love, they would be mated? His eyes flew open. "Married?"

~ ~ ~

Caitlin paused before opening her bathroom door. What would she say to him? She shook her head. The only thing she could. *If I had taken your blood, we would be bound for all eternity.*

Drawing in a deep breath, she opened the door.

Raven wasn't in her room. Maybe he'd gone to the living room. "Raven, we need to talk," she said as she walked down the hall. She stopped. Raven wasn't in the living room. He'd left.

Raven hadn't even told her goodbye. "Raven!"

Caitlin sank to the floor and let her tears flow.

Chapter Eleven

Caitlin lay in bed, watching her ceiling fan spin. Trying to sleep was getting her nowhere. She glanced at her bedside clock.

Six A.M. Caitlin groaned.

She had to get up in two hours, but she was so tired her body ached. She rolled over. Maybe she could sleep for a few seconds before her alarm went off.

Caitlin closed her eyes, but her mind returned to last night and Raven. She opened her eyes and focused on the glow from the streetlights shimmering on the wall.

Her thoughts drifted to the day she'd first met him. She'd been covering a story on teenage runaways. Raven wouldn't give her any information. She'd found out that Barbara Townsley had ruined it for all reporters with Raven O'Brien.

Later that night, Caitlin had run into Raven at the bowling alley. His team had needed a sub, and she volunteered. She'd never forget the look Raven shot her. His dark eyes pierced her as he ran his hand over his short hair. "Hell, we might as well forfeit the game," he said and walked away.

Caitlin smiled at the memory. After her third strike, he'd started talking to her. When they'd won the game, he'd asked her out for a burger. They'd been the best of friends ever since.

A tear trickled down her cheek, and she rolled over on her back.

If only I could sleep.

She must have dozed off some because she couldn't remember hearing Stacey come home. No matter how quiet Stacey tried to be, she always woke Caitlin.

She sat up. All night she'd thought of Raven. Her memories of him and last night kept her awake. She kept reliving how it had felt when he'd held her, when he'd kissed her, and when they'd made love. She couldn't get him out of her mind. Every time she breathed, she smelled his cologne.

She'd even gotten up and changed her sheets sometime around midnight.

Sometimes having sharpened senses was a real pain.

Caitlin hugged her pillow. She needed to talk to someone. Dammit, she needed to talk to Stacey.

Caitlin punched her pillow. Stacey wouldn't be up for another hour. "But damn it. I have to talk to her."

Caitlin slid from her bed and plodded across the hall. She lifted her fist to knock. Hell Stacy never got mad. "Stacey, I need to talk." Caitlin knocked.

No answer.

Caitlin knocked louder. "Come on Stace. I know it's not time to get up, but this is important."

Again, no answer.

"Stacey?" Caitlin slowly turned the doorknob. With her keen eyesight, she could tell the room was empty. She flipped on the light switch, hoping her sight had failed her. It hadn't. The room remained empty.

Stacey's hadn't slept in her bed. The only impressions on her white bedspread were Inky's paw prints.

Caitlin glanced around Stacey's immaculate room. Everything in the room sparkled, not a hint of dust anywhere. The crystal ball she'd given Stacey for her birthday shimmered in the light.

Maybe she'd been called into work last night. It's happened before, but I don't remember hearing the phone ring.

Caitlin backed from the room and closed the door.

"Stacey, are you in the kitchen?" She called, knowing Stacey wasn't in the kitchen or anywhere else in the house. She couldn't sense Stacey anywhere.

The living room lights were still on. Stacey usually turned them off when she came home.

Caitlin opened the curtains. Stacey's car wasn't in the driveway.

Inky rubbed against Caitlin's leg. He purred and stared up at her, begging for his food.

"Come on. I'll feed you, boy." She walked into the kitchen and opened a pouch of cat food.

"I hope there hasn't been another murder." Caitlin snatched up her cell phone and called Stacey's work number.

The phone rang eight times before someone answered.

"Is Stacey Parker there? I'm her roommate."

"Nah. She should be in at nine."

Caitlin bit down hard on her lower lip. Stacey never stayed out late. "Are you sure she isn't there?"

"Positive. Just me and the stiffs."

"Thanks."

"No problem—hey! Doctor Whenn walked in. Do you want to speak to him?"

"Please." Maybe he knew where Stacey was.

"Doctor Whenn," a male voice came over the receiver.

"This is Caitlin. Do you know where Stacey is? It doesn't look like she came home last night. I'm worried."

"No," his voice cracked with anxiety. "Do you know where Stacey went last night?"

"On a date. I thought Stacey came home afterward."

"Have you tried calling the man she went out with?"

That should have been the first number Caitlin called. "No. We're talking about Stacey. She wouldn't, you know, but I'll give him a call."

"Call me back when you find out something, Caitlin."

"I will." She hung up then searched through the tiny scraps of paper by the phone for Jeff's number.

If Stacey is there, I'm going to kill her.

After two rings, Jeff answered, sounding sleepy.

"This is Caitlin. Is Stacey with you?"

"No."

Caitlin's fear edged to panic. Stace didn't stay out all night. She didn't do hookups. Oh, God, please let her be all right. "Do you know where Stacey is?"

"Not in bed with me." He hung up.

She cursed and called him back.

"What!" Jeff answered.

"Don't hang up. Stacey didn't come home last night, and I'm worried," Caitlin quickly said.

"She went home last night. I know. I followed her."

Caitlin's anger gave way to icy premonitions. Stacey had a crystal ball. *Damn it! Don't think like that.*

She tried to focus, but Raven's words flooded her mind. She paced her small kitchen.

"You still there?" Jeff asked.

"Yes. Why did you follow Stacey home?"

"She complained about feeling dizzy. I offered to drive her home, but she refused. She said it was her sinuses making her feel that way. Anyways, I wanted to make sure she got home. I didn't stop. There was a silver Honda Accord in your drive. And FYI, it was around eight."

Raven's car. "Thanks." Caitlin returned the phone to its cradle and sank into one of the kitchen chairs.

This was all her fault. Stacey came home and saw Raven's car. She must have decided to give them some time alone and went for a drive. Oh, God, what if Stacey was in an accident.

After calling all three hospitals in town, Caitlin drew in a deep breath and bit her lip as she called Doctor Whenn again.

"Mountain Springs Morgue," a woman's voice came over the phone.

"Doctor Whenn, please."

"He's not here. May I ask who's calling?"

"Caitlin MacPhee. Please let him know that I've called." She hung up. Where could Stacey be?

Inky jumped into her lap, purring.

Mindlessly she stroked the cat's thick fur. Just sitting here wouldn't accomplish anything. She needed to find Stacey. Caitlin had to make sure Stacey was alive and unharmed, and safe. Then she'd kill her for making her worry.

Caitlin reached for the phone. She didn't want to do this, but she had no other choice. Her fingers punched Raven's number.

"Three, four, five. Why wasn't Raven answering?" She paced the small kitchen. "Maybe he's talking to someone."

"You have reached Raven O'Brien. I'm not available at this time. At the sound of the beep, please leave your name, number, and a short message and I'll get back with you shortly."

Twenty minutes later. "Raven, this is Caitlin. Stacey didn't come home last night. Call me." She disconnected and stood, catching a glimpse of the kitchen clock, seven, it seemed later.

~ ~ ~

Raven stared at the number on the caller ID. No way in hell he would talk to Caitlin, not now. He turned his attention to the ambulance pulling away from the crime scene, followed by a patrol car.

This time the killer had made a mistake. For some reason, he'd been in a rush this time. This victim was still alive. Victim? Hell. She's a friend. "God, please let her live long enough to tell us who did this to her."

Raven swallowed the lump in his throat. He had to keep his personal feelings in check. If he couldn't, he'd have to remove himself from the case and that was out of the question. He'd given up too much time and energy to find this bastard.

A low-lying fog gave the secluded church cemetery an eerie feel. The blue and red flashing lights shattered the darkness, revealing an elderly man sitting on the church steps, beside him sat a basset hound. The dog had as much gray around the muzzle as the old man had in his hair.

Raven walked over to the gentleman and extended his hand. "Mr. Hill, I'm Detective O'Brien. I understand you discovered the victim."

The man glanced up. "Yes, sir. Poor child. Will she live?"

"I hope so." God, he hoped she lived. "Mr. Hill, do you always walk your dog at two-thirty in the morning?"

"Ever since my Margaret passed last winter, Cleo here is all the family I got. She's an old girl and can't hold her water like she used to. So, I normally take her out about twice a night." He reached over and pulled the gray-muzzled beast toward him. "I couldn't let that poor child stay there dressed only in a rag. I had to put my coat over her." He looked up. "Did I do something wrong?"

"No, sir. You didn't." Raven gritted his teeth and swallowed the lump forming in his throat. Now wasn't the time to get emotional.

"She kept saying something about a ring. I think she might've been mugged. Don't know why anyone would do to her what they did, just for a ring."

The dog rested her head on the man's lap. Her large ears flopped to the brick steps.

"What did the victim say about a ring?"

"Just that. 'Ring, the ring.' She said it two or three times before closing her eyes."

Raven jotted down what the man said. "And do you always walk your dog here in the cemetery?"

"That's why I found that poor girl." The man's voice cracked, and a tear escaped his dark eyes and rolled down his weathered cheek. "She lay on my Margaret's grave." He buried his face in the hound's coat.

"Mr. Hill, I realize this is hard for you, but I have one more question. Did you see anyone else in the cemetery before discovering the victim?"

He shook his head, sobbing as he stroked the back of his dog.

"Mr. Hill, I'll have someone take you to the station. So we can get your statement."

He gave a faint nod. "What about my Cleo?"

"She'll come too." The muscles in Raven's jaw twitched. He turned and walked over to a uniformed officer. "Steve, get someone to take Mr. Hill and his dog to headquarters. See if you can get him some coffee or something to help calm him. Then, have someone drive him home."

"Sure."

Raven shoved his hands in his pockets as he walked toward the cemetery. He made sure to step around the graves, rather than on them. Superstition, but his grandmother always warned him about walking on graves. He walked over to Mike kneeling beside a grave. "Find anything?"

"Maybe." He placed a bloodstained leaf into a paper evidence bag. "Did you see her legs?"

Raven shivered. "Yeah. I saw. Damn bastard boiled her in oil. I'm no expert, but if I had to guess, I'd say he used motor oil. We'll have to wait for the lab results to know for sure. Has her necklace turned up? I've never seen her without it."

"Not yet." Mike stood and folded the brown paper bag closed. "You okay, Birdie?"

"Hell no. Damn it, Mike, last night I told Caitlin to get out of town, to take Stacey and leave. She wouldn't listen to me."

"Look, no one knew this would happen. And from what I've seen, I think snatching Stacey was a crime of opportunity for the bastard."

Raven fisted his hands. "You don't understand, Mike. I told Caitlin this would happen if she didn't leave. Now, I have to tell her I was right."

Mike stared into the darkness. "Do you want me to come with you?"

"No." He didn't know how Caitlin would react, and he didn't need Mike there if she fanged out. "I want to go over this area one more time before I leave."

"Sure. Where do you want to start first?"

After an hour, Raven glanced up at the sky. It looked as bleak as his soul. They hadn't found any more evidence or clues that would lead to Stacey's attacker. "I'm going to Caitlin's."

Mike patted Raven's back. "See you at the hospital."

Raven nodded then walked toward his car. The sun peeked above the horizon, giving the sky a crimson glow. What was that saying about a red sky in the morning? It didn't matter.

Twenty minutes later, he pulled into Caitlin's driveway and sat, looking up at the house. The living room and kitchen lights were on. She was up, probably getting ready for work. Hating what he had to do, he got out and trudged up the steps.

His mind went blank as to what he would say. He'd done this a hundred times in his career, and it never seemed to get any easier. He lifted his fist to knocked on the door. His arm was as heavy as lead.

What am I to tell her? I was right. She couldn't protect Stacey.

The door flew open, and Caitlin stood before him. She swept her wet hair behind her ears. Dressed in jeans and a sweater didn't look as if she'd planned on going into work. "Thank God, you're here. I've been trying to call you all morning." She stepped back for him to enter.

"Raven, I'm scared that something's happened to Stacey. She didn't come home last night. I've already called the guy. He told me she came home around eight. He saw your car." She stared up at him. Her eyes grew large. "Why are you here anyway?"

His throat suddenly went dry, and he swallowed. He had to push the image of Stacey's beaten body from his mind.

What words do I use? How do I tell her?

"Caitlin."

The color drained from her face, and she covered her mouth with her hand. "No." Shaking her head, Cat backed away, her body trembled. "I saw in your mind. I saw Stacey." Caitlin's voice trembled and her eyes shimmered.

"Caitlin."

"Don't come near me. You said this would happen. You said I couldn't protect Stacey and you were right. She was hurt because of me." Dark tears welled in her eyes.

"I was wrong. None of this was your fault." He took her in his arms and tipped her chin up.

Anger flashed in her eyes as bloodstained tears ran down her cheeks. "You're right," Caitlin screamed. "It's *our* fault."

Chapter Twelve

Fear shot through Raven. He stared at Caitlin's crimson tears. "Your eyes!"

"It's nothing." She wiped the back of her hand across her face. "Where have they taken Stacey?"

He grabbed Cat by the arm and pulled her toward the door. "Dammit, don't tell me that crap! Blood running from your eyes is something."

Caitlin dug in her heels and tilted her defiant chin up. Her bottom lip quivered. "Where is Stacey? I've got to see her." Her voice cracked.

Seeing the anguish on Caitlin's face, Raven understood her tears. He took her in his arms. "Your grief causes you to bleed."

"Why Stacey?" Caitlin sobbed.

"Shh," he whispered as he smoothed his hand down Caitlin's back. "They've taken her to University's Trauma Center."

He closed his eyes and held Caitlin. "When I saw her, I stared at her face and prayed what I was seeing wasn't real. Cat, I thought she was dead."

Caitlin's body shook. "I let her down. I should have done what you and Grandpapa wanted. I should have gone home."

He held Caitlin until her crying stopped and her breathing calmed. He tipped her chin up then wiped her eyes with his hand. "I know in my heart, even if you'd packed up last night, you couldn't have stopped this from happening."

"Stacey saw your car here last night. Jeff Morgan told me so."

His gut wrenched. He wasn't about to let Cat blame herself or what happened between them last night for the attack. "Since when has my being here ever stopped Stacey from coming into this house?"

"She may have seen us or heard us."

He shook his head. "Not hardly. Caitlin, think about it. Stacey couldn't have seen us through the closed curtains or the shut door. Stacey maybe a goddess in the morgue, but she doesn't have x-ray vision. And if she had seen me wrestling with you, do you think that would have stopped her from entering? Hell, no. She'd have broken through the damn door, and I'd have ended up with one of her frying pans against my head. Stacey came home last night and for some reason decided to go somewhere else. You had nothing to do with what happened to her."

Intense desolation swept through him. If anyone was to blame, he was for not catching the killer sooner.

Caitlin rested her head against his chest. She shuddered as she drew in a sharp breath. "You can't blame yourself, either. You've done everything possible to catch him. She pushed away from Raven and glanced up into his face. The shadow of his beard made him look older and tired. "Give me a minute to wash my face. Then could you drive me to the hospital? I need to be with Stacey. I'd drive myself, but." Her bottom lip trembled.

"I'll drive you. You're in no condition to be behind the wheel." He led her to the couch. "But first, I need to ask you some questions concerning Jeff Morgan."

Caitlin sat and pulled her legs up, placing her feet on the cushion. "Sorry about the bloodstains." She pointed to his jacket.

Raven shrugged. "It's dark anyway."

He sat facing her. "How well do you know Jeff Morgan?"

"Not very well. I know Jeff claims to be a writer, and he likes to drink."

"How did Stacey meet him? Through you or someplace else?"

"I guess through me. Jeff came into Lambert's the Saturday Vicky was here. We were having lunch."

"The day after your attack?"

She nodded. "Yes."

"The same day you and Townsley had words? Did he witness this exchange?"

"Yes, yes and yes." She bit her lower lip. "Stacey told Townsley to take a flying leap, and Barbra tripped. Then Jeff asked Stacey to tell him that he'd be rich and famous, because of what happened with Townsley. Do you think he did this to Stacey because of what happened when Barbara tripped?"

"I don't know. Right now, I'm trying to piece together a puzzle." He lifted her feet from the couch. "Go get ready. Wait a minute. Two more things, first, did Stacey wear rings?"

"No. Why?"

"The man who found her said she mumbled something about a ring. One last question, did Stacey have on her crystal necklace last night?"

"She always wore it." Caitlin stood. She stared into his eyes. "Stacey didn't have it when you found her?"

"No. Is there anything unique about it?"

Caitlin bit her lower lip and squeezed her eyes against the stinging in them. "Grandpapa," her voice quivered, "gave it to her the first time I took Stacey to Scotland for Christmas." Caitlin blinked and looked up at the ceiling. "There's nothing special about it. Just a simple gold chain with a rose quartz dangling from it. Stacey cherished it as if it cost a fortune. On the flight back, she told me that no one had ever given her anything so nice." Cat drew her arm across her eyes. "I never knew before then how hard Stacey's life had been." Caitlin sniffed and walked toward the hall.

"Find the necklace. Find the killer," Raven muttered.

Inky leaped onto Raven's lap. He stroked the cat's long thick fur. "You don't have any white on you, do you, boy?" *A solid black cat.*

Random pieces came together, adding to the puzzle he had to solve.

Raven pulled out his notebook and jotted down: Owns a black cat, works in the morgue, uses herbs, and wore quartz crystal.

"Ready?" Caitlin strode into the room.

He closed his notebook then placed it back into his pocket. "That was quick."

~~~

Caitlin held Raven's hand. She glanced up at him, realizing how much she truly needed him as they sat in the waiting room. Despite the reasons he'd given her that he had to talk to Stacey the moment she recovered from surgery, Raven stayed and waited with her during the long hours. He'd only left her side three times, to get her a coke, to make a call, and to speak with other detectives. Raven's presence had given her the strength she needed to hold her emotions under control.

Mike opened the door and approached them. His expression grim, but his lips curved in a faint smile. A man in scrubs followed him. "Cat," Mike greeted her. "Stacey's out of recovery. They've taken her to Intensive Care."

Raven squeezed her hand.

The man in scrubs extended his hand to her. "I'm Dr. Morrison. Are you a family member?"

Caitlin stood and stepped toward him. "I'm her roommate. Stacey doesn't have any family here. How is she?"

Raven placed his hand on her shoulder. "Cat, why don't you sit down?"

She glanced into Raven's compassionate dark eyes. "I'm fine."

Doctor Morrison cleared his throat and motioned to a room across the hall. "Detectives, if I may have a word with you?"

Caitlin locked eyes with Doctor Morrison. His exhaustion made it easy to connect with his mind. "If it concerns Stacey then I need to hear."

Raven narrowed his eyes at her.

Doctor Morrison blinked. "Very well. I'll be honest with you," he quietly said. "Miss Parker's injuries are severe. The next twenty-four to thirty-six hours will be the most critical. We had to remove her spleen. Miss Parker has second and third-degree burns covering forty percent of her lower body, mostly to her feet and lower legs. We are hopeful that we'll be able to save her limbs and that amputation won't be necessary. However, right now, there are no guarantees. She also has several broken ribs and a punctured lung."

Stunned, Caitlin repeated his words. The images she pulled from his mind sickened her. Despite his words, Caitlin saw in Doctor Morris's mind. He didn't have much hope of Stacey surviving. But, Stacey's strong. She'd survived the attack. She would survive. She had to survive.

Caitlin's knees buckled, she swayed and bit her lower lip until she tasted blood.

"Cat," Raven's voice broke through her thoughts. His arm slid around her waist, steadying her. "You okay, Cat?"

She nodded and turned her attention back to Doctor Morrison. "May I see her?"

Doctor Morrison nodded. "Follow me."

"I'll get some coffee," Mike said. "Then I'll be with you."

"Fine." Raven extended his hand. "Ready?"

They followed Doctor Morrison down the brightly lit hallway in front of the nurse's station.

The antiseptic smell stung Caitlin's nose.

Her stomach twisted as they turned the corner and came face-to-face with Barbara Townsley. Caitlin stopped in mid-stride while Doctor Morrison continued down the hall. She didn't want Barbara hovering over Stacey like a vulture.

Barbara smiled at her. "Little late for your morning edition isn't it?" Her accusing voice sliced the air and through Caitlin. "I understand the victim might make it." Her blood red lips turned into a smirk as she glared at Raven. "Lucky for you, Detective?"

Concentrating, Caitlin glared into Barbara's cold eyes. "There are some things in life more important than a story. Don't you agree? Like maybe food."

Barbara shook her head and swayed then turned toward her photographer. "Come on, let's get something to eat."

"But—"

"I'm starving. This can wait," Barbara snapped. "Not like she's going anywhere."

"As you wish."

Raven watched as the two left. "I thought you couldn't do that?"

"Simple minds are easy to manipulate. It'll wear off."

He slid his arm around her waist and led her through a pair of double doors. "We've put a guard outside Stacey's room."

Raven's thoughts echoed in Caitlin's mind. He feared the killer would know he'd made a mistake. "Do you honestly think he'd risk getting caught here?" She asked.

"Reading my mind?" Raven arched his eyebrow at her.

"I can't help it," she whispered. "It's Stacey."

He bent close to her. "I don't mind you walking around in my head, Cat."

The uniformed officer stood. "Detective."

"This is Caitlin MacPhee," Raven introduced her. "She has clearance."

"Yes, sir." The officer nodded.

Doctor Morrison placed his hand on Caitlin's shoulder. "Before you enter, you'll have to scrub and wear a mask, gown, and gloves." He motioned to the sink outside Stacey's room.

After scrubbing and gowning up, Raven pushed open the door for her.

A nurse glanced at them as they walked in then continued checking the IV The respirator hummed in the darkroom, as an EKG machine beeped. Stacey lay connected to machines Caitlin had no idea what they were or what they did, just as long as they kept Stacey alive. That was all that mattered. Caitlin inched closer to the bed, her legs grew heavier with each step she took.

Stacey's long beautiful golden hair had been shaved off. Cuts and bruises covered her face. Her eyes were black and swollen, and dried blood stained the corners of her mouth. Under Stacey's hospital gown, Caitlin could make out the outlines of the bandages covering Stacey's chest. Caitlin didn't have to see the wound. She knew the bastard had branded

Stacey just like his other victims. Caitlin perused the rest of Stacey's body. She had bandages on her legs and right arm. The stench of burnt flesh and blood permeated the air.

How could one human do this to another? The question turned Caitlin's guilt into anger. She would hunt whoever did this and make him know what a real demon was capable of doing.

Her fangs throbbed

Caitlin looked up. Her gaze fell to the unit of blood hanging next to the bed. She watched each drop of the dark, life-giving fluid drip from the bag.

"Caitlin, are you okay?" Raven turned her to face him. His eyes narrowed, and he hugged her, pushing her face against his chest. "Take a deep breath," he whispered against her ear. "Or we'll have unwanted questions."

"I'm fine." She glanced up to prove she was.

Raven frowned and took her hand.

She gently pulled away then carefully, lightly stroked Stacey's cheek. "He takes trophies," she whispered.

"You're right. Once we find the killer, I think we will discover evidence linking him to other victims."

"Who did this to you?" Caitlin stroked Stacey's cheek.

"I'm afraid she won't be able to tell you that for a while," Doctor Morrison answered. "We've sedated her to help with her pain."

Doctor Morrison took the chart from the nurse. "Are these the newest reports?" His lips pulled into a thin line.

"Yes," the nurse replied.

"I want another unit." He handed the chart back. "If we can stabilize her, she may have a chance. The next twenty-four hours will be the most crucial." He glanced at Caitlin. "However, she won't be out of the woods. I'm afraid she will have a long way to recovery, both physically and mentally. No one can live through what she did and come out unscathed."

Caitlin had never taken Stacey's blood, but they shared a bond. Perhaps it was strong enough. Caitlin held Stacey's hand

and eased into her mind, only to see a dark void. She shifted her gaze to the rich red line of blood.

Raven's phone rang, shattering the silence of the room.

"O'Brien," Raven answered. He stared at Caitlin as he listened then shoved his phone back into his pocket. "I've got to leave. They've found Stacey's car."

"I'm staying." Caitlin stared down at Stacey lying motionless. "Don't worry about me. I'll be fine."

Raven pressed his lips to her cheek. "I don't know how long I'll be. Here, take my keys." He folded her fingers around them then kissed her cheek again.

"I'll be fine." She sat down next to Stacey's bed.

~ ~ ~

Raven walked to the door, stopped, and glanced back at her. It felt wrong leaving her when she needed him.

"Trust me." Caitlin nodded. "I'm fine."

She didn't look fine to him. Damn it. He wanted to stay. Raven opened the door then stripped off his gloves, mask, and gown. His gut twisted at leaving Cat.

Mike waited for him. "How is she?"

"If she makes it through the night it'll surprise me."

"I was talking about Caitlin," Mike commented.

"So was I."

Chapter Thirteen

Raven stood on the edge of Half Moon Pond, watching as they pulled the black Honda civic from the cold water. Even if the mud covered the license plate, he'd still recognize Stacey's car. "He's changing his MO. This is the first time he's stolen the victim's car. Either that or he's someone Stacey knew and felt comfortable giving a lift." He looked at Mike. "Or, we have a copycat."

Mike nodded. "If her attacker approached her for a ride, I wonder if this Jeff Morgan saw who it was."

"That's one of many questions I want to ask him," Raven said. He shoved his hands deep into his pockets, turned, and watched as they loaded Stacey's car onto a flatbed. Water still gushed from the car's doors and under the trunk.

Reporters from the local News stations pushed through the police lines. "Get a shot of the car," one shouted.

Someone shoved a microphone in Raven's face.

"Detective O'Brien, the woman found this morning, is she another victim of the Rag Dress Killer?" A male reporter asked.

"No comment."

"Is this the victim's car?" another reporter asked.

"No comment." Raven motioned to several uniformed officers. "Get this area secured. Now!"

Raven walked away from the reporters, pulling out his notebook. He jotted down his thoughts. "Why did he steal her car?"

Mike followed close behind. "Maybe it wasn't him."

"If it wasn't then someone leaked about the brand." Raven drew in a deep breath. He knew the same bastard responsible for the other murders was also Stacey's attacker. He continued walking toward the water's edge. Had Stacey's attacker put the car in at the boat ramp so that he wouldn't leave any footprints? Muddy prints were found eight feet away in the dirt.

Raven looked around. He'd been to this park many times but had never noticed the surroundings. Lighted tennis courts, baseball fields, and a playground were all visible from where he stood. College kids came here at all hours of the day and night. Why risk the chance of being seen? Unless Stacey's attacker knew the area would be deserted when he dumped her car. Raven pulled out his notebook and made notes: Groundskeeper, or someone familiar with the park, maybe a coach, instructor, or trainer?

"Mike, how deep do you think the pond is?"

"Fifteen feet at the deepest. Why?"

"Just wondering what the chances are the divers will find anything else the killer tossed into this pond? I'm going to find Doon." Raven turned and walked over to a group of plain-clothed officers. "Where's Doon?"

"She's talking to Sergeant Cunningham." One of the officers pointed to the parking lot.

Raven nodded and walked off in the direction. A woman with a cane strolled toward him. He instantly recognized her limp. Jackie Doon had been the head of Forensics since he was a rookie. She hadn't changed at all. She still wore her gray hair pulled back into a long braid, and her glasses hung low on her nose. He wondered how they stayed there.

She smiled. "I understand, O'Brien, an anonymous tip about the car came into the station. Do you think the killer is playing games or do you think this is a copycat?"

"It's him. He branded Stacey just like the rest. How long before your people start working on the car?"

"The second they get it back to the lab. I'll stick around here for a while, just in case the divers find anything else."

Raven nodded. "Call me if you find a Rose quartz crystal on a gold chain. Stacey always wore it."

"I will." Doon touched his arm. "I'll take that car down to the last bolt if I have to. We'll find something on this son-of-a-bitch, or I'll be turning in my papers. He won't get away this time. He made a mistake. He messed with family. You don't screw with one of my people."

"Or mine." He cleared his throat. "Doon, I know I don't have to tell you, but Mike collected a bloodstained leaf from the cemetery."

She shook her head. "I've already got someone working on it. So far, I can tell you it's Stacey's type."

"What about the footprints we found? Do you think they will match any of those from the cemetery?"

Doon pushed her glasses up on her nose. "Just by eyeing it, I can tell you it's' the same size and brand of shoe."

"So, you're telling me that it's the same person?"

"I'm saying it appears to be the same size and brand of shoe." She peered over her glasses.

~ ~ ~

Raven knocked on the door to Apartment 32. He'd been here before. The second victim, Susan Holloway, had lived in Apartment 214, just across the parking lot.

"Yeah?" a man's voice came from the other side.

"Police. We'd like to ask you some questions." Raven stepped back.

The door opened. A blond man about five nine, in his late twenties or early thirties, stood in there. He wore jeans, a wrinkled t-shirt and was barefoot. "What can I do for you?"

"I'm Detective O'Brien, and this is my partner, Detective Wingate. We're looking for Jeff Morgan."

"I'm he. What's this about?"

"We'd like to ask you some questions concerning Stacey Parker. May we come in?"

"Sure," Jeff said. He opened the door and stepped back. "Have you found her? You know her roommate called me this morning. She sounded pretty upset."

Raven glanced around the small apartment. Laundry and mail cluttered the couch. An ashtray overflowing with butts sat on an end table. He noted the brand of cigarettes.

No wall separated the living room from the kitchen. From where Raven stood, he could see a half-empty bottle of Crown Royal Whiskey sitting by the sink. Trash overflowed the trashcan and dishes filled the sink. Pizza boxes littered the stove.

He'd bet the roaches left to find better living conditions.

To the left side of the room sat a computer on a desk littered with papers. Above the desk, newspaper clippings hung on the wall with thumbtacks. Two lawyer's bookshelves flanked the desk on either side.

"Have a seat." Jeff motioned to the couch.

Raven shook his head. "I'd rather stand. After your date, last night with Stacey Parker, did you bring her here?"

"Date?" Jeff glared at Raven then at Mike. "We didn't have a date. I met her at Pizza Max to go over some ideas for my latest book. It's about a Medical Examiner who stumbles upon a drug smuggling ring. You see, the smugglers use bodies to get the drugs out of the country. I wanted to find out what an M.E. does."

"And did Miss Parker give you your information?"

"Nothing that I couldn't find in a book. What I wanted to know was what it felt like to cut into a human. She told me I was too weird for her. Me. Weird? She should talk. Do you know what she dared to ask? Do you?"

Mike shook his head. "No. Why don't you tell us?"

"She wanted to know when I cleaned up this place last." Jeff made a swiping motion with his hand. "Hell, I work at a bookstore, go to school, and write. I'm not a Martha Stewart wanna-be. I mean I bought her dinner, the least she could've done was answer a few of my questions."

Raven met Jeff's gaze. "You brought her back here. Correct?"

"I just said I did. Didn't I? She isn't here, so, what do you guys want anyway?"

"Just want to ask you a few questions." Raven walked over to the computer. Scattered on the desk were newspapers with articles cut from each. "Last night when you followed Miss Parker home, did you see anyone?" He picked up an article. It was the story Cat had written on the victims.

"No."

"Are you sure?" Mike asked.

"Yeah. Look, what gives? Is she still missing?"

Raven glanced up. "No. We found her this morning. How long did she stay here?"

Jeff crossed his arms. "Not long. She couldn't get away from here fast enough."

"And why was that?" Raven asked

"I don't know. She started complaining about her head hurting after I offered her a drink."

"Did she take the drink you offered?"

"No, she picked up her purse and stumbled to the door. I thought she'd tripped over something, but she complained about being dizzy. Funny, for someone so dizzy, she wouldn't let me drive her home."

Dizzy or drugged, Raven wondered. He scanned the book titles on the shelf. *Witches and Black magic, Deadly Doses, Cause of Death,* the last book caught his eye *The Trick to Torture.* "Research books?"

Jeff grinned. "Yeah. You have to know how to kill someone if you're going to write about it. Hey! You guys know a lot about murder. How does it feel to find a stiff?"

"Sickening." Mike kicked something with his foot then bent down.

"Is that all? No rush?" Jeff frowned. "Man, that's not the emotion I need. I wonder what it's like to kill someone." He looked up. His eyes gleamed. "Do you think I could interview the killer once you catch him? That is if you catch him."

Raven couldn't believe this guy. He stared Jeff in the eye. "I might be able to arrange to have you put in the cell with him. When we catch him." Raven walked over to Mike. "What did you find?"

Jeff pushed Raven aside, bent down and picked up an earring. "Stacey must have lost this. She kept rubbing the left side of her head, probably knocked it off." He handed the earring to Raven. "See she gets it back. Will you?"

"Sure." Raven placed the crystal earring in a handkerchief then placed it in his pocket. "Thank you for your time, Mr.

Morgan. If you remember anything else or recall seeing anyone last night near Miss Parker's residence, you can reach me at this number." He handed Jeff a business card then opened the door, and stepped out into the hall. Mike followed.

Jeff pocketed the card then shut the door.

Raven reached inside his coat pocket, pulling out the handkerchief containing Stacey's earring. He dropped it into an evidence bag then sealed it. "At least we have his fingerprints."

"When are we running him in?" Mike asked as they walked toward the car.

"We're not."

"I saw enough evidence in there to hang him."

"Circumstantial."

"What?" Mike opened the car door. "Birdie, we found Stacey's earring in there. Hell, the man had a gallery of his victims, what more do you need?"

"You're right. There's enough evidence in there to get a warrant. But, my gut tells me Morgan isn't our man."

"Your gut? I don't give a damn that you outrank me. I'm not listening to your gut." Mike slammed his door and started the car. "Birdie, we have six dead women linked to this psycho, possible nine, and one who is hanging on by a thread. I'm telling you he's our man."

Raven held up his hand. "I'm not letting my feelings overrule my head. All I'm saying is look at the differences between our killer and this man. The killer is extremely meticulous. He hasn't left us the first clue to his identity. The dresses he makes are from old sheets that he has picked up either at yard sales or second-hand stores. Because of which, we haven't been able to track him down. He uses gloves, so we can't get fingerprints from the bodies. He makes sure to dump the bodies in areas that are grassy and near paved roads or parking lots. So he won't leave tire marks. Today was the first time we've gotten footprints."

"But look at all the evidence in Morgan's apartment," Mike argued.

"Morgan is a slob and strikes me as a braggart. If he's our man, I'm sure he would have been all too eager to taunt us, if for no other reason than to feel the emotion. Instead, he rambled on about the book he's writing. No, our man would be helpful and overly concerned all the while laughing to himself about getting away with it and making fools out of the cops. If Morgan's our man, he wouldn't have picked up Stacey's earring and handed it to us."

Mike turned the corner sharply. "Morgan lives in the same apartment complex as the first victim. The park where we found Stacey's car is only two miles from here, and if you cut across the park, you can be at Caitlin's in about thirty minutes on foot. Plus he just told us that he's a student."

"I know, but hell, Mike, everything inside of me is telling me he isn't the one."

"All right, so let's say I agree with you, I still think we should bring him in for questioning."

Raven stared out the window. "And we will, if for no other reason than to let the real perpetrator think he's not in any danger of being caught." Raven glanced at Mike.

"Use Jeff as a ploy?"

"Why not? It will buy us time with the media. You saw them in the park. They want a suspect, and this guy wants to know what it feels like to be a killer." Raven glanced at Mike and grinned. "Why not let him experience all the emotions of being a murder suspect? I'm sure he'll love the attention he'll get from all the reporters when he makes bail. I'm sure he'll love the attention he'll get from his neighbors if they don't kill him. Course, if that happens, we'll have to investigate his death. The downside would be the paperwork. God, I hate paperwork."

"Morgan certainly pissed you off." Mike stopped at a red light. "Caitlin's or the hospital?"

"The hospital. I know Cat is still there."

"Another gut feeling?"

"No. I know Cat."

Raven's car sat in the same parking space where he'd left it earlier.

"When we bring Jeff in for questioning, I also want a search warrant for his apartment." Raven opened the car door and slid out. "I'd like to get a better look at his files."

"You think he knows something we don't?"

Raven shrugged. "No, but he may have a different perspective."

Mike rolled his eyes. "Are you going to tell Caitlin what you're planning?"

He shook his head then smiled. "Make sure that Townsley gets wind of us bringing in Morgan."

"Hell, Raven, why not just hang the poor bastard yourself?"

"I won't answer that. See you in the morning." He tossed Mike the bag containing Stacey's earring. "Give this to Doon. See if she can get a fingerprint." Raven shut the door, shoved his hands into his pockets, and walked into the hospital. It was quiet now, no reporters only the staff and a couple of visitors sitting in the waiting room, probably expectant grandparents to be.

Raven stepped into the elevator. His mind slipped back to the graveyard. Even before he'd seen Stacey's face, he knew it was her. He couldn't explain it. All his life he'd had feelings about things. They weren't premonitions, just gut feelings. Why couldn't his gut lead him to this monster?

The elevator door opened and Raven walked toward Stacey's room.

The uniformed officer glanced up at him and nodded for him to go in.

Raven scrubbed and gowned up then opened the door. Only a faint light over Stacey's bed lit the room. He noticed a full unit of blood hung next to her bed. Damn, how much blood had she lost? A slight movement caught his attention.

Caitlin sat in the chair, eyes closed, her head leaning against the back of the chair, and her arms on her lap. She seemed fragile sitting there.

He bent down and brushed a kiss to her cheek. It was cold and her breathing shallow. The stress of the day had left dark circles under her eyes. He gently placed his hand on her shoulders, and her eyes fluttered open.

"Have you left this room at all today?" He asked.

"No." She shook her head. "I couldn't leave her."

"You don't look well. I'm taking you home."

He'd expected her to argue. Instead, she nodded and pushed from the chair only to have her legs buckle. Cat quickly sat. "I guess my legs went to sleep."

"Here, lemme help you." Raven helped Cat to her feet and slid his arm around her waist. She leaned against him as they walked to the door. She paused and glanced once more at Stacey. Once outside the room, Caitlin struggled to remove the gown. In the bright hallway light, her complexion appeared gray. "Cat, what's wrong?"

"Nothing just tired." She smiled at him. "Take me home."

Chapter Fourteen

Physically and mentally exhausted, Caitlin leaned against the wall of the elevator. Just the motion of riding down made her head throb. She'd pushed her mental limits by persuading Doctor Morrison to give her blood to Stacey. Caitlin closed her eyes, she could only pray her sacrifice was enough to save Stacey's life.

A sharp pain ripped through her. She gritted her teeth, giving up a pint of blood had been a dangerous move on her part especially, since her body couldn't replace her lost blood as quickly as a human or her brother. Glen could replace some of his blood, he inherited that trait from their father. Too bad she hadn't

Oh, the pain. The sooner she got home, the sooner she could feed. The Hunger gnawed her. She glanced up at Raven. The skin over the large vein in his throat seemed virtually transparent. She could see the precious red blood flowing through his vein. The sound of it was an alluring tattoo, calling her, increasing the pains of the Hunger.

Raven looked at her. His grim eyes narrowed. "What?"

"Nothing." She turned away. She desperately needed to replace the blood she'd lost. Her fangs budded and throbbed with the scent of Raven's blood filling the close confines of the elevator. "I'm tired, that's all. I need to get home."

"You look like death." He touched her cheek. "And you're cold."

"I'm fine, honestly." She closed her eyes and gripped Raven's arm. The Hunger's sharp pains tore at her stomach.

"Fine, my ass." He slipped his coat off and draped it around her shoulders. "You're sick."

"I don't get sick," she snapped.

Before he could argue, the door opened. Caitlin pushed by him, needing to put distance between her and the smell of his blood.

Her fangs throbbed. The scent of fresh blood filled her nostrils.

Lambert stood in front of a drink machine, fumbling with his wallet. The huge bandage on his right hand made it difficult. He smiled at her. "Caitlin, Detective O'Brien, could I bother you for some assistance?"

His blood teased her senses. She shouldn't stop, but she couldn't ignore his plea for help either. "Sure." She took the dollar from him and slipped it into the machine. "What do you want?"

"A Coke, thank you. Why are you here tonight?"

"Seeing a friend," Raven answered. He retrieved the canned drink, opened it then handed it to Lambert. "What happened to your hand?"

"I cut it, opening a box. I thought I would pass out before I got here."

Raven watched as Lambert took a sip from the can. "Do you need a ride?"

"No, I drove myself here. Thanks, anyway."

Thank God. Caitlin thought. She wouldn't trust herself to be in the car with Lambert in her condition. Hell, she could see Barbara Townsley's headlines. *Reporter Drains Blood of Wounded Shopkeeper.*

"Raven, I think we need to be heading home. See you later, Lambert." She placed her hand on Raven's arm. The pain intensified. And the smell of Lambert's blood didn't help matters. She didn't know how long she could hide her condition. Her fangs had budded. It was only a matter of time before her eyes turned.

"Detective, I heard there's been another attack. Is this true?" Lambert walked with them toward the entrance.

"Yes."

"Who was it? Another co-ed?"

"I can't discuss the case, sorry. Good-night."

The cool night air did little to ease her pain.

"What's wrong, Cat?" Raven asked. He slipped his arm around her and led her to his car.

"Nothing. Just get me home."

"Cut the bull. I know something's wrong. What is it?" He opened his car door and stared at her as she slid in.

She rested her head against the back of the seat. After last night, and her tears this morning, she didn't want him to see her like this. Vulnerable. Dangerous.

Raven shut the door and started the car. "Well?"

She closed her eyes. Once she got home, she could replace her lost blood. Too bad, it wouldn't be fresh. Fresh blood always eased the pain and restored her more quickly. "Don't worry. I'll be fine."

She didn't have to look at him. She could feel his gaze.

"For the love of Pete," he mumbled. "I'm sorry." He took hold of her hand and squeezed it. "I wish I could tell you that Stacey will be all right."

"She will be, physically anyway. I wish I knew how she would handle this emotionally."

Caitlin stared out the window at the streetlights as they drove the familiar roads. *What am I to tell Stacey, that I couldn't let you die, so I gave you my blood?*

A sharp pain pierced Caitlin and she doubled over. Five more minutes and she'd be home, five long minutes before she could ease the Hunger.

Raven sat quietly. He pulled to a stop at her street corner.

She peered out the window toward her house. There were more cars than usual parked on the side of the road. Someone must be having a party.

It was only a matter of seconds before she could end her suffering. She pulled her keys from her purse. Had she even locked her door this morning? God, it seemed so long since she'd left her house this morning.

A driver behind them blew his car horn.

Raven drove through the intersection.

"You missed my turn," she yelled.

"No, I didn't," he said calmly.

"I asked you to take me home."

"With every damn reporter camped on your porch? I don't think so."

The Hunger gnawed at her. Her canines fully extended with the drumming of Raven's blood hammering in her ears. "I don't care, Raven. Take me home." Another sharp pain gripped her. She needed blood.

"Damn it, Caitlin!" Raven drew in a deep breath. "I realize you want to be alone. I know you want to crawl into your bed, and you are a big girl and can handle those reporters on your own. But I care too much for you to submit you to those vultures."

He glanced at her. Tenderness filled his eyes. "You've been through enough today. Lemme take care of you tonight."

She closed her eyes. How could she tell Raven he couldn't? Her thoughts drifted back to Nam. It wouldn't be as bad now as then. She could fight the pain for a few more hours until Raven fell asleep then she'd go home. It wouldn't be any problem to get past the reporters. She just had to fade into her house, go to her hidden stock, and relief would follow. Simple.

"Very well," she said.

Raven reached over and patted her leg. "That's my girl. I have an extra toothbrush you can use. I'll even let you wear the pajamas my mother gave me last Christmas."

"Gee, thanks." Caitlin opened her eyes. They were already at his apartment complex.

Raven pulled into his space, stopped the car, and opened his door. "Ready?"

"Sure." *God, please, don't let me give into the pain.*

Caitlin opened her door and pulled Raven's coat tight across her chest. She shivered against the cold wind. It would be a very long night. Hopefully, Raven would go to bed soon.

"Are you cold?" Raven slid his arm around her.

"Just a bit."

"You've probably caught a chill. C'mon, I'll fix you some hot tea."

As she followed him down the hall to his apartment, she kept her face down, letting his large coat hide her red eyes and puffy upper lip.

Raven opened his door, flipped on the light then went to take his coat from her.

She held it tightly. "I'm still cold."

~ ~ ~

Raven stared at her. Something wasn't right. He stepped back and studied her. Her thin, petite body trembled. "Cat?"

"I'm fine." She walked toward the couch and grabbed the throw. "I'll take that tea now."

"Sure." He watched her as she sank into his overstuffed leather chair, wrapped the throw around her, and tucked her feet under herself. "Why don't I get a fire going first?"

"That's okay. I can do it."

He jumped as a fire sprang to life in the fireplace. "Next time I go camping, I'm taking you with me." Damn, what other magical powers did Cat have? Raven headed to his kitchen and filled his grandmother's blue willow teapot with cold water. "I've got Chai and orange spice, or would you like some old fashioned black tea?"

"Chai."

He placed two tea bags into the pot, retrieved two cups from the dishwasher then set them on the counter. "Milk and sugar?"

The microwave beeped.

"Both please." Cat shifted on the couch. She rested her head against its back. She glared at the picture he'd hung on the wall. "I can't believe you hung that thing over your fireplace."

"I told you I would hang it there." He poured the tea then carried it to her. "This should warm you."

Her ash-gray hand shook as she took the cup from him. "Thanks."

He studied her. Why wouldn't she look at him? "Here, lemme hang up my coat."

Caitlin shifted in the chair, keeping her head low, she sipped the tea he'd handed her. He noticed her bone-thin fingers wrapped tightly around the tiny cup. Her hands appeared weathered, dehydrated. Hadn't she'd told him she couldn't go for long periods without blood. "When was the last time you," he cleared his throat, "ate?"

"Three, maybe. One of the nurses brought me a sandwich and a drink. Honestly, I'm not hungry."

"No. I mean, when did you take blood last?"

"Oh." She lowered her eyes and raised the cup to her lips.

"Caitlin?" Raven knelt in front of her. "You need blood. Don't you? That's why you bit my head off when I didn't take you home."

"I'll be fine." She turned her face from him. "Honest."

"Bullshit!" He grabbed her chin and forced her to look at him. Her cheeks were sunken, but her eyes were bright red. He gently ran his thumb over her lips. Just as he'd thought, Caitlin's fangs had extended. "Cat, why did you go this long?"

She jerked free of his hold. "I didn't."

"Then what the hell—Oh. My. God. Stacey. You gave your blood to Stacey."

"She was dying." Caitlin's voice cracked, and she wiped at her eyes. "I couldn't sit there and watch, knowing I could save her." Tears rolled down her cheek.

"No, you couldn't." Raven stood and took the teacup from her. He sat it down then held his arms wide open. "Come here."

Caitlin went to him and fell into his embrace. He held her for a while before leading her back toward the couch and pulling her down on his lap.

With one arm around Caitlin, he removed his tie and unbuttoned his shirt collar with his other hand. "Take my blood."

She pushed from him and stood. Shaking her head, she backed away. "No."

That simple word cut him. As desperately as Caitlin needed blood, she still wouldn't take his. "Why? What's wrong with me? You think I've got something you can catch?"

"No, it's just—"

"What?" He stared into her eyes. They didn't seem as red now for some reason. "I'm waiting."

"If I take your blood it will bind us."

"So."

Caitlin closed her eyes. "You don't understand. You would belong to me, and I don't think that's a commitment you're ready for."

He stood and stepped toward her. "If I weren't ready for a commitment I wouldn't have made love to you last night."

Chapter Fifteen

"Admit it, Cat. We belong together." Raven slipped an arm around her waist and with his other hand tipped her chin up.

"You don't know what you are suggesting."

"Yes, I do." He tenderly stroked her cheek. "I can't stand to see you like this."

"I can't." She tried to push away from him.

He pulled her against him. "Why?"

She looked away. "I'll be able to know your every thought."

He didn't care. "You already do. You read me like a book. You know me better than I know myself."

He had to be in love. There's no other reason for his willingness to bleed for a vampire. Raven stared into her fiery eyes. He loved Cat and wanted her in his life.

"Take me home. Please," Cat pleaded.

Seeing Caitlin in so much pain was killing him. Why wouldn't she take what he offered? "What are you afraid of? That you'll catch something from me?"

"No!"

"Then what is it?"

"Nothing," she snapped. "And everything," she whispered.

Raven slid his hands up her arms. He gently rubbed her shoulders. "Tell me what has you so frightened?" he asked again, this time not as harsh.

"That I'll take too much!" She glanced over her shoulder.

"You won't."

"You don't know that."

Raven stared at her and silently counted to ten. She needed blood so desperately she could barely stand on her own, but she still had the strength to argue. "Okay, level with me. What didn't you tell me about yourself?"

She flicked a speck of imaginary lent from her shirt. "I told you everything."

"You're not a good liar. What is it? Will, I what? Go blind? Not be able to go out in the sun? What?"

"I lied! I've killed for blood." The grief in her eyes twisted his gut.

"Tell me, now. Everything."

"Fine. If you must know, I'll tell you. Perhaps then you'll take me home. Do you remember what I told you about Nam?"

"Yeah. The platoon you were with got hit, and you went for a few days without feeding."

"When I finally did take blood, I killed the man. He was a prisoner, but that doesn't excuse what I did. I didn't mean too. I didn't want too. But I couldn't stop myself. I killed for blood. Raven, please take me home. I wouldn't be able to live if I harmed you." Pain etched across her face, and she wrapped her arms around her stomach.

He couldn't stand it anymore and scooped her up in his arms. The hell with her reasoning. He loved her and wasn't about to watch her suffer any longer. "You won't take too much," he said placing her on the couch.

"But—"

Raven placed a finger over her lips, stopping her protest. "No, butts."

He knew she wouldn't jeopardize his life. It would be safe for him to bleed for her. She simply didn't realize it.

"How do you want to do this, neck, wrist, what?" He lifted his finger from her lips so she could answer.

Drawing in a shaky breath, Caitlin whispered, "Neck." She smiled weakly and straddled him.

He hardened under her weight. Now wasn't the time to think about sex. His heart pounded and his cock thickened as she unbuttoned his shirt and pushed the fabric aside.

"You're sure about this?" she asked.

The pain reflected in her eyes was more than he could handle. He framed her face and brushed his lips across hers. "More than you'll ever know."

"After this, I'll know."

Trailing kisses along his jaw, she set him on fire. Her lips moved down his neck. She licked, sucked, and blew on the sensitive area of his throat, driving him mad with wanting her. "Cat," he moaned.

When he couldn't take it any longer, he pulled her closer to him, running his hands down her back, pressing her tight against his arousal.

Her hands caressed his cheek. Her fingers trailed down his neck before she gripped his shoulder with incredible strength. Her fangs sank into his throat, and she drank from him, drawing from him the crimson gift, he gladly gave.

The sensation was the most erotic feeling he'd ever experienced in his life. He lifted his hips, pressing his groin against her heat. "Oh, Cat," he gasped. The climax she gave him ripped through him and with each draw on his throat, his trimers increased.

He cupped the back of her head, holding her. He didn't want her to stop.

Pleasure washed over him like a storm, carrying him to peaks he'd only dreamed.

Caitlin's fangs retracted, taking away the blissful haze he'd been enjoying. "You didn't take hardly a mouthful," he protested. "Don't you need more?"

"Believe me. I took plenty. Any more and *you* would need blood." She ran her tongue over the area she'd bitten then studied him. "How do you feel?"

The concern in her voice pleased him. "Fine. Vhy?" He used his best impersonation of Bela Lugosi.

She narrowed her eyes and smiled in exasperation. "Not funny. Seriously, tell me how you're feeling. Are you thirsty? Do you feel weak, cold, or dizzy?"

Raven cupped her face, meeting her now steel gray eyes. Her smooth skin no longer looked ashy and pale. His gaze dipped to her lush pink lips. He brought her mouth to his.

Their kiss sent new spirals of ecstasy through him, but tonight wasn't the night. He could wait. Slowly, he brushed his lips against hers, ending their kiss. "As I said, I feel fine."

Gently he caressed her silken cheek. "How are you feeling? You look a thousand times better than you did a few minutes ago."

"I feel a thousand times better too."

"Does it always work this fast?" He couldn't believe the difference in her. Caitlin's coloring returned to its healthy glow, her eyes had their twinkle back, and her body warmed against his.

She trailed her finger over the area she'd bitten. "No, but your blood is special." She looked up at him. Cat's lids slipped down over her eyes. "You will always be special to me."

"Just like you will always be special to me."

Caitlin shifted on his lap, bringing her leg around, so she sat sideways. "Have you ever had premonitions?"

That shocked him. "What? Why do you ask?"

"Your blood. I can tell." She straightened her back and stared into his eyes. "Raven, when I taste your blood, it tells me a lot. Blood is the life force of all living things. It's what makes us human."

"Yeah?" he asked, wondering where this was leading.

She drew in a deep breath. "You have the gift of Sight. You get premonitions."

"Are you telling me I can see into the future? Cause if you are, this so-called gift hasn't helped me solve any cases yet. And I could sure use it now."

"Now, who's keeping secrets?"

She was right. "Cat, you told me your secret." He ran his hand over his throat where she'd bitten him. "I have had feelings about things, but nothing more than that. Just gut feelings. No eerie visions, no voices in my head, no out of body experiences, or *deja'vu* sensations."

"Maybe you have the gene, but not the actual power." Cat yawned and rested her head on his shoulder.

He rubbed his hand over his neck again. He'd expected her bite to hurt. It hadn't.

"There won't be any noticeable marks in the morning, just in case you were wondering."

Something in her tone alerted him. Something still bothered her. Hmm, maybe she's worried about spending the night with him. "What, no hickey? Darn! I'd hoped to give Mike something to wonder about."

"Sorry, none that he'll be able to see." Her voice faded, and she shifted, leaning back against him.

"You don't have to worry about my telling the guys you stayed here tonight."

"I'm not." The melancholy in her voice stabbed him.

Damn, he was a jackass. How could he be so stupid? "Look, I know you're upset about Stacey. So am I, but worrying about her will only make you sick. You have to be positive."

"You're right." She covered her mouth as she yawned. "I didn't realize how tired I was."

Despite her tired act, he knew something bothered her. If only she trusted him enough to tell him. "I think you're right. I do have the sixth sense. And right now I'm getting a clear picture that you are not telling me what's eating you."

Twisting around, she glared at him. "I'm worried."

"Not about this?" He motioned to his throat.

"No."

He combed his fingers through her silky red hair, waiting for her to tell him. He could hold her all night if that's what it took.

"I don't know how Stacey will handle what I did. I gave you a choice. I didn't with her. What if she resents me?"

He held her snugly. "I know Stacey well enough to know she won't resent you. Hell, Cat, you risked your life to help save her. Of course, the downside is you'll have access to her mind, and I, for one, don't envy you that."

"You know, you can be a real smartass at times." She relaxed against him. Her warm breath tickled his neck. "I hope you're right. I hope Stacey forgives me." Caitlin yawned again and closed her eyes.

"Let's get you into bed. You can have my room tonight. I'll sleep out here." He knew she was tired, both physically and emotionally.

"You're not sleeping with me?"

"No." If he slept with her, he'd end up making love to her. In her emotional state, that would be taking advantage of her. He wanted to make love to Caitlin when she was both physically and emotionally alive. He wanted all of her, not just her body.

"You wouldn't be taking advantage of me," she slurred sleepily.

"Right, making love to a half-conscious woman isn't taking advantage of her. Tell that one to the judge." He stood then carried her back to his bedroom. He would have to watch his thoughts from now on. She'd warned him she'd know his thoughts.

"That's why I love you, Raven, always thinking of me."

His heart pounded. Cat loved him. Yeah, but for how long?

He pushed his bedroom door open then using his elbow he flipped on the light. Caitlin needed sleep. She'd been on an emotional roller coaster since last night. He placed her on his bed then strolled to his dresser. "You can put these on." He pulled out a pair of pajamas his mother had given him for Christmas. He'd never worn them. He hated sleeping in anything other than his boxers. "Cat?" Raven turned around.

Caitlin was already asleep curled up on her side. He smiled, removed her shoes and socks then pulled the covers over her. Kissing her cheek, he whispered, "Good night, Cat."

Night, Lover. She nuzzled his pillow.

Raven closed the door behind him and headed back into his living room. He paused in front of the hall mirror. He could barely see the faint white marks on his throat from Caitlin's bite. He'd thought for sure his neck would be bruised or something. All he'd felt was a sharp sting then incredible pleasure. He wished she'd bite him on a regular basis. Good, Lord! What was he thinking?

Raven picked up Caitlin's teacup and carried it back in to the kitchen. She'd told him his blood was special. Perhaps she'd ask him to bleed for her again. Maybe he was special enough to her that she might agree to be his wife.

His wife? Hell. Where'd that thought come from?

He shook his head. He might as well admit it. He loved Caitlin and wanted her in his life permanently. She wasn't like Beth. Caitlin was different. Maybe there was a chance for them after all.

Raven smiled. Maybe. He picked up his grandmother's teapot to rinse it out. At the sound of Caitlin's screams, he dropped the teapot into the sink, ran to the bedroom, and shoved open the door.

Caitlin screamed and thrashed as she kicked and slapped at her legs with her hands. "No! Stop! Please stop!"

He rushed to her and grabbed her, shaking her. Caitlin! Wake up! Caitlin!"

Her eyes flew open, and she stared at him. Her lips quivered. "Raven." She fell into his arms. "I saw the killer."

Cold chills ran down his spine. "It was only a dream." He gathered her in his arms and rocked her back and forth. "Just a bad dream," he said, brushing kisses to her hair, cheeks, and face.

After her crying stopped, he reached over to his nightstand and grabbed the tissue box for her.

He noticed she'd stripped out of her clothes and only wore her bra and panties.

Caitlin lifted her face and looked at him. The fear shining in her eyes broke his heart. "It wasn't a dream. I was in Stacey's mind. Somehow, I made contact with her. I felt what he did to her, Raven. I felt everything he did." A crimson tear rolled down Cat's cheek. "He tied her hands over her head, suspended from the ceiling in what appeared to be some warehouse or barn. Raven, he beat her like a damn piñata. Then. . ." her voice cracked and a lump form in her throat. "He lowered her into the hot oil. Raven, he tried to boil her alive in oil!" Caitlin's body trembled, and she clung to him.

Raven lifted her onto his lap. "Shh, it's over."

Violently Caitlin shook her head. "No. No. No. It isn't over." Dark tears streaked her face. "I saw his hands. On the left, he wore a silver ring with a large sardonyx stone."

Raven rested his chin on the top of her head. She could see into his mind, now that he'd given her his blood. So, why couldn't Stacey contact Caitlin? Logically it made sense. He hadn't told Caitlin about the ring. He'd only asked her if Stacey ever wore one. If what Cat said about her dream was true, then her dream could help identify the killer.

"Thank you," she said and nuzzled against his chest.

"For?"

"For believing me."

Boiling oil?

Had he told Caitlin how Stacey was burned? "Caitlin, you need to try to get some sleep."

She nodded and clung to him tighter.

After a long while, Caitlin tilted her face up. "Don't leave me tonight."

The plea in her voice melted his resolve. He wouldn't leave her now for any reason. He picked up the pajamas. "Put these on."

"They're stiff."

"I know, but I'd feel better if you'd wear them." He went into his bathroom to wash. If she didn't wear them, then he'd be stiff all night. After brushing his teeth, he ventured back into the bedroom. "You decent, Cat?"

Deep breathing came from the bed. The bathroom light lit Cat's face. She'd finally fallen back to sleep. Cat had decided to put on the pajama top, but the bottoms hung on the foot of the bed. He might as well wear them.

Raven slid into bed and snuggled closer to Caitlin. It would be wonderful to crawl into bed with her every night.

~ ~ ~

Raven woke to the shutting of a cabinet door. Someone was in his apartment. He eased out of bed, careful not to wake Caitlin. Quietly, he slid open the drawer to his nightstand and withdrew his sidearm. He glanced back at her before slowly opening the bedroom door and slipping out into the hall.

From where he stood, he could see the light on in the kitchen. Whoever this intruder was, he wasn't brilliant.

Gun ready, Raven eased toward the kitchen to find a man going through the refrigerator.

"Hands up and turn around slowly!"

"No need for that, son. Just tell me where you keep your cream." The man stood and faced Raven.

Raven lowered his sidearm. He'd never met the man, but he knew the voice. "Mishenka?"

Chapter Sixteen

"What are you doing, Mishenka? And for that matter, how the hell did you get in?" Raven placed his handgun on the table, meeting Mishenka's piercing blue eyes.

"I'm making myself a spot of tea. I slipped in under your door." He grinned wickedly. "Would you like me to explain how?" He pressed his long fingers together forming a triangle.

Foreboding overcame Raven, and he eased into a kitchen chair. "No. need. I've seen how your kind can slip in and out. I guess you're here to take Cat. Ah, Caitlin back to Scotland."

"That window of opportunity has closed." Mishenka lifted the top of the sugar bowl. "Now, where is your cream?"

"Milk's in the frig, but if you want, I've got instant creamer in the top left cabinet."

"Mmm, in that case," he opened the refrigerator and withdrew the milk carton. "I had to heat the water in a pan."

"You could have used the microwave."

Mishenka frowned. "'Tis a shame you broke your teapot. It appeared to have been rather old. Was it?"

Raven sighed. He'd forgotten he'd dropped the blasted thing. "It was my grandmother's."

He studied Mishenka, who appeared no older than his mid-sixties. The man fitted Raven's image of a vampire, tall, lean, and with an air of strength emanating from him, demanding respect. "If you're not here to take Caitlin home then what are you doing here? How did you know where to find her?"

"So many questions." Mishenka lifted the teacup to his lips.

His eyes lowered as if he were weighing Raven's questions. After a few long moments, Mishenka set the cup down. "My presence here should be obvious. Caitlin is my grandchild. I always know where she is." He eyed Raven.

"Better my coming here than her mother. Wouldn't you say?" Mishenka clicked his tongue, tsking, and shaking his head. "My daughter wouldn't approve of your apparel."

The ceramic tiles were cold to Raven's bare feet. He glanced down, realizing he wore only his briefs. He'd decided against the pajama bottoms. Caitlin had been right they were too stiff. "Come into my house uninvited and who knows how you'll find me dressed or undressed, for that matter."

Mishenka laughed, pointing a long finger at Raven. "I like you. You will make a good addition to our organization. Someday."

"Organization?"

A seriousness entered Mishenka's eyes, and he waved his hand as if to push Raven's question aside. "How bad is Stacey?"

Raven slid his chair back, stood, and reached for a cup sitting on the counter. Drawing in a deep breath, he poured himself a cup of tea. "I can't believe she survived."

The image of Stacey lying in the cemetery flashed through his mind. Raven stared into the amber liquid. "Last night Caitlin assured me Stacey would make it."

He froze and stared at Mishenka. If he knew where to find Cat, then he probably knew she'd given Stacey her blood. Raven clenched his jaw. He'd be damned if he would let that old man blast Cat for her actions. "Look, Mishenka—"

Mishenka held up his hand. "Before you say another word, let me inform you there is no need for you to protect Caitlin. Though, I admire your chivalry. I know what she did was out of love for Stacey. Had I been here, I would have done the same for her."

Raven relaxed his jaw. "What will happen now? I mean with Stacey." Raven sipped his tea. He couldn't imagine her drinking blood. Hell, he couldn't imagine Caitlin either, but she had taken his. The strange thing of it all, it seemed natural to him. Raven shifted. He would never hesitate in seeing to Caitlin's needs. All of them.

Mishenka cleared his throat. "We will take care of Stacey."

"How?" Raven stared into the old man's clear blue eyes.

"The way we have always taken care of those belonging to the family."

Getting information from the old guy was even tougher than Raven had expected. He decided to change his course of questions. "It didn't take you long to get here after Caitlin called you. You must have hopped the first flight."

Mishenka shook his head. "She did not call me." He leaned back in the chair and folded his fingers together. "I felt her grief. You see, my friend, my blood flows through Caitlin as it does in all of my grandchildren. In times of need, we feel each other's pain."

"You *always* know what she's feeling?" Shit! Did he also know what they'd done the other night?

"Of course." Mishenka waved his hand. "I knew the situation would *climax* sooner or later and I wanted to be here for Caitlin."

Heat rose in Raven's cheeks. "Wh—What did you say?"

"I knew Stacey's life would be in jeopardy. And Caitlin would share her blood. It was their destiny."

"Destiny? Bull. What happened to Stacey was because some nutcase fingered her as a witch. And that same SOB," he pointed toward the window. "Is still out there somewhere while six women lay cold in the grave. Destiny, my ass, there's no such thing. We all control our own lives."

"No, my young friend. Forces are controlling all of us. As you will see."

"Yeah, right, may-the-force-be-with-you and all that crap. Then let the force allow me to put that animal behind bars."

A deadly glow shimmered in the old man's eyes. The corner of his lips turned up. "I will see to it that the guilty one pays for what he has done. One way or another."

"Like hell." He had enough on his plate without having to deal with a vampire vigilante. Keeping his voice low and his anger in check, Raven met Mishenka's gaze. "You will not interfere with police work. You will not put yourself at risk."

Mishenka refilled his cup. "Not interfere with police work? You no longer wish my help?"

Raven gritted his teeth. "That's not what I meant. Damn it, Mishenka. It almost killed Cat, seeing Stacey lying in that hospital bed. What do you think it would do to her if you're harmed?"

A deep belly laugh erupted from the older man. "My dear young friend," he said and bowed his head. "Do you honestly believe I cannot take care of myself and all who are my responsibility?" He lifted his head.

Dark amber eyes, glowing with deadly fire, met Raven's gaze. Raven stared at the vampire sitting across from him. Mishenka's fangs glistened in the kitchen light. His fingernails had turned into long wicked claws.

"Believe me, young man, I won't be in any danger. Many have hunted my family and me including those of my kind." He shrugged. "They're dead. I am still alive."

"Grandpapa!" Caitlin shouted.

Raven jumped and turned. He smiled at the sight of Caitlin wearing his bathrobe. The sleeves covered her hands. "Sorry, we woke you."

"You didn't." Her wide-eyed gaze darted from Mishenka to Raven to his sidearm on the table. "What's going on?" She stepped toward Mishenka. "Grandpapa?"

He smiled warmly at her. "Nothing for you to be concerned over. I was only proving to this young man that I am quite capable of taking care of myself." Mishenka's appearance softened. His eyes gradually returned to their crystal blue, and his fangs retracted.

Caitlin pointed to the table. "So why do you have your gun?"

Raven allowed his gaze to travel over her. "I was protecting you from an intruder."

A blush colored her cheeks, and she turned back to Mishenka. "You didn't tell me you were coming." She smiled and walked over to him, hugging him. "Why are you here?"

"Why do you think? I felt your pain, knew your need." He nodded toward Raven. "It is a blessing your detective saw to your need last evening. You know better than to go without, unlike your brother, you cannot replenish what you lose."

Caitlin took the seat between him and her grandfather. She glanced from one to the other and crossed her arms over her chest. "It couldn't be helped."

Mishenka slammed his hand on the table. "No excuses! You were in a bloody hospital, Kitten. Don't tell me you couldn't find a spare bag somewhere. Or don't these American hospitals keep blood on hand?"

"They do, but that blood is for people who desperately need it to save their lives, Grandpapa."

"My point exactly. You are Dhampir. You should have taken what you needed."

Caitlin rolled her eyes and turned her smile to Raven. "He's always like this. Unbearable."

"I am not." Mishenka reached across and stroked her cheek. "What is it, Kitten?"

"Nothing. I'm fine. Just waking up, that's all."

Raven's gaze fell to her full lips. She worried her bottom lip and twisted a lock of her short hair around her finger. A habit of hers he knew so well. "You're worrying about Stacey."

"I shouldn't have left her last night."

"Cat, you were not in any condition last night to stay. You needed to rest. Besides, I'm sure her condition hasn't changed. If it had, the hospital or Mike would have called." He tried to sound reassuring, instead of like a cop.

"Kitten," Mishenka lowered his voice to a soft whisper. "Raven is telling the truth. But I sense something else is bothering you as well."

She released a heavy sigh. "I don't want to face Mr. Hamilton. Not today, I want to be with Stacey when she wakes." Caitlin closed her eyes. "Hamilton will want me to spill everything I know about Stacey, and I'm not ready to do battle with him."

"Kitten," Mishenka said. "Today is Sunday. You don't have to face your boss."

"Yes, I do. This is a big story. I'm a reporter. He expects me to come in today. I know him."

Caitlin's eyes were dull gray stones. Her mental exhaustion was draining her. Damn it. Cat needed to rest, not worry about her frigging job. Raven drew in a deep breath. "You're not up to it. Emotionally, you're burnt."

"It doesn't matter. It's what's expected of me. So is a story."

Raven reached across and covered her hand with his as much for his comfort as her. Just touching Cat, grounded him. "Tell him any information released now could jeopardize Stacey's life. Tell him I'll make sure you'll get an exclusive once we know Stacey's out of danger."

"He won't listen."

"Maybe not to you," Mishenka said. "But, he'll listen to me." Once more, that wicked gleam entered his eyes.

"No, Grandpapa. I have to deal with D.P. on my own. If need be, I'll resign."

Mishenka's eyes glowed. "You'd quit?"

Raven's gut twisted. If Caitlin quit her job, there wouldn't be any reason for her to stay. "Cat, think about this before you do something you'll regret."

She jerked her chin up defiantly. "I won't have my grandfather fighting my battles. If I can't reason with D.P. Hamilton, I'll quit. It's not like I can't find another job."

Mishenka stood and placed his cup in the sink. He leaned against the counter. His eyes appeared lifeless. "I won't fight your battle. All I'm suggesting little one is to allow me to persuade your boss not to release any information on Stacey. If you do not want my help, I'll gather my belongings and return to that lonely heap of stones your father calls a castle."

That manipulating old goat knew Caitlin wouldn't argue with him. Raven gritted his teeth. Didn't the old man see the emotional stress Cat was under and what it was doing to her?

"Grandpapa." Caitlin shoved from her chair. "I'm sorry if I hurt your feelings. You don't have to go back home. I'm just worried about you."

Oh, for crying out loud! Raven glared at the old goat.

Mishenka grinned over Cat's shoulder. "It is understandable that you are worried about Stacey. So am I, Kitten." Mishenka said. "But there is more than this bothering you. Isn't there?"

She rubbed her hands over her face.

Mishenka smoothed his large hand down Caitlin's back.

"I didn't give her a choice, Grandpapa. I broke one of our prime rules."

"You did nothing wrong. You preserved a life. That my dear outweighs any law."

"What about Stacey? I know how she feels whenever I feed. I've felt her revulsion and seen it in her eyes."

Raven watched Mishenka's reaction. If he blasted Cat, he'd pay hell.

The old man's eyes softened, and his facial expression grew tender. He caressed Caitlin's cheek with one hand and drew her into his embrace with his other. The love Raven witnessed warmed him and reminded him of his grandfather. *God rest his soul.*

"Caitlin," Mishenka said in a soothing tone, "when I first met Stacey I knew she belonged to us. I didn't know how or when. I always assumed her mate would bring her to us. Had hoped it would be your brother, but not the case. The point is, Stacey will not resent what you did. You saved her life. You are putting more guilt on yourself than is necessary."

He swatted Caitlin on her bottom. "Why don't you go and get dressed and I'll take you and Raven out for breakfast."

Raven held up his hand. "You don't have to do that."

Mishenka looked over Caitlin's head and his gray brows arched. "I've seen inside your refrigerator."

Raven stared at Mishenka then burst out laughing. The old coot would make his life miserable. And he thought things couldn't get any worse than what they were. That was before he had to deal with a manipulative, temperamental, old man. Correction; manipulative, ancient vampire.

Caitlin pointed at the clock on the stove. "Is that right, it's only six thirty?"

"Actually, it's six-fifteen. It's set fast so I won't be late for work." Raven stood and stretched. "If you'd like, we can run you by your place before we eat. Hopefully, the vultures have left, and you won't have to deal with them this morning." He figured Caitlin wanted to change her clothes since she hadn't brought anything with her. "I don't think Hamilton will be in his office before noon."

"Thanks, I'd like that, but why don't you go ahead and get dressed."

"If you don't mind." He left, glancing over his shoulder once more to see Caitlin smile at him.

~ ~ ~

Caitlin waited until she heard the shower running. "Grandpapa, I will catch whoever did this to Stacey."

"That my, dear, is why I'm here."

"He boiled her in oil."

"I know."

"Last night I entered Stacey's mind. I saw what he did to her. I felt her pain. I also saw a ring the killer wore." She shivered at the memories. "I recognized that ring. I've seen it before."

"Did you tell Raven?"

"Yes." She wrapped her arms around herself, remembering how he'd taken her into his arms last night and comforted her. In that one instance, he confirmed the love for her she'd seen in his mind. "He's a detective, Grandpapa. Raven won't act on anything until he has solid proof."

"Then young lady, I suggest you use your natural powers and find him that proof. Open your mind to the people around you. Listen to their thoughts, feel their evil, smell their desires."

"I don't have those gifts."

"You have stronger powers than you know. You've denied who you are, all of your life. Embrace your inner self, Kitten. You will find the one who did this to Stacey. It's time that you accept just who and what you are."

She drew in a deep breath, breathing in Raven's aftershave. He was already out of the shower.

Raven placed his hand on her shoulder. "Bathroom's all yours."

"That was quick." She stood on her tiptoes and brushed a kiss to his smooth cheek. "Five minutes, I promise."

Someone pounded on Raven's door. She stopped. Her stomach knotted.

Raven glanced at her before opening the door. "Mike, what's up?"

"Tried to get a hold of you last night, both on your cell and home phone."

Raven pushed his coat aside and stared at his cell phone. "I must have shut the damn thing off. What's going on?"

On weak knees, Caitlin walked closer to Mike. The room seemed to grow smaller with each step. "Is it Stacey?"

Mike smiled at her and shook his head. "I didn't mean to frighten you, Caitlin. As far as I know, she hasn't changed. The reason I'm here is a cruiser spotted someone breaking into your home last night. They brought in Barbara Townsley and a guy with her. I have to tell you though. You've got yourself one hell of a watch cat. Inky scratched the heck out of Townsley's face and hand. Hope Inky doesn't contract anything from her."

"Very, funny, Mike," Raven said. "Where's Inky now?"

"They brought him in as well. I took him home with me. The kids love him. You can pick him up on your way back from the station. Think you can come down and fill out some paperwork?"

Her grandfather placed his arm around her shoulder, giving her a firm squeeze. "Of course we can, young man."

A wave of nausea came over Caitlin. What if Barbara found her blood? Oh, God, how would she explain this? "That beyotch! What's she doing breaking into my house? Did she take anything?"

"No. Barb and her photographer were caught climbing in through a back window," Mike reassured her. "I guess I should say attempting to climb through your window. Barbara's butt was still hanging outside. I think she was too busy playing with Inky. I knew I liked that cat, for some reason."

Mishenka extended his hand to Mike. "I'm Mishenka Lucard, and you are?"

"Where are my manners?" Raven said. "Mishenka, this is my partner Mike Wingate. Mike, Caitlin's Grandfather Mishenka Lucard."

Mike shook hands. "Mishenka, that's Russian isn't it?"

"Carpathian. Officer Wingate, I was planning to take my Granddaughter and Mr. O'Brien out for breakfast, would you join us? I don't imagine this Townsley woman is going anywhere."

"I'll have to decline your offer. Thank you though." He glanced over at Raven. "The files you were interested in are on your desk."

Raven nodded. "Great. I think I'll have to take a rain check as well. This could be the break we've been looking for."

"What files?" Caitlin stared at Raven.

"Unsolved cases."

"I see." Caitlin smiled. Something was up. As much as she wanted to step into his mind, she didn't. She had too much on her plate to worry about what Raven was up to, besides she'd find out later.

"Caitlin, I'll warn you, Townsley may have already posted bail. When I left, she was going before a judge. That gossip sheet she works for wanted her out ASAP."

"Great." Caitlin gnawed her lower lip. How could she have forgotten about that dangerous witch?

Caitlin's stomach churned. *Please don't let her have found my supply of blood.*

Chapter Seventeen

"I thought the *Herald* was a reputable paper and not a bloody rag!" Caitlin glared across the plush office at D.P. Hamilton. She'd been arguing with him about Stacey for over an hour, and he still wanted all the details, including whether or not she'd been raped.

"Young lady, don't you ever raise your voice to me again or you'll find yourself out of a job." He loomed over his desk toward her. "All I'm asking you to do is fill in a few minor details. Did you and Stacey experiment in witchcraft?"

Caitlin's mouth fell open. Minor details? The man was heartless. "What do you think?"

"You're a damn reporter, woman. You must cover the news." He walked purposefully to the large plate glass window. "Look out there. Do you think we are the only news outlet covering this story?" He made a swiping motion with his hand. "Because if you do, you're wrong. There were at least fifteen different news reporters outside my paper this afternoon when I arrived, all waiting to get a statement from you, or didn't you notice them when you finally decided to waltz in today."

"Oh, I noticed. They were camped outside my front door this morning. I didn't tell them anything about Stacey, and I'm not telling you. She's my roommate, but more importantly, she's my friend." Caitlin glared right back at Hamilton. She wasn't backing down from him. Damn him to hell. She wouldn't turn Stacey into a media casualty.

Hamilton's jaw twitched, and he punched his left hand with his fist. "I don't give jack if she's your roommate or your lover," he said with no vestige of sympathy. "You have until four to get a draft on my desk, or I'm suspending you. Indefinitely. Understood?"

"Perfectly, D.P." Caitlin stood, smoothed her hand down her skirt.

"Fine." He grinned. "I knew you'd come to your senses." He walked to his door, yanked it opened, and motioned her to leave.

Caitlin nodded as she walked out. Her sight fell on her grandfather sitting at her desk. She wouldn't involve him. This was her battle.

D.P. saw her as his goldmine. His persistence proved to Caitlin none of the other reporters or news agencies had any information on Stacey or this new turn in the case and D.P. wanted to be the first to break the story. He didn't care who it hurt. News was news to him, and that's all that mattered. Caitlin shook her head. That and good ratings.

She glanced over her shoulder at his closed office door. She'd expected him to fire her or suspend her without pay. He thought he owned her, well he didn't. He wanted a cutthroat reporter who didn't give a rat's rear about anything but a story. Fine, in that case, he could hire Townsley back.

"It didn't go so well, I see." Mishenka stood. "Perhaps, I'll have a word or two with him."

"No, you won't. I won't compromise my friends or myself for a job. If he can't accept the information the police have released, that's his problem." She typed her password into her computer, pressed a few keys, and deleted everything from her files then formatted her hard-drive. "Because I just quit."

"You told him that, Kitten?"

She set the box she'd brought with her, just in case she'd needed it on her desk. "Nope. But, I'm sure he'll figure it out."

"You don't have to do this. All it would take is a few moments."

"No. I don't want you to interfere." She sighed and sat on the edge of her desk. "Grandpapa, Hamilton isn't someone I want to work for anymore. Okay?"

Mishenka cast his gaze skyward. "You are just like your father. Stubborn."

"All my life you or someone in the family have always bailed me out of my bad times. Let me handle my problems. Please."

"If you are planning to drive off a cliff. I'll walk to the hospital if you don't mind."

Caitlin ignored him and continued packing her things. She gathered her photos, nameplate, and the few knickknacks she'd received as gifts from her co-workers. The last thing she placed in the box was a pair of hideous red plastic vampire teeth Betty, D.P.'s secretary, had given her.

Caitlin swallowed the lump forming in her throat and lifted the box in her arms. "Let's go Grandpapa. I want to get to the hospital. Maybe Stacey's doctors will have some good news for us."

"As you wish, Kitten. Here, let me carry that for you." He reached for the box.

"It's okay, Grandpapa. I've got it." She walked past Hamilton's closed door. She knew he'd seen her through his windows when his door flew open.

"Where do you think you're going?" he bellowed.

She kept her pace and her eye on the exit. "Home."

"You walk out, and you'll never work for another paper again! Do you hear me?"

She heard and so did everyone else at the paper that day. Typing and conversations stopped. Silence fell over the normally loud room. Her co-workers, the sectaries that were in and even the mail boy stared at her and Mishenka as they kept walking toward the entrance.

"MacPhee. You're fired," Hamilton roared.

She stopped, turned, and met his glare. "Correction, sir, I quit," she spoke in a calm, level tone.

Mishenka opened the door for her, and the bright sunlight warmed her face. Perhaps this was the start of new things ahead. This exit wasn't as dramatic as when she'd left Hollywood years ago, but it felt just as good.

"Should I inform him I own this paper along with over a hundred other publications?" Mishenka asked.

A laugh bubbled up inside of her. Oh, it would be so worth the look on D.P.'s bulldog face. "If you did that it would kill him."

"True." Mishenka grinned. He glanced over his shoulder. "Then again, there are other ways of dealing with people like him." He slipped his arm around her waist.

"Grandpapa, leave him alone. Please." She knew her grandfather too well. He could make a man go insane, drive him to the point of taking his own life. She couldn't have that on her conscience, nor would she be able to face Raven. "Besides, it's past time for me to change careers anyway. I've been thinking of writing that novel. Royce once told me I should try to get some of the stories I wrote during the Vietnam War published. I may do just that, so leave old D.P. alone."

Mishenka twisted his lip. "If you insist."

"I do."

"Very well. I'll leave that fat, slimy, parasite alone, but it would have been so gratifying to see Hamilton squirm. Do you know the last time I was permitted to have a bit of fun?" He lifted an eyebrow. "It was when I went to retrieve your mother from that barbarian she married. Though I will say, over the years I have grown fond of your father. I like his evil streak."

Caitlin groaned. She knew better than to argue with her grandfather. He thought highly of her father, and she knew it. She glanced at him out of the corner of her eye.

His smile warmed her. It was good to have someone from her family with her, someone who understood her.

"I'm glad my presence makes you happy. I was about to think I wouldn't see a smile on your face." He winked at her. "Now, what about Raven?"

She opened the door of her Mustang and placed the box on the back seat. "What about him?"

"Don't you think it's time to bring him into the family?"

She shoved her seat back then slid in behind the wheel. "I hope Stacey's condition has improved." She shut the door, put the key in the ignition, and started the car.

"You're avoiding the question, Kitten. He has a right to know he is your mate. You've already taken his blood and joined him to you. Among the other things you've done with him."

Out of the corner of her eye, she saw him glaring at her. How could her grandfather go from joking one second to lecturing the next? "This is not the time, Grandpapa, to discuss my love life."

"Then when will it be the time?" Irritation rang in his voice.

Caitlin shifted gears and kept her sight ahead. She had too much on her mind as it was, to be thinking about Raven. She just wanted to wake up from this nightmare.

"When Stacey's home," she snapped. "When Raven catches this maniac. When—" Her eyes stung. It had to be the bright sunlight. "When everything is right in the world. When Raven no longer fears, falling in love with me."

Mishenka reached over and placed his large hand on hers, giving it a reassuring squeeze. "He will come around."

Caitlin pulled into the hospital parking lot, immediately spotting Barbara Townsley's car. With any luck, they wouldn't see Barbara or any other reporters.

Drawing in a deep calming breath, Caitlin willed her fangs to retract. She wasn't in the mood to play nice. She wanted to even the score with that witch. She wanted blood.

As they took the stone steps to the hospital, Caitlin noticed how peaceful and beautiful the grounds were. A cardinal perched on the split railing fence surrounding a small garden. Hyacinths pushed up through the ground and tiny buds already formed on the trees. Spring had arrived early. Stacey would love this. She loved this time of year. Hopefully, there wouldn't be another hard freeze.

Caitlin paused. "I don't know if the officer outside Stacey's room will let you in, Grandpapa."

"Why not? She's legally my daughter."

"Excuse me?" Caitlin stood there staring at him, blank and amazed. "When did you arrange this? Never mind." She held up her hand. "Knowing you, you had Royce arrange everything this morning."

"Last night." His eyes softened, his smile faded. "You're not upset are you, Kitten?"

"Of course not. Surprised, but not upset." She studied him. He wasn't looking at her, and he'd blocked his thoughts from her. "Stacey doesn't know. Does she?"

His grin returned. "Well, no, not as yet, considering the child's been in a drug-induced sleep."

"Grandpapa." She pulled him over to a bench. "You can't adopt Stacey without her knowing. It isn't legal. I'm sure the police have been trying to find Stacey's family. What will you do when her real mother shows up?"

"Believe me," he lowered his voice. "Your cousin Royce has taken care of all the details. Trust me it is as legal as need be. It pains me to say this, but that poor child doesn't have any family, except us. Stacey's mother died soon after she placed Stacey in foster care."

"But—"

He held up his hand, silencing her. "By doing this, we can transfer Stacey to another hospital. One where we have connections." He leaned closer to her. "How long do you think it will be before the doctors here start noticing miracles in her recovery?"

"I've made a mess of things, haven't I?" Her stomach twisted in knots and her head began to pound.

"No, you haven't, Kitten." Mishenka's gentle blue eyes sparkled. "You gave her another chance to live. You gave her the family she didn't have, one that she craved. A family who loves her."

Caitlin blinked against the burning in her eyes. Pollen. It had to be the pollen in the air. She stared at the bright yellow daffodils. "Does Vicky know?"

"All of the family knows about Stacey, even the Wolfes. I've already spoken to Sara and Vaughn. If need be, they will be here at the slightest word from me."

"No."

Mishenka held up his hand. "Do not reject their help. Royce, Vaughn, and Glen have been hunting longer than your detective has. And if need be, Tristan and the pack can and will smell out the bastard. Besides, it would be heartbreaking if anything happened to Raven before you claimed him. Now, try to smile, for Stacey. She wouldn't want to see you worrying about her. I fear she will blame herself for being attacked."

Caitlin slid her arm around her grandfather's waist. "Come on. Let's go see her."

A pent-up breath escaped Caitlin as they made it to the elevator without seeing any reporters. "Well, we made it this far."

The elevator door slid opened to their floor.

Jeff paced in the hall. He looked up at her. "Caitlin? I'm glad to see you. These bitches," he pointed to the nurse's station. "Won't tell me how Stacey is doing." He held a small arrangement of daisies.

One of the nurses glanced at Caitlin. "Are you family?"

Mishenka stepped forward. "I'm her father." He reached into his coat pocket and withdrew an envelope. He paused before he removed the papers and handed them to the nurse. "This should explain everything."

"Mr. Parker—"

"Lucard," Mishenka corrected her.

The nurse's eyes narrowed as she read over the papers. "Mr. Lucard?" She glanced at Caitlin. "This way." She led them through the double doors. "I apologize. I'm Officer Cannon."

"I'm Caitlin MacPhee. Stacey's my roommate. What's going on?"

"I'm here on Detective O'Brien and Wingate's orders. Everyone entering Miss Parker's room is thoroughly checked. You will have to leave your purse with me, and I will have to ask you, sir, to empty your pockets."

Mishenka stroked his chin. "I assume Raven believes the killer will try to attack Stacey here. Are you also checking all hospital staff that enters her room?" His eyes grew dark. "If I were the killer, I would try to acquire access to her by posing as an orderly, or nurse. It would be quite simple to slip a deadly dose of something into her I.V." He nodded. "Yes, an overdose of morphine would go unnoticed long enough for him to make his escape."

Officer Cannon's eyes became blank, and when she spoke, her voice was monotone. "As I said, we are checking ID's on everyone who enters the room. We've also installed a concealed video camera in the room. We've taken all precautions to protect your daughter, sir."

Caitlin groaned. She couldn't blame her grandfather but damn him. If Raven saw this, he'd have kittens.

"Very good." Mishenka smiled.

Officer Cannon blinked and returned his smile. "You can go down the hall. Officer Thomas will see to you." She walked back through the double doors.

Caitlin turned, meeting Raven's dark glare. Oh, fudge sickles "Raven. Where did you come from?"

"What the hell just occurred?" He stepped toward Mishenka.

"Simple my boy, I was acquiring information." He placed his hand on Caitlin's shoulder. "Making sure *you* were doing *your* job."

"Raven." Caitlin looked at him. His eyes were harsh when he glanced at her. "I didn't see you when we came in here."

"I was standing over there." He pointed to an adjacent hallway. "Why didn't you tell me your family had adopted Stacey? Didn't you trust me to know that bit of information? I felt like a complete ass when Mike informed me of it this morning."

She'd had enough. First D.P then her grandfather, now Raven. This bullying bullshit was ending. Caitlin lifted her chin and boldly met Raven's black gaze. "I would have told you if I had known. Since you want to act like an ass, then go ahead. I don't give a rat's rear anymore." She pushed by Raven. "Coming, Grandpapa?" She strode toward Stacey's room.

Raven grabbed her arm and pulled her back. "I'm sorry, Cat." Bending down, he placed a firm kiss on her lips, taking away her anger.

They were both under a lot of stress. Caitlin placed her hands on Raven's chest and glanced up at his now warm eyes. "I am, too. Do you know how Stacey is doing?"

"Her condition hasn't changed."

Caitlin swallowed. "Did you know Jeff Morgan is here?"

Raven's jaw twitched. "Yes. I think Mike may be right. So far, Mr. Morgan is the only person to show up asking about Stacey." Raven slid his hands to her waist. "We're bringing him in for questioning."

Caitlin gritted her teeth and clenched her fist. "You think he did this to Stacey."

Chapter Eighteen

"Raven, answer me." Caitlin stared at him. Sudden anger flared inside her. She had to know the truth. If Jeff were the one responsible, she'd make sure he'd pay. *Dearly.*

Raven sighed heavily, grabbed her hand, and practically dragged her down the hall past Stacey's room to a waiting room. "You're safe here."

She snatched her hand from him. Damn it! She'd had enough of his manhandling, yanking her here, and there. It stopped now.

Caitlin looked around the room. Dust angels glistened in the sunlight shining through the large picture window. A drink machine hummed in a corner. A large palm tree occupied another corner next to the window.

They were alone. Good.

"I am sick and tired of you yanking me here and dragging me there. What's eating you, Raven?"

He crossed his arms, and his lips thinned. "Oh, let's see. First, I'm no closer to catching this ass than I was a year ago. Second, your grandfather just pulled some mojo on one of my officers. And third, your inability to control your temper. I think that about covers it."

"My temper? What do you mean by that? I'm not the one with a flippant attitude."

He raised his dark eyebrow in amusement at her. "Do you need me to hand you a mirror?"

Her fangs retracted, and she groaned. "Oh, good God!"

Raven smiled and shook his head. "My girlfriend, the vamp. How did it go with Hamilton?"

"I quit." Girlfriend? That one word sent flutters through her.

All expression slid from his face. "So, you'll be leaving town?"

"No. I can find another job and, if not, I've got enough money put back to survive."

He sighed and walked to the window. His shoulders rounded with the stress he carried.

Her bubble of joy burst. She knew Raven was tired. She knew he was frustrated about the case, but this wasn't like him. Maybe she could help him. She pushed into his mind.

"Don't do that." His warning tone stunned her and forced her from his consciousness.

She stared at him. He'd felt her trying to enter his mind. "Then tell me why you're acting like a caged tiger. Is Morgan the one responsible for everything? Is he?"

Raven pushed his hand through his hair. "I don't know. Everything inside of me is screaming no. Except for the reporters and you, no one else has tried to see Stacey. That's what has me so baffled. Why hasn't the killer attempted to see her?"

"Maybe he doesn't know Stacey's alive." Caitlin wrapped her arms around his waist and leaned against him, wanting to ease his tension.

"Then he's deaf, dumb, and blind, and doesn't own a television, or knows how to read."

"The media." She stared at him. The tension, and stress he carried inside bunched his shoulders. Raven was a volcano about to erupt.

Raven glared over his shoulder at her. "The photo of Stacey's car pulled from the lake is on every paper in this damn state. This morning every television station had Stacey's license photo plastered on the screen as their reporters did the story about her. If he didn't know her name, he does now."

He cast his eyes skyward. "Someone from here, the hospital, or even the station released information that Stacey had survived the attack, and was in critical condition." He pushed from the window and turned, slipping his arms around her. "The killer knows."

"He won't harm her again. I'll see to that," she promised.

"How? More hocus-pocus?" Raven leaned his forehead against hers. "I don't want you to become the target of this asshole. What if Mike saw your grandfather pull that stunt with Cannon? How did he do that anyway? When did he bite her?"

"Grandpapa doesn't have to bite people to bind their minds."

"Great, one more thing I have to worry about."

"You don't have to worry about him or me."

"Don't tell me not to worry about you. I've heard that line often enough from you."

"Touchy, aren't we?"

He brushed his knuckles gently across her cheek. "Where you're concerned, yes."

She smiled at his admission. "Did you find anything helpful in the files you received?"

"Nope. They were more confusing than I'd hoped. In the past twenty-one years, there have been three murders similar to the ones that have happened here. Two, remain unsolved. I was positive I would find something in them." He glanced away. "Maybe I have," he whispered and moved from her. "Ready, Mike?"

Caitlin caught off guard by Raven's sudden change, turned.

Mike smiled at her as he walked toward them. "Your grandfather told me you two were down here. Have you seen Stacey yet? How is she?"

Caitlin lowered her gaze. For the briefest of seconds, she'd forgotten about Stacey. When Caitlin spoke, her voice broke, miserably. "No. I haven't seen her today." She forced a smile and met Mike's gaze. "I was telling Raven I'm now unemployed."

Mike threw his hands in the air. "They fired you? Why? You're a damn good reporter."

"I quit. Hamilton wanted me to tell everything I knew about the case. He didn't care the victim was my roommate, my best friend. He saw it only as an opportunity to sell more papers." She caught the sight of her grandfather strolling toward them with a newspaper tucked under his arm.

"I was very proud of her, Detective Wingate. She stood up for her beliefs." Mishenka's eyes shimmered with pride.

Mike blinked and stepped back. "I'm sorry. What were you saying, Mr. Lucard?"

"How proud I am of my granddaughter." He placed his hand on her shoulder. "Shall we look in on our Stacey, Kitten, and let these gentlemen get back to solving this hideous crime?"

"Sure." She glanced at Raven then swiftly looked away from his dark scowl. He knew her grandfather had pushed into Mike's mind. She had to pretend not to notice. She had to act as if everything was normal. Then once she had Grandpapa back at her home, she'd wring his bloody neck.

She understood this was his way of helping. How many times had she sat at his knees and listened to him retell of how he'd used his powers to get information during the French Revolution and both world wars. She risked a glance at Raven. "Call me if you find out anything. Please."

"I'll do better than that. I'll see you tonight. There are things we need to discuss." Raven's terse tone cut through her, despite him brushing a kiss on her cheek as he left.

"Once we solve this case," Mishenka said. "I'm sure your young man will be more civil."

She gritted her teeth as she scrubbed. Dealing with her grandfather at times felt like dealing with a temperamental three-year-old. Once she helped her grandfather gown up, she drew in a deep breath and opened Stacey's door.

The shades were open, allowing the sun to brighten the room. The room smelled of roses and heather from the many beautiful bouquets that filled the room.

Mishenka removed a card from one of the arrangements. "I had the local florist deliver these, in case she woke up. I wanted Stacey to know how much she means to our family."

How could Caitlin stay mad at her Grandfather when she knew everything he did was out of love and his need to help? She just hoped Raven would understand and not be angry with her or Grandpapa. "They're beautiful. I'm sure Stacey will think so, too."

Stacey lay motionless, hooked up to the same strange instruments as she'd been to last night. Someone had washed the blood from Stacey's face. A nurse must have bathed her this morning. They'd even changed her gown. Caitlin caressed Stacey's cheek. "Wake up, please wake up."

"Such a gentle soul." The weight of Mishenka hand on Caitlin's shoulder had her tipping her head toward him.

"She didn't deserve to suffer as she did." Fury almost choked Caitlin. Stacey wouldn't harm anyone. She was always thinking of others instead of herself. During the holidays, she would fret over not doing enough to help at the local homeless shelter. How could anyone have done this to her?

The shadows on the wall grew long as the day slipped by. Caitlin glanced over at Mishenka. "If you want to go and get some lunch, go ahead. I'm not leaving her."

"You won't do her or yourself any good if you're exhausted. Come with me. You need a break."

"I want to be here when she wakes."

A male nurse entered the room. "Doctor Whenn was in this morning to see her. You must have missed him." After the nurse replaced an I.V. bag, he pressed several buttons on one of the many machines. "Her pulse is steady."

"Why isn't she waking up?" The words caught in Caitlin's throat.

"Are you a *real* nurse or an undercover police officer?" Mishenka asked before the nurse could answer Caitlin's question.

"I'm a real nurse." He turned his attention to Caitlin and smiled. "I'll see if Doctor Morrison can speak with you. He can answer your questions." He scribbled something on Stacey's chart then left, pulling the door closed behind him.

Caitlin bit her lower lip until it throbbed. Something was wrong. Stacey should be recovering faster than she was. After all, Caitlin's blood flowed through Stacey. What had that bastard done to prevent her from healing? Caitlin took

Stacey's limp hand and held it. "Your coloring is healthier today, and your bruises have faded. Honest."

She looked up at Mishenka. "Grandpapa, she looks like she's only sleeping. Come on, Stace. Wake up. Come back to us."

Caitlin's guilt weighed on her heart like a metal beam. Had she been actively hunting this man instead of trying to cover a story or court Raven, Stacey wouldn't be laying in this hospital bed.

"This isn't your fault. Nor is it Raven's. This madman is a chameleon," Mishenka's voice lowered to barely a whisper. He stood with his back toward her, staring out the window. "Raven took the young man we met by the nurses' station in for questioning."

"He said he was, but I think Raven is wrong. Jeff only had a date with Stacey."

"Did Raven tell you he found Stacey's earring in Mr. Morgan's apartment? Or about the newspaper articles this Morgan had pinned to his wall?"

Caitlin gripped the bed rails for support. "No. He didn't mention any of that."

"Perhaps, he wanted to protect you. Or his suspect."

Maybe. Caitlin smoothed Stacey's cheek. It all made sense. Why didn't she see the connection? Jeff lived in the same apartment complex as Susan Holloway, the second victim, and he attended classes at night. Maybe he knew the third victim, Anne Thompson? He could have met her on campus.

Caitlin moved her hand to Stacey's. "Only you know who did this to you."

"Only she knows," Mishenka repeated.

Caitlin brushed a kiss to Stacey's forehead. "Please wake up. No one will ever hurt you again. I swear."

Stacey arched her back. Her eyes flew open and sheer terror shown on her face. She gasped and fell limp on the bed. Her lips began turning a faint shade of blue.

The alarms on Stacey's monitors sounded.

Nurses rushed into the room. They shoved Caitlin and Mishenka aside. Doctor Morgan ran in shouting orders. A male nurse grabbed Caitlin by the arm and pushed her and Mishenka from the room. "Wait out here." The door shut.

Trembling, Caitlin grabbed Mishenka's hand. Her knees went weak. Tears stung her eyes. "Grandpapa."

"I'm sorry. So, very sorry." Fear etched Mishenka's wrinkled and gray face. His weathered hand shook. "I didn't know this would happen."

He hadn't. He couldn't have. "Grandpapa? Did you force Stacey's mind? Tell me you didn't."

"Kitten," his voice cracked. "I didn't mean to hurt her. I thought I could see an image of her attacker." He bowed his head. "I only saw a shadow of a man. I couldn't see his face. I can't even tell you the color of his hair. I'm sorry, Kitten."

She hugged her grandfather. "I want you to stay here until you find out about Stacey. There is something I have to do. I'll be back shortly."

Without waiting for him to reply, she turned and left. A short time later Caitlin pulled out of the hospital parking lot.

Raven had a suspect. There was one way of finding out if he was the killer or not.

She parked her car across the street from the police station. Using her powers, she faded. Floating across the street brought back memories of Nam. She would fade from sight to search the jungle for prey. It didn't seem wrong to hunt the enemy, especially when she didn't kill them. Funny, wasn't that what she was doing now? Only this time she knew where to find him.

Strangely, she found the thought of hunting satisfying. All of her life she'd tried to hide what she was, tried to be more human. Being in this ghostly form released her from her inhibitions. She was Dhampir, not a human, not a vampire, but a child of both.

I am Dhampir.

Slipping under the heavy metal door was easy. Pushing through the cinder block wall into the interrogation room took more concentration. After today, she'd make it a point to practice fading more often.

Caitlin emerged from the wall and took in her surroundings. Raven loomed over Jeff, sitting at a long metal table while Mike leaned against the far wall.

Raven slammed his fist onto the table, making her jump. "One more time, Morgan. Did you know Anne Thompson?"

"Not personally. Look, how long are you going to keep me here? It isn't a crime to write about murder. Is it?"

The vein in Raven's throat swelled. "Only when the murders are real, and you've written about them before they took place." Raven snatched a piece of paper from a file. "I cut her, and she cried. I burnt her, and she screamed." He glared at Jeff. "Did you or did you not write this?"

"Yeah, I wrote that. That doesn't make me the murderer."

Mike tossed a file at Jeff. "You wrote these two years ago. Two years before the death of Anne Thompson. Two years before the attempted murder of Stacey Parker."

Anger emanated from Jeff. "You're not going to pin this on me. I didn't kill anyone, and I certainly didn't attack Stacey."

Anger raged inside of Caitlin, and she pressed her hand against the wall, grounding her. All of the victims had been cut and burnt. If Jeff were the one who attacked Stacey, he would not leave this room alive.

Raven looked up directly at her, and his eyes narrowed. She swore he mouthed her name. He couldn't have. He couldn't know she was there. Could he? No, there was no way. Yes, he'd given her blood, but they hadn't shared blood yet, and they were not connected.

She couldn't hold this form for much longer. Caitlin seeped deeper into the wall. She'd already lost her sense of direction. Perhaps she should slip out and wait until Jeff was alone. She couldn't risk Raven catching her here. There was no way she could explain to him what she was doing.

The door to the interrogation room opened, and another man entered. "The hospital is on line three."

"Thank you," Raven said. He glanced at Mike. "C'mon, this may be our break."

A rush of air escaped Jeff as Raven and Mike left the room.

This was her chance. Staying in her ghostly form so she wouldn't show up on the surveillance cameras, Caitlin moved behind Jeff. Swiftly, she grabbed him, tilted his head, and bit into his flesh. She let his head fall limply onto the table.

Chapter Nineteen

Caitlin swallowed the warm, rich blood. Jeff wasn't the killer. He'd tried to grope Stacey, and she'd slapped him. That explained how she'd lost her earring. He hadn't hurt her.

Guilt flooded Caitlin, souring her stomach. She'd attacked an innocent man. Her shame overshadowed the sweetness of his blood.

She glanced around the dimly lit, gray interrogation room. The surveillance camera pointed down at her and Jeff. She couldn't be caught on film or seen by whoever stood on the other side of the two-way mirror in front of her. She had to maintain her phantom state.

Drawing in a calming breath, she lowered her mouth once again to his throat. This time she gave him pleasant dreams instead of forcing herself into his innermost thoughts. She left him dreaming of writing the best seller that had been eluding him. It was the least she could do.

After easing Jeff's head down and resting it on his arm, she pushed through the wall. Slowly she made her way down the hall, and out of the building. Raven wouldn't have any idea what she'd done. Maybe she'd tell him. Then again, maybe not. He wouldn't understand. The memory of his anger at the hospital was still fresh in her mind. It was obvious he didn't approve of the use of supernatural powers.

Staying in her ghostly state, Caitlin floated across the street. She'd slipped into her car. "Well, I've eliminated one suspect. A few thousand more to go."

~ ~ ~

"Repeat that." Raven's knees buckled, and he gripped his phone tighter as he listened. The noise and commotion of the station made it difficult for him to hear what officer Cannon said. His knees buckled, and he leaned against his desk, not believing what he'd heard.

"She had a heart attack?" he asked, making sure he'd heard correctly. "I understand, Cannon." He hung up and met Mike's questioning gaze. "Stacey's had a heart attack."

"How the hell is that possible? The woman isn't even thirty. Was it a reaction to some medication she'd received?"

"From what Cannon was able to find out, the doctors are contributing Stacey's heart attack to shock. Stress from her attack."

"Jeez. How's Caitlin? Did Cannon say?"

Something disturbing replaced Raven's feeling of shock. "Caitlin wasn't there. Her grandfather said she had to go for a walk."

Sinister images built in Raven's mind. A walk or revenge? He pushed from the desk and quickly headed to the interrogation room.

Mike ran after him. "Hey! Where are you going?"

"To get some answers."

Raven shoved open the door and pushed the fearful thoughts from his mind as he shook Jeff. "C'mon, Morgan."

"Hmm, what?" he groaned.

Relief washed over Raven. Jeff was alive. Caitlin hadn't broken in and killed him.

Jeff stirred, yawned, and stretched. "Oh, it's you two. Back so soon?"

Mike shut the door. "Yeah, we're back, Sleeping Beauty. Now, that you're well rested, we're going to ask you once more, what happened the night of the twentieth?"

"For the last time, Stupid. I met Stacey at the pizza place."

"Pizza Max?" Raven asked. His gaze fell to the two small white marks on Jeff's throat, just above his jugular. Caitlin had been there.

Jeff rolled his eyes. "Do you know of another decent pizza place in this damn town?" He held up his hand. "Never mind. As stupid as you are it's no wonder you two haven't been able to catch this creep."

Raven lunged at Jeff, grabbing him by his shirt collar, lifting him from his seat. "Damn you. I've had enough of your mouth."

"Raven. Let him go." Mike pried Raven's fingers from Jeff's shirt. "He isn't worth losing your job."

Raven glared at Mike then shoved Jeff away. "You're right. He isn't." Raven balled his fist and walked to the far side of the room. Hell, what was wrong with him? Just because Caitlin bit the guy didn't mean she'd had sex with him. Didn't mean she hadn't either, a small voice said.

Bitter jealousy twisted inside him. He glared at Jeff, wanting to punch him until he was a bloody pile of garbage.

Get a hold of yourself, O'Brien. This guy isn't worth losing your badge over. You can trust Cat. You always have and always will. She's a far better woman than Beth ever was.

Raven glared across the room. He still wanted to punch the crap out of Morgan, just for the pure joy of it.

"I get it," Jeff said, straightening his shirt. "You're playing good cop, bad cop." He looked at Mike. "I guess you're supposed to make me feel like you're my only friend. Right?"

Mike smiled. "Nope. I'm the bad cop. You see, I think you did it. My partner here believes otherwise." Mike slammed his hands on the table in front of Jeff. "I think you killed the other six women and tried to kill Stacey Parker. I think that once we search your apartment again, we'll find evidence to this fact."

"What evidence? You searched my place already and didn't find a damn thing. You can't arrest me just because I had a date with the victim. I know the law too, Jack."

Raven crossed his arms. "Good. Then you're familiar with the term *probable cause.*"

"What?" Jeff rose from his seat.

"Her earring was in your apartment." He wanted to wring that bastard's neck. Morgan hadn't killed the other victims, of this, Raven was sure. But it didn't mean Morgan hadn't tortured Stacey.

"Yeah. So. I didn't hide it from you did I? No. I gave it to you."

"True. But then again, what were you to do, with us standing there? Say it belonged to your sister? No. You picked it up and came up with a story to cover your ass. What you didn't count on, was our finding her necklace inside your desk."

"Her what?" Jeff's mouth dropped opened. "Look, if you're trying to frame me—"

"Shut up!" Raven walked to the table. He gripped the edge to keep from punching Jeff. "How did her necklace get in your desk drawer?"

"Hell, if I know. One of you probably put it there." He stared at Raven. "Seeing the only way you'll solve this case is by framing me."

Raven snatched Jeff from his seat and slammed him against the wall. He bit his lip on impact.

"Once more. How did Miss Parker's necklace get in your desk drawer?" Raven growled.

"Raven," Mike warned.

Blood ran from the corner of Jeff's mouth. "Screw you." He spit in Raven's face.

Raven wiped his face then drew back his fist, and stopped. This worm wasn't worth being taken off the case. "You have the right to remain silent." *Damn, it felt good to say those words.*

~ ~ ~

Raven had said he'd drop by to see her tonight. Caitlin stared at the kitchen clock. It was already ten. She'd try calling him one more time, before going to bed.

Sleep, that's what she needed. Maybe she'd wake up, and all this craziness would turn out to be a nightmare.

"You don't get reruns of *Mr. Bean* or perhaps *Benny Hill* here?" Mishenka called from the living room.

"No, Grandpapa."

He mumbled something about American television before walking down the hall with Inky cradled in his arms. She'd told Mishenka he could sleep in her room and she'd take Stacey's room. He still blamed himself for Stacey's heart attack.

Caitlin closed her eyes. Whatever that bastard did to Stacey, the memory of it frightened her so much it caused her heart to stop. If Caitlin ever got her hands on whoever did this, she'd give him something to fear. No, not if, when.

Caitlin snatched up her keys. Raven had shut off his phone. Like it or not, she needed to talk to him.

Fifteen minutes later, Caitlin knocked on his door. She held her breath. She could sense him inside. She also sensed his anger. He was ignoring her. Fine. She leaned against his doorbell.

The door flew opened. "Come in." Raven still wore his dress pants, his shirttail was pulled out, and the first three buttons were unfastened. He stepped back for her to enter.

She smiled at him. "You said you were coming by my place tonight. I waited."

"Things came up." He shut the door. "We've arrested Jeff Morgan." His dark eyes belied his anger, or was it disappointment she saw?

"Why?" She stepped toward him with open arms.

He backed away. "Don't."

Her arms fell to her sides. Fine. Raven was pissed at her. Again.

The urge to press into his mind tempted her. "Talk to me. Why did you arrest him?"

"Sit." Raven flopped down onto the leather recliner. He picked up the bottle of whiskey sitting on the coffee table. "We searched Morgan's apartment and found Stacey's necklace. He'd hid it in the back of his desk drawer."

"Oh, God." Caitlin's throat closed up. She gasped. "This can't be."

"It looked like it had blood on it."

"No, no, no. Jeff didn't do it." She met Raven's cold glare. He sat staring at her, and she looked down. She couldn't meet his gaze. She had to tell him the truth. Raven would hate her for it, but she couldn't permit an innocent man to be arrested when the guilty one still walked free.

She met Raven's tempestuous gaze. "Someone planted Stacey's necklace in Jeff's apartment. He wasn't the one who attacked her. I know." Caitlin held her breath, waiting for Raven to ask how she knew.

He took a swig from the bottle.

She swallowed. "Grandpapa tried to enter Stacey's mind today. I don't know what happened. She suffered a heart attack. Grandpapa blames himself." Tears stung Caitlin's eyes. She wanted Raven to hold her. "I understand why he did it, but I had to get away from him. I had to find answers for myself."

Raven sat rigidly. His expression grew grimmer as he stared at her.

Drawing in a breath, Caitlin willed herself to continue. "Grandpapa saw a shadow of Stacey's attacker. I had to know if it was Jeff."

Raven leaned forward in his seat. "Go on," he whispered.

His soft-spoken, unemotional words added to her anguish and shattered the last shred of her control. Raven was all police detective and didn't care about her feelings. He wanted the facts, nothing more, and nothing less.

Fine! If that's how he wants it, she could be just as cold as he. "I am Dhampir. I went there with two things in mind. To find out if Jeff was the one responsible and if so, I planned to kill him." She closed her eyes and balled her fists, digging her nails into the palms of her hands. Blood pooled in her palms.

Damn it! She wasn't going to do this anymore.

"You broke into the station and acted like a vampire. All this time I've had the feeling you didn't like that part of yourself. I see now it's all been an act. But, then again, you were an actress. A damn good one."

"I've been a lot of things in the past two hundred years, but never honest about who or what I was, until today. Now, I know who and *what* I am. I did what I had to do. I had to know if Jeff was the person responsible for Stacey's injuries and the deaths of the other women."

Raven leaned his head back and stared at the ceiling. "Tell me, did he get his rocks off when you bit him, as I did?"

She'd never had a stake driven through her heart, but now she knew how it must feel. "How can you ask that after what we've shared?"

"Because of what we shared." His jaw twitched, and his eyes became black pits. "When I found out about Beth, it hurt. When I saw your marks on that bastard's throat, I wanted to kill him." Raven drew in a deep breath and released it. "Then you."

"Oh?" She stood and grabbed the fireplace poker then tossed it at him. "Go ahead. Run it through my heart. Then you'll have to take my head. Staking me alone won't do the trick. You won't have to worry about disposing of my body either. Just sweep my ashes into the fireplace."

The poker rolled off his lap.

She snatched it up again and thrust it at him. Her voice rose in volume, yet dropped in pitch. "Do it! If you think that little of me. Do. It!"

Raven glared at her. "You're out of your mind."

"I'm not crazy. I'm tired of being something I'm not." She met his condemning eyes. "I went there to kill Jeff, not give myself to him. Just because I take a person's blood doesn't mean I make love to them. I've taken blood from many in my lifetime, but *none of them* experienced what you did. Not one."

Unable to bear the pain flickering in Raven's black eyes, she turned away. "Jeff felt burning pain as I bit into his throat. When I realized he was innocent, I felt guilty for my action and gave him a peaceful dream. *That's all.* Had he been guilty, I would have made him suffer even more. You and Mike would have found Jeff's dried husk of a body crumpled on the floor with his throat ripped out. Needless to say, Detective, you would have had another murder on your hands."

"I would have hunted you down. You know I would have."

She turned and marched back to the couch. She flopped down, crossing her arms over her chest. "You would have tried. You might have even traveled to Scotland, and you might have found my parents. That's as far as you would have gotten."

"You're wrong," his voice trembled. "I would have found you, even if it took me a lifetime."

"And what, brought me back here to face your justice? Do you think my family would permit that?"

"No, they wouldn't. Your family would protect you at all cost," Raven's voice sounded dull and troubled.

She closed her eyes. Why was she staying here? She shoved from the couch. "Protect me? No, Raven, you have it wrong. For my actions, for risking exposing us, I would be tried by the Council and punished according to my crimes. *If* I were lucky, I would get imprisonment. If, not, then I would be held by my father and Glen, while Vaughn ripped my heart out with his hand. Since he's the Council's Enforcer, it would be his responsibility to carry out the Council's verdicts. So, you see Detective justice would be served. And my family would suffer emotionally for my crime. Think how you would feel if you had to execute your sister or one of your brothers." She strode to the door. Her hand rested on the doorknob. "Good-bye."

"Cat." Strong arms wrapped around her shoulders and pulled her against a rock hard chest. "Forgive me for being a jealous ass. I had to know the truth. I had to hear you say it."

"Say what? Killing a human would mean my death? That justice would be served?"

"Cat, I'm sorry."

"You didn't trust me." She pushed away. "That hurts the most."

"I was hurting." His arms drew her back against him and tightened around her. "You don't know the things I imagined. The pain I felt. I acted like a jerk. I know that. Forgive me." He kissed the back of her neck. "Please," he begged. "I would never—Oh, God, Cat. I would never hurt you. I spoke out of anger. You have to believe me."

A hot tear splashed on her neck.

Her resistance melted. She turned and clung to Raven.

He framed her face and kissed her tear-streaked cheeks. "Even though I couldn't see you, I knew you were there."

"You felt me?"

"Yes. When Mike and I returned to the room," he closed his eyes. "Oh, Cat. Don't ever put me through that again."

The bond between them was stronger than she'd thought. She couldn't keep anything from him any longer. She willed herself to look into his eyes.

"I attacked an innocent man. I grabbed Jeff and tore into his throat with no mercy. Jeff is only guilty of trying to feel Stacey's breasts and get into her pants. She slapped him, and he backed off. When I realized his innocents, I felt sick." Tears blurred her vision.

A rush of air escaped Raven, and he tipped her face up, savagely capturing her mouth. Raven's arms tightened around her, crushing her to him as he forced his tongue into her mouth. His five o'clock shadow scraped her cheek. Fragments of his thoughts flashed in her mind. Raven had thought she'd made love to Jeff.

Caitlin pushed away. She drew a long deep breath. "Raven, I've got to tell you something, and I don't know how you'll take it."

His face became like granite, and he stepped back. "Is this where you tell me you only want to be friends? Because if it is, I *don't* want to hear it."

He walked toward the fireplace. His head lowed as he rested his arms on the mantel, under that hideous painting of her. His shoulders rose then fell, and he looked over his shoulder, he met her gaze. "Cat, what we shared the other night was a hell of a lot more."

"Do you love me?" She'd dreamed of the moment when he told her he loved her, not of her forcing the confession from him. She eased down onto the couch.

He turned and flung his arms wide. "How can you ask me that? You've been in my mind. You know how I feel about you."

"In your mind yes, not your heart," she tossed back. Sitting rigidly on the couch, she tilted her head and stared at him. She didn't need to hear the words. She wanted to hear them.

In two steps Raven towered over her then dropped to his knees and took her hands in his. "I love you, Cat. I didn't want to admit it. I didn't want to be hurt again." He lifted her hands to his lips.

She slid her arms around his neck. "I love you, too."

"Move in with me. We can live together. Say yes." He pulled her close and captured her mouth again.

She kissed him briefly. "I can't move in with you. Not yet. Not until you know everything."

His eyes grew dark. "You're engaged to someone else, one of your own. Your grandfather mentioned something about knowing your mate. Your family has arranged a marriage for you, haven't they?"

"No. That's not what I've got to tell you."

"Your family won't approve of you getting involved with a human."

"No. Grandpapa likes you. Besides, my father is human, remember?"

"Then what's the problem?" Raven challenged.

She never thought she'd be the one proposing. "I don't want to live with you. Well, I do. I want more. Will you marry me?"

All color drained from his face, and he fell back on his rear. "Marry you?"

Chapter Twenty

The clock chimed the twelfth stroke of midnight. Caitlin stared at Raven sitting on the floor.

The color edged back to his cheeks, and he opened and closed his mouth like a fish. "Marry you? Think about this. I'm human. One morning you'll wake up and find yourself saddled with a fat, gray, and old man. Do you want that?" He pierced her with his dark gaze.

Before she left this night, she would make Raven see they belonged together. This fight, she would win. "We will grow old together. When we consummate our union, I will take your blood then give you mine. You will live as long as I do. You will age as I age. We will be joined together for all eternity."

He raised a dark eyebrow. "How much blood?"

She twisted her fingers in her short hair and worried her bottom lip. Why did Raven have to ask *that* question? Raven went for a knockout in round one.

"Cat, how much blood will you take? All of it? Will you drain me dry like they do in the movies?"

Some things were best left unsaid, but he'd asked, and she wouldn't keep anything from him. Then again, she wouldn't volunteer any information he didn't ask for either. "No. Not *all* of it." She drew in a deep breath. "I will take all, but your last life-giving drop. Then, I will open a vein in my throat and press your lips to the wound. You will drink my blood. This ritual will join us together, body and soul for all times, even past the grave."

"But, I'm human."

"You know, I hate repeating myself, but I will a million times if that's what it takes for you to understand we will both be old and gray together." She waited for him to respond.

What was he thinking? "Don't you see, we are already joined? You already can sense my presence."

"Because I gave you my blood."

Show no signs of relenting, she told herself. "No. You sense me because we belong together. Don't you understand? I have lived for two hundred years. I have shared blood with many humans over that period, and not one human could feel my presence. I knew where they were, what they were thinking, but they had no control over me. You do."

"You still have one up on me. You know my thoughts."

She studied his stone expression. He wasn't making this easy. "Once we are mated, you will be able to hear my thoughts as easily as I hear yours. You will know what I'm feeling and where I am at all times."

Raven sat silently, stroking his chin, and staring at her.

Damn. The temptation to enter Raven's mind drove her crazy. The ticking of the clock didn't help. "Will you say something?"

He nodded. "You're still not telling me everything. Are you?"

Staring into his impenetrable black eyes, Caitlin prepared for round two. Why had she fallen for a detective? She wanted children, at least two, a boy, and a girl would be nice. Did Raven want children? They'd never discussed this subject. What if he didn't want kids? The other night he referred to her getting pregnant as an unexpected consequence.

The torment churned inside her.

She conceded. The only way to find out was to ask. "No, I'm not. During this blending of our blood, is the only guaranteed time I can become pregnant. That is one reason why there are so few of my kind in the world. Many of my people are childless because they miscarried the child created during their joining."

A faint smile pulled at his lips. Or was it her imagination?

"So you can have my child. I hoped you could, but I wasn't sure," Raven said, matter-of-factly.

"You hoped I could?" The knot in her stomach eased, and a sigh of relief escaped her. "You want kids?"

"Of course. I'd like to have two or three." Raven's eyes darkened, and his face grew somber. "Beth never wanted children. She didn't want to lose her shape, or give up her free time."

Her fangs lengthened, and her back stiffened. *Beth this. Beth that. Beth! Beth! Beth!* "I am not Beth! I will not cheat on you! I will not leave you!"

Raven held up his hands in surrender. "I know you're not Beth. You're not shallow." He ran his fingers through his hair. "Cat, look. When I married Beth, I was young, stupid, and horny as hell. She married me because she thought my family had money. Go figure, a rich police sergeant. When she found out otherwise, she started nagging me to take my detective's exam. She pushed me. I guess I should thank her for that." His voice dropped to nearly a whisper. "To tell the truth, neither of us was in love with the other."

Caitlin shuddered inwardly at the thought of being in a loveless marriage. Round three went to him.

Raven rose to his knees and took Caitlin's hands in his. His dark eyes brightened, and his face softened as he stared at her. "I didn't know what it was like to be in love until you entered my life."

Caitlin leaned forward, brushing a kiss across his lips. His admission had been dredged from a place deep within his soul. "You honestly love me?"

His eyes shimmered and his lips curved. "Blood rituals and all."

His answer shocked her. "You don't have a problem drinking my blood?"

"Not at all." His smile faded. "What else haven't you told me?"

Without warning, he'd slipped back into his ironclad, unfeeling, just-the-facts-ma'am mode. Caitlin didn't know how he would take what she had to tell him next. She knew how close he was to his family.

The bell rang for round four.

"Raven," she forced out. "In a few years, you will have to sever all ties with your family."

~ ~ ~

Raven stood, walked to the fireplace, and gazed up at Caitlin's portrait. He'd not expected her to ask that of him. The anguish of having to choose between his family and the woman he loved nearly overcame his control. He had to stay firm. He had to remain in control of this discussion. "I love you, and I would do a hell of a lot for you, but I don't know if I can do what you're asking."

"Despite how much your family loves you, they will become suspicious when you stop aging. They will ask questions you won't be able to answer without risking the lives of others." She drew in a breath. "I'm sorry," she whispered.

Caitlin's hollow, lifeless voice drew him. Raven glanced over his shoulder and turned. Her head bowed, chin resting on her chest. She looked so small and defeated. "Cat."

She lifted her head, and the pain in her eyes froze him. The events of the past few days had taken a toll on her. She wasn't as invincible as she thought. And he'd just added to her torment. He had to make Caitlin understand how he felt without hurting her even more. "Growing up, my brothers and I were close. We still are close. When Beth left me, Usher and Edgar pulled me out of my slump."

Inhaling, he calmed himself and stepped toward the coffee table. He picked up the files he'd been going over before Cat came. "Caitlin, Edgar risked his job to get me these files." That statement didn't help. Raven tossed the files back on to the table. "Edgar suggested they may help me with this frigging case. He believes our serial killer could have killed before, as a juvenile. I agree with him."

Raven then pointed to the photo of his mom and dad. He was grabbing at straws and knew it, but he had to make her understand. "My parents are old; my father's health isn't great. I can't turn my back on my family. You of all people know what family means."

His mind felt like a bowl of spaghetti, lose and stringy. He didn't know what else to say or do to convince Cat he couldn't turn his back on his family. He needed them as much as he needed her.

Gracefully, Caitlin stood. She stepped forward and wrapped her arms around his waist. "I know the meaning of family." She melted against him, resting her head on his chest. "We'll find a solution."

Gathering her in his arms, he breathed in her scent and never wanted to leave her embrace. "Cat."

She lifted her head and smiled at him. Her eyes were moist from unshed tears. The mere sight set his heart pounding out of control. He loved her with all his heart and soul. He couldn't leave her. He couldn't leave his family either. Somehow, he'd find the way to keep both. He framed her face. "I love you. I want to share my life with you."

"I hear a 'but' in there."

He stared into her silvery eyes, framed with long thick lashes. "I want both. Can you put up with my family, until my parents die? That's all I ask."

Her smiled melted his heart. "Only if you can put up with my family for the next thousand years or so?"

He captured her mouth, tasting her sweetness. Damn, never in his life did he want to have to choose between his heart and his family. Yeah, he was a spoiled, greedy bastard. He wanted his cake and eat it too. He slid his hands down her back, roaming over Cat's bod, pressing her closer to his throbbing groin. He sensed the fire he'd awakened inside of her.

She rubbed against him.

His tongue teased and danced with hers. Cat's fangs, budded. He carefully skidded his tongue around the needle sharp points. A snake's fangs couldn't be as sharp. Hmm, what would happen if he just lightly ran his tongue across their tips?

A moan slipped from Caitlin, and she clutched him tighter to her. She kissed him with a passion and desire that sent his blood pounding to his head and turned his knees to rubber. Damn! Had he thought her teeth were erogenous zones, he'd suck on them long ago. *I have to remember this*.

He had to get them both horizontal fast. Raven lowered Cat to the floor and lifted his lips from hers. She was beautiful with her rumpled hair, kiss-swollen lips, and fiery red eyes that mirrored the passion burning in his heart. He wanted her forever. He had a choice to make. And he knew what his answer would be. There was no going back.

He smoothed her hair then kissed the tip of her nose, followed by her eyes.

Caitlin purred in his arms.

Slowly, he planted kisses in the hollow of her neck, gently nipping the skin.

She clawed at his back.

Raven chuckled. *Another hot spot.* Oh, he was learning so much about his love.

He trailed baby kisses up her neck to her jawline, and finally, he kissed her soft mouth.

Caitlin pressed her lips to his, caressing them more than kissing them.

His hand slid down her taut stomach to the swell of her hips. This was it. There was no going back. After tonight he'd be hers. No other woman would ever share his bed. And that made his heart pound even faster.

Lifting his lips from Caitlin's, awkwardness replaced desire. His gaze roamed over her body tucked beneath him. Her full breasts raised and lowered with each breath. He didn't want to screw this up, but damn if he didn't feel like a pimply faced teen in the back of his daddy's car. But before he took tonight one step farther, he needed to make sure she wanted this, wanted him too.

Caitlin's hand lightly caressed his face then slid to the back of his neck, pulling him closer to her lush mouth. "Why did you stop?"

His lips brushed against hers as he spoke. "You know where this will lead?"

Chapter Twenty-One

Raven studied the glow in Caitlin's eyes, trying to read the emotion shining in them. He shifted his weight, rolled to his side, and drew in a deep breath. He wanted her, now and forever. "The choice is yours. If I understand you correctly, this act will bind us tighter than if we were to stand before a priest."

Other than her biting her lower lip, her face lacked expression. Yeah, she'd make a damn good poker player.

Seconds ticked past. The anticipation of Cat's answer was unbearable. Raven stared at her, wishing he could read her mind as easily as she could his. "Cat?"

Her gaze suddenly turned dark, and way too serious. "You can get a divorce when a priest joins you. The bond of the blood ritual will bind us so tightly there can be no divorce. We will be as one. Not even death can separate us."

Raven took her hand and placed it over his heart. "Isn't that how it's supposed to be?"

"Yes, but—"

He gently placed his hand over her mouth. "No buts, just yes or no." He lifted his hand and kissed her.

Caitlin smiled and snaked her arms around his neck. Her smile grew to a full grin. She pulled him on top of her with incredible strength. "With this act, I thee wed."

"Till death do us do part," he added.

She slid her hands down his shoulders and around to his chest. Her fingers seared a path to the waist of his pants. "One more question, carpet burn or no carpet burn."

His heart pounded as she freed him, taking his cock in her hands. She slid her fingers from his base to his crown. "I don't mind either way," she purred against his ear. Then licked the side of his neck.

A shudder ran through his body. "Let's continue this back in the bedroom," he gasped when Cat slipped her hand further down and cupped his balls.

"Not partial to carpet burns?" She nipped at his earlobe.

Laughing, Raven rolled from her, kicked off his pants then scooped her up in his arms. "Not really." He wasn't about to make love to her on the floor of his living room, this winter, maybe in front of a roaring fire, but not tonight, not when there was a mattress waiting for them.

He pushed open his bedroom door. Great! He'd forgotten to make his bed, and the room looked like hell. His dry-cleaning hung over the treadmill, a heap of dirty clothes filled one corner of his room, and his dresser drawers hung open. He usually straightened things when he returned home, but not tonight. He had other things on his mind. Maybe Caitlin wouldn't notice his sloppy housekeeping skills.

He barely made it into his room when she slid from his arms. Laughing, Caitlin back from him. He stared into her violet eyes, losing himself in their fire, as she unbuttoned her blouse then tossed it across the room. She licked her lips, keeping her eyes locked with his as she slid one strap of her bra down her arm then the other strap down her other arm. Cat held one arm over her breast as she unfastened her bra. Smiling and revealing her fangs, she dropped her bra on the floor as she did a little shimmy. Damn, he'd blow his wad just from watching her. Next, she slowly slid her panties down over her hips. As she revealed inch by inch of her gorgeous self, he grew harder and harder.

Finally, Caitlin stepped out of her panties. She picked them up and twirled them around her finger. They flew off her finger, landing somewhere among his mess. "I don't know why you're worried about your room. I'm the one who didn't make the bed this morning." She licked her bottom lip.

"Reading my thoughts again?" He reached for her, wanting to touch her.

Caitlin dodged him. Her gaze roamed slowly down his body. He'd had enough of her teasing and grabbed at her again.

"Anxious are we." She batted his hand away.

The beauty of her naked body taunted him, as much as her lusty smile. "Woman, you have no idea," he whispered.

Cat, angled her head, her razor-sharp fangs peeked out from her lips. A sane man would run from seeing her fangs, but damn, all he could think about was the sensation he'd felt when she drank his blood. His dick throbbed.

"Then catch me." Caitlin leaped into his arms, wrapping her legs around his waist and her arms around his neck.

"Cat," Raven laugh out her name as he stumbled back, slamming shut the bedroom door with his back.

"I want you now." She slid down on his cock, taking him completely inside her in one swift plunge.

Raven pushed into her, meeting her thrust for thrust. His arms supported her as he slammed into her furiously, his back up against the bedroom door. The door banged in rhythm to their lovemaking. No, this wasn't making love, this was a claiming, a primal statement that he was hers just as much as she was his. This was a fast and furious claiming against the door.

"Make me come, Raven. Make me come," Cat song out as she dug her nails into his shoulder. She lowered her mouth to his in a torrid kiss that branded him. He knew any moment now Cat would sink her fangs into his neck, finally claiming him. Raven tilted his head, to give her better access.

Cat's inner muscles tightened. She was getting close. He could fill her trimmers. He held her tight as he plunged deeper into her, meeting her thrust for thrust. "Come for me. Come on Cat. Come on my dick." His balls drew up tight. He wouldn't come until she had. They would do this together.

Cat cried out as she tightened her legs around his waist, increasing her pace and thrusting harder down onto him. Her inner muscles tightened. She flung her head back, screaming his name as she climaxed. He gave in to his own release, filling her with his seed. Cat's head fell forward, resting on his shoulder as her muscles continued to milk him with the waning of her orgasm.

Raven didn't know how long he'd rested against the door, afraid to move, unsure if his legs would support them. Damn, they felt like overcooked spaghetti. His cock softened and slipped from her warm body.

"I think my bones have turned to mush," Cat murmured against his neck. "Wow. Simply, wow."

He chuckled as he carried her the few feet to his bed then placed her in the center of it. Her body glistened with sweat and their lovemaking. "Damn, you're beautiful."

"You're not bad yourself." Caitlin held out her hand to him. "Come here."

"Let me get a cloth so I can clean you."

"No." She rolled her head back and forth across the pillow. "Hold me."

Raven slid in bed then cradled Caitlin in his arms, their bodies still moist from their lovemaking. His mind drifted. She hadn't taken his blood when they made love. She hadn't joined them together as he'd hoped.

He breathed in her scent and pressed a kiss to her lips as he fought off the disappointment sinking into him. Or was it more hurt that he felt? Raven wanted to know why Cat hadn't taken his blood. He wouldn't push the issue tonight. Raven exhaled. Cat would tell him in her own time. Right now, he'd concentrate on her featherlike caresses. Her thumb and forefinger encircled him and she ever so lightly stroked him up and down. He didn't think it possible to be hard so quickly after what they just did, but damn. Raven rolled to his side and lightly caressed Cat's breast. When they grew pebble hard, he leaned over her, teasing her nipple with his tongue.

~ ~ ~

A moan escaped Caitlin as her fingers lightly stroked Raven's long firm shaft. She was still enjoying the bliss from their lovemaking. If you could call it lovemaking. There was a moment she thought the door wouldn't survive. Noisy, loud sex ran in the family. She had vivid memories of nights she'd buried her head under the pillow waiting for her parents to quiet. What would they do about Raven's parents and his family? Her father would understand Raven's determination to keep in touch with his family. Her brother, Glen, and her cousin, Royce, would too, as would Vaughn. She wasn't sure about Uncle Alan. He now ruled the clans but listened to Grandpapa. What would they do if Uncle Alan ordered them to sever ties with Raven's family? Raven wouldn't agree.

"Why do I have a feeling your mind is someplace else," Raven asked. He teased her earlobe lightly, sucking it into his mouth.

"I'm right here," she murmured and snuggled closer to him. He smelled of spice, and sex, and his unique scent, which made her blood pool to her center. She wanted him again, and from the fell of his hard shaft, he wanted her again, too.

She'd think of something. Somehow, they would make Grandpapa understand that Raven didn't have to give up his family. Times were changing. They needed to change how they viewed the outside world. Not all humans wanted them dead.

"Earth to Caitlin." Raven stroked her hair. His disappointment washed over her, pulling her from her thoughts. She'd hurt him by not claiming him.

"Hmm, I'm just enjoying your caress."

He nipped her neck, sending a wave of heat straight to her core. "I can't seem to get enough of you."

Her fangs lengthened. "When's your lease up?"

"Hmm. What?" Raven asked. His hand had slipped between her legs.

She blew in his ear. "Your lease?"

"Six months." He leaned up, stared into her eyes. "Why do you want to know?" A lazy smile curved his lips as he continued to caress her.

"I guess I could move in with you and let Stacey have the house."

Both eyebrows shot up. "You're serious?" His hand stilled, and she rocked against it, wanting more of his touch.

"Of course." She bit her bottom lip. "We can get married once Stacey is out of the hospital."

"And this case solved." He shook his head. "Not an option. Six months, that's my final offer." Raven drew his hand away, leaving her wanting.

His statement aroused old fears and uncertainties in her. Perhaps she'd been right not to claim him. "I don't understand what you're saying," she forced out, her voice quivered more than she'd liked.

"You move in now, today. Ah, in the morning. You can bring your things over, and *we will* be married within six months. No arguments."

October, when the mums were in bloom. Warmth flooded her. "No problem."

Raven's gaze roamed over her. In the darkness of the room, she saw the questions in his eyes. "What about your family? What will they think about your moving in with me?" he asked.

"Trust me. My folks won't have a problem." Heck, her parents wed while Grandpapa laid siege to the castle. Uncle Alan and Aunt Emma had lived together for a year. Of course, she'd been his housekeeper. Then there were Vaughn and Rose, but that's another story. "I'll be carrying on a family tradition."

She lightly drew her finger down his chest, moving lower. "What about your family?" She cupped him.

He drew in a sharp breath. "They would care, but wouldn't say anything."

She circled him, stroking him slowly. Raven closed his eyes and leaned his head so far back, his Adam's apple stuck out. "So it's settled. I move in with you?"

~ ~ ~

Raven opened his eyes and studied Caitlin. She lay on her side, resting her head in her hand, while she continued to gently stroke him. Her thumb smoothed over his head, spreading the drop of pre-cum over his crown. Her short red hair, draped across her eyes, giving her a sexy, sensual look. "Hmm, there's just one problem. You can't cook," he teased.

Her head snapped up, and her small fingers quickly moved up his side, tickling him. "But you can."

"Cat, you're not playing fair." He stilled her hand.

She giggled, and her warm breath teased his cheek. "I never do." She rolled on top of him and bent toward him, kissing him. Her breasts grazed his chest, and a moan escaped him. His cock hardened even more, and his balls drew up with her not so innocent caresses. It was all he could do not to grab her and shove deep into her. Pure mischievousness gleamed in her eyes as if she'd read his mind. Maybe she had. Cat shifted then lowered her body, taking him into her warm, slick, sheath.

He liked a woman who wanted seconds.

His hands skimmed up her legs and thighs. He kept their upward movement until he gently caressed her silky smooth breasts.

Caitlin set the tempo of their lovemaking again. He sat up, wrapping his arms around her waist. He lowered his mouth to her breast, running his tongue around her areola before lightly biting her nipple. He shifted to her other breast, giving it the same treatment as Cat squeezed her walls tighter around him. It took everything in him to keep from coming. Nope, his lady would come first.

Something clicked in his mind. He'd figured out why Caitlin hadn't taken his blood. *Damn, was he slow?*

He licked the side of Cat's neck then gently nipped at her soft skin where her neck and shoulder met. "I love you. I want you in my life forever. I don't want another second to go by without you." He leaned back and met her gaze. "Claim me, Cat. Make me yours forever. I love you."

"I love you. Have loved you for so long." She tightened her arms around him, holding him in an iron grip. He angled his head, giving her better access to his neck as he slid one hand around her waist, and his other to the back of her head, pressing her to his throat.

Her fangs brushed against his throat. "I love you," she cried out.

"And I you, forever and always."

Her fangs pierced his jugular. The soft touch of her mouth pushed him over the edge. He thrust deeper into her as his body surged with pure hot pleasure. It rolled over him repeatedly. He continued to pulse and come into her as she drank from him. He had never had an orgasm continue for so long.

As Caitlin drank from him, a cold sensation crept into his arms and legs, mixing with the pleasure of his orgasm washing over him. His body became a battle between fire and ice.

He was dying.

He didn't want her to stop taking from him. Raven didn't want the pleasure to end. His arms became heavy and slipped from her. His chest burned with every breath. *Thirsty, God, he was thirsty.*

He slipped into a crimson cloud, floating in the red haze.

"Drink, my love," Caitlin's words echoed in his mind.

Sweet, hot liquid filled his mouth, quenching his parched throat. As much as he wanted to, he couldn't swallow.

"Raven, you have to drink." Caitlin's voice pulled him from the crimson cloud engulfing him.

He opened his eyes and gulped, forcing down the thick liquid.

Blood.

His cold arms and legs tingled with fire. Warmth surged through him from his fingers to his toes. His heart pounded in his ears. He wrapped his arms around Caitlin, clinging to her. Like a man dying of thirst, he fastened his mouth over the wound in her throat and drank from her. How he wished his blunt teeth were fangs. He bit down, wanting more of the elixir she offered.

Soft moans of pleasure escaped Cat's lips. Her fingers threaded through his hair and her body quivered around him, milking him. Pure ecstasy assaulted him. His balls drew up again, and his body shuddered as he filled her with his seed, once more.

Raven closed his eyes again, savoring the erotic sensation. *Damn, how many times could he come in one night?*

The red haze again clouded his brain. Images flashed through his mind. Battles. Bombs fell from the skies, people screaming. He was running through the jungle trying to escape the fire.

Napalm.

Men were falling in front of him. *My God, he was in Nam!* What hellish nightmare was he living?

Suddenly he stood on a stage, singing in some speakeasy, and all he could think about was his girdle riding up his ass.

My God! I'm in Caitlin's mind. I'm seeing her life. I'm living her life.

His confusion eased into curiosity, and he wanted to learn everything about her.

A red tidal wave swept him through two hundred years. Events and images of people flashed through his mind, drowning him in the whirlpool of her life. When it finally ended, he fell limp against her. His body drenched in sweat.

He knew everything about Caitlin. Even though he'd only met her sister and grandfather, he knew every member of her family and loved them as much as she did. Raven's heart swelled when he felt how much she loved him, how much she worried about him. How much he'd *hurt her* earlier. Never again would he distrust her.

Raven opened his eyes and stared into her loving face. "I was in your mind. I felt—no. I experienced your life. What you felt, what you saw." He nuzzled her neck.

"I shared your life as well." She smiled at him. "You were such a brat to your brothers."

He chuckled. "You, my love, were no angelic child either." His gaze fell to her throat and to the large hideous wound he'd created. *Oh, God!*

All pleasure left him, and his shriveled cock slipped from her. "What in the hell did I do to you?"

Caitlin lifted her hand to her neck. A tender smile curved her lips, and her eyes shimmered. "You made me your mate. Marked me as yours for all to see."

He reached to touch the wound but pulled his hand back. "I hurt you. Why didn't you say something?"

"You know you didn't hurt me. You shared my pleasure, just as I felt *yours*."

She was right. Raven had experienced her woman's pleasure. He eased back to the mattress, his eyes focusing on her bloodied and bruised throat, the hideous wound. *That I caused*. It had to hurt. "How do you feel?"

Caitlin grinned and wiggled against him. "Very satisfied. Very happy. And very loved." She rolled from him then slid from the bed. Cat strolled to the bathroom, pausing to glance over her shoulder at him. "Don't go anywhere."

He grinned and folded his arms behind his head. He was exhausted, but he wasn't about to let her know. "I'll be waiting for you."

"Good, cause I think I want seconds, or would that be thirds?" She laughed and flicked on the light switch.

"My eyes." He quickly shut them against the blinding white-light.

"Not funny, Raven."

He opened his eyes and shut them again, covering them with his hands. "Cat!"

Caitlin was beside him, pulling his hands from his face. "What is it?"

"No, the light. It's too bright. Why is it so bright?"

"I don't know. Your body is changing. But this isn't normal."

"What do you mean?" Changing? He didn't feel any different. A little tired, but what did he expect after what they'd just done. Hell, he came at least four times tonight. Shit. "How am I changing?"

He opened his eyes once more, only to shut them and turn his head. The simple 40-watt light was brighter than the noon sun. "Cat, what's happening to me?"

She left him.

Panic came over him. "Where are you?"

"I'm turning the light off." The bed dipped. "I'm here." She stroked his face. "Your body is growing stronger, and I guess your eyes are becoming as sensitive to light as mine are."

Drumming echoed in his head, easing his fears. He listened. "Your heart is pounding."

"You can hear that?" He didn't miss the shock to her voice.

"Yeah, I can."

"Sleep and let your body heal."

He kissed the palm of her hand. "I feel like a fool."

"Don't," her voice quivered.

A warm, soft cloth covered him. He opened his eyes and saw Cat clearly in the dark room. Caitlin sat worrying her lower lip, as she cleaned him. "What are you doing?"

She brushed his hair from his eyes. "Taking care of my mate."

"Come here. How could I be so lucky as to have you in my life?" He drew her next to him.

~ ~ ~

Caitlin snuggled against him. Her throat tightened. If she spoke, she'd lose control completely. *Because you loved me enough to accept me for who I am.*

"No, it's you who accepted me as I am." He pressed a kiss to her temple. "I don't ever want you to change," Raven slurred, before giving in to the dark healing sleep.

Caitlin watched Raven slumber. She had to tell Grandpapa. Perhaps he would know why Raven's changes were so drastic.

She wiped her tears. She'd cried from the heartache and pain she'd experienced in Raven's mind over his failed marriage, and every emotion he had during all the important aspects of his life. *She* was the one blessed to have a man such as Raven for a mate.

~ ~ ~

The alarm buzzed and Raven slammed his hand on the clock, shutting off the annoying sound.

Caitlin slept with her head on his shoulder and her leg wedged between his. He carefully slid her head onto the pillow without waking her then eased her leg off his.

He stood and stared at Caitlin, not believing his luck. After so much wasted time, she was his. Period. End of discussion. She would be moving in today. She was his, and he'd be damned if they would wait six months. They'd be husband and wife by summer. Simple. Now he had to persuade Cat.

After he showered, he stood in front of the mirror and examined his neck. There were no visible marks on his throat.

He didn't feel any different. He brushed his teeth, noting they didn't look any different either. The only change so far, he didn't like a light. He opened the bedroom door careful not to wake Cat. She didn't have to go to work, and he'd call her house and inform Mishenka of her whereabouts. He didn't need the old man suddenly appearing.

Hmm. Mishenka's presence complicated Caitlin's moving in. The old man seemed too old-fashioned to permit his granddaughter to live in sin. Raven shook his head. He and Cat were mated and belonged together. Period.

After dressing, Raven quietly strolled into the kitchen and placed a cup in the microwave. He had time to make himself breakfast. Unfortunately, he didn't have much to cook. He slid a bagel into the toaster then removed his cup from the microwave.

During their lovemaking, he'd been in Caitlin's mind. He saw what she'd seen in Stacey's mind. Cat was right. That ring was familiar. Raven had seen the ring before, now if he could only remember, who'd he'd seen wearing it?

Maybe? He retrieved the files from the living room that Edgar had sent.

He flipped through them. Nothing.

Raven unfolded a paper towel and drew the ring the best he could. Mike was the artist, not him. They'd visit David

Hawkins today. Maybe Hawkins had information that could lead to the owner of the ring. While there, he'd look for a ring for Cat.

~ ~ ~

Caitlin placed her hand on Raven's shoulder and kissed him. He smelled of spice and his unique scent. She trailed her fingers across his smooth-shaven face. "What are you doing?"

He glanced up at her, drew her down onto his lap, and kissed her again.

"Kissing an angel," he told her.

More like a Banshee, the way I look. She combed her fingers through her tangled hair.

"I think you look pretty sexy with wild hair." He growled and winked at her.

She grinned. *Raven, you heard my thoughts.* She waited for his reaction.

"I did. I heard them last night, too. And I didn't even have to try. I heard them as loud as if you spoke them." He leaned back and met her gaze, his black eyes shining like polished onyx. "I won't be able to hear anyone else's thoughts, will I?"

"Yes and no. You will be able to hear my parents' brothers,' sister's, and cousin's thoughts because we have shared blood. But their thoughts won't be as easily heard as mine. In time you will learn to ignore them." She shrugged and picked up the paper towel. "What's this?"

"You were right. I should have listened to you yesterday. This ring will lead us to the killer."

"You saw it in my mind?"

"That and a million other things, love. I was you in Nam, and on some stage with a girdle crawling up my ass." He nuzzled her neck, breathing in her sweet scent. He nipped at her throat, then kissed it. She turned her face toward him and captured his mouth. "Now, that's what I call a good morning kiss," he said, before capturing her lips again.

She snaked her arms around his neck. Her eyes shimmered. "I know a better way to say good morning."

"I do too." He laughed and handed her the phone. "But don't want your grandfather popping in on us. Better call him and let him know you're safe. We can tell him the rest tonight."

"He knows."

Chapter Twenty-Two

"How much does your grandfather know?" Raven groaned.

Caitlin sifted on Raven's lap so she could see his frown better. He hadn't touched his bagel or his tea.

His thoughts flooded her mind. He worried about how her family would take the news of their mating. "Grandpapa knows we have mated. He doesn't know how great a lover you are, nor does he know about your stamina."

Raven's ears turned a bright red. "Cat! I would hope you didn't tell him that."

She laughed. "Nor does Grandpapa know about the little birthmark on your tush."

Raven lowered his head, resting his forehead on her shoulder. "Did he call while I was in the shower?"

"Well, not with the phone anyway. Grandpapa sent me a mental message." She placed the paper towel with the drawing of the ring back on the table.

"Mishenka told me he knew when you were in trouble, but I didn't think he could honestly send you psychic messages."

"It's one of his powers. He does it all the time."

"Oh, Jeez. You're telling me your grandfather was in your mind. When we were. . ." Raven stared at her, eyes wide and mouth opened.

"Of course not. Grandpapa wouldn't do something that crude. At least, I don't think Grandpapa would," Caitlin teased.

Raven rolled his eyes. "Can you do that, enter your family members' minds?"

"To a limit. I mean I can't talk to my parents in Scotland. If I could do that, I wouldn't have the phone bills I do."

"Is Mishenka ticked about us?" He slid his arms around her waist. "About us not getting married first?"

"Concerned, I would say." She picked up his uneaten bagel. "Is that all you are having for breakfast?"

Raven glanced at the bagel. "As it's the only thing in the house, yes." He twisted his lips. "Not what you would call a romantic morning after. Cat, get dressed, and I'll take you out for breakfast. I'll ring Mike and let him know I'll be a little late." He slid his arms from around her waist and lifted her off his lap. Then he swatted her on her derrière. "Go on." He grinned.

Caitlin hurried back to the bedroom, retrieved her clothes from the floor, wishing she'd brought something else to wear. But, last night when she came over, she hadn't intended to spend the night. *Liar!* In the back of her mind she knew damn good and well she'd they'd end up in bed again.

She glanced at the bed and decided to pull the sheets and comforter up. At least doing that made the room look a little better.

Raven was so proud of that bed. He'd made it from a wrought iron gate he'd purchased at an antique market in Lancaster. She smiled at the memory. They'd taken her Mustang that day. Once Raven purchased the gate, he realized he'd had to leave his find until he could borrow a truck. Thank goodness, the dealer had been willing to deliver the gate. Raven had worked for months on cleaning and polishing it. She ran her hand over the smooth finish.

Most of his furniture he'd purchased at antique markets in the area. He had good taste.

"Glad you like my taste," he said from the doorway.

She whirled around.

He stood with his arms crossed, leaning against the doorframe. His dark eyes roamed over Caitlin, and a lustful smile curved his lips. "Lady, you don't know how tempting you look."

Heat rose in her cheeks. "I thought I would straighten up the bed a bit. Give me five minutes, and I'll be ready. Did you already call Mike?"

"Yeah, and I also rang Mishenka. He'll meet us at the café."

She quickly showered then dressed. When she opened the bathroom door, Raven was sitting on the bed staring at a file. He placed his hand over a photo and stared at the image before removing his hand. He repeated the action.

"Cat, look at this."

"Sure." She stared at a black and white mug shot of a teenage boy, about fourteen she would guess. "What about it?"

"Does he look familiar to you?"

"No."

Raven covered the photo again with his hand, leaving only the eyes exposed. "What about now?"

Cold, unfeeling eyes seemed to glare back at her. "I don't know anyone with eyes like his."

Raven closed the file. "I know those eyes. I don't recognize the name, but I'm sure I know this kid. Only he isn't a kid now. He's in his thirties." Raven opened the file again. "Lenard Richardson," Raven repeated the name. He shook his head. "C'mon. This can wait until I get to work." He stood and held out his hand to her.

Caitlin took it. "If this kid was convicted, can't you check if he changed his name?" She followed him from the room.

"I could if he'd been convicted. They sent him to a mental hospital. He was released at the age of sixteen to child services and placed in a group home. Once he turned eighteen, his file was sealed."

She stopped and picked up her purse from the couch then took Raven's hand. "I take it this is one of the files Edgar got for you?"

He closed the door behind them and slid his arm around her waist. "Guess we'll take two cars?" He stopped. "How is your grandfather to meet us if he doesn't have a car?"

A sense of mischief filled her. "Guess he'll fly." She glanced at Raven out of the corner of her eye.

He pinched her rear. "Not, funny."

She giggled. "Grandpapa more than likely will walk. He likes walking, and the café isn't that far from my house."

"So, Mishenka can fly?" Raven stepped out into the sunlight and threw his arm in front of his face.

"Your eyes?" Caitlin asked.

"Yeah, but not as bad as last night." He blinked and reached into his coat pocket, pulling out his sunglasses. "Much better. Now, about your Grandfather?"

Raven opened her car door for her. He bent down and kissed her then shut her door.

"He can fly. So can my uncle, and Vaughn. I'm not sure about my cousin Royce. I know he can fade, but there is something else special about him. I'm not sure." She shrugged. "My grandmother is from the DuMond Clan. When she gets mad, she looks more like a gargoyle."

Raven pursed his lips and nodded. "DuMond. Demon. Got it. See you in five." He strode to his car.

Hmm, she'd never related the two like that before. But then again, she wasn't the detective like Raven. Cat rolled up her window then followed Raven as he drove through town. She'd driven these same roads before, but this morning they seemed different. New, almost. Matter of fact, everything seemed different.

The drive to the café took only five minutes. The sun was shining. Raven and she were mated. And everything was right in the world.

Except, it wasn't.

Stacey fought for her life in the hospital. A killer prowled the streets. Raven had received her sensitive eyesight, which may or may not be a good thing. What else had he received from her that they didn't know of, yet?

She parked her car next to Raven's, and he opened her door, then helped her out, brushing a kiss to her cheek.

A frown quickly replaced his smile, and he drew her into his embrace. "Don't do this to yourself. Stop it. I'd rather be sensitive to light than not have you in my life. Stacey will make it. Mike and I will catch this madman. And I also have your sensitive hearing." He slid his arm to her waist. "C'mon,

I see your Grandfather is waiting inside for us." Raven opened the restaurant door for her.

Mishenka sat at a table near the front. He stood and smiled. "It's time that you two arrived. I was beginning to think I was in the wrong place."

She brushed a kiss to his weathered cheek. "We would have been here sooner, but I wanted to straighten up things. Have you ordered yet?"

"Of course not. It wouldn't be proper." Mishenka extended his hand to Raven. "Welcome to the family, my son."

When Raven accepted Mishenka's hand, he pulled Raven to him and embraced him, slapping him on the back. "Shall we eat? I'm famished."

Caitlin took a menu and handed it to Raven.

Mishenka leaned across the table. "We can arrange for your departure to be . . . shall we say pleasant, for your parents," he spoke in a low whisper.

Caitlin lowered the menu. She placed a hand on Raven's knee, stilling him. His anger washed over her. "Raven's parents are up in age. Don't you think it would be best to let nature take its course?" She met Mishenka's icy glare. Oh, how he hated to be challenged. Too bad.

"Very well. We'll discuss this later." Mishenka held up his empty cup to a passing waitress. "More coffee, please."

By her grandfather's actions, she knew he didn't approve but was willing to wait before approaching this subject again, or until he could take matters into his own hands. That thought chilled her. She knew how manipulating he could be.

The waitress returned with a coffee pot. She took their orders then quickly departed.

"You will consider joining the family business, correct?" Mishenka stirred his coffee. A cocky expression played across his face like he'd won some prize.

"Just what is your family business? I thought you were a historian." Raven sipped his coffee, staring over the rim of his mug at her grandfather. She'd seen that same look on Raven's face before. Great. They were heading into a pissing contest.

Mishenka's grin spread across his face. "Much like what you do now. Only the pay is far better." He nodded. "And according to my grandsons, bigger toys."

"I see. Who do I see about a position?"

Caitlin rolled her eyes, understanding her grandfather's plan. He was recruiting Raven. She should have told Raven what her brothers and father did for a living. The subject had never come up. But then again, how could she have explained to Raven that her family members were, for no better name, mercenaries—hunters without explaining other things to him as well. The last case her brother and cousins worked on involved the kidnapping of a senator's daughter. The young woman had been returned safely, and her kidnappers were *dealt with*. No question asked, no witnesses, no media. The young woman's memories had been effectively modified, so she didn't have to suffer from what had happened to her.

Caitlin swallowed the knot forming in her throat. Raven would never agree to those tactics. She risked a glance at him.

"You're right, Cat. I wouldn't. But from what I saw last night, I had an idea of the *family business*." He stared stone-faced at Mishenka. "Just wanted confirmation."

Mishenka folded his fingers together and sat back. "Once you meet the rest of the family and see how we handle certain issues, I'm sure you will make an excellent member."

"Perhaps. Once I retire from the force."

"That may not be an option. Events happen in one's lifetime to change their plans for the future. Some of these things have already taken place." Mishenka's jaw twitched.

"Grandpapa, after we finish eating, why don't we go to the bookstore? I'm sure you'll be able to find something to read. You complained yesterday about not having a good book," Caitlin intervened, hoping to head off an argument between Raven and her grandfather.

"If you wish."

Raven cleared his throat and squeezed her hand. He looked directly at Mishenka. "You're right. Something wonderful has happened to change my life. Cat and I are mated. But, we will be getting married. We haven't talked much about the wedding. Whatever she wants is all right by me."

"A traditional wedding. Yes?" Mishenka nodded and fixed her with a pointed look. "I assume, Kitten, you will want to wait until Stacey is out of the hospital."

"Yeah. Have you spoken to the hospital today?"

"A hospital, but not the one she's at currently. I placed a call to your cousin, Quaid Wolfe. He will handle her transfer to West Grove. Hopefully, we can have her moved as early as the day after tomorrow."

"West Grove?" Raven glanced at Caitlin with a perplexed expression. "That's a private hospital, in Texas." He had to have pulled that information from her memories. "You didn't know he was having her moved either?" It was a statement, not a question. In the short time, Raven had mastered extracting information from her mind. He probably didn't realize he's doing it.

"Grandpapa, do you think it's safe to move Stacey?" She glanced at Raven then her grandfather. "I mean, is she stable enough?"

"Quaid has spoken to Doctor Morgan, who has informed me it would be perfectly safe to move her. Especially with all the precautions, Quaid has set in place. Stacey's safety and wellbeing are of utmost importance."

"Stacey is in protective custody." Raven crossed his arms over his chest. "What if this creep tries to get at her while she's being moved?"

The wicked laugh that came from Mishenka chilled Caitlin's blood. "We can only hope he does," he said. His eyes flashed an evil red.

"I don't like it. Stacey should remain where she's at," Raven gritted out between his teeth.

"As I am quite aware," Mishenka stated. "However, West Grove is a far better facility and has doctors who specialize in her *unique* condition." He leaned closer to Raven. "Some staff members where she's at, are already saying her fast healing is a miracle. How long before others will also take note?"

"I understand," Raven conceded. "But, I don't like it."

Caitlin glanced from Raven to Mishenka. The two of them glared at each other across the table, neither willing to yield. God, she now knew how her mother had felt all these years.

She was thankful when the waitress brought their food.

They didn't discuss anything else until the waitress brought the check. Then Raven and Mishenka argued like children over who would pay the bill. Raven reached for the check, but Mishenka snatched it up first.

Caitlin snatched the bill from Mishenka's fingers. "I'll pay the blessed thing. You two are acting like children." She pushed her chair back. "I can't believe the two of you."

"What's wrong with her?" Mishenka asked.

"She's been edgy since Stacey's attack," Raven responded.

Edgy? No. What was wrong with her was their frigging pissing contest. She'd seen it coming but had hoped she was wrong. She had half a mind to turn around and tell them both off. Men! Why did her grandfather have to have things his way? Why couldn't Raven not argue with Grandpapa? Caitlin bit her lips. For the same reason, her father argued with Grandpapa.

Raven slid his arm around her waist. "You should have allowed me to pay for that."

"Don't worry about it." She held out her hand and received her change.

"Your grandfather has a way of getting to me. I'm sorry if I made you mad."

You didn't. Are you coming over tonight? You can stay the night. She sent him her thoughts.

Call me old-fashioned, but I have a problem sleeping with you with your grandfather in the house.

Caitlin stared at him, amazed how rapidly he'd adjusted to his change. The possibilities of what Raven would do with his new abilities both excited her and made her wary. Over her lifetime, she'd witnessed some, few, but some human mates who abuse their new powers. She knew Raven and could trust him. Everything by the book.

Mishenka stood behind them. "I would have paid for breakfast."

"You can buy lunch," she told him.

Raven walked her to her car, opened her door then kissed her passionately. "See you later."

"Quite hot-blooded isn't he." Mishenka smiled as he shut his door.

"Grandpapa." She pulled out of the parking lot.

"Your mother is very pleased you have mated. However, you will have to make Raven understand the workings of our family. We do things to protect ourselves. I would hate to say what would happen if he chose not to follow our rules."

She slammed on the brakes. "What are you hinting at?"

Chapter Twenty-Three

The car behind them blew the horn, and the driver flipped her off as he yelled obscenities out the window. She pressed her foot to the accelerator.

"My lord, child!" Mishenka roared. "Are you trying to kill us?"

Gripping the steering wheel so tightly she thought she'd snap it in half, Caitlin glared straight ahead. "Answer me," she hissed.

"Very well." Mishenka's tone dropped to a whisper. "Raven is your mate, your responsibility. What will you do when his family starts asking questions you cannot answer?" He placed his large hand on her shoulder. "I love you, Kitten. I'm only trying to protect you. I don't want to see you hurt."

Damn, why did Grandpapa always know what to say to take the storm out of her sails? "I love you, too. But you have to permit Raven time to adjust. He has to leave his family when the time is right for him. We can't make that decision for him."

"I will do all that I can to help him and you when the time is right." He grinned at her. "You cannot blame an old man for wanting to protect his granddaughter. Can you?"

"You're right I can't, but you can't blame me for protecting my mate either. And I will protect him." She parked in front of Books and Java. "Let's go find you something good to read. Lambert keeps a great selection of books."

"I'll be the judge of that," he grumbled.

Great, so she'd ticked him off. She didn't care. Raven was her mate, and she'd protect him with her life. Even against her family if need be. Caitlin yanked opened the heavy oak and stained glass door.

"Ms. MacPhee, how are you doing?" Lambert smiled as she entered.

"I'm holding up."

He came around the counter. Caitlin noticed the bandage on Lambert's right hand. "How is Stacey doing?" Concern echoed in his voice.

"She's still unconscious. Still fighting."

"We are praying that she lives," Mishenka added.

"Lambert," Caitlin said. "I'd like you to meet my Grandfather Mishenka Lucard."

"A pleasure, sir." He held out his hand.

Mishenka hesitantly shook hands. "Yes, well, we don't have time to dilly around. Where may I find your suspense section?"

"Back left corner."

Mishenka gave a curt nod and headed in the direction of his quest.

"I'm sorry, Lambert. Grandpapa isn't normally this terse. I think the stress is getting to him." She motioned to his hand. "How are you doing?"

He glanced down. "I'm learning how difficult it is to be one-handed. And it itches. I guess that's a good sign it's healing. Caitlin, may I call you Caitlin?"

She eyed him. "Sure."

He reached over and took her hand. "If there is anything I can do, please do not hesitate to ask."

"That's very sweet of you."

He blushed and let go of her hand. "I realize this isn't the proper time to ask, but if I don't, I may not have the courage."

As casually as possible, she asked. "What?"

"Would you have dinner with me sometime?" His face suddenly reddened and Lambert lowered his gaze. The man was so shy.

She stared, tongue-tied for a few seconds. "Ah, Lambert, I don't know what to say. I'm very flattered."

"But, I'm not your type."

"No, that's not it. I'm engaged to Detective O'Brien."

"Oh, I didn't know." His smile seemed forced. "Then congratulations. Excuse me." He backed away then turned and stepped behind the counter.

"She hadn't meant to hurt his feelings. Heck, he'd never given her the impression he was interested in her. But, then she'd probably never saw it as she only had eyes for Raven." Drawing in a deep breath, Caitlin went in search of Mishenka. She found him in the history section. "I thought you wanted suspense. Have you found anything you would like to read?"

"Changed my mind and I've read everything here. Shall we go?" He replaced the book he'd been thumbing through back on the shelf.

She didn't see Lambert as they left the store. She'd hurt him. She hadn't meant to, and it bothered her, but heck she hadn't thought the man even knew her first name. She shouldn't worry about Lambert. This town was full of young women dying to meet a wonderful guy, and she'd bet Lambert would find his Miss Right.

"You were rude to Lambert. It's one thing to be mad at me, but you didn't have to take it out on him. He's a kind soul." Caitlin shut her car door and started the engine.

"Kind soul. Huh. He struck me as a self-indulgent man." Mishenka turned on her radio then searched the stations for some classical music.

She had too much on her mind to worry about a temperamental old man who wasn't getting his way. Caitlin shifted gears. She turned left onto her street. *Crap on a stick!*

Parked in front of her home sat not one, not two, but three news-vans. One belonged to Townsley, one to the *Herald*, and the Local News 6 van sat across her driveway, blocking her. "This is ridiculous." Caitlin turned her wheel sharply, driving over the curve then across her lawn. She laughed as one reporter jumped out of her way as she parked in her driveway. "Grandpapa, don't say a word to them." She flung open her car door and got out. She wasn't in the mood to spar with the press.

Barbara Townsley and two other reporters ran toward them. "Has Stacey Parker's condition changed?" Someone asked.

Barbara shoved a microphone in Caitlin's face. "How does it feel to be canned?" She sneered then loudly asked, "Do you think that Jeffery Morgan is the person responsible for your roommate's attack?"

"No comment." Raven had told her they were holding Jeff, if for no other reason than to see if the killer would show his hand.

"What sort of black magic did Miss Parker practice?" A male reporter asked.

Caitlin pushed past the reporters. She tripped, stumbled, and caught herself. She turned and glared at Townsley, before turning back and walking up the front porch steps, knowing full well Townsley had tripped her.

"Do you practice witchcraft? Are you a witch? Do you worship Satan? Do you worship the goddess? Are you Wiccan also?" Questions were shouted at her from all directions and microphones were shoved at her. She just wanted to reach the safety of her home, and close out the ugliness of the world.

"Please leave me alone," Caitlin demanded.

"Can you explain to us the Wiccan religion?" Another question. They didn't care about her grief. They didn't care about Stacey or the other victims. All they cared about was selling the story.

"What religion do you practice?" Another person asked.

Closing her eyes, Caitlin gripped the doorknob. Her parents raised her as a Christian. When her mother took her father as her mate, she'd also embraced his religion. Caitlin knew of *Yeva*, the Creator. So close were the two religions, the one from an ancient world her people came from and the Christian religion of Earth, she often wondered if the worshipers of *Yeva* hadn't influence Christian practices.

What am I? Caitlin thought. She's been asking herself that question a lot lately. She'd been baptized at birth, took her first Holy Communion at age seven, but at times her faith had failed her. Like now. How could a merciful God allow Stacey to suffer as she had? She'd been abandoned by her mother, always searching for a family, and then tortured by a madman. Why? Why had such a gentle soul been treated so bad?

"Miss MacPhee, did Miss Parker practice witchcraft?"

Anger raged inside of Caitlin. Her fangs budded. They only want to find something ugly about Stacey to justify what happened to her and the others. They wanted to justify Stacey's attack and make it *her* fault.

"Witchcraft? Wicca?" Mishenka tsked and placed his hand on Caitlin's shoulder, stilling her. "Young man, you know nothing about the Wiccan. They are not a bunch of broom-riding, wart-nosed hags. What religion do you practice? Do you attend a church, temple, or mosque? If so, how often?" He fixed Barbara Townsley with a hard glare. "And you Madame. What are you? Are you a daughter of Eve or Lilith? Before you start assuming the worst about any faith, I suggest you do some research. Let us not forget Hitler massacred thousands of Jews because of their religion. Across the world, as we speak, innocent people are murdered because of religion. It's ironic that in nearly every religion love, peace, and tolerance are taught. Yet, we butcher people who believe differently." Mishenka tsked and shook his head.

Silence fell over the group of reporters.

"What is happening in this town is not about religion. It is about a man who is victimizing innocent women in your community. An animal who is murdering women, torturing them. And you, all you want to do is humiliate these women even more." Mishenka turned the knob and opened the door. "You make me sick."

Caitlin drew in a long steady breath. When would this nightmare end? She stepped into the sanctuary of her home.

Mishenka shut the door behind him. "Forgive me, but I had to say something. They do not care about Stacey or the victims. They are jackals, feeding on the misery of others to sell a story." He closed the curtains.

"Why did you ask Barbara Townsley if she was a daughter of Lilith?"

"To see her reaction. As angry as that woman is, I wondered if perhaps *she* wasn't the murderer." He shook his head. "No such luck. So perhaps my question will urge her to spend a few hours on the Internet looking up Lilith to understand what I asked. But, I doubt it. She doesn't strike me as a very intelligent person."

A faint smile pulled at his lips. "Had I asked that question of Stacey, I would have had a very stimulating discussion on my hands. As it was, I received only a blank stare." He placed a kiss on Caitlin's forehead. "Go and change. Then we will see how our little Stacey is doing. Yes?"

Caitlin gave a curt nod and made her way down the hall. She paused outside Stacey's bedroom before turning and walking into her room. Grandpapa hadn't opened the shades.

Standing in the darkened room, Caitlin mechanically, she shed her clothes and cried. How could she have been so selfish? She wiped her eyes. Last night she and Raven made love, mated and she'd forgotten about everything, about Stacey. How could she be so self-centered? She headed into her bathroom. She didn't have time to dawdle. They had to get to the hospital.

The hot water washed over Caitlin's back, relieving her tensed muscles. Twelve hours ago, things had seemed brighter. Raven had slept in her arms, and the ugliness of the world vanished. Her hand spanned her flat stomach. Had she done the right thing last night by mating with Raven? She loved him, would die to protect him, but Grandpapa was right. Would Raven's refusal to give up his family put her's in jeopardy? Would she be forced to give up her true love and live miserably for the rest of her life? Oh God, she would die without him.

~ ~ ~

Raven stared at the photo. He couldn't get the face out of his mind. He knew those eyes! But the name? He'd sent a copy of the fingerprints to the lab.

"You're awful quiet this morning. You thinking about Caitlin?" Mike set a cup of coffee on the desk. "Rogers made it today."

"In other words, we can use it to clean the drains." Raven pointed to the mug shot. "Look at this photo and tell me if this kid looks like anyone you've seen lately? He'll be thirty-five now."

Mike eyed the folder. "Is this one of the files your brother sent you?"

Raven nodded and leaned back in his chair. "Look at the eyes."

Mike flipped through the pages. "He murdered a psychic healer but was acquitted?"

"Yeah. Madame Zigana treated this kid's mother for cancer. When the woman died, the boy went berserk and killed Zigana. He strangled her then cut her hair. When the woman's employees discovered them, the boy was running her hair across his fingers."

Mike shivered. "Where does," he glanced at the name, "this Lenard Richardson live now?"

"That's the clincher. I ran the name through DMV. Nothing."

"You're telling me that there isn't a Lenard Richardson anywhere in this state. What about the rest of the U.S."

"They've found plenty." Raven pushed from his chair and snatched up his car keys "Come on."

Mike followed, reading the report. "We going to interview one of the Lenard Richardson you found?"

"Nope. There isn't a male that fits this guy's age with the same name. I think he's changed his name. I should have something back on the fingerprints. I wish the boys in the lab could have lifted a clear print off of Stacey's necklace. We're going to see Hawkins again."

Mike buckled his seat belt. "One more time, why?"

Mike's going to start wondering if I've gone insane. Raven drove the block to the jewelry store. "To see if Mr.

Hawkins knows anything about a ring." Raven opened his car door.

"And how do you know about this ring?" Mike followed.

"It's a hunch." Yeah, he knew what Mike thought, that they were wasting time.

The bell over the door chimed as they walked in. Raven spotted David Hawkins standing in the back of the store. The smile on his face faded as recognition entered his eyes.

"Gentlemen," David Hawkins greeted them.

Raven removed a piece of paper from his coat pocket. "I'd like to ask if you've seen this ring before." He handed the drawing to Hawkins. "I realize it's a crude sketch. The ring is silver or silver colored metal. The stone is sardonyx. Can you tell me anything about the stone?"

"Sardonyx? The Egyptians engraved scarabs on it and wore them as talismans. It's a semiprecious stone known as the gem of courage. Roman soldiers would wear sardonyx to enhance their bravery in battle. Later, Christians wore crosses carved from the stone." He met Raven's gaze. "They believed it protected them from the *evil eye*."

"You know a lot about its mystical legends," Raven commented.

"It was my wife's hobby. She was into all that kind of thing. You know, birthstones, healing stones, that sort of stuff." He sighed. "It appeals to the college kids. They always seem to want to know what special meaning or power stones have. You'd be surprised how many students come in here thinking they can purchase a good ruby to help them with their finals. They think the stone will give them knowledge. Go figure."

He shrugged. "We don't sell much sardonyx." Hawkins slowly lowered his gaze to the paper. "I've seen this ring or one like it." He handed the paper back to Raven. "Wait here." He turned and left.

"Some hunch. How did you know what the ring looked like?" Mike asked.

Raven lowered his gaze. He had to tell Mike something. The man wasn't an idiot. Raven drew in a deep breath. Damn, he hated to lie. "The day Cat stayed with Stacey in the hospital, Stacey mumbled something about sardonyx." He looked at Mike. "I know what you think about my gut feelings."

Mike grinned. "Well, your gut has paid off today."

"We'll see." Raven glanced into the showcase. His attention fell to a ruby and diamond engagement ring. Two heart shaped rubies flanked the round cut diamond stone. Their dark color of the rubies mesmerized him. Two heart shaped drops of blood. He smiled. *Crimson hearts.*

"Here we go." David Hawkins placed an open book over the showcase, covering the diamond and ruby ring. He pointed to a color photo of the ring in question. "According to this," he said. "Inquisitors wore a ring very similar to that one, to protect them from the evil thoughts and impulses of the witches they were questioning." He chuckled. "Makes you wonder who were the ones really practicing witchcraft, the Inquisitors or the poor souls they were torturing."

A cold chill ran through Raven. "Do you know of anyone who has a ring like this?"

Hawkins shook his head. "Mostly kids who are into the gothic look. You can pick one up at the medieval festival this summer."

"This one's not a copy." Raven didn't know how, but he knew the particular ring had been around since the Inquisition, placed carefully, and safely kept in a carved rosewood box.

"I wish I could be of more help." David Hawkins closed the book. "Here, if you want to take this with you, you can."

"Thanks." Raven lifted the book. His gaze fell once again to the engagement ring. "One more thing."

"Sure."

"Can you hold that ruby and diamond ring for me? I'll be back this evening."

David Hawkins smiled. "Sure thing. I'll put it aside along with the matching wedding bands. Would you like to see them?"

"Please."

Mike slapped Raven on the back. "Have you asked Caitlin?"

Raven grinned at Mike and nodded. "Last night. Hopefully, we'll be married within six months. Sooner, if we can solve this case before then."

David Hawkins opened the showcase then removed two gold bands. The smaller ring was a continuous circle of rubies and diamonds. The larger band, his, Raven thought, had a small diamond flanked by two smaller rubies. A little flashier than he'd pick out for himself, but if Caitlin liked it or wanted their wedding bands to match then he guessed he could wear it. "Hold those as well. What time do you close?"

"I'll be here until nine. If you can't come back tonight, don't worry, I'll hold the rings for you a week."

"Thanks," Raven said.

Hawkins' smile faded. "I understand you've arrested someone."

Mike met Hawkins' gaze and nodded. "He's being questioned."

"Do you have any leads? I mean other than that ring?" David Hawkins pointed to the book tucked under Raven's arm.

"Not many." Raven extended his hand to Hawkins. "Thanks for your help."

Mike followed Raven outside. "Why didn't you tell me sooner about you and Caitlin, Birdie?"

"I don't know. Guess I didn't think about it until I saw that ring." Raven opened the car door and slid in behind the wheel. "I hope Cat likes it."

"She will."

Mike picked up the file and opened it. "Damn. Reading this gives me the creeps. If this kid didn't get psychological help, he probably turned out to be a sociopath."

Raven glanced at Mike. "Sociopaths are self-serving people. With them, someone else is always to blame. Their mothers were too demanding. Their fathers were drunks, et cetera, et cetera." He made a right turn and headed back to the station. "I'm calling the Forensic Artist who does age progression in Harrisburg. I wonder if he can scan that photo and possibly age it for us."

"Do you honestly think this kid is behind the murders?"

Raven glanced into his rearview mirror. He wouldn't tell Mike he'd had another feeling. If he could see a photo of that kid as an adult, Raven knew he would recognize him. Maybe the fingerprints would match. So far, this was their only solid lead, and it wasn't much.

"Your gut again?" Mike muttered.

"I believe the guy's name is Kurt Lehr." Raven ignored Mike's jab. "If I remember correctly, he needs a picture of both parents. All we have is this kid's mother." Raven pulled into the station parking lot, parked the car, and opened his door.

"The aging process may not be accurate, but it's worth a try." Mike grabbed the file and followed Raven into the station.

~ ~ ~

Caitlin twisted the gold chain around her finger and stared at Stacey, sleeping peacefully. The burns on her legs seemed to be healing. The nurse even commented on the speed of Stacey's recovery. *If only she'd wake up. If only she would tell us who did this to her.*

The gold chain untwisted and hundreds of multicolored spheres danced on the wall as the crystal spun around, reflecting the day's last rays of sunlight. Grandpapa was right. They would have to move Stacey before the doctors here became too suspicious of her quick recovery.

The door opened, and Mishenka entered carrying two canned drinks and two newspapers. She recognized them as *The Herald* and *The Informer*. "Why on earth did you buy Townsley's gossip sheet?"

"To see what the witch printed about you and Stacey." He tossed the papers onto the chair. "You should go for a walk. You've been sitting there for over eight hours." He handed Caitlin a drink can. "And you haven't had anything to eat since breakfast."

"Thanks. I'm fine."

He snorted as he took his seat, and noisily opened the paper.

"I've been thinking. You're right." Caitlin shifted on the chair. Her rear was numb.

His face lit up. "It's not often my grandchildren tell me I'm right. What am I right about?"

He was trying to make her relax. Trying to get her mood to lighten. "Moving Stacey."

"I see. I ran into Doctor Morrison by the drink machine. They've cut back on her sedatives. Raven should be able to question her soon. Doctor Morrison believes that she may be awake enough to answer some questions as early as tomorrow. We can only hope."

"She's been moaning more, and I thought I heard her call Inky's name." Caitlin twisted the chain around her finger. It had been a Christmas gift from Stacey. For some reason, she'd needed to wear it today.

"That bloody bastard," Mishenka hissed. He lowered the paper. His eyes blazed red, and his nails had lengthened.

In all her life, Caitlin couldn't remember ever seeing her grandfather lose his control or temper over something as simple as an article. "What is it?" She took the paper from him.

Rag Dress Victim expected to live. A neighbor confirms women practiced witchcraft.

Her stomach knotted, and she handed the newspaper back. Why had D.P. printed that lie? "Grandpapa?"

Mishenka turned to her. His eyes softened and his lips twisted. "Between that woman Townsley and now this," he slapped the paper, "you'd best be on your guard."

She expected a story like this from Barbara, but not Mr. Hamilton. She wasn't worried. Angry and betrayed, but not worried someone would burn her at a stake. "Raven will have kittens when he sees the paper."

"I'd like to see that, but not as much as Hamilton screaming beneath my grip." A sinister glow burned in Mishenka's eyes, and he stroked his chin.

"Grandpapa, do not go after Hamilton. He isn't worth the trouble."

"No?" He looked her in the eyes. "We once numbered in the millions. Because of slanderous tongues, thousands of our people were slaughtered.

Even now, I'm not so certain we do not have enemies hiding among our friends and Council members," Mishenka's voice dropped to an ominous tone. "If anything happens to you because of this story. He will pay."

Chapter Twenty-four

"At least Barbara spelled my name correctly this time." Caitlin tried to make light of Townsley's article. She didn't need her grandfather getting into a blood-rage. "I like this story better than the one Hamilton published." She glanced at Mishenka. He'd taken the chair by the hospital window. His lips were still pulled into a thin line.

"Mr. Hamilton has put you at risk." He pointed his finger at her.

"Perhaps, but if the story Townsley wrote about me being a vampire didn't make me a target, why would this? Why was Stacey his target?"

Caitlin drew in a deep breath and stared at Stacey. Her burns had healed so well Doctor Morrison had reduced Stacey's pain medication. She wasn't moaning as much either when the nurses changed her bandages. It's only a matter of time before she could tell who did this to her.

Caitlin ran her tongue over her budding fangs. She'd make whoever responsible know hell. Her stomach churned with anticipation. She quelled the rage inside her before she succumbed to it.

Mishenka lowered his paper. "One must always guard against the rage. If you give into it, you must live with the consequences. I've known many who have gone mad because they could not wash the blood from their hands." He lifted his paper and continued to read.

"You've given into it and have killed. So have Uncle Alan and the guys. None of you have gone mad." She was just as strong as they were. Stronger.

Once again, Mishenka lowered his paper. His eyes were soft, not hard, as she'd expected. "When you were a girl, you accompanied your father and me hunting. I'll never forget the thrill I experienced when I watched your father steady your arm as you drew back the bow. You brought down a stag with your first shot."

"Papa was proud of me."

"Yes, he was. Still is, the proof is how many times over the years I have heard the retailing of the tale. The only difference is I believe the last time your father told it, the stag was charging and nearly had you on its horns when you dropped it. However," Mishenka folded his fingers together. "I'll also never forget the look in your eyes when you realized the stag no longer lived. Killing a man, even one who deserves to die is much worse than killing an animal."

"You're wrong, Grandpapa. I could take down this animal, and it wouldn't bother me." She'd struggled for so long with what happened in Vietnam. Perhaps if she told him what happened then, he wouldn't worry so much about her. "Grandpapa, I have killed."

"I know Kitten. And it almost killed you. Do not think for one second that I do not know what you and all of my grandchildren are up to every moment of the day. You children are my life. When my body dies, my spirit will live on in you and your children." He smiled at her.

The door opened, and Raven stepped in, carrying a bouquet of yellow and white daisies. Despite the smile on his lips, his anger washed over her. "Hey, love. Mishenka. Doctor Whenn said Stacey might be awake enough in the morning to enjoy these." He bent down and brushed a kiss to Caitlin's lips. "I've got some time before I have to meet Mike. How about I take the two of you to dinner?"

"A wonderful idea," Mishenka said.

"I'm not hungry," Caitlin replied taking the flowers from Raven's hand.

"She hasn't left this room, at all, today." Mishenka fixed her with a glare. "She'll make herself ill."

Raven frowned. "You look like you could use some fresh air."

"Do I look that bad?" Caitlin asked.

"No. Just furious."

Mishenka rumpled his paper. "She won't listen to me. Have you seen this?" He turned the paper for Raven to read.

"I've seen it," Raven said and glanced at her. "And don't tell me not to worry about you."

She swore Raven's eyes flashed red. "You and Grandpapa think I'm in danger. I'm not. I can protect myself." She placed the flowers on the table. "

Raven shook his head and smiled at Mishenka. "I swear Hamilton and Townsley crawled from the same cesspool." He fixed her with a harsh stare. "I don't want you to go anywhere alone. I wish I could string Hamilton up by his balls."

Mishenka's eyes glimmered and his mouth curved into a wicked smile. "Don't tempt me, son."

Son? For a second time, Grandpapa called Raven 'son.' Her heart filled with joy. Grandpapa had finally accepted Raven.

Raven smoothed his hand over his hair. "After Mike showed me that article, I wanted to drag Hamilton out of his office and pound him to a bloody pulp."

"I, for one, wouldn't have objected if you had." Mishenka folded his fingers together. "But there are more effective measures that can be taken against him. More *diabolical* ways, of dealing with a man, of his caliber."

"As an officer, I have to warn you against saying such things." He turned and smiled at her. "As someone who loves your granddaughter very much, keep it legal."

Caitlin shoved to her feet. "Oh stop it, both of you." She glared at them. "I wasn't, nor will I ever be, in danger. Like I've said before, I can take care of myself."

"She takes the fun out of being old," Mishenka teased.

Stacey moaned.

Caitlin quickly took her hand. "I'm here," she whispered. "Grandpapa and Raven are here, too."

Raven wrapped his arm across her shoulder and hugged her. "She's going to make it."

Raven's scent comforted Caitlin, and she leaned against him. "Why did this animal choose Stacey as his victim?"

Raven's rough hand tenderly stroked her cheek. "Only he knows."

Caitlin stared deep into his black eyes. "You know something. Tell me," she demanded. She looked deep into Raven's black eyes and in his mind saw glimpses of photos. He'd gotten a break in the case. "Do you have enough evidence to make an arrest?"

He furrowed his eyebrows. "What arrest?" His eyes grew large, and his lips thinned. "You've been taking a stroll inside my head again. What else did you see?"

They were mated. Seeing into each other's minds was as natural as breathing. She swallowed. Raven wasn't Dhampir. He was human. "Just the photograph. Tell me what you've found out."

Mishenka stood, tucking his paper under his arm. "I don't think this topic is beneficial for Stacey's ears. Though her eyes are shut her ears aren't." He bent over her bed and brushed a kiss to her forehead. "Shh, child. Do not fear. You are safe. Dream of the times you were in Scotland. Remember the fragrance of the heather in bloom. Remember how it made the green fields purple." He smoothed his hand over her hair. "Sleep. We will return shortly." He glanced over his shoulder at them. "Perhaps this would be an excellent time too, as you say, grab a bite to eat."

"I agree," Raven said and slipped his arm around Caitlin's waist.

"Raven, you, and Grandpapa go on without me. I don't want to leave her. If she wakes, someone should be here."

"I know you don't want to leave Stacey. It's just after seven. The cafeteria is still open. We can go there. You have to eat." Raven fixed her with a compassionate look. "Or do you need another kind of nourishment?"

"I'm fine." She tenderly stroked his cheek. Raven would let her take from him until she'd killed him. "And I'm not hungry for food either."

Mishenka placed his hand on her shoulder. "I understand how you feel, but you haven't left this room since we arrived. Please come with us, if for no other reason than to stretch your legs. Stacey will be fine."

"Love, you have to take care of yourself." Raven's velvety smooth voice pleaded with her. "We won't be gone long, and there is an officer outside. She won't be alone."

"Fine." Caitlin followed Raven from Stacey's room.

Mishenka pulled the door closed behind him. He walked on the other side of Raven. "I take it your brother came through with the information you needed to solve this puzzle."

Raven paused before pressing the elevator button. "I've spoken with Edgar."

The elevator door opened and they stepped into it.

"And what did he tell you?"

"He added more pieces to the puzzle."

A sinking sensation crept over Caitlin. She slammed her hand against the stop button. She tried to see into Raven's mind, but he blocked her as easily as if they'd been mated for centuries.

"Not this time," he said.

"Tell me."

Raven casually reached over and restarted the elevator on its downward journey. "Later."

Why wouldn't he tell her what he'd found out? Because he knew she would go after this monster herself. Her fangs budded at the thought of making whoever had harmed Stacey pay with his blood.

"That is exactly the reason," Raven whispered close to her ear. "The last thing I want is for you to get hurt."

The elevator door opened.

Jeff Morgan stepped aside, permitting them to exit.

"Jeff, why are you here?" she asked.

He glared at her and stepped into the elevator. "My grandmother is ill."

"I'm sorry to hear that. I hope she gets well soon." She wished she could have thought of something better to say. Sympathy wasn't one of her stronger points.

Jeff placed his hand on the door, keeping it from shutting. "I've got to know something." He stepped out of the elevator. "What the hell did you tell him?" Jeff motioned to Raven.

"About what?" Stunned, she tilted her head back to meet Jeff's glare. Raven tugged on her arm.

"About me? What lies did you tell him? I didn't do anything to Stacey. Do you know the hell you caused me? Because of you, I have a police record now."

Raven pushed her behind him. "You don't have a record. You were never booked. You were only questioned, and I suggest you go see your grandmother before you end up getting a record."

Caitlin eased around Raven. "I didn't cause anything," she snapped.

"Bull! You women are all alike. A bunch of lying bitches. Do you know what he put me through? They threw me in a cell, where I was questioned. No." He faced Raven. "Interrogated would be a better word."

A wicked laugh came from Raven. "Well, now you know what it's like to be questioned." He pinned Jeff with a dark look. "Put it in one of your books. Now, if you'll excuse us." He turned, grabbed Caitlin by the arm, and led her down the corridor.

"I hate that guy," Raven snarled.

"Why," her grandfather asked. "You have my granddaughter's love. That young man has nothing. You should pity him."

"Whatever," Raven mumbled.

They walked in silence to the hospital cafeteria. Raven held the door for her and Mishenka.

The place was nearly empty except for a few late eaters like themselves. A young couple laughed at one table, at another table, an elderly man sat sipping a cup of coffee and toying with a piece of the pie.

With food tray in hand, she followed Raven as he made his way through the maze of empty tables to a booth against the far window and away from everyone.

It was obvious to her Raven didn't want to take the chance of anyone over-hearing what he would say. Either that or he didn't trust her to keep her temper.

Mishenka slid into one side of the booth. "You do have a temper, Kitten."

"I do not, Grandpapa." She slid in across from her grandfather. At least compared to her sister and father she didn't have a temper.

"You are more like your father than you think."

Caitlin huffed and waited until Raven had placed their plates on the table before asking, "Why did he pick Stacey?"

Raven slid in beside her. "Because she reminded him of someone who'd hurt him in the past. Perhaps his lover, but I think it was someone in authority who harmed him or a loved one. All of the victims reminded him of that person. Women with long hair, light colored eyes, and who in his mind practiced witchcraft of some kind or another."

Raven reached into his coat pocket and withdrew a white envelope. "Someone who may have looked like this." He handed her the envelope.

Anxiety gripped her, knotting her stomach, and killing her appetite. Carefully she pulled a black and white mug shot from the envelope and studied the image of a woman in her mid to late forties. Her long hair draped over one shoulder. She was dressed like a carnival gypsy. "Who is this? Or should I say was this?" She handed the photo to Mishenka.

"At the time of her death she called herself Madame Zigana, but she had as many aliases as she did convictions. Her real name was Sally Harris. She would milk her victims of every penny they owned, all the while promising she'd cure whatever ailed them. All she delivered were false hopes. In her final case, her greed destroyed three lives; hers, her mark, Elizabeth Richardson who was terminally ill, and Richardson's fourteen-year-old son." He handed her another photo. The same one she'd seen that morning on his kitchen table.

Disappointment seeped into Caitlin. "How long ago was this taken?"

"Twenty-one years ago. We don't have much information on a father. Parents could have been divorced, or the father could have died, or never in the picture to begin with."

Mishenka shook his head. "Humans with a terminal illness might seek out any form of treatment, no matter what the consequences. Rich or poor, insured or not. This Madame Zigana fed on the desperate." He handed the picture back to Raven, and he slid it into its envelope.

"Lenard Richardson," Caitlin said as she stared at the photo of the boy. An absent father, a mother facing certain death, a horrible future for a young boy to face. No wonder his eyes looked so cold. The name didn't mean anything to her. *But his eyes.* "You think the murderer is copying this particular case?"

"No. I think that boy is the one responsible. All we have to do is find him. He isn't going by Lenard anymore. Mike and I have contacted a forensic reconstruction artist to see if he can tell us how this boy might look like as an adult. We should know something tonight. Maybe."

She swallowed. "Can't you check his fingerprints and see if anything comes up?"

Raven's jaw twitched. "We're doing that, love. Unless he's committed a crime, purchased a handgun, or applied for any number of jobs that require fingerprinting, the only name that will come up is the one we already have."

"And you're sure he isn't in prison somewhere or something?"

"Positive," Raven said through clenched teeth.

"It only gets worse, lad," Mishenka said with a chuckle. "Did she ever tell you she cut her hair once to pass herself as a lad? She wanted to become a Pinkerton agent."

"She told me." Raven smiled at her.

Lifting a spoon to her lips, Caitlin tasted the thick creamy broth. As good as her beef stew tasted and smelled, she didn't have an appetite. She wanted this nightmare over and the guilty punished. She wanted Stacey to wake-up and not be mentally harmed by what had happened to her. She needed to get on with her life with Raven.

~ ~ ~

Raven forked a piece of meatloaf into his mouth. He didn't want to think about the case anymore tonight. He wanted to enjoy his time with his mate. *Mate*. Caitlin was his mate, and nothing in this world or the next would change that fact. He felt his coat pocket, felt the ring box where he'd placed it. He glanced at Caitlin. She wasn't eating. She stared into her bowl, mindlessly moving her spoon back and forth. Her anguish soured his stomach. "Cat?"

"I'm fine."

He placed his hand on her arm. "I'll find him. I swear."

Chapter Twenty-Five

Raven reached inside his coat pocket. His fingers curved around the velvet box. He'd wanted to wait to give Cat the ring. He wanted the time to be right, to be romantic, and not in a hospital cafeteria. He turned and studied her. Slowly she moved her spoon back and forth before lifting the creamy broth to her lips. Stress and worry had etched fine lines on her beautiful face. In the last few days since Stacey's attack, Caitlin had aged. Her smile no longer reached her eyes. Raven sighed. More important, he wanted to see her smile again. "Cat," he said and covered her hand with his. He withdrew the red velvet box from his pocket.

"Is that for me?" Her eyes widened.

"Maybe," he teased and nodded.

Caitlin slid her hand from under his and took the box. Slowly she opened it. Her eyes brimmed with tears. "Raven, it's beautiful."

His hand shook as he placed the delicate ruby and diamond ring on her finger.

The ring fitted perfectly.

The small diamond sparkled with intense fire in the dim light of the cafeteria. He'd wished he could have afforded a larger stone for Caitlin. She deserved much more than he could offer on a detective's salary. He wanted to give her a large home with a big yard where their children could play, nice clothes, a newer car. He wished he could give her the entire world.

"You have," she whispered. "You've given me your heart." Caitlin looked up at him.

The love shining in her eyes dissolved all his doubts. No matter what life threw at them, they'd survive as long as they were together. He lowered his head, brushing a kiss over her lips. "Six months, no longer." His own eyes stung. Must be the pollen in the air.

Mishenka cleared his throat. Loudly.

"May I?" He held out his hand to Caitlin. "I say," He glanced at Raven, "you have exquisite taste. Then again, my Granddaughter did choose you. That should say something about you." His full smile wrinkled his eyes and revealed his even white teeth. "Very lovely. Now, if you two would permit me, I need to discuss a matter of grave importance."

Raven met Mishenka's gaze, knowing the old man was up to something. He didn't strike Raven as a man needing permission to speak his mind. "We're all ears."

"Yes, well." Mishenka leaned closer, his smile faded. "You two are joined as one. I have given your situation much thought. I'm not a cold, heartless old man." Mishenka's eyes grew dark and impassive. "After our discussion this morning at breakfast, I decided to speak with my son Alan. I told him much about you, Raven. Alan is eager to meet you. He believes as I do that you will make an excellent addition to our. . ." Mishenka stroked his chin. A faint smile curved his mouth. "I believe the word I'm looking for is agency. You would be doing much the same as you are now. The only difference being the pay, making it possible for you to give my Granddaughter the things she deserves."

It was one thing for Caitlin to invade his mind, but having Mishenka invade his thoughts was unnerving. He held up his hands. "Cat and I have already discussed this issue. Your offer is very tempting. However, I have obligations here to my job and my parents. I can't just up and leave everything." He stared deep into Mishenka's eyes. "And stay out of my head." He glanced at Caitlin as she squeezed his hand.

"When you agreed to become Caitlin's mate, you also agreed to accept the rest of her family as well." Mishenka's eyes narrowed. "As I told you earlier today, things happen in one's life to change one's plans. The offer to you will remain open as long as you live."

Raven gritted his teeth. He wouldn't upset Cat any more than she was already. He'd pick the right time and place to continue this argument. He wouldn't give in to this conniving old coot. He locked gazes with Mishenka. *I respect you, but you will not control my life.*

Mishenka gave a faint nod and glanced at Caitlin. "As for you, Kitten, I think you should either go home or return to Raven's flat. You're exhausted and need to start taking better care of yourself."

"I'm fine," Caitlin said impatiently. "I want to be here when Stacey awakens. I have to know she'll be all right."

"Dear little one," Mishenka's voice softened. "Trust me, Stacey will be fine. In the morning, you will see. By the time she is ready to be moved to West Grove, she will be our old Stacey again." He lowered his gaze. A shadow concealed his eyes. "Nonetheless, she will have scars."

Raven pushed his plate from him. Mishenka's remark was an understatement. How could anyone survive what Stacey had and not be scarred, mentally and physically?

"I still don't want to leave until I know for sure." Caitlin lowered her gaze to her ring and twisted it around her finger.

He understood Caitlin's need to be near Stacey, but Cat had to think about herself. Raven brought Caitlin's hand up to his lips. "Love, you're mentally exhausted. You need to take a break."

"I don't need you telling me what to do, too," she snapped.

She was the most stubborn woman he'd ever known, but in the last two years, he'd learned how to handle her. Carefully, very carefully. "How about this? You go back to your place, grab a shower, and pack a change of clothes then return here. You'll feel better. I'll stop by as soon as I'm finished at the station. You can decide then if you want to come home with me, go back to your place, or stay the night here. The choice is yours."

"An excellent idea," Mishenka said.

~ ~ ~

Caitlin worried her lower lip. Damn, Raven. She couldn't argue with him. He wasn't telling her not to stay, and a hot bath would make her feel better.

"Besides." Raven kissed her hand again. "Don't you think it's time to feed Inky?" He raised an eyebrow. "You know how much Stacey loves that cat."

Ouch! Raven didn't pull any punches that time. "All right. I yield." She glanced at her wrist. In all the commotion of the morning, she'd left her watch on Raven's nightstand. "What time is it?"

"Almost eight." Raven slid from the booth. "I told Mike I'd be back at eight."

"After all the years working with you, Mike knows to add thirty minutes to whatever time you tell him." She winked. "Grandpapa, I shouldn't be long. With luck, I'll be back at or before ten. Do you want me to bring you anything from the house?"

"No. Take your time."

Raven's arm wrapped around her waist. "I'll walk you to your car."

The cool evening air reminded her of Scotland.

The days were getting longer. If she were back in Scotland, she'd be helping her mother prepare for *Eostre*, the celebration of the spring equinox. She loved the festive celebration of new beginnings, new growth, and renewal. This time of year was perfect for joinings. There she went again, thinking of herself as Stacey laid suffering.

"You're in deep thought. Want to share?" Raven asked.

No, she didn't. She didn't want to tell Raven she was a selfish bitch who only thought of herself and no one else. "I'm just thinking about home. It's almost *Eostre*. My mother is probably driving Papa mad with all her plans, along with everyone else in the household."

"Spring cleaning? My grandmother was like that. She'd have a weekend set aside she'd expect my mother to come and help clean. My mother would drag my brothers, sister, and me along. When we were older, we were the ones who did all the moving and cleaning while my mom and grandma gave orders." Raven grinned at her. "As silly as it sounds. I miss those days."

The images of Raven sweeping and dusting made her smile. "It's not spring cleaning. Every year my parents give a huge party that lasts for days. Most, if not all, of the family, come. There are games, feasting, and dancing. When I was a child, it would rival Christmas as my favorite celebration. Still does." She looked up at the stars.

"There have been so many years I didn't go home for the celebration, not because I couldn't, but because I didn't want to at the time. I didn't want to be lectured by my father, my brother, or some other member of my family about finding my place. You know, doing something with my life." She looked at Raven. "You don't honestly know what you've gotten yourself into, do you?"

"It sounds like a very loving family." He bent and kissed her briefly.

"Last year I promised Stacey we would try to make it home this year." Her throat tightened. "I guess I lied."

Raven stopped, he turned her and placed his hands on her shoulders. "You didn't lie. Easter is still four weeks away. Stacey will be fine by then."

"It's not her body I'm worried about it's her mind." Caitlin stepped into Raven's embrace. "A person can only take so many times being kicked in the teeth before they snap. Stacey's been kicked more times than I could handle."

Raven's arms tightened around her, shielding her from the outside world. "This time she has all of us. She has a family to pick her up."

She sniffed. "Stacey will be surprised when she hears Grandpapa adopted her."

"She doesn't know?" Raven's eyes darkened, and he shook his head. "Why doesn't that surprise me?"

"Because you know my Grandpapa doesn't mean any harm. He only does things he thinks are for the best. As much as I hate it when he interferes, it is nice to have him around." Caitlin leaned against Raven as they walked toward her car.

"Don't tell him this, but I rather like your Grandfather, despite the fact he irritates the hell out of me." Raven chuckled. "I'm just waiting for him to march us to a church."

"Why?" She stopped and gazed up into Raven's eyes.

"We're not married yet, and he knows we've been sleeping together. He isn't blind."

"Grandpapa follows the ancient ways of my people. He believes in *Yeva,* the Creator. To him, once I claimed you as my mate, we were married." She went up on her tiptoes and kissed him. "For better or for worse."

"Yeva. I wonder if she is where we get our Goddess from?" Raven's arms pulled her closer to him, his lips pressed against hers. His tongue slid into her mouth. His kiss was soft, slow, and passionate. He hinted at the pleasures he had in mind if she decided to go home with him. He lifted his mouth, ending their kiss. "I'd marry you this very second."

The sharp blade of reality cut her. "If you didn't have to meet Mike."

"Cat—"

She placed her fingers over his mouth. "I didn't mean it the way it sounded."

Raven's eyes darkened, and his lips thinned. "Stacey is up there," he pointed to the hospital, "because of this bastard. He has to be stopped. I've been beating myself for not catching him sooner. But damn it to hell, every lead turns into a dead-end."

"I wasn't blaming you." A shard of guilt twisted in her breast. "I'm blaming myself. I've been going over my notes from all the interviews for this story. I've even gone as far as to try to read David Hawkins's mind and you know what I did to Jeff. I'm this supernatural being, and I'm helpless. I want to hunt this bastard down and make him pay, but who do I punish?"

"You don't punish anyone. The law does." His words were harsh and raw.

"The law? What if the killer has already left the country? What if even after Stacey wakes up and tells us who did this to her, we still can't find him?"

"We'll find him."

"I hope you're right." Tears blurred her vision. "All day I thought about you, about me, about us. I thought about being in your arms, and I'd glance at Stacey, and I would see her burned and broken body. I felt so damn guilty and ashamed."

Caitlin turned away and wiped her eyes. How could she be thinking of celebrations, of weddings, of making love to Raven, when her dearest friend fought for her life? "How can I be so happy and so miserable at the same time?"

Raven turned her and wrapped Caitlin in his warm embrace. Silently he held her, allowing her to cry. His hand caressed her back. Only after her sobs stopped did Raven force her to meet his tender gaze.

"You've worried about Stacey. You've watched over her, and you inflicted pain on yourself, helping to heal her." He hugged Cat, resting his chin on her head. "Don't ever think of yourself as being selfish again. In the morning, once you're able to see and speak to Stacey, things will be better."

"I want this nightmare over." Despite his words, she still felt guilty.

Raven pulled his handkerchief from his coat pocket and dabbed her tears. "It will be. I can't promise you when, but it will be." He brushed a kiss across her lips.

Hesitantly she stepped back. She didn't want to leave Raven's embrace, but she knew she had to. "You've got to go."

A faint smile curved his mouth. "When this is over, we'll go visit your family. I want to see your family's castle you've told me about, and yeah, I saw it in your mind, but man   A castle."

"Only because you're hooked on Game of Thrones." She laughed.

Raven reached behind her and opened her car door. "Go take a nice long bubble bath, and I'll see you when I get back.

Lock your doors and don't stop anywhere. Go straight home. I'm still concerned about those articles."

"Aye, aye, captain." She saluted. "What time do you think you'll return?" she asked.

He shook his head. "Ten."

"I'll be here." She rose up and gave him a quick kiss then slid behind her wheel. Raven shut her door then strolled to his car. After he'd driven away, she started her engine and pulled from the parking lot.

It was easy for Raven and Grandpapa to tell her everything would be fine, that Stacey wouldn't be harmed. They hadn't lived with her or been there the night Stacey discovered Caitlin's secret. They hadn't smelled the fear emanating from Stacey or seen the panic in her eyes. They weren't there as she begged for her life, fearing she'd be attacked.

Once Stacey had calmed down her reaction was much like Raven's and turned to curiosity.

Caitlin turned on the radio. She needed a distraction. She needed to think positively. Stacey would be fine. Hadn't she accepted things, even to the point of mothering, sometimes excessively? Stacey made sure that Caitlin didn't go for long periods without taking blood, almost to the point of nagging.

She stopped for a signal and shivered, remembering the time Stacey had put cinnamon in the blood to give it a different taste. That experiment created the worst concoction Caitlin had ever tasted, but she didn't have the heart to tell Stacey.

Maybe Grandpapa and Raven were right. Maybe Stacey was strong enough to overcome what that bastard did to her. Maybe Stacey wouldn't have any problems with the knowledge she'd been taken into the inner circle of the family, or the fact her lifespan had been extended, considerably.

Caitlin impatiently stared at the light, willing it to change. Just ahead, the lights at Books and Java drew her attention, almost like a moth to a flame. She could use a good cup of coffee. The stuff she got out of the machines at the hospital tasted little better than Stacey's experiment.

The light changed and Caitlin pulled into the parking lot.

Lambert stood vigilant at his post behind the cash register. He smiled as she got out of her car.

Caitlin strolled through the open the door and breathed deeply. The rich coffee aroma teased her nose as she walked into the store. Except for Lambert, the place was empty.

He looked up at her and his smile faded. "Are you all right? You look like you've been crying."

"I'll be fine once I get off this emotional roller coaster." She forced a smile for him. "What would help is a cup of real coffee and a good romance to read to help me escape for an hour or so."

"Then you've come to the right place. I just finished putting out this month's new releases. There are some that look promising." His smile returned, wrinkling his eyes. "As for the coffee, I've just made a fresh pot."

"That's great."

He turned his back as he prepared her coffee. "Cream?"

"Of course." Stopping by here was good. Things would get better.

"Has Miss Parker's condition changed any?" Lambert asked as he grabbed a cup from under the counter.

"She's improving, but hasn't awakened yet."

"Cinnamon?"

She had to laugh. "No, thank you."

"Did I miss something?"

"No, I had a bad but funny experience involving cinnamon."

Lambert handed her the large coffee, topped with whipped cream. "You and Miss Parker are very close. Almost like sisters."

She took a long sip of the rich hot liquid then licked the cream from her lips. "Now, this is coffee."

"All you need is your book."

"And I'm getting that now." She walked toward the back of the store. She picked up a book and read the back cover. It sounded good.

Her vision blurred and she became dizzy. She really did need this coffee. She took a large gulp.

Everything began to spin. What was wrong with her?

"Caitlin," Lambert called her.

She turned to him for help.

He grinned at her, his arms crossed over his chest. The fingers of his left hand drummed against his right arm.

She'd never noticed him wearing a ring before.

Oh, God.

The world went black.

Chapter Twenty-Six

For a Monday night, the station was busy. Raven leaned back in his chair and studied the photos of Lenard Richardson. Thanks to modern technology and the proper software, Kurt Lehr had kept his promise. He'd aged the photo of the boy, using only the mother's face. It would have been more helpful if they had a photograph of the father. The boy didn't favor his mother. However, what Kurt did to the photo help. The aged face seemed familiar.

Someone kicked his desk. He glared at the uniformed officer leading a handcuffed man toward holding.

Raven tried to focus on the photos spread out in front of him. Choosing another picture, one with lighter hair, Raven stared at the haunting eyes. He still couldn't identify the face. Who in the hell was this man? The chaos surrounding him made it hard to concentrate.

A shadow covered his desk. He looked up at Mike. "Thanks for the coffee. Anything on the prints?"

"I'm on my way to the lab now. What to come?"

"No. I still can't shake the feeling I know this guy. Here, you have a look. Kurt kept the face clean shaven."

Mike took the picture then angled his desk lamp. "There's no doubt. He looks familiar to me, too. What about the color of the hair? Maybe that's it." He handed the photo back. "Give him darker hair."

Raven sifted through a folder. "You mean like this?" He pulled out more pictures. "Look through these. Kurt had sent several photos with different shades and styles of hair. He'd even put glasses on a few. I think it's the weight. What if we made the face thinner?"

Mike shrugged. "I don't know. I'm going to check on the prints. Maybe they've got the results back."

Raven picked up the original photo of the fourteen-year-old boy. *Who are you?*

What was he missing? All the photos were strewn across his desk. Somewhere in the mess was the answer to this bastard's identity. But where? The proverbial needle in the haystack.

Panic sharp and vivid seized Raven, closing his throat. Cold sweat beaded his forehead. He couldn't breathe. He loosened his tie and gasped.

Lambert. Caitlin's cry forced its way to the front of Raven's mind.

Through a blurry haze, Lambert stood, arms crossed, fingers drumming on his arm. He threw his head back, laughing.

Raven opened his eyes and stared at the familiar eyes. "You son of a bitch." He stood, grabbed his keys, and headed toward the car.

"Raven! We've got a match," Mike yelled. "Lenard Richardson is Lambert Rollands."

"I know." Raven paused long enough for Mike to catch up with him. "He has Cat."

"Oh, shit. Did he call? Is he holding Caitlin hostage?" Mike followed him down the corridor.

"No."

"Then how do you know that he has her?"

"I just do." Raven shoved the heavy metal door open and ran toward the car. There was no time for him to explain. He couldn't sense Caitlin.

"Come on, level with me on this." Mike slid into the car seat as Raven put the vehicle in reverse.

Caitlin was at the bookstore when he'd felt her panic. That's where he'd start. Ever since he'd taken her blood, he'd known where she was at all times. She'd told him they were joined as one. And they were. Why couldn't he sense her now?

He's drugged her.

"Raven."

How could he explain this to Mike?

You don't.

Mike reached for the radio and Raven pushed his hand away. "Don't call for back-up. We've got to do this alone."

"Damn it, Raven, I'm your partner. I'm tired of you keeping me in the dark. What the hell is going on?"

Mike deserved to know some of the truth. "My grandmother said I had the gift. Call it the six sense or ESP. You can call it any frigging thing you want. Whatever the name, I have it. Every time this bastard killed. I've had dreams about it. I would know how and what he did to those women before we'd found the bodies." He glanced at Mike then at the road. "There was a time I even wondered if I was the frigging murderer. I can't explain it, Mike. All I know is that he has Caitlin and I can't feel her. I know she isn't dead."

"You feel Caitlin?"

"Yeah. Part of the gift." He parked in front of the dark bookstore and opened his door.

Mike followed, drawing his gun. "I don't think we'll find the door open."

"Like that would stop me."

"We don't have a search warrant."

Raven glanced at Mike, before he kicked in the front door, setting off the alarm. "I don't need one."

With lights flashing, a police car squalled to a stop in front of the bookstore.

"It's Sue and her partner. See what you can find, I'll deal with them," Mike said. He walked toward the two officers. "This may be a college prank."

Whether Mike believed Raven or not, Mike's actions proved he had Raven's back. "Thanks." Raven nodded and strolled toward the deli counter. Everything was neat and organized. Lambert was a meticulous man. *Let's hope he made a mistake.*

Nothing looked out of the ordinary, but the smell of burning coffee drew Raven's attention. He stepped behind the counter. The coffee pot had been left on and the coffee cooked to the bottom of the pot. "Mike!"

"Find something?"

"This pot is still on, and everything else was cleaned." Raven bent down and looked at the different flavors, careful not to touch anything. There had to be a clue here somewhere.

"Looks like someone was in a hurry to get out of here. Look at this."

Raven stood. "What?"

Mike pointed to the antique cash register. "See, it's closed. He didn't take the money out of it tonight." Mike used a pencil and pressed the No Sale key, the drawer open, revealing its full contents.

"Where did he take her?"

"Detective, I've found something," The female officer called.

Raven found Sue kneeling beside a coffee cup lying on the carpeted floor. Raven took a pen from his pocket and rolled the cup. A woman's lip color smeared on one side. "That's Cat's color."

~ ~ ~

Her head throbbed, and her chest hurt as if she'd been stung by a million fire ants. Caitlin hadn't felt this bad since the time she tried to out drink Glen. What had happened to her? The last thing she remembered was drinking a cup of coffee at Lambert's. She remembered feeling dizzy. Then Lambert standing with his arms crossed over his chest laughing at her. He wore the sardonyx ring.

Oh, God! Lambert's the killer.

If she stayed motionless, she might have a chance to escape.

Where was she? Still lying on the floor in Lambert's store?

She listened for his breathing, to pinpoint his whereabouts. All she could hear was the pounding of her own heart. Caitlin forced her eyes open. Her vision was blurry. Where in the heck was she? Cobwebs and ropes hung from the wooden rafters. She wasn't in the bookstore unless she was in the basement.

She drew in a deep breath to clear her head. A musty damp stench and something else filled her nose. She took another deep breath recognized the stench of blood and seared flesh.

She licked her upper lip. The metallic taste teased her tongue. There was the faint scent of other blood in the room, old, dried blood. Her stomach turned.

Caitlin tried to sit. She couldn't move her arms or legs. She lifted her head as much as she could, trying to see what held her. Metal clamps bound her wrists and ankles to a wooden table.

She wasn't wearing her clothes, only a thin cotton shift.

Her slight movement sent paralyzing pain to her chest.

Tilting her head back, she stared up at the ropes. Fear knotted her stomach. Her vision had cleared enough for her to see the dark stains on the ropes dangling above her. She rolled her head to one side. In the dark corner, she could make out what appeared to be knives and other unfamiliar implements.

Each time she moved, the fabric scraped her chest causing excruciating pain. In the back of her mind, she knew why.

Like all the others, she'd been branded.

She wouldn't end up like them. She wouldn't end up like Stacey.

Concentrating, Caitlin tried to fade. Nothing happened. She still had too much of the drug Lambert used on her in her system.

Caitlin, where are you? Raven's voice echoed in her mind.

I don't know. Lambert has me bound to a table. He's cut my nose and branded me.

Get out of there! Fade, dammit.

I can't. I'm too drugged, but don't worry, he isn't here.

Where are you?

In a basement or warehouse, I think.

Which is it? His fear washed over her. *Never mind. I can sense you again.*

"Did you have a nice nap, witch?" Lambert stood at the foot of the table glaring at her.

Raven, Lambert is here.

Hold on. I'm almost there.

Where the hell can I go? She met Lambert's glare. "I'm not a witch." She couldn't show any fear, even if it held her in its icy claws.

He snickered. "That's what they all said. In the end, they all confessed to their evil, just like you will." He stepped closer to her. "As you have already discovered, you cannot use your black magic against me."

She had to stall until she could free herself. "Why do you think I'm a witch?"

He touched her hair, gently petting her as if she were a rabbit. "You have such beautiful hair. All witches have beautiful hair. It was a shame Mr. Fisher cut yours. It would have made a lovely addition to my collection."

"My hair? That's why you consider me a witch."

"No." He pulled the shift covering her and exposed her breasts. "You have, or should I say had, the devil's mark."

A sharp pain pierced her. He'd burned the three moles between her breasts. The hideous red brand glared at her.

"I searched your body. They were the only marks I found, but they were enough to prove my speculations. You are a follower of Zigana. Confess, and your death will be painless."

"I'm not a witch."

He tore the shift exposing her more. "God is the salt of the earth." Lambert held up a bowl. "Bless this and drive the evil from within." He reached into the bowl then rubbed salt into her burn.

Gritting her teeth, Caitlin willed herself not to scream. She wouldn't give him the satisfaction. Instead, she stared into his cold, emotionless eyes. "Yea, though I walk through the valley of the shadow of death, I will fear no evil."

His hand struck her face, hard. "Demon! You are not worthy enough to speak such things." He turned and walked toward the knife-laden table. "I will pull out your tongue!"

"Then I cannot confess. Can I?" Closing her eyes, she tried to fade. Her wrist seemed to move more freely.

Lambert grabbed her hand with one hand and held a pair of pliers in his other hand. He bent her index finger back and pulled on her nail. "Who are your sisters?"

Blood oozed from around her cuticle. "You've already met her. She's in Scotland," she forced out as calmly as she could, despite the pain.

"I plan to remove each of your fingernails. One at a time until you tell me the names of those in your coven."

"Why are you doing this?"

"Because you are a follower of Zigana and need to be saved." He stopped pulling on her nail.

"I'm not a witch, and I don't know anyone named Zigana."

He smiled at her. "You are such a liar." He let go of her hand and leaned close to her face. His hot breath fanned her cheek. "At first I had hoped, I was wrong. But you lived with a witch and, as I feared, she cursed you."

Where was Raven?

I'm coming through a window. His voice eased some of her worries.

"What made you think I'm a witch? I mean other than the moles on my chest. There had to be something else."

Lambert nodded. "There was the lie about your attack. You were never attacked. You attacked an innocent man, who because of God's help was able to weaken you when he cut your hair." He fingered her hair. "But you were still strong enough to send the man sailing through the air. I spoke with Ms. Townsley. She is a good woman. She told me how you caused her to lose her job. She also told me of her interview with Mr. Fisher and how he saw your eyes turn red." A cold evil gleam sparkled in Lambert's eyes, and he tightened his grip on her wrist. With a quick jerk, he yanked out her fingernail. He held it up for her to see.

Caitlin clenched her teeth refusing to scream. The pain shot up her arm all the way to her jaw. She glared at Lambert.

This was a nightmare. There was no reasoning with him. "We're not back in the seventeen hundreds, and this isn't Salem." He was insane. In his mind, he was right, and she was a witch.

He calmly tapped the pliers on her middle finger then gripped her nail. "Enough talk."

"I agree," Raven said. "Move away from her Lenard."

Raven. She was safe.

"Do not call me that." Lambert looked up. "I see your witch has you under her spell." He glanced at her. His right eye twitched. "You must be one of Satan's favorites, and he has sent this misguided man to save you." Lambert made the sign of the cross. "But don't worry, Detective, I *will* save your soul."

Caitlin gasped. The terrifying realization hit her. Lambert had booby-trapped the place. "Raven, watch out!"

Lambert kicked something and the landing where Raven stood, collapsed.

"Raven!" She screamed as Raven fell helplessly to the concrete floor.

Caitlin turned her head and strained to see that Raven was all right. She swore she heard bone breaking.

Lambert causally strolled over to Raven and kicked the gun out of his limp hand. "I know you are not dead, but is that a bone I see protruding from your leg?" He nudged Raven then placed his foot on Raven's broken leg.

Raven grabbed Lambert's foot, trying to pull him to the ground, but Lambert pressed down on Raven's injured leg, snapping the protruding bone, and forcing Raven to let go. "You can't get away. We've got this place surrounded." Pain scratched Raven's voice.

"Oh, please, Detective, do you take me for a fool?"

"No, a sick animal."

"You flatter me." Lambert returned to Caitlin. His lips pulled into a thin line. "I had wished to save your black soul. However, I cannot take the chance of being captured before my job is finished." He stroked her cheek then turned away from her.

Lambert faced Raven. "I think I will kill you first." He raised Raven's pistol and pointed it at him.

Despite her blood flowing through Raven's veins, a gunshot to his head would kill him because he was only newly embraced. She struggled against her bonds.

"I'll make this quick," Lambert said.

Caitlin's bonds gave way. "Lambert," she called.

He faced her. His eyes grew wide. "How? Magic." He aimed the gun at her and fired.

Caitlin laughed, not even flinching as the bullet passed through her shoulder. She advanced on him. "I'm not a witch."

He fired again, missing her, and backing up until he was pressed against the table covered with knives. "Only a witch could have broken free of those metal clamps. Only a witch is unaffected by bullets. You are not human."

~ ~ ~

Raven struggled through the pain to reach for the gun he kept in his ankle holster. He couldn't let Caitlin go through with what she was planning. It would tear her apart inside to kill. She might not know it, but he did.

"Your right. I'm not human. Something worse." Caitlin snarled, revealing her fangs.

"Vampire," Lambert whispered. He reached behind him then lunged at Caitlin.

Raven raised his pistol. His finger smoothly squeezed the trigger. His ears rang with the discharge. The smell of cordite stung his nose. He watched as Lambert slid to the floor.

Raven gazed at Caitlin's wide eyes and ashen face. She looked down. His gaze followed. "No!"

Caitlin sank to her knees. A knife protruded from her chest. Lambert had jabbed it in her to its hilt.

Dragging himself across the floor, Raven reached her. He pillowed Cat's head on his lap and tried to pull the knife from her chest.

Caitlin's hand covered his. "Don't. Mike. He wouldn't understand. Don't."

Raven's tears splashed on her cheek. "Caitlin, don't leave me. Let me pull it out then you can drink."

"No. Don't worry," She rasped. "Thirsty. The darkness. It's pulling me."

Cat's memories of Glen, Vaughn, Tristan, and Royce explaining to her about the dark sleep. The healing blackness where she wouldn't feel the pain anymore filled Raven's mind. Then nothing. His connection to Cat was gone. She surrendered to the wonderful void where nothing mattered at all.

Raven cradled Caitlin's limp body in his arms. She couldn't be dead. He could still sense her life, felt her heart beating in his. It was the connection to her mind, her thoughts he couldn't feel.

"Raven." Mike knelt beside him. He placed his hand on Raven's shoulder, giving it a firm squeeze. "I'm sorry."

Mike stood and stepped away. He placed the call. Officer down.

Raven smoothed his hand over Caitlin's face. She was sleeping. She had to wake up. She had to open her eyes.

Behind him, he heard voices. Other officers had arrived at the scene. Raven pulled the torn shift up, covering Caitlin's breasts. He didn't want her to be embarrassed when she woke.

The paramedic checking Caitlin's pulse glanced at Raven then lowered Cat's wrist and shook his head. "We've got another one to be tagged and bagged."

"Show some damn compassion," Mike yelled and shoved the paramedic.

Mike gripped Raven's shoulder. "Let her go, man."

Raven jerked away.

"There's nothing you can do for her. She's dead."

Raven stared at Mike. "No. She isn't dead. She isn't." He shook her. "Wake up. Dammit, Cat, *wake up.*"

Chapter Twenty-Seven

Raven brushed a lock of hair from Caitlin's ash white face. In the dim light, she appeared to be sleeping. That made sense. She'd slipped into some form of coma. Once her body healed, she'd wake up. His gaze fell to the blood-soaked shift she wore. She'd lost so much blood. She needed his blood. He had to find a way to help her. "Mike, I need to be alone with Caitlin."

"For God's sake, Birdie, let her go." Mike grabbed Raven's arm and pulled him free of her. "If you don't let these guys tend to you, you'll die."

Raven tried to jerk free. She wasn't dead. He had to do what he could to help her. She needed him. Didn't they see that? "Lemme go!"

"You'll bleed to death." Mike drew back his fist.

Raven fell against the cold concrete floor. His head throbbed.

"I'm sorry, Birdie," Mike said.

"Go to hell!"

An oxygen mask was placed over his face. Pain shot through him when the paramedic added pressure to the wound to stop the bleeding. Raven gritted his teeth and turned his head.

The Coroner placed Caitlin's limp body on a black vinyl bag.

"Wait a minute," Mike said. He bent over Caitlin's body. "Okay, you can take her now." He turned, and tears glistened in his eyes.

The Coroner zipped the bag closed, sealing Caitlin inside.

Raven's heart winced. She wasn't dead, but there was no way he could convince anyone of that, not without disclosing her secret. To save her life, he'd have to risk the lives of her family members.

Events happen in your lifetime to change your plans for the future. Mishenka's words slammed to the forefront of

Raven's mind. He squeezed his eyes shut against the pain in his body and soul.

Caitlin, where are you? He couldn't feel even the faint beating of her heart.

The paramedics strapped him to a gurney, rolled him from the building then placed him inside an ambulance. Before the doors were shut, he watched as the coroner pulled away, taking Caitlin. Raven closed his eyes.

The wail of the siren stopped. They were already at the hospital. Raven tried to lift his eyelids. He was so weak his lids felt like they were made of bricks.

Without his connection to Caitlin's mind, he felt more alone than he'd ever been in his life.

A voice shouted orders. They wanted units of blood. Someone pushed up his sleeve. Raven slid opened his eyelids enough to watch a woman tied a tourniquet around his arm. Damn, he hated needles. He closed his eyes. He didn't want to see what she would do next.

"Get him to surgery, stat," a male voice ordered.

Using all the strength Raven could, he opened his eyes. "Wait," he forced out. "Mike. Where's Mike?"

"I'm here, partner." Mike squeezed his hand.

"Mishenka. Find Mishenka." Darkness overcame him.

~ ~ ~

Raven opened his eyes. He was in a dark room. It didn't look like a recovery room. Where was he? A dim light glowed over his bed. What was that nagging beeping?

"Well, it's about time you woke up." Mike's voice drowned out the annoying beeping sound.

Raven turned his head. "Did you find Mishenka? Did he get to Caitlin in time? Is she all right? Talk to me, Mike."

Mike exhaled and shook his head. "Your parents came in last night. They've been here with you all morning. They left about an hour ago. I took the liberty of giving them your keys. Your brothers are coming in tomorrow."

"My parents were here? I thought I dreamed of them." He pressed the button next to his bed, raising it to a sitting position. He glanced out the window into the darkness. Street lights were on, and he could see other lights in the distance. This didn't make sense. "How long was I out?"

"It's Thursday night."

"Thursday? Not Monday?"

"You were in surgery for nearly nine hours as they worked to repair your leg. Then you slept all of yesterday and most of today. You'd opened your eyes, mumble something then fall back to sleep."

"Tell me about Caitlin."

Mike stood. "Maybe I should get the nurse."

"Maybe you should tell me what the hell is going on. Where is Mishenka?"

Mike shook his head again then moved his chair closer to the bed. "We almost lost you, too, Birdie."

Raven clenched his teeth. A soothing peace crept over him. Caitlin wasn't dead. Deep in his soul, he felt her heart beating again. He knew she'd not left him. "Tell me about Caitlin."

"I'm sorry, Raven. She was dead at the scene. When we brought you in, I went looking for Mishenka." Mike lowered his head. He rested his arms on his legs, letting his hands dangle between his knees. "I don't know how to tell you this?"

Raven's jaw twitched. He hated it when Mike beat around the bush. Why couldn't the man say what was on his mind? "Tell me."

"Stacey died Tuesday morning. A little past midnight."

"What?"

"When I found Mishenka, he was on his way to the morgue with Stacey's body. She'd suffered another heart attack and died. Doctor Whenn said he thought Stacey's heart couldn't take the stress of what had happened to her. There are things Lenard or Lambert or whatever the hell that bastard's name, did to Stacey, things too horrible for her to remember. Anyway, Whenn wouldn't know for sure what caused Stacey's death until after the autopsy. I had to tell Mishenka about

Caitlin. I felt so helpless watching that old man cry." Mike shoved his hands into his pockets and paced.

Autopsy? Raven's gut twisted. He'd not thought about that. An autopsy would kill Caitlin, but she wasn't dead. He could feel her heart beating. "Do you know the results yet of the autopsy?"

"Mishenka would not allow them. He said an autopsy violated their religious beliefs. So, the official cause of death for Stacey was listed as heart failure and for Cat, acute blood loss due to the stabbing."

Raven smiled. *Religious beliefs, my ass. Thank you, Old man.* "Where is Mishenka now? I have to speak to him."

"You can't. He left yesterday morning to take Caitlin's and Stacey's bodies back to Scotland."

Raven turned his head and stared out the dark window. "He's already left?"

Mike nodded. "Yeah, one of Cat's brothers and cousin were with him."

"Damn that old man!" Raven glared at the I.V. sticking into the back of his hand. "I'm getting out of here, and you're going to help me."

"Like hell I am." Mike shoved Raven against the mattress. "You're not going anywhere."

"How will you stop me? Strap me to this bed, or are you planning to run me up with some more drugs? Huh, what are you going to do to stop me?"

Mike eased his grip. "Not a damn thing. If you're so hell-bent on killing yourself go right ahead." He backed away and flopped back down onto the chair. "I won't stop you."

Raven stared at the ceiling. He'd underestimated Mishenka. The man was more conniving than Raven believed possible. He drew in a deep breath. He had to think. He knew Caitlin was alive, he could feel her. All he had to do was find her.

"Birdie," Mike called. His tone no longer angry, but soft and compassionate. "I know how much Caitlin meant to you, but she's gone. Mishenka lost both a granddaughter and a daughter. Caitlin's family is mourning, just as much as you are. I wish I could take away your hurt."

Mike stood and reached into his pocket. He stared at the item he held then drew in a breath, and extended his hand. "I thought you'd want this," he said, dropping Caitlin's engagement ring on Raven's palm.

Tears stung Raven's eyes. He would find her again, and she'd wear his ring once more.

His search would begin, now.

Fisting his hand, the stones on the ring dug into his palm. "Tell me more. Tell me everything about her brother. I need to know." They had to already been in town and more than likely in on Mishenka's little plan.

"From what I gathered, he and Caitlin's cousin arrived sometime Monday while you and Caitlin were at the hospital with Stacy. They said they wanted to surprise Caitlin, to be here for her and Stacey. Caitlin's brother seemed quiet. Guess he was in shock about finding out about his sister's death."

Raven swallowed the lump in his throat. Mike had said the word, 'death.' "What did her brother look like?"

"Tall, about your height, with jet-black hair, and eerie blue eyes."

"Glen." Raven knew the man, though he'd never met him. "What about her cousin? Describe him to me. Was he a man about six-nine or more, short platinum hair, green eyes or did he have dark blond hair and blue eyes?"

The latter. Mishenka introduced him as Royce. The man stayed on the phone most of the time I was there." Mike shrugged. "Making arrangements."

Raven made mental notes. Anything Mike told him could help him find Caitlin. "By any chance did you overhear any of the conversations?"

"Yeah. As I said, the man just made travel arrangements. He spoke with a Vaughn Madoc first, then made a call to a Percy Westmoreland. And he made a call to an agent Culpepper. When her cousin did get off the phone, he informed me he'd already made plans to ship Caitlin and Stacey's things overseas. The movers were there today."

Culpepper? Agent Culpepper, Edgar's boss, was a Culpepper. Naw, that would be too much of a coincidence. Vaughn Madoc, Raven knew that name. Wonder if Vaughn's in the states or Europe. "You went by Cat's today?"

Mike nodded. "Birdie, I've got to tell you, the place had been cleaned out, not even a speck of dust over the door frames. For sale sign already in the yard."

"What about Inky?" Raven asked. He knew how much that cat meant to Stacey. Caitlin would want to make sure he'd have a good home.

"Caitlin's brother said they would be taking Inky with them to Scotland. I think Mishenka is attached to the cat." Mike stood. He patted Raven's shoulder.

Raven opened his hand and stared at the ring. "Thanks." He glanced at Mike. "I'm sorry for how I acted. I'm just…"

"Hey, man, you don't have to apologize. I know what she meant to you."

Tears stung Raven's eyes. "It's late. Why don't you head home? Hug Jeanette."

"Will you be all right?"

"In time." He patted the cast on his leg. "Don't worry. I'm not going anywhere tonight."

"I'll see you tomorrow," Mike said and left.

Alone except for that damn beeping. Raven glared at the machine he was hooked to, wishing he could silence the blasted thing.

Placing his hand over his heart, he closed his eyes. He and Caitlin would be together again. This, he swore.

~ ~ ~

Channel surfing at six o'clock on a Friday night was not how Raven wanted to spend his evening. It wasn't like he could do anything else. It sucked that nearly every station had something to say about the case. That was the last thing he wanted to see. Raven clicked the remote several more times before settling on Scooby-Doo.

Great, witches.

Raven clicked off the *TV*. He couldn't wait until he could get out of this Hellhole. Thank God, he'd convinced his brothers to take their parents out for dinner. Raven couldn't believe how old his mother and father looked today. His mom seemed to have aged ten years since Christmas. His parents didn't need this stress.

He's glad his parents understood his need to take time off from work. Raven explained to his folks he planned to travel through Europe, maybe even to Scotland. Mike hadn't filled them in about Caitlin, telling them she had been a friend and was the last victim of the serial killer he and Mike had hunted. Mike was the only one, who knew Caitlin and Raven were lovers. Mike. Good old Mike.

Raven's mind still spun with all the information Mike had that afternoon. The police were still searching Lambert or Lenard Richardson's warehouse. They found Lambert's gruesome collection of his victims' hair, jewelry, and clothing along with Lambert's detailed journal. Apparently, Lambert removed his victim's jewelry and cut their hair once he felt they were dead or close to it like with Stacey. According to Mike, Lambert vented for twenty-two pages about his mistake with Stacy. The lunatic had been positive she would die just like his other victims. He also wrote about cutting his hand in an attempt to sneak into Stacy's room and finish what he'd started. Thank God he was frightened off by the police presence. Raven shivered. No one suspected Lambert.

The other good news, Mike arrested Townsley. Cat's family spoke with the DA, citing Townsley's article deliberately placed Cat in danger. The Prosecutor agreed with them and had a warrant issued.

Raven twisted Cat's ring around on his pinkie. It would be great if Townsley stayed in jail, but Raven knew she wouldn't. That rag she worked for would have her out in no time, stating freedom of speech. He couldn't waste his energy worrying about her. And he sure as hell wouldn't waste energy worrying about internal affairs. He knew they would start an investigation into the case. Raven expected there would be questions as to why he'd not requested backup, and how he'd known where to find Lambert.

Raven would have to come up with plausible answers for the investigators. He wouldn't say anything to jeopardize Caitlin or her family.

Strong perfume stung his nose, and he turned toward the door. A mixture of emotions seized him. His heart pounded with joy and apprehension. His questions would be answered. "Victoria, Vaughn, come in," Raven greeted. Damn, Vaughn was bigger and more menacing than he appeared in Cat's mind or the photographs.

Victoria smiled, and Vaughn closed the door then leaned against it, ensuring no one would enter without them permitting it.

Victoria sauntered across the room and eased into the chair beside his bed. "You look like something the cat brought in."

"Where's Caitlin?" Raven's gaze roamed over her. For sisters, Victoria and Caitlin were as far apart as the east was from the west.

"Home. Where else would she be?"

"How is Caitlin? Is she all right? I've got to talk to her."

The smile faded from Victoria's face, and she glanced over her shoulder then back to Raven. "Caitlin's as well as can be expected. As for you speaking to her, that depends on our conversation."

He studied Victoria. She sat stiff and expressionless, staring at him. With her black hair, pale eyes, and ruby lips, she looked every bit the vampire. Raven didn't know if he wanted Victoria's help, but right now, she and Vaughn were the only ones who could lead him to Cat. "So talk," he said.

Victoria ran her fingers through her hair and crossed her legs. Smiling, she folded her fingers together. Her long blood red nails nearly extended to her wrist. "My sister died, Mr. O'Brien. That fact cannot be changed."

He sat and glared at her. "Cat is alive. I can feel her, so don't sit there, and lie to me."

"Vic," Vaughn uttered, crossing his arms, and glaring at her. "That's one."

She huffed and fidgeted in her seat. Her body language spoke volumes to him. Victoria was hiding something. "Alive to you, yes. To this town, no. And because of the national media attention, this case caused, my sister, is also dead to this part of the world. I'll be honest with you, Raven. My grandfather could have prevented a lot of this if he had only acted, but he chose to meddle, and play one of his bloody games. Because of this, we had to do some major damage control. Glen, Royce, Tristan, and Vaughn," she motioned to the man behind her. "As you are already aware of, arrived Sunday night."

"Mike said you came in on Monday." Raven flicked his attention to the giant leaning against the door.

Vaughn shrugged. "Some of us were here Sunday. We should have been here from the start." His eyes glowed and sent a shiver through Raven.

"You were here! And you allowed Cat to be kidnapped! I thought you're kind sensed when others were in danger."

Vaughn exhaled. "Usually we are immune to the effects of drugs. However, the concoction given to my sister was created especially for our kind. I sensed her once she woke and arrived shortly after you."

"Yes, well, as I was saying." Victoria rolled her eyes. "The guys came in to help in case you or Caitlin needed them." Victoria huffed. "And it was a bloody good thing too after the debacle Monday night. Vaughn could not act with so many humans present. However, once she arrived at the hospital, he and Glen acted quickly to remove my sister and Stacey from there to save Caitlin's life."

"What do you mean." He jerked too quickly and pain radiated up his leg.

"My sister lost a great deal of blood. Unlike our brother, my sister and I cannot replace our blood loss as fast. We require blood to heal, from anything other than minor injuries. That bastard jabbed a knife through her heart."

"Cat told me a stake through her heart wouldn't kill her."

"Technically, she was right. As I said, the guys had to act quickly because of my grandfather's muck. Fear not. With the help of our liaison, they were able to take care of the police investigation. They have also taken care of the media. And for your information, I'm personally taking care of Barbara Townsley." An evil smile spread across Victoria's lips. For some reason, Raven didn't give a damn what she did to Townsley. "Don't worry. I won't kill the bitch. But I'm having fun. She's squirming under the civil suit for contributing to the wrongful death of my sister. Maybe she'll think twice about writing lies. Anyway." Victoria flicked her hand. "After we spoke with your family tonight, they know you and my sister were dating."

"My parents? My family?" He glared at her then at Vaughn. "You played mind games with my family?"

Victoria smiled and rolled her eyes. "Calm down. We didn't fry any brain cells."

"Victoria!" Vaughn straightened. "Raven, we took your family out for dinner, there were no mind games. *I* told them you and Caitlin had been dating." Vaughn's eyes were glowing red orbs, and he turned his attention to Victoria. "That's twice, Vic. I already told you I would not put up with your shit."

Victoria flinched. "Sorry."

Raven glanced at his left hand. On his pinky, he wore Caitlin's engagement ring. He didn't like what he was hearing. They'd erased Caitlin from his life. "Let me just cut through the bullshit. If I ever want to see Caitlin again, to see *my mate again*, I have to play by Mishenka's rules, correct?"

Victoria reached into her oversized purse. She pulled out a large envelope and placed it on her lap. "If that's how you want it."

"What's that?"

"Your new life, if you choose to play my grandfather's game."

Raven stiffened at the challenge. "And if I decide not to play by Mishenka's rules, then what?"

A tight smile pulled at Victoria's lips. "Then we have been ordered by my grandfather to erase your memory. I'll be honest with you, Raven. You and my sister are joined as one. I can't remove the love you have for her. You will always mourn for her. You won't know for who or why you're mourning."

"And Caitlin?" His voice broke. "What would happen to her?"

"My little sister would live the rest of her life miserably ever-after, and possibly die in a few short years, instead of a thousand. Raven, we are a cursed people. We are not demons or creatures from Hell. We are beings that are driven by a primal force to find our one and only true mate. To claim them, produce children with them, to live happily ever after in their arms of as long as fate will allow. To deny ourselves this union is self-destruction. For many of our kind, when our mate dies, we soon join them."

"What are Mishenka's terms?"

"Simple. You leave tonight on a flight to Scotland, never to return here." She shrugged. "But then I don't know why you would want to come back here, anyway."

"My parents are old. Granted, I don't see them as much as I should, but I still see them, and if they need me, I'm there for them. How do you explain my sudden disappearance to them?"

Victoria lips curved into a wicked grin. "Didn't I tell you that part? You die."

A low growl escaped Vaughn, and he glared at Victoria. "That's three. Leave. Now."

"But."

"No. Buts." Vaughn grabbed Victoria by her upper arm, lifted her from the chair and walked her to the door. "You know what I have endured. What he is enduring and yet you still want to act like this." He opened the door and pointed into the hall.

The torment of the past few days overwhelmed Raven. Unashamed, he let his tears fall. "Do what you were sent here to do." Raven glared at her and Vaughn. "But I will find Caitlin, and we will be together again."

Victoria slinked out into the hall, patting Vaughn on the arm. "He's all yours. Do be gentle with him."

Chapter Twenty-eight

The wind blew Caitlin's hair as she stood on a rocky cliff eighty feet above the North Sea. The waves crashed against the stones below her. She watched the churning waters below her and breathed in the cool salt air. Storm clouds darkened the horizon. It had been four weeks, two days, and fourteen hours since Raven held her in his arms. So many times, she'd picked up the phone to call him, and hung up the second it rang. This had to be Raven's decision. If he wanted a life with her, it had to be his choice, not hers. She wiped the tear from her eyes. The memory of his touch, his smile, his kiss, burned in her mind.

Caitlin touched her chest. Despite her healing abilities, her burns were still visible. Her fingernail had barely grown back. Even with the blood Grandpapa had given her, it would be sometime before she was completely healed.

The crunch of gravel drew her from her empty thoughts. She turned toward the sound. Stacey smiled and inched her wheelchair forward. She grew stronger each day, but it was still too painful for her to walk.

Burns always healed slowly.

Faking Stacey's death had been another of Grandfather's ideas, his way of protecting the family.

Caitlin shook her head. "Why are you in that antique thing when Father brought you an electric one?"

"I like this one. Besides, I'm building up my arm muscles." Stacey struggled with the wicker-backed wooden wheelchair. Her face reddened as she strained to move the cumbersome thing over the flagstone walkway.

"Let me help you," Caitlin said and started toward Stacey.

"No." Stacey held up her calloused palm. "I made it this far. I can make it the rest of the way up this hill."

"You shouldn't be out here."

"And neither should you," Stacey countered.

"But you've not healed well enough."

"And you were puking up your guts this morning." Stacey tilted her chin up and frowned. "You've lost too much weight. It's not good."

Caitlin conceded. "I couldn't stay in that house another second with Grandfather. I feel like every day that passes without Raven contacting me is a victory to that old goat."

Stacey's frown softened. She reached up and clasped Caitlin's hand. "I wish I knew what to say. Have you tried calling Raven? He may not have the number here. You don't have cell coverage up here, and if you did, you no longer have the same cell number you had in the States."

"Maybe you're right. But it hurts each day that I don't hear from him. At times I find myself wondering if Raven doesn't want to speak to me. I can't go back to the States. I feel so helpless." Caitlin sighed. She squeezed Stacey's hand and looked out over the sea again. She needed to change the subject before she broke down crying. "We've hardly had any time alone since we've been here."

"You've been pushing yourself too hard," Stacey said. "So much, so this is the first time I've seen you, that you were not cleaning something."

Dark clouds swirled above, and thunder rumbled in the distance. "I've been busy, trying to keep my mind off Raven by helping mother prepare for *Eostre*. Most of the family will be arriving by week's end."

"By the way, your mother told me Glen and Victoria are coming in tonight. I'm a little nervous about seeing everyone."

"You shouldn't be. You know them." Caitlin bit her lower lip and looked at Stacey. "Do you regret what we did to you? What I did to you?"

"Regret what?" Stacey's eyes widened with surprise.

"Grandfather adopting you without your permission. My embracing you, bringing you into the family by giving you my blood."

Stacey stared at Caitlin for several long minutes. "I've been given a family, a slightly weird one, but a family nonetheless. You saved my life. You've changed my perception of what is normal." Stacey grinned. "I mean until I met you, vampires only existed in the movies. Then we have your cousins, with the two spirits who have the changing-into-a-wolf thing down to an art, you could have warned me about that part. First time I saw Tristan drop trou, and turn into his wolf, I almost had a heart attack for real. Geeze! I bet he still has the claw marks from Inky. Oh, and to add to all of that, Quaid wants me to go back to school to finish my education to be a General practitioner. He's spoken to me about being his liaison here as Healer. He's offered to sponsor me and Royce has said he'd pay all expenses. And you want to know if I regret what you and Grandfather, and everyone else have done for me?" Her soft green eyes shimmered. "How long do I have to think about this?"

Caitlin stared at her dearest friend. Any fear she'd had vanished with Stacey's smile. "Honestly, Stacey, you have absolutely no regrets at all?" She had to ask once more.

"The only regrets I have are what. . ." Stacey shivered. Her hand went to her short golden hair. "Is what Lambert did to me?" She gripped Caitlin's hand. "My nails, thanks to your blood are growing back, my hair is growing back, Quaid has told me with time, my scars will fade and won't be as noticeable. And he said that I'd be able to run again. I know with time the nightmares will eventually end. As soon as he thinks I'm well enough, I'll have a great job working with him while I continue my education. I mean, the guy is like hot! Even if he does turn into a wolf. And I am a cat person. Still, can we say, hottie-toddies? I have no regrets about becoming your sister. Legally." She twisted her lip. "Or am I your aunt?"

Strong arms wrapped around Caitlin's waist, pulling her back against a solid chest.

"I believe Mishenka made you her aunt and *ma* sister." Caitlin's father placed one of his large hands on Stacey's shoulder. "What are you lasses doing out here? Don't you see that storm a brewing?"

Caitlin gazed up at her father. "We're just talking, Papa. Besides, the storm is still far away."

His rough hand tenderly stroked her cheek. "You are as cold and damp as a gravestone. It's not good for you in your condition." He glanced at Stacey. "And you shouldn't be out here either. I should thrash the both of you."

"We love you too, Papa," Caitlin said then kissed his bristled cheek.

He growled low in his throat. "Stacey informed me you haven't eaten at all today. Is that so?"

Caitlin glanced at Stacey then at her father. "I'm not hungry. My stomach is still queasy." It wasn't, and she knew she shouldn't lie to her papa, but she just wasn't hungry, and she wanted to be alone.

"It's peaceful out here," Stacey said, breaking the silence.

"Aye, it is. The sea has a way of calling to us. As a lad, I would sit at my *seanair*, my grandsire's knee, listening to stories of the sea."

Thankful for the change of subject, Caitlin looked back over the sea. "When I was little, I would sit out here and watch the tall ships."

Her father smiled and raised his bushy red eyebrow at her. "When *yer mither* and I were newly mated, we would come out here and stand for hours. You were conceived on this very cliff."

Stacey gasped. "Ew. Gross. TMI."

"Papa, I think you're embarrassing Stacey."

He chuckled then glanced at her. His grin shown in his eyes as he cupped Caitlin's cheek. "I remember the night well. The stars lit up the sky, and the sea was as wild as it is now. And just like now, Mishenka had been up to his old ways of meddling. Come, let's get you both inside." He turned Stacey's chair toward the gatehouse.

Caitlin pulled her wrap tighter across her chest. "Has Babushka and Grandfather left for the market yet?"

"Aye, they have."

"Good. Then I think I'll go back." She turned and walked down the path.

"Little Bit," her father called.

She paused. He hadn't called her that in years. Slowly she gazed into his tender eyes. "Yes."

"I'll not grudge you your anger, lass, but you need to think about the bairn, growing inside of you. This sullenness is not good."

She stood on the rocky cliff, the wind blowing in her face. No longer could she hide her anger or pain. "I cannot forgive that bitter, old man for forcing Raven to choose between his parents and me. How can I? Grandfather knew Raven freely gave me his blood when I needed it. Grandfather knew we were mated. He knew all of this, and he still interfered." Hot tears rolled down her cheeks and trembled with rage. Her father opened his arms, and she fell into them.

The wind blew harder, and thunder rumbled in the distance.

"Oh, ma, child, let out your anger. It is not good to keep it inside of you." Her father held her until she stopped crying, then he dried her tears. "Looks like we'll have a rough go of it tonight. Come along, the both of you." He pushed Stacey down the walkway.

Small raindrops began to fall. A car horn blared.

"Looks as if Glen and Victoria have arrived early," her father said, his smile gleaming in his eyes.

Caitlin turned in time to see the 1947 black Cadillac drive through the portcullis. Chills ran down her back, and her heart pounded. Caitlin glanced at her father. His smile grew, and he nodded. She ran down the slope, nearly tripping on the loose rocks. Her heart pounded wildly in her chest.

The car pulled to a stop, and the driver's and front passenger doors opened.

Raven stepped from the car.

Her gaze dropped to the cane he leaned on and memories of him lying, bleeding on the warehouse floor flooded Caitlin's mind.

"Cat." He took a step toward her, and she flung herself against him. Raven stumbled back against the car.

Caitlin clung to him, kissing him. She didn't care who watched.

Her father laughed, her brother made some crude comment, but she didn't care. All she cared about was Raven. He was solid and real, and in her arms and that was all that mattered.

His love for her flowed through her, giving her life, removing the heartache she'd suffered these past few weeks.

~ ~ ~

Standing in the pouring rain, Raven framed Caitlin's face with his hands. He broke off their kiss and gazed into her eyes. She was in his arms. So many nights he'd dreamed of this moment, of holding her again. His gaze roamed over her. She'd lost weight, too much, he thought. "I've missed you so much. I love you."

He'd never thought he could feel so much joy. He pulled Caitlin tighter into his embrace and lowered his mouth for another kiss. God, he'd missed the taste of her, the feel of her.

"I thought I'd never see you again." Caitlin placed her hand against his chest, stilling him. Dark tears streamed down her pale cheeks. "I've felt so dead these past weeks. Why didn't you try to contact me?"

Lightning flashed across the sky, and the rain fell harder.

He now understood her weight loss. He'd have to tell her the truth, but not now. "I tried," he said.

"You tried?" Confusion gleamed in her eyes right before he felt her entered his mind. A sensation he once hated and thought he'd never experience again. Now, he welcomed the connection and opened his mind to her.

Cat's eyes became two glowing amethyst flames. "I'm so going to kill him," she whispered, before claiming Raven's lips again.

Glen placed his hands on their shoulders, giving them a firm shake. "Don't know if you two lovebirds have noticed, but it's raining. Shall we continue this reunion in a much drier place?" He nodded toward the large gray stone house. "Father and Stacey have gone ahead."

"We're coming," Raven assured Glen. In the past month, he and Glen had become fast friends. More than friends. They were brothers.

"How is Stacey doing?" Raven asked Caitlin. "On the way from the airport, Glen told me she was healing. I should have said something to her when we arrived, but once I saw you, you were the only one on my mind."

"I'm sure she understands. She's surprised us all." Caitlin slipped her arm around his waist. "I thought Victoria was also coming."

"She's coming in with Royce and his parents tomorrow."

"Royce? You've met my cousin?"

"A week ago, when I arrived in London, he and Percy picked me up at the airport. You should have warned me about Percy. The man had hot pink hair."

"I don't think any amount of warning would have prepared you for him," Cat laughed, and the sound was music to him. "But a week ago? Why didn't you call?"

"I'll explain all in a moment." Raven maneuvered the steep steps instead of taking the ramp built for Stacey. He'd worn a brace for the past few weeks so as not to raise suspicion about his quick recovery. Vaughn had warned him because of the media coverage of the case, and Raven's involvement, they had to be careful. Everyone had a camera phone these days.

Raven wasn't surprised. While still in the hospital, he'd been approached to write his story, from D.P. Hamilton of all people. Raven simply flipped the asshat off, then went back watching *Star Trek* on his tablet.

Anyway, once, on the ferry, Raven removed the cumbersome brace from his leg. He wanted all reminders of that nightmarish event gone from his life. Glen took the brace from Raven and unceremoniously tossed the damn thing into the North Sea.

In awe, Raven paused on the steps and stared up at the ancient castle. The place was more than he'd imagined. But one thing puzzled him. "Why aren't there any windows on the first floor?"

"To keep our enemies out," Cat answered. A smile graced her beautiful face, and her gray eyes seemed to shimmer.

Inside he faced a circular stairway. He hadn't realized how out of shape he'd gotten in the past weeks. "You Scots like stairs."

Cat laughed as she mounted the stairway.

Once they reached the great hall Raven was formally introduced to Cat's parents, Ian, and Angelique MacPhee. Cat's mother hugged him and kissed his cheek. With her ebony hair and bright blue eyes, Angelique didn't look old enough to be Caitlin's mother. Hell, the woman barely looked older than Cat. And Ian, with the few strains of gray in Ian's auburn beard he appeared a little older than Raven, himself.

Ian shook hands then slapped Raven firmly on the back, nearly knocking him to the floor. For a reason Raven couldn't explain, it felt as if he'd known them his entire life. Cat had her mother's smile and her father's eyes.

Angelique stepped back. "You both are soaked to the skin. Your bags have been taken to your room, Raven. Caitlin will show you where it is. Straight away with the both of you and get out of those wet things. I'll be serving tea in the parlor at four. Hopefully, your grandparents will be back by then."

Caitlin took Raven's hand. "This way."

He followed her up a comfortably wide and straight staircase then down a long hall. Beautiful lavish tapestries hung on the stone walls. The electric wrought iron wall sconces resembling torches lit their way and added to the medieval look. At the end of the corridor, a suit of armor stood guard next to a door.

"This is my favorite room," Cat said. "Our room." She walked in then shut the heavy wooden door behind him.

Raven surveyed the enormous room. His suitcases were neatly placed at the foot of the bed. Hunter green velvet bed curtains adorned the large mahogany, poster bed. Someone had already lit a fire in the fireplace. His gaze fell to the cradle next to the fire, and he quickly looked at Caitlin. So many things had happened he'd forgotten. "Cat? The baby? Is it okay?"

Her eyes met and held his gaze. Her hands slowly covered her flat stomach. "Strong and healthy."

"Oh, Cat." He went to her and swung her up in his arms, kissing her.

Her hands framed his face then tenderly smoothed down the front of his shirt. *Make love to me.* Her words echoed in his mind.

He lifted his lips and stared into Cat's violet eyes. The tips of her fangs peeked from under her lips. Raven eased her down onto the bed then slowly undressed her. His heartbeat pounded in his ear, and he quickly shed his clothes then joined her.

They moved together in a symphony of magic.

It had been a month since he'd held her, made love to her. Raven took his time worshiping Caitlin's body. Telling her with every touch, every kiss how much he loved her and missed her. He brought her to pleasure first with his hand, then a second time with his mouth. Once Cat came down from her second orgasm, Raven entered her. The warmth of her tight walls nearly undid him before he could bring Cat to pleasure a third time.

Cat trailed kisses along his neck. Raven tilted his head giving her more access to his throat. Her fangs scraped the area where his neck met his shoulder. Raven cupped the back of Cat's head, urging her to take from him. Caitlin's fangs pierced his throat, pushing him over the edge and he clung to her, reveling in ecstasy.

Her fangs retracted, and she fell against the pillows. Raven rolled from her and leaned upon his arm, watching her. He took pleasure in the smile curving her lips, knowing he'd loved his lady well.

"Don't think I'll be able to walk for a while." Cat grinned at him then rose up and brushed a kiss to his chin. "I've missed you so much."

"And I you." He leaned over her and kissed her tenderly before he stood from the bed.

"What are you doing?" She eyed him strangely.

He'd waited long enough for her. He'd be damned if he waited another second. Raven took her hand in his and knelt. "Caitlin MacPhee, will you marry me? As soon as possible?"

"Yes!"

"Then I think you should wear this." He removed her engagement ring from his pinky then slipped it on her finger.

"I thought I'd lost it. I thought Lambert or whatever his name had taken it for a trophy." She squeezed her eyes.

Raven scooped her up in his arms and held her. "It's over. He'll never hurt anyone again."

Sitting on Raven's lap, Cat rested her head on his shoulder. "I need to hear everything from you. I need to know what happened. Why didn't you have one of the guys contact me?"

He couldn't keep the truth from her any longer. "Like I told you and as you saw in my mind, I tried to contact you. Your grandfather refused to allow me to speak with you whenever I called the landline. He even went as far as blocking my number." Raven smoothed his hand down her back. "Glen told me this place didn't have good cell reception, something he and Royce are looking into changing. Percy is checking into installing a receiver of some kind. Anyway, after a while, Royce decided to use Mishenka's interference to our advantage, by letting him think he'd won." Caitlin was in his arms again, and no one would ever keep them apart. Oh, yes, Raven knew he'd have to travel with his new job, but no one would ever purposely separate them again. No one.

Caitlin rested her head on his shoulder. "No wonder Grandfather always answered the phone. I've been so stupid. Forgive me?" Warm tears splashed on his shoulder.

"Love, you have nothing to forgive. You did nothing wrong." Raven wiped Caitlin's tears from her cheeks.

"I blamed you. I should have known you were trying to get to me."

He pressed a kiss to her gorgeous red hair. It had grown and now brushed her shoulders. "Your grandfather is a manipulative old bastard. When Victoria and Vaughn came to me in the hospital, Victoria gave me Mishenka's ultimatum. I'll be honest with you I felt totally hopeless." Raven kissed Caitlin's forehead. "I love you more than anything, but I couldn't just forsake my parents, my family, not like Mishenka wanted me to."

"But you did. You're here." Fear etched across Cat's face, and she bit her lower lip. "You're staying, right?"

"I'm never leaving you again." Raven tenderly caressed her cheek. "There will be times in our lives when we will be apart, but we will never be separated again. You are my mate, for now, and forever. I will fight to keep you at my side."

She shook her head. "I don't understand. Mishenka told me you'd refused," her voice cracked, and she rested her head on his shoulder. "He told me he'd ordered Vaughn to erase your memory of me."

"No more tears." Raven drew in a calming breath. "I refused to play by his rules and apparently so did Royce, Vaughn, Tristan, and Glen. To be honest with you, I think it was mostly Vaughn's idea considering the grief he suffers because of Rose." Raven kissed Cat's lips then wiped the tear from her cheek. He had to tell her everything. "After Victoria gave me Mishenka's ultimatum, I was so distraught I told them to do what they were sent to do, but I would find you. Victoria left me alone with Vaughn after he tossed her out of the room." Raven laughed. "I think your sister put her toe over the line just a bit with him. Damn Cat, I'm not going to lie to you. Vaughn is downright intimidating. Even after spending a month with him, I still don't want to end up on his bad side."

"So, what happened?"

"Vaughn asked me if I was willing to compromise. I said yes. Then he told me of their plan. I move over here, I work with them, but I will still be able to have ties with my family."

"Why didn't they tell me? Why didn't Glen say a word? All this time, not one of them said a damn thing to me. They knew what I was going through." Caitlin's eyes glowed. "They knew I was grieving you. Did Vic know too?"

He shook his head. "Victoria wasn't let in on their conspiracy. Don't be hard on the guys. They couldn't tell you. Royce, Vaughn, all of them, they understand Mishenka's powers. They know he likes to walk around in their heads at any given time. To prevent him from knowing what they were doing, so that he could not interfere, they each one of them acted separately. Together, but separately."

"I don't understand," Cat whispered. Her eyes filled with curiosity.

"Vaughn checked me out of the hospital and moved me to West Grove. To the rehab facility. That's where I met your other cousins. While I was at the facility, Tristan visited me almost daily. And when he didn't show up, Peter, Paul, Morgan, or another member of the Wolfe clan did. Tristan and Vaughn were the two who visited the most." Raven brushed a stray strand of hair from Caitlin's eyes. It seemed like a lifetime, two lifetimes since he held her in his arms.

"Then what?" She nuzzled his chest.

"Once Quaid decided I was well enough, he released me. That was two weeks ago. I spent a few days with my family before I flew out a week ago for England. Royce and Percy picked me up at Heathrow. I stayed with Royce at his flat in London. When Tristan put me on the plane in Atlanta, neither he nor I knew who would pick me up in London. So, love, you can't be mad at them. They knew what you were going through and it tore them up inside to have to keep it from you."

Caitlin sniffed. "What about your parents?"

Raven kissed her lips again and smiled. "As I was saying, your brothers and cousin, came up with their own set of rules. Ones I can accept, rules that will allow me to see my parents until they die of old age. First, I resigned from the force and told my parents I needed a change. They understood after everything that happened. Mike, not so much, but he knows how much I love you, so yeah, I guess deep down, he understood, too."

"What else?" Caitlin chewed on her lower lip and stared deep into his eyes.

"I have a new identity. I'm still Raven O'Brien, but I'm a British citizen. Even went to Eton and graduated from Cambridge. I have no idea how Royce pulled that off, and frankly, the cop inside of me doesn't want to know. I'll be working with Glen at Scotland Yard under an Inspector Kelly. During my week with Royce, I had my job interview. From what I understand Kelly not only knows about the family but has helped in keeping the family secret. He is the liaison here in the UK, while Edgar's boss is the American liaison. Small world, huh?"

"He has. What else? What about your parents, how are you still going to see them?"

He smiled at her. "Because of your death, we won't be able to return to the States for several years, but under Royce's rules, my parents will be able to visit us here. Glen did tell me when the time comes, he and Royce will make sure you, and I can return to bury my parents. As far as my siblings go, according to Royce, he's still working on that issue. Your brothers and cousin understand my ties to my family and they are willing to help. I know what I asked was a lot. I know in time I will have to cut ties with my brothers and sister and their families. Royce is giving me a chance to come to terms with it."

"Grandfather is going to have a fit. Oh God, do you realize what he will do to the guys when he finds out what they've done?" Caitlin's smile faded, and her fear stabbed Raven in the heart.

"They understand the risk they've taken for us. As far as Mishenka goes, I don't give a damn if he has a frigging heart attack." Raven lowered her to the bed. Having Caitlin sit on his lap was arousing enough, but naked as well, tempted him beyond reason.

They were a little late for tea. Okay, they were extremely late for tea. But Raven didn't give a damn. When given the choice of making love to his beautiful mate or having tea, Raven would always choose to make love to Caitlin.

"You ready?" Caitlin glanced up at him as they stood before a massive wooden door.

He drew in a deep breath. Raven was ready as he would ever be. He looked forward to seeing Mishenka again. Giving Cat a nod, he pushed opened the door.

All eyes turned to them as they entered the immense room.

"I take it, we're a little late," he whispered to Cat.

She squeezed his hand tight. "Just a little."

Raven's gaze fell to Glen and Stacey. Glen looked out of place with his long, unruly, black hair. He'd changed out of his suit. He now wore torn jeans, ragged tennis shoes, and a worn wool sweater. He held up a cup and nodded. A glint of humor shimmered in his ice blue eyes.

Raven shifted his gaze to the fireplace, a roaring fire heated the room. He'd never seen a fireplace so huge. He could stand straight inside it. Hell, he bet Vaughn could stand up inside of the blasted thing.

"At Christmas, we burn the yule log in it and hang our stockings from the mantel."

Glancing around the room, Raven nodded to Caitlin's parents. They sat in the center of the room with Mishenka and a petite woman with graying black hair who appeared to be in her mid-sixties. Raven knew better. Sara, Mishenka's mate, was probably pushing a few millennia.

Angelique smiled at Cat and him. "Join us, please."

She motioned to the other woman. "Mother, this is Raven."

"Mrs. Lucard," Raven greeted and gazed into the palest blue eyes. When he took her hand a slight jolt of current ran up his arm and through his body.

Sara patted the cushion next to her. "Sit and call me *Babushka*. That is what all my grandchildren call me." She smiled at Caitlin. "Isn't that so, dear?"

"Yes, *Babushka*," Caitlin agreed.

Raven met Mishenka's glare. "Cat, why don't you sit next to your grandmother? I'll take this chair." He wanted to sit where he could see the underhanded, conniving, old weasel better.

Mishenka lowered his teacup and licked the red liquid from his lips. His eyes narrowed and changed to a brilliant red as his fangs descended.

Caitlin's grandmother glanced from Mishenka to Raven then back to Mishenka again. She exhaled, then turned her attention back to Raven. "Tell me about the gift you have, your second sight."

"My sight?" Why would Caitlin tell her grandmother about that? "My grandmother told me I had inherited the gift, from my grandfather. They're just feelings. However, during the case, I would have dreams. I would know how and what he did to those women before we'd found the bodies." But I can't control it. I can't call upon it, it just happens."

"A pity, you were never trained." She placed her cup on the cart then looked directly at him. "I will not let your gift go to waste. We'll start your training, and in time you'll learn to harness your power." Her eyes shimmered. "It will take time, but I do not think it is too late for you to learn to control your gift. And if your children are blessed with your gift, they will learn to master this power." Sara seemed almost giddy with the prospects.

Glen pushed Stacey's chair over to them. "I thought we'd join this little party."

"How are you doing, Stacey?" Raven asked, taking in her appearance. Her golden hair had grown out to a pixie. But through the thin blouse she wore, he could see the hideous cross burned into her chest.

"I'm good." She lifted the hem of her skirt, showing him the twisted flesh on her legs. "My legs are healing. Good news, I'll never have to shave them again. And Quaid feels with time my scars will fade." Stacey laughed. "Gotta look at the positives."

He opened his mouth then shut it, not knowing how to respond to Stacey's proclamation.

Mishenka slammed his cup down, causing Stacey to shudder. He pointed his finger at Raven. "You have betrayed this family."

Raven met Mishenka's gaze. "I haven't betrayed anybody, but you have. You have broken one of your own laws. A law *you* wrote in blood *yourself*." He glanced at Glen. In the past four weeks, Tristan, Vaughn, Glen, and Royce each had trained or rather educated Raven on the laws that governed the Dhampir. They drilled the rules into his head to the point he could recite them in his sleep. Most importantly, Vaughn and Royce had trained Raven how to argue with Mishenka. And win.

"I've done no such a thing." Mishenka's eyes took on an evil glow.

Raven sipped his tea and stared directly into Mishenka's eyes. Rule number one, never look away. "Oh, yes you did. You came between a mated couple. In your blood, you wrote, no one should divide a truly mated couple or jeopardize the life of the unborn. You broke one of your own ten commandments. To do so is punishable by death. You jeopardized the life of an unborn child, my child, and the life of its mother, my mate, your granddaughter, and for what reason?"

The flame in Mishenka's eyes died. "To protect the family from those who wish us destroyed. By keeping in touch with your family, they and others will see that you have stopped aging. Questions will be asked. How do you plan to answer these questions?"

Glen placed his hand on Mishenka's shoulder. "Grandpapa, I've met Raven's parents. They are old, and will pass before they suspect Raven of not aging."

Mishenka knocked Glen's hand away. "I will deal with you and your three cohorts later." Mishenka glared back at Raven. "What about your brothers and sister? Are they old as well?"

A low growl emitted from Glen and his icy blue gaze turned red. "A touch of gray to his hair and a little makeup to add wrinkles and none will be the wiser. What angers you, Grandpapa, is not the fact Raven wishes to keep in touch with his family, but he—we disobeyed you. Again."

Mishenka's fangs lengthened. "You will pay for this insolence. The four of you will pay."

Sara set her cup down and took Caitlin's hand in hers, bringing Caitlin's hand up, and kissing the back of it. "My dear husband, you mean the five of us will pay." She smiled at Mishenka. "Who do you think came up with this idea? Hmm?"

"You?" Mishenka glanced at his wife and wagged a finger at her.

"Of course, me. We already have one of our grandchildren morning the loss of his mate. Did you honestly want to watch another of our grandchildren suffer?" Horns budded from Sara's forehead. "Did you want to risk the life of the child she carries? I love you with all of my heart, you foolish old man, but I would not allow another member of our family to suffer."

What anger and hate Raven had, vanished. He pitied the old man. Mishenka truly believed vampire hunters or a rival clan would storm the gates of this castle and drive wooden stakes into his cold, shriveled, ancient heart.

Mishenka had seen more than his share of death in his thousand plus years. Glen had spoken of the clan wars when it was Dhampir against Dhampir and about how humans had hunted the few that survived. Glen also hinted of rumors of rogues within the Council. Then add the increase of technology, everyone having cell phones and facial recognition software everywhere, then perhaps there was justification for Mishenka's paranoia.

Raven met the old man's glare. "Mishenka, if the hunters come I will fight with you, to protect the family."

Mishenka sat up and lifted his empty cup to his lips. "Do not ever defy me again." He turned his glare to Glen. "And that goes for you as well."

Raven sat back and crossed his arms. "Don't *you* ever try to come between Caitlin and me again."

Mishenka gave a faint nod. "You do not realize how powerful I am, human. I can crush you with my hand."

Raven rolled his eyes. "Yeah, and I can be the biggest thorn in your ass."

Ian laughed. "I like you, Irish. You have a strong will. You'll do well by my daughter, of this I'm sure." He stood and placed his large hand on Raven's shoulder. "Welcome to the family, lad."

Epilogue

The light of the midnight moon danced on the waters below. The sea air filled Raven's lungs as he sat on the cliff, his arms around Caitlin as they snuggled under a warm blanket. They'd snuck out of the house, leaving their son, Ethan, sleeping in his grandmother's arms.

It had been three years since Raven moved to Scotland. In that short time, he'd grown to love the country and its people. Tomorrow, his brothers and sister would arrive with their families. They'd be here a week and planned to do the touristy things, like a ride on a double-decker bus, gape at Big Ben, visit Madame Tussauds. He didn't mind. He knew the time he had with his family was running out. Already they wanted to know when he planned on returning to the States.

Raven sighed. He wished his parents were here. They both passed away shortly after Ethan's birth. His father died first then his mother of a broken heart six weeks later. *They are together, as it should be.*

Caitlin smiled at him. "They're always with us, in our hearts. And as far as your brothers and sister goes, we still have a few more years to worry about what ifs."

"Reading my thoughts again, love."

"Of course."

"I'm glad Mishenka will not be back from Japan while Edgar, Usher, and Lenore are here. I could see your grandfather causing trouble."

"Hmm, he and *Babushka* are enjoying their time with Stacey. She deserved this trip after she graduated with honors. She pushed hard for her degree. She's a doctor now. I'm glad Quaid gave her some time off. Of course, he told her it might be a long time before he gives her time off again."

"Mishenka probably didn't give Quaid a choice in the matter, manipulative old coot."

"Admit it. You love grandfather as much as he loves you."

"Yeah, he has a way of growing on you. Just like a boil."

"Oh, you. You are as stubborn as my father."

He nipped the tender flesh of her throat. "So, I'm like your father."

Her eyes shimmered. "He once told me I was conceived on this very cliff."

"Were you, now?" He kissed her, lowering her to the ground. Raven didn't know what tomorrow would bring, or even the next few years, but for now, all that mattered right now, was loving Caitlin.

Don't miss Crimson Moon! The Crimson Series, Book 3

Crimson Moon
By
Georgiana Fields

Prologue

"Mommy, what do they want?" Shelby clung to her mother as they ran into her room. Men dressed in black had broken into their home. Her father had grabbed her and shoved her at her mother telling them to go. They had run upstairs. Her mother locked the bedroom door, then pushed the dresser against it.

"I want Daddy."

"Shh, or they'll hear you." Her mother brushed a lock of hair from Shelby's eyes. "Always remember your father, and I love you," her mother whispered. She opened the window.

"Mommy, why did they break into our home? I'm scared. I want Daddy."

Her mother clutched her chest, gasped, and sank to her knees. Tears streamed down her mother's cheek. "Your daddy can't help us now." She kissed Shelby then lifted her out the window. "I want you to run and don't stop running. Find your Uncle Tristan. He'll protect you."

"But he lives a long way."

"Honey, listen to me. We don't have much time. Do as I say."

Shelby tightened her arms around her mother's neck. "I can't. It's too high, and it's dark out there."

Someone pounded on the door. An ax blade split the door panel.

"Shelby, change into your wolf form and run. I'll slow them down so you can get away. If I can, I'll come for you. If I can't, I'll always be with you, here." She placed her hand over Shelby's heart then dropped her to the ground below.

Shelby fell and rolled. She stood and looked up at her mother.

"Change! Run! Run, don't stop," her mother shouted.

Shelby ran into the woods behind her house. Her mother's scream shattered the silence. Sharp pain ripped through Shelby's chest as if someone had torn out her heart. She stumbled and stared back at her home. Flames lit the sky, giving the blackness an orange glow. The scent of sulfur filled her nose and burned her eyes. She sniffed. If she waited here, Mommy could find her.

Two huge cats burst through the underbrush. They batted at her with their enormous paws. Shelby screamed and ran deeper into the woods. She had to get away. She had to run faster. Their claws scratched and cut into her back and legs. One caught and tore her nightshirt. In the distance, the voices of the bad men grew louder. They chased her. She changed into her wolf form and ran for the swamp. Her father had told her if she followed the swamp north, it would take her to Uncle Tee. Her lungs burned. She had to find her Uncle Tristan. He'd know what to do. She'd be safe until Mommy and Daddy came for her.

Chapter One

Bees swarmed around the multiple floral arrangements. The smell of freshly dug earth mingled with the overpowering scent of flowers. Tristan surveyed the crowded area. It's been over 100 years since the entire family had gathered, including those from around the world. Some family members he hadn't seen since he was a teen.

His Great Uncle Mishenka stood stone-faced while his cousin. Royce stared at the ground. A wealth of emotion glistened in Royce's eyes. Vaughn's arm held Rose tight to his side, her cheeks streaked with tears.

Tristan's knees buckled. This couldn't be happening. "Oh, God," came from somewhere deep inside him. Tears stung his eyes and blurred his vision. His father stared at him. His eyes glistened with unshed tears.

Tristan blinked. He couldn't look at the ground, at that hole. He looked skyward. To Heaven. To where Peter and Jean were now. His heat ached. He could imagine the pain his parents suffered. Last night he'd found his mother crying. In his entire life, he'd never seen her cry.

This couldn't be happening. This couldn't be real. He balled his hands into fists. His nails dug into his palms and blood dripped from the wounds. He'd find the ones responsible for this and send them to Hell.

It seemed like yesterday he'd spoken with his brother Peter. How could he and his wife be dead, murdered? And where the hell was Shelby?

"Ashes to ashes, dust to dust." The priest opened his hand. The dirt fell onto the casket. Jean's body and Peter's ashes forever together.

Hot tears trickled down Tristan's cheeks. He swallowed the lump in his throat. It had been over a week since he received that call. Nine whole days. Nine days, fourteen hours, and twenty minutes give or take a few, and Shelby was still missing. She was a child. Only four years old. How could she survive all this time alone in a swamp? She had to be hungry, cold, and terrified. Where could she be? He'd searched the woods behind the burned ruin of her home, and he'd be back there tomorrow, today if possible. He knew she had to be alive. He could still feel her in his heart. Oh, God, please protect her.

"Tristan," his brother Quaid called. "Come on." He placed his hand on Tristan's shoulder. "Everyone's going back to the house. Come on Bro, let's join 'em."

Tristan pulled away and shook his head. "I'm staying."

"It's not right to watch them fill in the grave. Besides, Mama needs us, all of us. There's nothing else to do out here. Come on. The women have laid out a huge spread of food. You need to eat."

"Let me be, please." Tristan turned his back. Quaid may have been born second, but he was the Alpha, destined to take over the control of the family someday. Quaid was stronger than Morgan, stronger than any of them. So strong, Quaid never showed any emotion. Nothing. Not even now.

"No. You need to be with family, now, not alone."

"Leave me the Hell alone," he snapped. "You're not Alpha, yet."

"That's enough, you two," Royce bellowed. He strolled purposely toward them.

Tristan glared at his cousin then turned his attention back toward his brother. "I'm not like you." Tristan met Quaid's glare. He seemed older. His hair had grayer, and his eyes were dull. "If I go into that house, I'll lose it."

"For your information, Useless, we've all lost it. And as far as being Alpha, I don't want it. You can have the damn job. Why don't you go and challenge Gramps for leadership?" Quaid shoved Tristan.

"I said enough," Royce, bellowed louder.

"Don't you ever call me Useless again." Tristan shoved back. This was between him and Quaid. "Stay out of this, Royce."

Quaid's eyes glowed. "The night we received the call, I tore my clothes from my body and ran into the desert. I ran so damn far I wore my pads off. And in case you're thinking about taking your frustrations out on Morgan, don't. When I'd returned, I found our older brother, Mister live-and-let-live pounding the brick wall in the barn and turning his fists into hamburger. His bones were sticking out of his hands, and he couldn't feel a damn thing! And for the record, our sister, Miranda, hasn't slept. For that matter, no one has. And let's not forget Paul. After all, he and Peter were twins. How do you think he feels, especially when he looks in the mirror every damn day?"

Tristan pushed his fingers through his hair then turned his anger toward Royce. "You heard the chatter of Fagan taking a girl. You knew. You knew he'd planned something and you didn't do a damn thing."

Royce's cold blue eyes glowed, and the tips of his horns erupted from his forehead. So his cousin was pissed---tough shit. "You're right. I didn't do a bloody thing, because I didn't have confirmation, not a drop of hard evidence. All I had was chatter! So, Tee, tell me, what I should have done? Hmm? Who should I have contacted? Tell me who should I have warned?" Royce let out a slow breath. "Look the Council is in on this. Peter was one of theirs. They won't allow his and Jean's deaths to be in vain."

"The hell with you and the Council. You know as well as I do, all they'll do is slap Fagan's hand. You didn't find Jean's body. You didn't see what they did to her! What they'll do to Shel." His throat tightened and his vision blurred with unshed tears. Oh, God, the hell Jean went through before death took her.

Quaid grabbed Tristan's shoulders and forced him around. "Look at me, damn you. You're not the only one in this family hurting. You're not the only one worried about Shelby. We all are." Quaid's eyes softened, and he let go of Tristan. "Of all of us, you and Peter are more like the wolves we choose to be.

Father once told me wolves howl because they carry the sorrow of the world."

"I failed Shelby." Tristan let his tears fall. He didn't care anymore. "I lost her tracks in the swamp. I lost her scent. I failed."

"Losing her scent doesn't mean you failed, Tee." Royce placed his hand on Tristan's shoulders. "You know the team. They are doing everything in their power to find her. We have our best hunters searching for her. We know Fagan doesn't have Shelby. I know this. You know this. You know we have someone on the inside."

"Have you heard anything from them?" A faint glimmer of hope flicker in Tristan's heart. Please say yes.

"No. I haven't. Unfortunately, I feel Fagan has figured out their identities. I suspect that's why we didn't know about the attack ahead of time." Royce pushed his hand through his hair and let out a rush of air. "Look, we haven't found Shelby yet because you and Peter taught her how to survive. You should take pride in that. We'll find Shelby. Fagan will pay for this, with his life." Royce pinched the bridge of his nose. An action Tristan had seen Royce do whenever he debated with himself on what information to reveal. Despite the blood, he and Tristan shared, Royce had the power to block everyone from his mind. The bastard was that strong. "I've issued a kill on sight for Fagan and his inner circle. The Council stands with us. Just for your information. So, I think it will be a little more severe than a hand slap."

"Shit," Quaid hissed. "You declared war."

"No, Fagan declared war when he murdered Peter, raped, tortured then murdered Jean," Royce replied.

Tristan glared at Royce. "Then we have to find Shelby, fast. If Fagan gets his hands on her, he'll use her as a bargaining chip." He met his brother's worried expression. "Quaid, I'm leaving. I'll drive straight through. This way, I can rejoin the search for Shelby by tomorrow evening."

Royce shook his head. "No. I want you to go through the maps you and Pete used. Plot out all the places between your apartment and Peter's home where you and he took Shelby camping. Places that would be familiar to her and her wolf. Then track her that way."

"I need to be on the ground, not going over maps."

"Royce is right, Tee. We know Shelby ran north. She's heading for you. Shit, Bro, it wouldn't surprise me if this very second she's camped out on your front porch."

"I don't have a porch," Tristan said as he watched the gravediggers fill in his brother and sister-in-law's shared grave.

~ ~ ~

A thick fog hugged the swamp, and a dog howled in the distance. Nicole shivered, looking back at Toby. His porch lights cast an eerie glow, making the shadows dance like wandering spirits in the night.

Tonight she'd stick to the road when she ventured home. She rubbed her shoulder. Toby had been rougher in his training tonight than he'd ever been. Still, Nicole beamed, she'd finally pinned the behemoth of an old man. "Well, I'd best be heading back." She went up on her tiptoes and kissed his scruffy chin. "Take your time reading those books. I've almost finished the latest one. "

"And don't tell me anything about it this time." Small dimples pitted his dark weathered cheeks. "Um, you thought more about going back to school and finishing your degree? I told you I'd help."

"Yep. I've already applied. With luck, I'll start in the fall. But I'm not fooling myself. Once I finish, I still may not get into the Veterinarian school." Toby grunted at that. "Anyway, I'm off for the next two weeks to work on the house."

"I know. You've already told me a quadrillion times."

"I'll cook breakfast in the morning." She grinned at him.

"Usually when you offer to cook, you want me to do work around your place."

"You know me too well." She laughed.

"All right." Toby clasped his hands behind him. "You going out with that Timothy boy again? He seems nice. A little on the shy side."

"No. He freaked when he saw Pogo and informed me animals belong outside. Besides, he kisses like a fish, wet and slimy."

"Didn't need to know that."

"So, on that note, stop playing matchmaker. I'll find a guy when I find a guy."

Toby harrumphed. "When hell freezes over, at the rate you're going. All the men you date are either too bossy, too prissy, too redneck, too this, or too that. Girl, hate to tell ya, there ain't no such thing as a perfect man, except me." He grinned. "And I'm too fuckin' old."

"Anyway, the Rangers released the fox today. It made me feel good to see him run off into the brush." She hated talking about her nonexistent love life. One of these days, she'd find a man who made her tingle, who didn't mind getting his hands dirty, smelled of the outdoors, and loved animals. And he must love kids. Definitely must love kids. Yep, one of these days.

"The way you have with animals you'd make an excellent vet." He rocked back and forth on his heels as he fixed his dark eyes on her. At well over six feet in height, Toby towered above her. "UGA has an excellent school, but they ain't the only one in the country."

Not the least bit intimidated by his dark stare, she crossed her arms and tilted her chin up. "One step at a time. Let me finish my degree then we'll talk about UGA. If they don't accept me, then there are other universities. Who knows, I may end up as a Tiger or a Gator. I know how much you love those two Universities."

"Uh huh, maybe my ass. As far as you dating, Girlie, you got to start taking risk! Stop being a tin man, hollow inside with no heart, no zest. Throw caution to the damn wind! Reach for the fuckin' stars! Have some faith. Dream! And give a poor guy a second chance!"

"Thump--thump." She pounded on her chest. "Still sounds hollow. Nicole turned and stepped down.

"Bullshit. Ice your shoulder, and put shoes on Girlie. Damn, I'd like to make it through one spring without you getting snake bit."

"Yeah, yeah." She rotated her stiff shoulder. "Didn't you tell me to throw caution to the winds and all that crap?" She checked her back pocket for her phone then wiggled her fingers good-bye, not one bit daunted by his glare. "Nite."

Toby's hounds barked and yipped. One jumped the fenced enclosure and ran up to the porch. He licked Toby's hand then ran off the porch, glancing back at them and barking.

"Something's got the dogs going. Sure you don't want me to take you home?"

She shoved her hands into her pockets. "I'll be fine. Betcha it's this fog that has them spooked."

"More like them, damn poachers, again." Toby's dark eyes searched the direction of his hen house and the swamp.

"Those poachers," she corrected and hoped he was wrong. The swamp was a national wildlife refuge, but that didn't stop poachers from coming.

Cypress was a sleepy little backwater town, located south of Waycross and west of Folkston, even though most of the town's people considered Cypress a suburb of Folkston. Cypress had a bank, gas station, a local Waffle House, a small grocery, plus a few other restaurants for the tourists. In any case, Cypress was located close enough to the swamp for poachers to enter the park by one of the many branches or creeks that flowed into the area.

Toby grunted.

In the distance, a shotgun sounded, and a dog yipped in the darkness, knotting Nicole's stomach. "Toby!"

"Those sons-of-a-bitches. Because of them, there ain't a panther in this area." He reached inside his house and withdrew his shotgun. "Stay to the road, girl, I'm a-goin' hunting."

"I'm calling the rangers. Let them handle this." She knew pleading with the old man was futile. Toby was a swamper. His family had lived in the Okefenokee since before the Civil War, or as Toby called it, 'Okefenok'.

He yelled, "Rangers, hell. I taught most of them pups the ins and outs of this place." He snatched up a large flashlight and stormed off toward his boat. "Get your ass home, girl."

Nausea rose in Nicole's throat, and she stepped off the porch. You didn't argue with a man like Toby. In his eyes, he was protecting his home and his critters. "Please, God, let him come back safely. Don't take him from me, too."

Nicole pulled her jean jacket tighter as she jogged toward home. A dark figure darted across the road in front of her and into the woods, more likely a bobcat or a raccoon, by the size of it. In any case, she quickened her pace.

The fog grew heavier as she neared the river and the gentle night breeze ruffled the Spanish moss hanging on the trees. Most people see the swamp as spooky. To her it was beautiful. It had been a place for her to heal, a place for her to lose herself in the bewitching black waters. Here she found solace.

The loud call of a Barred Owl announced her approach. A gunshot blast echoed across the swamp, followed by the roar of a motorboat. A light flashed on and off, signaling someone or something. Crap on a stick! Why hadn't she paid more attention to Toby when he tried to teach her Morse code? "Please, Toby, don't be foolish."

Above, a helicopter searchlight lit up an area not far from her home. "You are under arrest," a voice blared from a bullhorn.

Relieved the rangers were out there, and Toby would be safe, Nicole ran the short distance down her driveway. She came to an abrupt halt. The side door of her garage hung open. She'd shut that door.

A muffled sound came from within. What else would happen tonight? "Who's there?" Nicole called. "Answer me. I know someone is in there."

Nicole peered into the darkness. The faint glow from her porch light shone through the front windows but didn't offer enough light to see anyone or anything. "If you want a place to sleep, or if you need something to eat, just ask." She didn't mind helping someone in need, but it griped the heck out of her when people stole.

Gritting her teeth, she stepped into the doorway and felt for the light switch. Finding it, she flipped on the overhead light. Everything seemed as it should. She'd recognized the massive shape of her Chevy truck in the darkness before she'd flipped on the light.

She looked around. Her tools and welder were still where they belonged.

Something moved in the far corner of the garage. Nicole grabbed a huge monkey wrench from the table. She should run screaming for the house and call the police. But wouldn't she feel foolish if her intruder turned out to be a raccoon or 'possum? Just to be on the safe side and to give her a larger escape route, she pressed the garage door opener. She could see her porch. Ready to throw the wrench at whomever or whatever and run, she eased around her truck.

"Oh, good God." Nicole froze, staring at the unnatural sight before her.

Curled on the blood-soaked cement floor a half child, half wolf creature lifted its head and tried to crawl away.

Nicole's fear melted as the creature completed its transformation. A small girl, bleeding and naked, scooted into the corner. The tiny child couldn't be more than a few years old.

The child pulled her knees tight against her chest. Tears pooled in the child's eyes and rolled down her pale cheeks. "Please help me," she pleaded. "I hurt. I want Mommy."

Staring into the girl's huge golden brown eyes, Nicole remembered herself huddled in the back of her closet, nude, beaten, and pleading for help. Her Grandmother Ruby had stood over Nicole, glaring down at her, telling her that she'd gotten what she'd deserved. Ruby had grabbed Nicole by the hair and dragged her from the closet.

Shoving the memories of that horrific night from her mind, Nicole shed her denim jacket. "No one will hurt you." She stepped closer to the child. "You're safe here."

Nicole knelt beside the girl and covered her with the jacket. Pain etched across the tiny child's face. Nicole stared at the hideous gunshot wound to the girl's outer thigh. It appeared the bullet had grazed her, but the deep wound bled profusely. The poachers hadn't shot a dog. They'd shot a child, and she needed medical help. Nicole swallowed the knot forming in her throat, hoping to hide her renewed fear. If she didn't get the kid some help, she would bleed to death. "I know you're hurting. I'm going to help you."

"You are? The Hunger is so strong." The girl's eyes turned an unnatural glowing red. She lunged at Nicole, knocking her to the concrete floor. Despite the child's small size, the girl pinned Nicole with incredible strength and bit into her throat.

Check out the first book in the Crimson Series, Crimson Dreams:

Crimson Dreams

Book One of the Crimson Series

Chapter One

"If I had your brother here, Simon, I'd cut out his heart and serve it to him on a platter." Rose Kelly didn't care if everyone in the restaurant stared at her. How could this happen!

Sitting across from her in a Versace suit he probably found at a consignment shop, Simon snickered. His dark brown eyes sparkled with humor as he leaned across the table.

"That's the problem. My dear, Scott isn't here, to be honest with you, I don't think he has a heart. Besides, if he were here you'd have to get in line to kill him, right behind the FBI, his investors, his creditors, and me. Now stop being so damn dramatic. It's not like you won't be able to find work elsewhere, Rose. You're the best I know in this business. Hell, the economy is bouncing back. You'll be fine. You always land on your feet. But the simple fact is my brother is an ass who stole everything he could from the company. Baby, Victorian Dreams is bankrupt. We're broke! Shit! I wouldn't be surprised if he didn't steal the damn coffee maker."

She slammed her hands on the table, jarring it. The wine in her glass splashed onto the white linen tablecloth. "How could this happen, Simon? Didn't you know what he was doing? I have to go into work tomorrow and tell everyone what's happened. My God, Simon, these people have families."

He released a heavy sigh. "What can I say, he is my brother. Now, tomorrow you're going into work to tell everyone what's happened, and you're going to divide this up as you see fit." He tossed a manila envelope toward her. "It's all I could come up with for severance pay."

Rose studied Simon's face. Gone was his ever-present grin. "Where will you be?"

He stabbed the air in front of her nose with his finger. "Hopefully, not dead."

"I'm serious, Simon." She stared at him across the table. *He has the nerve to tell me I'm overreacting.*

"So am I, Rose." He motioned for the waiter. "Another whiskey."

Rose rubbed her forehead to ward off the headache she felt coming. "What about my ten o'clock appointment with Mr. Madoc? He's flown in from England, you know."

"Right now, Rose, he is the least of my problems." Simon glanced at his watch. "I would love to discuss this more with you, but I have another meeting with someone who may be able to keep my ass out of jail."

Rose tossed a twenty on the table.

He handed the bill back to her. "Keep your money. Oh, and make sure you and everyone get all your shit cleared out tomorrow. Once the auditors get involved, you won't be able to keep as much as a paperclip."

"Good night, Mr. Becker." Rose tucked the envelope into her purse, then pushed away from the table to stand, and bumped into the waitress. Rose cringed at the sound of breaking glass and turned. The waitress had spilled her entire tray of drinks on a customer.

Scarlet-faced, Rose handed the drenched man a napkin. "I'm so sorry about this."

She glanced up and looked into the most compelling pair of pale green eyes she'd ever seen.

"It's all right, Miss."

Behind her Simon laughed loudly and clapped. "Rosie, you always know how to make me laugh."

More heat rose in her cheeks. Rose snatched her purse and ran out of the restaurant. Dodging people, Rose made her way through the hotel lobby and toward the elevator.

Every time she found happiness, it seemed the universe had thrown her a curve ball. Rose pressed the button and waited for the elevator doors to open. How would she tell her co-workers they didn't have jobs anymore?

"Tough break." A man's deep voice came from beside her.

She glanced up but didn't recognize him. "Yeah, it is," she said, keeping her eyes on the elevator door. What was taking it so long?

"Can I buy you a drink?"

She faced him. He was tall, dark, and rather handsome, despite the eye patch covering his left eye. "No, thank you."

"At least permit me to escort you to your car, you look upset."

As pleasant as he seemed, something warned her not to be alone with this man. "Someone's picking me up. Thank you," she lied.

"Then I'll wait with you until he comes."

The elevator doors opened, revealing laughing, and smiling people dressed for a formal wedding. She stepped into the elevator, followed closely by the stranger. As the doors closed, she pushed them open and quickly exited. Rose took the stairs to the parking garage.

The parking deck smelled of exhaust and gas. The dim lights cast eerie shadows on the walls. Loud footsteps echoed behind her. Rose glanced over her shoulder. No one.

Her heart pounded, and the tapping of her high heels echoed with each step she took. This was a perfect place for a mugging or worse. Instinctively Rose yanked her Taser from her purse.

She wasn't usually paranoid, but with the recent killings in the area, she wouldn't take any chances. She glanced over her shoulder again to make sure she wasn't being followed.

Rose drove home with her windows up and car doors locked. Instead of going her usual route, she took the long way. Something about the man at the elevator gave her the willies. Neither his scarred face nor his mannerisms put her off. She didn't think he was the serial killer plaguing the city, but something threatening emanated from him.

Rose pulled into her building's parking garage and checked to see if anyone had followed. Feeling confident no one had, she ran to the elevator with her keys in hand. Once inside her apartment, she locked the doors.

Rose flipped on the lights. Normally the dark didn't bother her, but she felt more at ease as if the light would keep the bogeyman away.

Weary to the bone, she flopped onto her couch then dug around in her purse for her phone. Denny had called four times. As much as Rose cared for the old man, she just couldn't bear to talk with him. Tomorrow would be soon enough to deliver the bad news.

She flicked her finger across the screen, searching for her news app, catching the latest podcast.

"A man's body was discovered late this afternoon, making it the fifth homicide this month. FBI agents working with the Atlanta Police Department Task Force have little information about the killer or killers. And now for the weather."

Rose saved the file to her SD card before exiting the program and set her phone on the table beside her. "That's not what I wanted to hear. I know about weather in June, hot, hazy, and humid." Sighing, she picked up the photograph of her late husband from the coffee table. "Richard, if I learned one thing from your death, it's that I'll survive no matter what life throws at me." She replaced his photo next to their wedding picture. "I'll get through this, too."

Life had handed her another kick in the teeth.

Resting her head on the back of the couch, she glanced around her studio apartment. Her employment with Simon would have been her stepping-stone to starting her own business.

Why was she such a damn jinx? No. Negative thinking wouldn't solve her problems.

She wouldn't permit Scott to snatch away her dream. She'd start her business now! After all, she ran the company, not Scott or Simon. Heck, they thought gingerbread was only something you ate. She was the one with the contacts and the knowledge. "Yes!"

Rose shoved from the couch and headed straight for her roll-top desk. Logging onto her laptop, Rose opened her files for last year's tax forms and bank statements. She examined the numbers. Rose stretched, she'd gotten numb from sitting so long. She rubbed her hands over her face before she took a second look at the numbers. As crazy as this was, it just might work. What she needed were time and a miracle. A huge miracle. Rose drew in a deep breath. "It's a gamble." She sent the file to her phone before strolling toward the shower.

~ ~ ~

At eight, the bell over the office door rang. Rose looked up from packing up her desk and out into the lobby. Denny strolled in. He carried a white paper bag and two cups of coffee. This wasn't the worst day of her life, but it would be for so many.

Denny pushed open her door. He strolled in, then plopped the bag on her desk. "Tried calling you last night." He gave her a mock frown. "You know they found another body. You didn't kill Simon, did ya?"

"I heard." Rose smiled up at the tall black man who'd been both friend and confidant over the past ten years. His gray hair hinted at his advanced years. How in the devil would he find work at his age? Over the years, he and his wife Nancy became family. Damn, she'd let them down. "And no, I didn't kill Simon—he isn't the one I want, anyway."

Denny handed Rose a cup. "Double shot of espresso, black, no cream, no sugar. I hate to tell you, but you look like hell."

She took the cup, then gulped the hot liquid. "Thanks, I needed this. I've been up all night. Close the door, please."

He pushed the door closed with his foot. "No one's here but us. Must be something pretty bad for you to want the door shut."

She nodded and stared at the wall behind him, focusing on her degree from Savannah College of Art and Design.

"Let me guess. Pretty Boy finally got caught with his hand in the cookie jar."

Tears burnt her eyes, but she blinked them back. She'd sworn long ago not to let anyone see her cry, and she'd be damned if she'd start now. "How'd you find out?"

"I could lie, but I won't. Maggie and I heard Simon talking on the phone. He sounded pretty scared. I kinda feel sorry for the guy."

Rose exhaled and met Denny's gaze. "Our fearless leader gave me the job of telling everyone the news." She glanced at her phone on her desk, then back to Denny. "I've got an idea. But I know it won't be a solution to our imminent situation."

A smile curved his lips. "You never do stay down long. What is it?"

"I want to start my own company. But Denny, I'm worried about you and Nancy."

"There's no need for that. Nancy and I are going to be fine. We paid off the house, we don't have any bills, and we have insurance through her job. Besides, this will give me time to go down to Cypress, Georgia and look in on my dad. Don't like him living in that swamp, but, hell, he's lived there all his life." He looked at the empty boxes by her desk then back at her. "Feel like eating? I got us some biscuits. If you need help packing, I'm here."

She shook her head, her jaw tensed.

At nine-thirty she stood in her office, staring into eight sets of eyes. "I know you've all heard rumors. Well, I hate to tell you they're true. Simon's brother has allegedly embezzled from the company. As of last night, Victorian Dreams ceased to exist."

"Allegedly, my ass," someone said as the room erupted with curses.

She held up her hands. "I know you all are pissed—Hell, I'm pissed, but Simon, I don't know how he did it, and I'm not sure I want to know, but he came up with a month's severance pay for all of you."

One of the carpenters, Tim, stood and stepped forward. "I know I can find work anywhere, especially with the growth going on around this town. But I need insurance. What about our 401k and that stuff?"

Rose clenched her teeth. She willed herself to remain calm. "From what Simon's told me, it's gone. It's all gone. There is a warrant for Scott's arrest, and, from what Simon told me last night, the Feds have frozen all of Scott's bank accounts, including the accounts here."

"You mean the accounts the Feds know about, but what are they going to do for us?" another man asked.

"Not a damn thing," someone else replied. "Ever realize Becker rhymes with pecker?"

Rose felt their pain. Damn, she hated Simon even more for not having the balls to do this himself. "I don't know. I realize you have families, and I'm sorry I don't have more information for you."

Maggie, the office manager, pushed her hand through her black hair. "Honey, I don't blame you for this mess." She glanced around. "I don't think any of us do."

When the bell over the door chimed, Rose glanced out into the lobby. Her heart dropped to her stomach. She'd expected her ten o'clock appointment, but in walked the guy she'd dumped drinks on last night. Simon must have told him where to find her. She stared at the stranger through her office window. He looked around the lobby like he owned it. An air of self-confidence and authority emanated from him. "Let me see what this gentleman wants."

Rose opened her door then strolled into the lobby. Good grief, the man was a giant. He had to be at least six foot nine or taller. Surely, he had to be a professional athlete or something. Her gaze traveled over him. Last night she hadn't noticed his devilishly handsome good looks or his height. Strolling toward him, she took in his broad shoulders and trimmed waist.

Her eyes traveled back to his face. The square set of his jaw suggested a stubborn streak. She forced a smile and stared up into his pale green eyes. They seemed to penetrate her soul. "I'm sorry about last night. If you give me the bill for your cleaning, I'll be more than happy to pay it."

The man cleared his throat and ran his hand over his short blond hair. "That's very courteous of you, but I'm not here about my dry cleaning. I'm here about my home."

Rose bit her lower lip, not believing what he'd just said. The man looked more Scandinavian than British. "You're Mr. Madoc. From England?" Duh, as if his accent didn't give it away.

He inclined his head. "The same. And you are?"

So totally screwed. Rose had an office full of people to worry about and now this. She wanted to kill Simon, but orange just wasn't her color. "Rose Kelly. Sir, I'm sorry, but Victorian Dreams will not be able to restore your home."

"What?" He didn't raise his voice, but it rang with irritation.

Rose squared her shoulders and looked him in the eyes. "Victorian Dreams is bankrupt. It no longer exists. I'm sorry for your inconvenience."

"Inconvenience—Madam, you call flying from London to Atlanta a mere inconvenience? What about the money I've already paid?"

The doorbell rang again as Simon entered. "I had thought you, and everyone would be gone by now."

"Simon, Mr. Madoc to see you." She nodded toward the sexy giant, then marched back to her office. She slammed her door, rattling the glass. "Let them deal with each other."

Rose met the eyes of the people she'd worked with for the past five years. "If there are no other questions, I suggest you pack-up your belongings as quickly as you can."

She stood fighting back the tears for what seemed an eternity before Denny gave her a bear hug.

"I'll give you a call later." He kissed her cheek, then picked up his envelope. "Keep in touch," he said to the others.

As he opened the door, Denny smiled over his shoulder at her and left.

The others in the office shook her hand and followed him out the door. Maggie lingered behind until she was the only one left. Maggie took Rose's hands.

"Thank you for giving me a chance."

Maggie's simple expression of thanks nearly broke Rose's self-control. She pushed the door closed and turned seeing the boxes on the floor. Anger swept through her, pushing aside her sadness. Snatching up a box, Rose propped it up with her knee and raked everything on her desk into it. Her coffee cup broke. She picked out the broken pieces and tossed them into the trash. The sound of smashing glass surprisingly comforted her.

Someone banged on her door. She looked up through the glass in her door and moaned. Simon glared at her and pounded again on her door. Reluctantly Rose opened it. "What now, Simon?"

"That bastard is planning to sue me. Me, for breach of contract."

"Can you blame him?" She didn't have the patience for Simon's whining and heaved the box from her desk.

"If I knew where Scott was I'd beat him to a bloody pulp, then chunk his ass into the Hooch."

"Don't say that to the FBI when you talk to them, or they may dredge the Chattahoochee River." She tried to step around him, but he blocked her way.

"They wouldn't find him. Hell, he's probably lying on a beach somewhere." Simon smiled. "Look, Rose, we both know who really ran this company. Yeah, it was mine and my brother's, but you were the brains and the backbone. Shit, Scott, and I saw this business as a way to make a quick buck. You were the one who made us successful. What I'm trying to say is why don't you do this guy's house? Take it on freelance."

"Maybe." Rose kicked the door open with her foot. There were important things to consider, like the next chapter of her life.

Once outside, she set the box beside her jeep. Someone touched her shoulder. She jerked around and came face to face with Mr. Madoc. Or rather face to chest. The man was huge.

"Let me help you." He reached for the box.

She stepped back. "That's all right. I can handle it. Thank you."

"Look, I'm sorry about losing my temper in there. After all, Mrs. Kelly, your day hasn't been a bed of roses, either."

Rose worried her lower lip. "Don't worry about it."

He withdrew his wallet, then handed her his card. "I would like to speak with you concerning renovating my home."

She noticed the white band on his finger where a ring had once been. "I don't think you understand. There is no company."

"You are the person I want—not Victorian Dreams—not the company. You come highly recommended. And from what I've been told, you're the person I need to restore my place. Please, call me. I'm staying at the Swiss. I've written the number to my room on the back." He smiled at her, then turned and strode down the sidewalk.

Rose took in his tempting physique. He moved his muscular body with strangely familiar ease.

She glanced at his card. "V. Madoc. Hmm." She'd always wanted to see England, but she had more important issues to deal with first. She shoved the card into her pocket and went back into the office. Simon sat in her chair, waiting for her.

"I saw you talking to the Brit. Are you going to do him?"

"What!"

"His house." Simon grinned.

She lifted the last box from the floor. Drawing in a deep breath, she left for the final time.

Six hours later she soaked in her tub. After she'd left Simon sitting at her desk, she'd driven to the gym and worked out for two hours, which did nothing to relieve her stress. To make matters worse, she'd stopped by the bank. Her banker informed her she wouldn't qualify for a loan as large as she would need, not enough collateral. Rose moaned and closed her eyes. Another bump in the road.

At times like this, she wished she wasn't on her own. God, what she wouldn't give to be able to pick up the phone and talk to her parents. Everyone she'd ever loved had died, her brother, her parents, her grandparents, and finally Richard.

Enough of this pity-poor-me crap. Hadn't her grandmother always said when life slammed the door shut crawl through a window?

Rose opened her journal. She stared at the blank page. The day from hell, part two she wrote.

Her phone rang. She should ignore it…But. "Hello."

"Mrs. Kelly, please?" inquired a male voice with a heavy British accent.

"Who is this?" As if she couldn't tell from his accent who was calling.

"Vaughn Madoc. I hadn't heard from you and wondered if you'd thought about our conversation."

"You don't give up, do you?"

"Not when it's something I want. Will you have dinner with me? I'd like to discuss my offer."

"Your offer?"

"About my home? It's five o'clock now, say seven?"

"I didn't say yes, yet."

"But you will, if for no other reason than to repay me for last night's drenching."

She laughed. Very well, she'd meet with Mr. Tall and sexy. Maybe she'd found her open window. "Where shall I meet you?"

"I've heard the Abby is a nice place."

She swallowed. "It is." Expensive, too.

"Good. I'll meet you there at seven."

At seven-ten Rose walked up the stairs to the Abby. She spotted Vaughn dressed in a black suit, sitting at the bar. She also noticed the looks she received from the other women in the bar. Pure envy was plastered on their faces when he came over to her.

~ ~ ~

Vaughn let his gaze travel from her light reddish-brown hair swirling about her shoulders, to her full breasts, and down her long legs to the sandals on her dainty feet. The teal sleeveless dress she wore set off her hazel eyes. Damn, the mere sight of her affected him in ways he hadn't experienced in over a hundred years. He ran his tongue over the tips of his fangs and offered her his arm. "I'm glad you decided to join me."

Confident, she took his arm. "I was curious about this offer of yours."

The host showed them to their table.

Getting control over his beast, Vaughn glanced around the luxuriantly decorated restaurant before ordering their wine. He hadn't been this nervous in centuries. He met her gaze. "As I see it, we can help each other. I have a home in desperate need of repair, and you are unemployed."

Her hazel eyes sparkled in the candlelight. "True. But aren't there qualified restoration designers in England."

"Yes, there are, but I want you. As I have told you before, I have done my research. Restore my home. If your work is as good as your reputation, and from what I know about you it is, I'll help you start your own company. Isn't that what you want, your own business? I have the resources to get your business started."

He knew he'd surprised her. She chewed on her bottom lip. A habit of hers he knew so well.

"Just what do you know about me? And how did you know I wanted to start my own company?"

He smiled. Rose's curiosity was doing the work for him. But how could he get Rose to commit? "You're capable. You're honest." He shrugged. "I simply deduced you wanted to start your own company after seeing your distress about Victorian Dreams closing." He motioned toward her. "Your turn. What do you wish to know about me?"

The waiter brought their wine.

He watched as Rose ran her fingers slowly up and down the stem of the glass, imagining her doing the same to a particular part of his body. "I noticed the white band on your hand, were you married?"

Vaughn glanced at his hand. The ring had not been off his finger since their wedding day. He felt naked without it. Why did she have to ask about that? "A long time ago, next question."

"How did you get my number?"

"Simon. It was the first thing he offered me when I threatened a lawsuit."

Rose nodded. "Tell me about this home of yours. I understand all old English houses have a resident ghost."

"No ghost, I can assure you. However, there have been rumors of a vampire or two."

A faint smile pulled at her lips. "Vampires? Well, if they look like Alexander Skarsgård, Stuart Townsend, or Brad Pitt, I think I can deal with them."

Vaughn laughed. "I can assure you they are not as mundane as Hollywood vampires."

"Vampires don't frighten me."

"No?" He remembered her reaction when she'd first discovered his true nature and tried not to laugh. "So, you will take my offer?"

"I'll be honest. You make it very tempting, but I can't afford to go over to England for who knows how long."

"I will pay your roundtrip fare to England, plus provide housing for you and all expenses while you are there." Another argument countered.

"I need time to get my personal life in order. Also, I'm not familiar with the building codes of your country. It may take quite some time to restore your home."

"I have spoken with contractors who are willing to assist you. Fly back with me. Give the place a look and give me your opinion on what repairs should take priority. You can then fly back here and take care of what you must, then return to England and stay until you complete the job."

"You've thought of everything."

"When it comes to obtaining what I want, yes."

During the delicious meal of roast lamb, Vaughn described the house and the visions he had for it. He wanted to restore the place to its original splendor. He smiled at Rose. She'd listen to him ramble on about his home just as she'd listened to him ramble on about the case, all those years ago. His plan had to work. He would get her to England one way or another. He would not take no for an answer.

Vaughn sipped his wine, then lowered the glass. "How did you get started in this business?"

She looked as if she were weighing his question. "I became interested in restoration and preservation while researching my family roots. I fell in love with the pictures of some old homes and dreamed about living in one someday."

"Simply from pictures?" He asked, wanting to put all the missing pieces together.

"My grandmother loved to travel during the summer. She called it our road trip vacations. Anyway, simply put, I fell in love with the Victorian homes I saw across the country. . . Some were in complete disrepair." She glanced up into his eyes. "I felt a need to save them."

After their meal, he walked her to her car. "I have a favor to ask you. I would love to see Stone Mountain and other areas of this great city, but I don't know anyone here. Would you mind showing me around, if you're not doing anything?"

A faint smile curved her lush lips. She opened her car door, then slid into her seat. "Call me in the morning, and I'll give you my answer."

"About my house or showing me around your city?"

"Both." She winked at him, closed her door, then started her engine.

He stood in the dark and watched as her car's taillights faded from his sight. He'd waited over a hundred years to see her again. He could wait a few more days.

A cold shiver ran down his back, a feeling he'd not experienced in a long time. He narrowed his eyes and turned to the shadows.

Philip was here.

Biography

Georgiana Fields

Born in coastal North Carolina, Georgiana Fields spent her summers on the Atlantic Coast, where she developed a love for the ocean, nature, and coastal ghost stories and legends. As a child, she used to love listening to her aunts tell and retell stories and legends surrounding New Bern, N.C., and other coastal towns.

She married her high school sweetheart and moved to Georgia where she worked for the American Red Cross as a Medical Technologist.

Georgiana currently resides in North Georgia with her husband, two dogs, and two cats.

While she loves nature, horseback riding, and scary movies, she currently spends most of her time writing paranormal romance and suspense, where strong women, sometimes don't know their own strength.

Connect with Georgiana here:

https://www.facebook.com/AuthorGeorgianaFields

https://www.instagram.com/fieldsgeorgiana/

https://twitter.com/georgianafields

http://georgianafields.com/

http://amazon.com/author/georgianafields/

https://www.goodreads.com/AuthorGeorgianaFields